LOVE HIM NOT

"Tara K. Reed's *Love Him Not* possesses all those juicy traits of modern-day courtship: the support of great friends, the goosebumps over the guy, the over-thinking as intimacy grows or ebbs, and the delirium when things go right. Readers guide the loveable Elle Masters toward many futures with Mr. Wright in this fun, witty book. The author manages to find nearly every real-life situation a couple endures on the way to (potential) romantic bliss, which makes the story relatable and incredibly hard to put down."

—*Patience Bloom, Romance is my Day Job*

"Tara K. Reed creates a world that feels like your new favorite TV show: quick, funny, warm, populated by characters you love, love to hate, and some you'd love to...ahem...get to know very well. Plus, she makes YOU the star of these completely binge-worthy adventures. Get ready for your close-up, darling, and crack this spine."

—*Zageris and Curran, 'MyLady's Choosing' and 'Taylor Swift: Girl Detective'*

TARA K. REED

Love Him Not

ABOUT THE AUTHOR

Tara K. Reed is the accidental writer from Toronto, Canada, not that chick from Sharknado. When her career in public relations was cut short by a jerky plot twist, she wrote her first interactive novel. She was voted Most Sarcastic Female at her high school prom, which she went to alone—not that she thinks about it. She can fit her whole fist in her mouth (which makes the prom thing surprising), and sing with her mouth closed, though not at the same time. She once appeared on a romance novel cover with her husband, and believes book reviews beget good karma.

www.Doorflower.com

For Roy, for everything

EVERYTHING YOU NEED TO KNOW ABOUT READING THIS BOOK

This book is nonlinear, meaning you don't read it from cover to cover -- unless you want to wind up in a rom-com directed by Quentin Tarantino (which could be kind of epic). More importantly, it's written using the second person -- BUT you're not YOU anymore. See, Love Him Not is as much a game as it is a book. A role-playing game where you embody a character. THE character. The lead -- Elle Masters!

As Elle, you'll make hundreds of choices about your burgeoning relationship with Nick Wright. (He's the guy. Maybe THE guy.) Be they simple decisions, complicated decisions, or sexy decisions, as Elle, you'll experience the outcomes of your choices, good, bad and downright ugly. Along the way, you'll encounter 60 different endings. WARNING: Most of them are unhappy -- snotty tissues, incoherent rambling, fist-shaking, whatever happened to feminism, throw this book across the room in protest unhappy. But once you dust off the jacket/tape together your screen and try again, you'll hopefully have some laughs, take some chances, and find an ending or two that downright satisfies -- even if it means Elle winds up, gasp, alone.

Outside Forces

We rarely admit it, but we all seek outside perspective on our love lives, be it from friends or magazines or books. I have -- it's what inspired this novel. And while Love Him Not is founded in oodles of popular dating advice books, video games, and good ol' cultural observation, it's important to state clearly: THIS IS NOT AN ADVICE BOOK. I am certainly not a dating expert. There are no "wrong" or "right" choices, nor hidden moral meanings from the author, and no judgment toward you (or Elle). The only thing I'd judge you for is not soaking up a chance to break every rule, verbalized, institutionalised, or otherwise, without real-life penalty.

You personally may not like each option put in front of Elle. Some choices may seem obvious, others ridiculous, and some outcomes cliche or unfair. That sounds like modern romance to me -- a battlefield of over-analyzing and second-guessing, selfish and well-intentioned mistakes, missed opportunities and misunderstandings, unbalanced compromises, disappointments, and heartbreaks. Of course, often followed by looking back with confusion, frustration, and ire, while somehow skirting our fair share of any blame. Which reminds me...

On Mr Wright.

Every so often, you're gonna hate Nick -- when you don't love him and want to jump his bones. With no view into his world, you're left to make assumptions about what he does, why he does it, and who he does it with, which may make it occasionally tempting to write him off as Mr. Wrong. But remember, just as Rachel, Valerie, and the media influence Elle's not-always-stellar choices, Nick, too, has unseen pals and men's magazines who get into his head and relationships, so try not to be too hard on him. And should you find yourself carrying around negative Nick feels, just remember that every time you start over at the beginning, or double-back and switch directions, you change time! That makes holding a grudge against Nick like being mad at him for something he did in a dream. If there's ever a time to forgive and forget, it's while reading a book that cannot impact your real-world life. Speaking of which...

On Elle.

She's a gal you'll hopefully empathize with. She's got a good heart, a good sense of humour, and as good a sense of self as any of us do in our 20s. However, she's not always confident navigating a courtship with a guy she really likes, let alone one who could be the missing link between Matt Bomer and Henry Cavill. Like anyone trying to hang on to that kind of perfection, Elle will occasionally be faced with opportunities that are less "Tell our kids about this someday," and more, "Tell no one. Ever!" I know, because I put them there. The same way I know she's only headed down the road to scandal if YOU (in this instance you're still you) set her on the path! Something to chew on when you find yourself still holding a grudge against Nick for past timelines, even after we had that great talk. (Let it go.)

But How Does It Work?

It's simple: start the story as you would any other, reading until you're presented with your first dilemma! Decide between the two options and advance to the appropriate SECTION number (NOT PAGE number) to see what you've gotten Elle into -- or out of. And so it goes. Until you die. Well, you won't "die," but your relationship will. (See "throw book" above.) But then you get dozens of chances to do it over again!

For maximum heartache, download the 'Heart-A-Track' via www. Doorflower.com. Cross off each section as you go so you don't miss a single choice or ending. You can also get the 'Love Him Not "Happy" Endings Map' in case you want to skip the trials and head straight to the fibrillations!

Going Off Book

If you've gotten this far, you're probably a Doorflower. It comes with perks, including character-curated Spotify playlists and Pinterest boards, like my Total eQuips of the Heart ecard collection, games, crafts, and contests! Learn more at www.Doorflower.com. And don't forget, reviews are great karma.

PROLOGUE

When you hear the front door to your apartment open, you let out a groan.

Hell. Never should have given them a key.

"Elle Olivia Masters, we're coming in!" You recognize Val's stern but feminine voice and the clack of her high heels. Unannounced visit, full name, pumps after eight p.m. She means business.

"I'm naked," you call out. "In a compromising position."

"Promises, promises," says Rachel as she enters your bedroom, clad in her usual leather jacket and motorcycle boots. Val walks in next. Her dress would be long on most people, but at 5'11, it might as well be a mini-dress.

"Let's do this," Rachel says. "I've got an appointment for meaningless sex."

"I'm sure he'll wait." Val points to the pile of stuff in front of you. More accurately, the pile of romantic mementoes from Boyfriends Past emptied from a shoebox you keep in the back of your closet. "P.S. I told you so."

Rachel rolls her eyes. "It's not an 'I told you so' if we agree." She's five inches shorter than Valerie, but what she lacks in altitude, she makes up for in attitude.

"Why are you here?" you ask.

"We're tired of your moping, sweet cheeks."

"I'm not moping. I'm just blah."

"Kissing cousins," says Val.

"Fine. I'm tired of dating."

"Because of James?" asks Rachel. "The talented penis who says 'irregardless' and 'supposably?' Who you were going to dump anyway?"

When it comes to James, Rachel likes to say you were more 'heels over head' than 'head over heels' given you only dated him for three months because of his bedroom prowess. Exclusive, yes, but more joined at the *hips* than at the hip. There was no spark. No romance. Nope. And then a few weeks ago, it abruptly came to an end.

Since Valerie can't get enough of weddings and you loathe them, Rachel dragged you along as her plus one to a friend's nuptials. Distracted while formulating a plan to sneak out your table's centerpiece (a fish bowl full of Skittles), you didn't realize the bride had tossed the bouquet until it hit you - in the face. You spent the rest of the night looking for ways to ditch the damn thing, but thanks to the glares you received from all the single ladies for the rest of the night, you carried it home, tossed it on the counter and forgot about it.

James spotted the bouquet the next day while getting a (naked) glass of water in your kitchen and had a meltdown. A naked meltdown. Whether a convenient out or genuine panic, he decided *you* were in love (you weren't) and expected a ring (you didn't), more flowers (no thanks), a white dress (nope), another ring (uh uh), and a ton of bills (not even close).

You didn't bother to tell him the true story of the mystery gardenias. Instead, you took the opportunity to be the dumpee instead of the dumper, something you were going to do…just as soon as the sex got boring. And faster than you could say, "That's *my* charger!" James and everything he ever left at your place were gone.

So, okay. Rachel's right. You've been moping *a little*. But not over James. It's over every other guy you've invested in only to wind up delivering or receiving the "it's not you, it's me" (and the occasional "it's definitely you") speech. Each split left you more disillusioned than the last, and now you're a romantic pessimist who thinks more about divorce than of marriage.

You sometimes long for the old days, like high school and college, when you were resilient and optimistic about love, your raging hormones guaranteeing that each time you fell down, you'd get up and dust yourself off.

Valerie's lucky. She still views love like that - a true romantic. When you and Rachel met her in the SFSU dorms, her textbooks were outnumbered only by well-worn copies of Jane Austen, romance novels, and magazines promising foolproof ways to catch and keep guys. When she wasn't in the chemistry lab she was testing her ongoing romantic hypotheses, using whichever guys she was crushing on as her subjects.

Rachel's more of a free spirit. Her philosophy is "if it feels good do it." A philosophy nurtured by the fact she just doesn't care about attention from the opposite sex, which guarantees she'll receive it. It doesn't hurt that she's a knockout either.

After college, you each found careers. You're a public relations wiz. Valerie used her degree in biology toward optometry school and later joined the family practice with sights on opening her own. Thanks solely to her photographic memory, Rachel graduated with a degree in human sexuality, but it was her music fetish that led to her dream job: freelance music supervisor for TV and film.

You outgrew boys in favor of men. Valerie graduated from romance to self-help books and now lives by her own hybrid set of dating rules. Rachel's rule is no rules at all, especially not about men. You fall somewhere in the middle. You've given up the notion that a book alone will lead you to everlasting love but are too neurotic not to apply *some* strategy to relationships. You just can't remember the last time you cared enough about a romantic prospect to second-guess your every move, or analyze his. Strangely, you miss it.

That is why you're currently camped out on your queen-size bed pouring over mementoes from the shoebox time capsule, obsessing over the coulda, woulda, shouldas for each and every boyfriend, hindsight proclaiming what you'd do differently if given the chance.

There are countless couples-portraits taken with an outstretched arm, bent ticket stubs, and flowers with petrified petals barely hanging on. Each one sparks memories of times you were affectionate to the point of annoying, passionate to the point of complaints from the neighbors, and so addicted to each other that you used up a year's worth of sick days in a week to avoid being apart until dinner.

Fortunately for you, however, you've got friends willing to cut you off from selective-memory fueled nostalgia, and they're right in front of you.

Rachel snaps her fingers in front of your face. "So tired of dating you're going to build a shrine with the contents of your Heartbreak Box?"

"You're mean," you say.

Rachel smiles and nods. "I am."

Valerie examines the pile. "Not only," she says, "are there no pictures of James in that mountain, but I don't see any of the last five guys you've dated."

She's right. There isn't so much as a movie stub from your time with James. Or Will. Or Spencer. Or Dan. Or Other Will. You're not becoming less sentimental with age; there just hasn't been anyone worth adding to the box in awhile.

"Not *that* box anyway," says Rachel, and you realize you were talking out loud. "I wonder if it has anything to do with the fact you date guys you have no future with instead of having the occasional one night stand to satisfy your sexual needs."

"I don't do that."

"Yes you do," says Valerie.

"I don't want to have one night stands. Not on purpose."

"Everyone *wants* to have one night stands," says Rachel. "Your problem is you have long-term stands."

"Hey, remember how awesome it was when you guys were downstairs in your apartment?" you ask. "Ah, that was the day."

"You know I'm right. You waste time with guys you're lukewarm over - including that guy, Luke - but when you meet a guy with actual potential, you go bat-shit crazy, leading to a break up. It's your thing."

"That's surprisingly insightful," says Val, adjusting her glasses. "I'm inclined to agree."

"Ironic, given the bat-shit crazy part is usually your fault, but thanks."

"Is not!"

"Puhleeze." Rachel laughs. "You're a walking self-help section."

"What's wrong with getting advice?" She gives you a sideways glance that says, *Don't pretend you've never borrowed those books.*

"I ask for that advice," you say. "Sometimes."

"*See.*"

"And sometimes it works."

"And," says Rachel, "sometimes it blows up in your face."

"I suppose the fact your advice comes from personal experience makes it superior?" Val asks.

"When it's followed."

"Actually," you say. "You're both wrong as often as you're right."

"Can we agree you waste precious time with guys you don't love?" Val asks.

"Seconded," says Rachel.

"*Whoa*. Who's to say how long it takes to fall in love?" you ask.

"Six months," they say simultaneously.

You sigh. "How do I make you leave?"

"Promise to come out with us tomorrow night," says Rachel.

"No chance."

"Oh, you're coming," she says. "The rebound orgasm you've earned could very well be at that bar."

"Yeah," says Valerie. "Are you going to let a tramp like Rachel steal it from you?"

Rachel shrugs. You all know she's never had to steal a guy in her life.

"The *last* thing I need is another guy," you say.

"Actually, the last thing you need is an orgasm," says Rachel. "First you need to find a guy who can give you one."

"Fine, but I pay for nothing."

"And we pick your outfit?" asks Val.

"Fine."

"Deal!" they exclaim.

"Perfect. Now *please* get out. Enjoy your meaningless sex, Rach."

"Here's hoping I get to wish you the same tomorrow."

Ten minutes later, the shoebox is back in the closet and you're staring at your bedroom ceiling. Your friends are right. You don't want to be single. You *want* to find your someone. But why is it so hard?

On paper, you're a catch. Credible, unpaid, non-related third parties have told you you're smart, pretty, witty and fun to be around. You've got a job you don't love all the time but are great at. You make good money, own a car, have your own place, and don't expect a man to pay your way. You'd totally date you!

And yet you've watched a Prince Charming transform into a Prince of Darkness overnight. More than once.

Maybe it makes you jaded, even cynical, but you could insert any girl into your story and it would ring true. Couldn't you? You'd never consciously settle. Would you? You don't need to think about being less picky. Or should you?

No need to worry about it tonight. What are the odds you'll meet a major prospect on your first night out post-break up? Rebound sex, possibly, but a genuine Maybe Mr. Right? Unlikely.

Continue to section 1.

I

From prologue...

"That'll never work," Rachel says about a pair flirting across the room: a pretty blonde wearing a flowered dress with a Burberry clutch, and a shaggy brunette guy in Chuck Taylor sneakers, tight jeans, and a graphic tee under a cardigan.

"Why not?" Val asks, tilting her head.

She waves a hand dramatically. "She's air-kisses, he's air-guitar."

"Shakespearean. Or maybe Springsteenean?"

"Decent one-night stand at the least."

Val toasts the preppy-hipster hybrid. "Go forth and fornicate."

"Thirty minutes before they split," says Rachel, another of many wagers she and Val have going tonight.

"Fifteen," counters Val. "Twenty bucks."

"On."

Your friends were at your apartment when you got home. They'd set out your sleek "bar" pants and a lilac halter-top. While you changed and freshened up your make-up and hair, they drank and loaded your purse with ID, lip-gloss, a condom, keys, another condom, your phone and emergency cab fare.

Fast forward thirty minutes and you were bypassing the line outside Mixed in Union Square and taking in the usual scene: guys in suits and loosened ties, girls in their most fetching, work appropriate clothes. People come for the four-dollar cocktails, but stay for the meat market it becomes by seven o'clock. Ironic, given the location used to be a meatpacking plant.

Drinks in hand, you settled at your usual spot at the center of the top floor railing - the perfect locale for people watching, your favorite pastime.

"Wow, your set of rings connected by chains is so sexy," Rachel says, her high-pitched words synced with the mouth of a pixie-like girl on the level below.

Across from Pixie is a guy wearing an unfathomable number of accessories.

When he speaks, Val says in a deep voice, "Thanks, sweet thing. My rings are my favorite of all my peacocking devices, including this ridiculous Abraham Lincoln hat."

"Let's get out of here and make little douchebag babies."

"*No way!*" you say, shocked as Abe takes Pixie's hand and they walk toward and through the exit doors.

The three of you break into laughter; Val's loud but musical, Rachel's silent as she doubles over, and you, well, no one likes the sound of their own laugh. The three of you are undoubtedly a spectacle.

Val likes this vantage point for easy scoping of eligible bachelors. When you glance downstairs, you don't tell her she's clearly missed the standout in the charcoal grey suit. For a moment, you think he's looking at you, too.

You turn to the DJ booth and see the usual heavy-set guy in the same red Adidas warm-up suit he always wears. There's a set of turntables, but you're sure he just plugs his iPhone into the sound system and plays the same top 40 playlist he's been updating since the '90s. It's okay by you, since you stay *far* away from the dance floor unless you're drunk enough not to care about the music. Speaking of which…

"*Fuck!*" Rachel plucks a twenty from her cleavage and holds it out to Val. You follow her gaze to Bess and Tess (so nicknamed earlier by Rachel) faux-lesbian grinding for a group of half-drunk guys, probably because the fake laughter and uncomfortably long bouts of eye contact didn't work. Desperate times.

"Keep it," Val tells Rachel. "Our bar-crossed lovers are still here."

"Do you think the fact Bess wore leopard print the same night Tess brought out the zebra number bumped up the desperation time table?" you ask.

"It lives!" Rachel hooks an arm around your shoulder. "Welcome back to the world of the judgmental."

"Everything has evolved so much," you play along. "What is this beautiful duck face girls make in the pictures they take every five minutes?"

Rachel raises her full upper lip until it touches her pert nose. "This is how I always look."

You laugh and cover her face before looking downstairs. The same guy is looking your way again, but it doesn't mean he's looking at you. You finish your drink. "Who needs?"

"Me." Val holds up her empty plastic martini 'glass.' "Your round, Rach."

"I needs to dance," Rachel says, her energy building to a bounce.

"I'll go see Levi," you offer. Rachel produces the twenty from her bra. "Are you a stripper now?"

"Show Girls had a *profound* effect on me." She takes Valerie's arm. "Dance floor, Jeeves. The Mantis is hungry." Perfectly timed, the beginning beats of Nelly Furtado's Man Eater pump through the speakers.

Val leads the way to the stairs. "Sorry, but it's a barren wasteland down there." *She didn't see him.*

The three of you saunter down the wide, winding staircase to the main level. Rachel glides to the heart of the dance floor with Val in tow. You feel bad for the eager guys they end up next to, as they're sure to see Rachel flip the switch from happy-go-lucky to hey-go-fuck-yourself at any moment. You wedge your way through clusters of people and when you finally reach Levi's line, you find yourself shoulder to shoulder with Mister Mystery Guy. He's exactly your type: good looking and taller than you.

"Hi," he says. You turn toward him and he offers his hand. "Nick Wright." His voice, low and just a little rough around the edges, sparks a twinge in your tummy.

You shake his hand. "Elle."

"What are you drinking, Elle?"

"What's your budget?"

He has a great laugh. "Sky's the limit."

"A chocolate martini in a diamond encrusted glass, please."

"Excellent choice."

A moment later, he hands you your drink. "Sorry," he says. "Plastic is all they have left."

"No problem. I've already got two in my purse."

He places a hand on the small of your back and leads you away from the bar traffic. And so begins the banter. Concentrating is made difficult by his royal blue dress shirt, which intensifies his blue eyes.

"Obligatory 'what do you do' question," he says.

"I run a chain of upscale brothels," you tell him. "Twelve locations across the U.S. with plans to expand into Canada. You?"

"Rock star," he says naturally. "I'm a nobody here, but I'm basically Japan's David Hasselhoff."

In truth, he works in finance - something about high wealth and "The Market." *Who cares? He's gorgeous!* Wavy brown hair, perfect teeth and, if Clark Kent taught us anything, he's packing serious muscle under that shirt - fitting given he's got a major Henry Cavill thing going on.

"Obligatory 'where do you live' question."

"With my folks." When you say nothing, he continues. "In a basement apartment. We just share a front door…fridge…washer and dryer."

Your eyes widen with each detail until he puts you at ease with a playful grin. "I live *at* my parents' place in Nob Hill. They live in the Bahamas."

Oh, thank god.

"Too bad. I like a man who lives with his parents. The guys I meet are far too independent. It's refreshing when a guy doesn't have his act together, you know?"

"I can imagine. You live at the brothel?"

"My own room in each location. It's nice. Homey. Plenty of armed guards around to make a girl feel safe."

"Are you 'working' tonight?"

"Not for years now. Just supervising."

"Here?"

You turn him slightly to the right. "The girl in the red? Kiki." You turn him toward the animal print twins. "Bess and Tess. And finally…" You turn him to face the guys you saw him with earlier, one of whom is chatting up a cute girl. "Seems your friend has taken a shine to Lauren."

"Ted could use a sure thing."

"For five hundred bucks, he's got one."

"Five hundred?" He whistles slowly.

"Eight hundred, but any friend of yours…"

He smirks. You love a good smirk, and he's got a *great* one.

Gah! Why?

Why do you meet this hot, funny guy on the rebound? This isn't a rebound guy!

The gentle pressure of his hand on your arm brings you back to the moment. *Yep. Okay with the touching.*

"Excuse me a moment?" he asks. "Gotta loan Ted some cash. And you may want to check in with your friends." You look over your shoulder and find Rachel and Valerie watching intently.

He recognizes them. He was *watching you earlier.*

"They probably think they're being stealthy."

He squeezes your arm. "I'll be right back," he promises.

When you turn around, Rachel and Valerie are there.

"Your surveillance skills are seriously lacking," you say.

"Surveillance?" says Valerie. "We're gawking." She adjusts her Prada frames. "So?"

"Cute. Smart. Funny."

"Super fucking cute," says Rachel. "*Bitch.* That was my round."

"Still is."

"Rebound!"

"I-"

She looks down at her drink. "On your six."

When you feel Nick's hand on your arm again, you look up and note the adorable way his eyes crinkle when he smiles. He extends his hand to your friends.

"Valerie Hayes, Rachel Winters," you say. "This is Nick Wright."

Rachel chokes on her drink.

Wright! You just got that.

Valerie pats Rachel's back. "Nice to meet you, Nick."

"Same," he says. "Any chance you ladies would like to join me and my friends at a nearby spot?"

You want to go. *Badly.* Is that wise?

Nick gives you a moment to talk amongst yourselves.

"I wanna go," you say. "Should we go?"

"No!" says Val. "End it on a high note."

"Of course you go!" Rachel says as she sizes up Nick's cute pals. "And how could I call myself your friend if I let you go it alone?"

To see where the night ends, turn to section 10.
To end the night here, turn to section 15.

2

From section 41...

"Last relationship," you say with a light tone. "Go."

Nick's eyebrows rise in surprise as he reaches for his beer. *What were you thinking?* He takes a thoughtful sip as you lean into your backrest, bracing for the consequences of bringing up exes before you've even had dessert.

"Beth," Nick says, returning his glass to the table. You're relieved when he smiles. "That was a short one. She was cool, and we got along really well. Then a month into things, I arrive to pick her up and she's still getting ready. I figure I'll catch some highlights, so I sit on the couch, reach for the remote... And right next to it on the coffee table is a copy of Here Comes The Bride, or something like that, with *at least* two dozen color-coded sticky notes sprouting from it."

You cringe inwardly. You think you know where this is going...

"She comes out of the bedroom and I casually ask, 'Are you in a bridal party?' 'No,' she says. I ended it before my tux fitting. How about you?"

"Same exact thing," you say, wiping your mouth with a napkin. "Weird."

Nick smirks. "Had a sticky note-laden bridal mag, did he?"

"Something like that." You give him the Cliff's Notes version of your break up with James, trying to sound detached without sounding sociopathic. You even work in the facts you don't really like weddings and didn't even see the bouquet coming.

"James sounds like jerk," says Nick. "And hey - at least you proved that ridiculous legend of the bouquet toss to be false."

"That I did."

Well, it looks like Nick's and your ambiguous feelings about marriage are on the table. That doesn't foreshadow misunderstandings down the road.

Turn to section 33.

3

From section 15...

With what is hopefully a demure smile, you place your phone in Nick's hand. He focuses on adding himself to your contacts list, and you take the opportunity to memorize his features. His long, straight nose, steely - yes, *steely* - diamond-shaped blue eyes, deeply set under slightly arched brows. His wide mouth, the bottom lip slightly fuller than the top, framed by a strong, square jaw dusted with five o'clock - or more accurately, eight o'clock - shadow. You're mentally tracing your fingertips across his chin to his ear when he looks up.

"All set," he says, pressing the phone back in your palm. He lets his hand rest on yours a beat longer than necessary, setting your arm to vibrate. "Sure I can't change your mind?"

"Rock-solid resolve," you say, hoping he can't tell that you now know his face well enough to accurately describe him to a sketch artist.

"Worth a shot." He pauses briefly. "I'm glad we met."

"I am, too." You hold up your phone. "I'll call you."

He leans down and kisses your cheek, lingering for a moment. "Hope so."

You hate to see him go, but you love to watch him walk away, with his broad shoulders and long, easy stride. He exits with his friends and you immediately wish you'd gone with him. You consider making a break for the door to catch him, but cut the thought short with a brisk shake of your head.

Stop it.

A guy like that, plus liquor, equals an excellent chance of you waking up in a strange apartment, swearing you "don't usually do this kind of thing."

Your friends are waiting at the bar with congratulatory smiles and a round of champagne. Val hands you a plastic flute.

"Fancy. Toasting the new prospect?" you ask.

"Toasting that you're smart enough to reject Rachel's advice in favor of mine," Valerie says dryly. "That and I just like ordering champagne."

You cheers each other and take a sip, setting off a domino effect: Valerie gags, Rachel's face sours into a Renee Zellweger impression, and you spit the liquid back into the cup.

"Blech," says Valerie. "Whose idea was *that*?"

"Disappointing four dollar champagne," says Rachel. "Color me surprised. Let's head home. I've got some hooch…everywhere."

The three of you walk outside and you deeply inhale the crisp San Francisco evening air. It's been a good night. Once you're all seated in a cab and headed back to the Marina District, you grin. "So, when do I call him?"

Their answers are simultaneous, but not unanimous.

"Tomorrow," says Rachel.

"Monday," says Valerie.

"*Whatever*. The three-day rule is crap in general, and even if it weren't, it doesn't apply here. It wasn't a two-minute meeting at a hardware store. You talked for at least an hour and he asked you on a date for tonight. The iron is hot. Strike."

Valerie rolls her eyes and turns to you. "He's into you, no question, but if you call him tomorrow, you lose *all* the power you just gained by not going with him - though I'm still deciding how many points to deduct for taking his number instead of giving him yours."

"She *gets* points for that. She's the only one with a number. *That's* power."

"Then all the more reason to wait three days."

Both arguments are valid, but Rachel's means you get to talk to him sooner. What's a girl to do?

Good guys come to those who wait? Turn to section 44.
She who hesitates loses the hot guy? Turn to section 56.

4

From sections 24 and 59...

The following night, you lie on the couch, exhausted from the long workday and an intense, break-of-dawn workout. You will your limp body to stand and Thriller-walk the fifteen steps to your bathroom so you can wash off your makeup and change into your P.J.s.

But it's so far...

And you've got at least a few years before you *need* to worry about your skin. Besides, there are two episodes of Real Housewives of Wherever waiting for you on your Tivo.

Yes.

What you need is a night of judging the actions and emotions of other women, pretending to be superior while lobbing snarcastic comments at the screen. That's exactly what you need.

Pores be damned!

You're scrolling through the recordings menu when you hear your phone. Adrenaline zips through your veins at the possibility it could be Nick. You spring up and off the couch and jog to your phone in the next room.

It *is* Nick!

"What would you say to an ice cream delivery?" he asks after a quick hello.

"They deliver ice cream?"

"I don't know about *them*," he says. His voice is low with a sexy rasp that would make a banana split. "But I do."

Ice cream sounds extraordinarily good right now. Anytime, really. Ice cream and Nick?

Even better.

To defer dessert to another night, turn to section 17.
If you scream for ice cream, turn to section 14.

5

From sections 19 and 12...

You tell Nick you'll meet him for dinner.

Valerie believes it's a bad sign if a guy doesn't pick you up for a date at the outset of a relationship. She says it either means he's not that invested or just has bad manners, both of which are deal-breakers in her book. (Unless she really likes a guy, in which case she conveniently forgets that particular rule.)

You finally fall asleep after deciding it's more likely he's anticipating having to work late that night and doesn't want to risk being late. That or maybe his car's in the shop. No big deal.

You pull up out front Perbacco and are quickly reassured when you spot him waiting to meet your cab. He opens your door with a smile and extends his hand to help you out of the car. You kiss his cheek.

"Hey," he says, keeping hold of your hand. "You look great."

"Thanks. You, too."

Yes he does. He looks like he just came from work, dressed in a tailored grey pinstripe suit with a baby blue dress shirt and silver tie. The man knows how to work his eye color - no denying that.

Over a delicious dinner, you tell him that Rachel's playing with Valerie's head by swapping her treasured new ballet flats with an identical pair Rachel bought in a smaller size. She's done it each morning this week, sending Val to work in old shoes and a foul mood, only to be bewildered when she comes home and slips on the flats, which fit perfectly again.

He tells you he's been pulling late nights all week, putting together a huge RFP for a Fortune 500 company looking for a new...financier? Broker? A new whatever it is that Nick does.

After a bottle of wine and a shared brown sugar crumble, Nick excuses himself to the men's room. You're considering suggesting a drink somewhere else when the server drops your check in the center of the table.

You look at the leather folio and wonder if you should pay the bill. You can certainly afford it. He paid last time. Besides, you'd hate for him to think you're a girl who expects a guy to pay for everything, which he might if he comes back from the bathroom and sees the check just sitting there in front of you. Hmm....

To pay, turn to section 30.
To let him pay, turn to section 40.

6

From section 59...

Ten minutes ago, you were performing a sweaty, tangled, rhythmic dance with Nick, followed by a firework finish. Now you lay on your side with his arms wrapped around you from behind. You've come down from your coitus high and are now thinking relatively rationally.

What the hell did you just do?

You barely know him and you *slept* with him. And you like him - a lot - which actually makes you feel worse. You didn't even attempt to follow the "not until I know his middle name" rule - not that it really works. If it doesn't come up in conversation naturally, depending on how attracted - or flat out horny - you are, you usually just ask him, negating the point. It used to be "not until I know his mother's maiden name," but guys started to look at you like you wanted to hack into their online banking. Either way, you suppose it means this was bound to happen now-ish one way or another, so...good for you. Get yours!

Except when does this ever turn out well?

You're glad Nick can't see your eyes, which are surely bugging out of your head.

"Everything okay?" he asks and kisses your bare shoulder.

"Of course," you say, too quickly. "Why do you ask?"

"Your body just went from *very* relaxed to *very* tense."

Get out immediately.

"It's just-" You turn to face him. "I forgot I told Val I'd drop by to talk to her. About something *really* important. Or I'd stay. But I should go."

Stop talking.

Nick seems surprised. "Oh. Yeah. Okay."

You gather your clothes and duck into the bathroom to dress. Your skin is red from heat and whisker burn. You finger comb your hair into submission and wipe at your smudged mascara with a tissue. When you exit the bathroom,

Nick's wearing the daylights out of a pair of sweatpants that show off those crazy v-shaped ab muscles your brother calls The Adonis Belt.

Yep. You're outta here.

Sure you're full of anxiety, but that doesn't mean you have to be a *total* liar. Once at your building, you head straight for Valerie's apartment. You knock loudly until she answers. With one look at your mussed hair and raccoon eyes, she shakes her head. "You slept with him."

"I couldn't help it," you tell her. "I'm weak!" If only she'd seen him in those sweatpants.

"Then…why are you here?"

You look at her like the answer is obvious. "I didn't want to seem needy, so I left."

"Right. Better he think of you as easy. Or that you were using him for his bod."

You hadn't thought of it that way. "Do you think he'll call?"

"Honestly?"

"No."

"He'll call."

Continue to section 18.

7

From section 33...

You draw out a sip of wine as long as possible and then fidget with the stem of your glass, alternating glances at Nick with multiple false starts of "Um" and "Well."

It's a simple question: Are you close with your brother? Honesty is always the best policy *your ass*. Now you understand why people lie. Liars are brilliant. Maybe even kind.

Noting your clear distress, Nick asks, "Is it okay that I asked? I don't mean to pry. The sibling dynamic can get complicated. I get it. *Believe me.*"

You wince a little. "Yeah, see that's kind of the thing." A flicker of confusion crosses his face, leaving a puzzled twist on his pretty, pretty mouth. You exhale.

"Okay." He holds your gaze steadily.

"It's just that I'm *really* close to Rory. He's the greatest human being I know. And so when you said you had a twin, I thought of how great it would be to know someone who'd *get* how close we are and not be, you know, threatened by it."

He raises a speculative brow at you. "And because of me and my Rory..."

"Well, you looked sad talking about your sister and I don't even like to imagine not having the relationship I do with my brother, especially if he had a kid."

You are making this so much worse.

You look down. "I just didn't want you to feel bad."

"You felt sorry for me?" You look up and regret it instantly. Nick's expression is unreadable.

When are you ever going to learn to just lie, lie, lie!

Mortified, you blather into your lap. "I'm *so* sorry. I mean, not sorry as in pity, but sorry as in regret that I made you feel like I felt sorry for you-"

He finds your hand under the table, pulls it toward him and gives it a squeeze.

You look up, likely doing a stellar Bambi impression, and are relieved to see his face is once again just plain old chiseled, and with a grin to boot.

Jerk.

He laughs. "I'm sorry. I couldn't resist. You were so adorable." You try, unsuccessfully, to look mad. "Worried about my feelings, huh?"

"Just a little. Fellow man and all that." You can't believe he did that to you - such a Rachel thing to do. He picks up his drink and studies you for a moment, making you even more self-conscious. "What?"

"Nothing, you just surprised me." He takes a sip.

"Wait 'til you see me fit my whole fist in my mouth," you deadpan and he chokes, banging his chest as he coughs. You offer him a napkin and a smirk.

Two can play at that game.

Turn to section 42.

8

From section 93...

You stay where you are, but don't mind in the least when Nick drapes his arm over your shoulder and leaves it there for the rest of the evening.

He could easily pull you closer - and given the smoldering look in his eyes whenever you turn to him, you're pretty sure he wants to. The fact he doesn't shows you he's a gentleman, which just makes him all the more tempting. You keep yourself in check though, with the exception of occasionally resting your head on his shoulder as you listen to the band.

An hour later, your body betrays you with an involuntary yawn and you reluctantly agree when Nick suggests getting the bill so he can take you home. As you walk to the car, he wraps an arm around your shoulders and brings you close to him to protect you from the chilly night air. The ride home is comfortably quiet and he rarely lets go of your hand. He even raises it to his lips for a kiss.

It seems like just a few minutes before you arrive at your building. He parks and climbs gracefully out of the car before walking over to open your door and offering you his hand. Then, in case you needed more proof of his good manners, he walks you to the lobby doors.

You're digging through your purse for your keys when Nick asks, "So, any plans for next weekend?"

You try to hide the ripple of excitement creeping up your spine. "I usually fight crime on the weekends, but the city can fend for itself for a night."

"Great, I'll give you a call." Then he leans in and you finally get your hug, complemented by a sweet, soft kiss on the lips.

You like him. You *really* like him.

Turn to section 9.

9

From sections 13 and 8...

"Clingy!" Valerie fumes as she transfers pasta from a pot to a glass bowl, slopping sauce everywhere. "*He* thinks *I'm* clingy."

She's referring to Marcus, a guy she dated on and off until he abruptly ended it, telling her he needed space.

"Still bitter after a week," Rachel says from the couch, her socked feet propped on your lap. Grinning, she drums on her thighs with a pair of pencils. "Thought you didn't care."

"I'm not *bitter*," Valerie says, struggling to cover the bowl with plastic wrap. "I just can't believe he'd say that when I never even *suggested* getting together. *Not once.*" With a frustrated growl, she balls up the uncooperative cellophane.

You laugh. "I dunno, V," you say, motioning to her hands. "Even plastic wrap seems to think you're too clingy."

"*Ba dum chh.*" Rachel drums out a rim shot.

"I hate you both," Val says, tossing the ball at your head. "And I'm not bitter."

You turn to Rachel and exclaim, "I can't believe it's not bitter!"

"It looks and sounds just like regular bit-" Rachel is cut off by an oven mitt to the face, courtesy of Val. "Dude. So violent."

Between their squawks, your phone rings and you free yourself from Rachel's legs. "Girls, girls. Try to get along," you say, en route to the kitchen. You brighten at the sight of Nick's name lighting up the screen. "Actually, go ahead and kill each other."

"Are you at war?" Nick asks when you answer.

"Mud cage-fighting match." You pick up your keys from the counter and wave backwards at your friends on your way out the door. "I'm moonlighting as a ring girl for extra cash."

"And now I know why I didn't get *that* gig."

You laugh and open the door to the stairwell, climbing up three flights to avoid losing cell signal in the elevator. "What's up?"

"Nothing really," he says. "Just thought I'd call and say hi. So…hi."

Your heart fills with happiness and you don't even feel the burn of the final fifteen steps. "Hi back."

You float into your apartment and over to the couch where you enjoy your first call-for-no-reason from Nick, twirling your hair around your finger as you chat, flirt and tease each other. It's one of those rare occasions where being reminded of high school doesn't suck.

Thirty minutes later, your ribs are sore and your eyes are wet from laughter. And then it comes - a moment of silence. Yup. Just like in high school, you feel a little jolt of alarm that your call is about to end.

To get off the phone, turn to section 43.
To keep talking, turn to section 111.

IO

From section 1...

You and Rachel say a quick goodbye to Valerie, who has to be up early, and hop into a cab with Nick and his buddies. You drive a few blocks and stop in front of Fluid.

Nick is an attentive guy. He helps you and Rachel out of the car, and then takes your hand with a gentle squeeze. He leads you through the doors and then a cluster of people, settling on a spot that isn't too crowded. He only leaves you long enough to get drinks for the three of you.

How sweet. And, more importantly, how cute!

You love this part.

As time passes, you note that it's one of those perfect, spontaneous nights where everyone gets along and having a good time is contagious. The music is loud, but that just makes conversation more fun. Each time Nick speaks his lips brush against your ear. When you stand on your tiptoes to talk to him, he steadies you with a hand on your hip.

You're soon comfortably tucked against him with his arm draped around your waist. To strangers, you probably look like a couple, and that's okay with you. Nick appears okay with it, too, pressing the occasional kiss to your temple.

Rachel holds court with his friends at the edge of the dance floor. They flirt with her and she with them. She even gets them to dance, which, from the looks of it, is not a frequent occurrence for either guy.

You've had more than a few drinks and are feeling just fine when Ted asks if he can get you and Nick another round.

For last call, turn to section 28.
To call yourself a cab, turn to section 77.

I I

From section 232...

Or... not at all.

"You should go," he says suddenly. "You're young. See the world. Pad your resume."

You search for sarcasm or hostility in his words but hear none.

"You want me to go?" you ask, wounded.

He gently grasps your shoulders. "No. I don't *want* you to go, but I wouldn't stop you." His arms wrap around you tightly. "Truth is, if it were the other way around, I'd have a hard time saying no. No offence."

"None taken."

This was not a good plan. Not only did it *not* have the desired effect of making Nick realize he can't live without you, but you can't even run to Ireland to hide for two months *because there is no trip to Ireland.*

You never expected him to be supportive. Grand gesture and/or declaration of undying love followed by ring shopping, sure, but not this.

Over the next weeks, you follow Val's careful instructions to limit the fallout from your half-baked caper. You arrive at Nick's on Tuesday, bummed out because it turns out your boss didn't get approval from her own boss before offering you the position. Still, you might use your vacation time to join the girls in Ireland for a couple of weeks.

And he's with you a week later when you hear the news that Val's aunt and uncle accepted an unexpected and *tremendously* profitable offer to sell and vacate their house by month's end, putting the final nail in the coffin of your never-actually-happening trip.

When you feign disappointment, he is the best boyfriend in the world and does everything he can to cheer you up, which, of course, makes you feel awful. And just when you thought it couldn't get worse, tonight you come home to the most romantic thing anyone's ever done for you.

You turn on the lights in your apartment and are blinded by a sea of green and gold. There are streamers with four leaf clovers hanging from the ceiling, pots of gold-wrapped chocolate coins, and a tray of cupcakes decorated with marshmallow charms. Most surprising is the green artificial turf covering the floor and some of your furniture, creating the effect of rolling hills.

Nick turned your apartment into Ireland.

"Happy St. Patrick's Day!" he says, emerging from the bedroom in a *Kiss Me, I'm a Good Kisser* tee shirt. "Whaddya think?"

That I totally don't deserve you. "It's amazing. And confusing."

He takes your hands and pulls you into the center of the room. "Last month, I said I'd support you if you moved for six months, and I would have, but I was so relieved when it fell through. Which, I know, makes me kind of a jerk." *If you only knew.* "Before that, though, I promised myself I'd give you this when you came back."

The next thing you know, Nick's down on one knee, holding up an open box - with an engagement ring in it. The tears start flowing immediately. Not adorable happy tears either - snotty, guttural, tortured, baby seal barks. You cover your face with your hands.

Nick stands and gently pulls your arms down before smoothing back your hair. "What's the matter?"

"*Me,*" you blubber. "I lied to you. About the trip, about the job, about *losing* the job, and about the house falling through - all of it."

He wipes away a tear from your cheek with his thumb and tilts your face up to look at him. "I know."

"You know?"

He nods. "Valerie felt really bad. Said it was a plot in an Amy Adams movie and she thought it would work for you, too. Who do you think helped me bring Ireland to you?"

As relieved as you are to have that Irish monkey off your back, you can't help the anger bubbling up inside of you. *What you did was shitty, but…*

"So you, what, picked out a cubic zirconia and staged a fake proposal to get back at me?"

He reaches into his back pocket and produces an invoice, which he holds up, careful to cover the bottom half. In the corner is a jeweler's logo. "Receipt for the ring," he says, his lips curling slowly upward.

"And?"

"Look at the date."

You can't believe it. It's dated one week after that talk with Nick all those months ago, long before the Irish ruse. "You've had this all along?"

"Yup," he says smugly. "I was pretty sure what I wanted then, but I didn't want to mislead you, so I bought it and hung on to it until I was sure."

Groan. "After I told you about Ireland."

"Before. Like *right* before. I was going to propose that night."

"And even after I lied?"

"Oh, I'm not thrilled about it, but it clearly wasn't easy for you. The hoops you jumped through over the last couple of weeks prove that. And they were kind of amusing." He holds the box up again. "So... We getting hitched or what?"

You throw your arms around his neck. "Only if we can go to Ireland for our honeymoon."

"Not a chance, lass." He laughs into your hair.

Turn to section 34.

12

From section 69...

Two hours later, you lay on the couch, fighting sleep during an episode of Forensic Files. You elect to turn in early, but it takes a moment for your brain and body to cooperate. You finally sit up and turn off the TV before carrying your water glass to the kitchen.

You place it next to the sink and automatically set your cell phone to silent and connect it to its charger. You cross the floor and shut off the overhead light, only to see a soft blue glow immediately fill the room. It's nearly ten o'clock, so it's either one of the girls, or your mother's calling to tell you somebody died. In case it's the latter, you pad back to the phone. To your surprise, the display reads, *Nick calling...*

Suddenly, you're not so sleepy.

You consider letting it go to voicemail, enjoying a fleeting thought of him wondering where you are or who you might be with, but that would just lead to you staring at the ceiling all night, kicking yourself for not picking up.

"Hello," you answer. Your voice is gravely.

"Oh. Sorry. Did I wake you?" Nick asks. "Christ, it's almost ten. I didn't even look at the clock."

You smile. "Don't worry about it. I thought you might be a last minute client. I'll switch back to my regular voice now."

"Moonlighting?" You hear amusement in his voice.

"I volunteer for a phone sex hotline on Mondays," you tell him casually.

"Generous of you."

"I'm a giver."

"All the same, sorry for the late hour. I just pressed send on a report to my department head and wanted to touch base."

"You must be tired," you say, silently thrilled you were his first instinct after a late night at work.

"Wrecked. I'm about to head home, but I wanted to see if you'd have dinner with me on Friday."

You wait an impatient beat. "Sounds good."

"Great. How about Italian? I know a terrific place in SoMa. We can meet there at 7:30. I'll make a reservation."

Your car's scheduled for its annual tune up on Friday, so you're without wheels *and* you'll be in heels, ruling out BART. You could ask him to come get you, but you don't want to be a pain in the ass.

Take a cab while your car's under maintenance, turn to section 5.
Ask for a ride and risk looking high maintenance, turn to section 93.

13

From section 93...

"*Excuse me,*" comes an impatient male voice from somewhere. "*Hello.*"

Snapping back to reality, you pull away from Nick's mouth. It takes a moment for him to notice you have company.

He untangles his hand from your hair and turns to your server. "I'm sorry about that," he says with a small smile. You can't help but blush.

The server breathes deeply, obviously annoyed but not willing to risk his tip. "I just wanted to see if I could get you anything else."

Nick looks at his watch. "Wow. It's 10:30," he says. How long have you been kissing? "Just the bill, please."

"Coming up," your server says and disappears.

"Sorry," he says, stroking your cheek. "I'm dog-sitting and if I don't get home soon, I'll be replacing my mother's... everything."

You're a little disappointed as you walk arm-in-arm out into the cool night air.

"Actually," says Nick. "Are you in a hurry? You could come meet Cat."

"I thought you said you were dog-sitting."

"I did. Cat is the dog's name."

"Seriously?" You laugh.

"Oh, yeah. You've never seen a dog more like a cat."

"Oh, I don't know. What kind of cat-dog is it?"

"Golden lab puppy." He smirks, knowing fully the power of the puppy.

To shake a paw, turn to section 94.
To tell him "Down, boy," turn to section 9.

14

From section 4...

Individually tempting, ice cream and Nick combined leaves you no recourse but to give in. This is why you give Nick the green light to bring over a pint of Chunky Monkey.

A spoonful after he arrives, you're couch-dancing with Nick - and Ben & Jerry are the only ones going soft. Hands in hair, over backs and thighs, soft noises and sharp intakes of breath - the classic make-out session.

Overheating, you begin to remove your already unbuttoned sweater - not necessarily to go all the way, rather to be comfortable while making a decision as to...whether to go all the way. Nick braces his weight on his forearms and leans back to look in your eyes.

"You okay?" you ask breathlessly.

He laughs softly and kisses your jaw. "Very much okay," he says. "Better than okay." He plays with a few strands of your hair. "And I think we should pause here."

Isn't that my line? "Yeah?"

"Yeah. I mean, I'm not saying I *want* to stop, but we probably should."

Your body completely disagrees with him, but your rational brain says, *Such a gentleman. Prioritizing my welfare over his gratification.* The rational part of your brain sounds an awful lot like Valerie.

You continue to kiss and laugh as you redress, and then snuggle on the couch for a while before he has to head home. Afterward, you notice the now melted pint of ice cream. You weren't thinking clearly, so it's a good thing Nick was thinking clearly enough for both of you.

Tonight was a success. You spent some time with Nick, nothing got out of hand (even if it crossed your mind), and now you have melty ice cream to polish off with a jumbo straw and a spoon.

Turn to section 72.

15

From section 1...

"*Come on!*" groans Rachel.

"No, Val's right," you say. "I like him. I'm not making him Rebound Guy."

"So don't sleep with him."

"You saw him, yes?"

"I'll chaperone."

Valerie guffaws. "Every mother's worst nightmare." She turns to you. "Good choice."

Rachel opens her mouth again to protest, but Val grabs her arm. "Stay," she says and waves you on. "Go ahead. We'll stare really obviously from over here."

You walk across the floor to where Nick is listening to that blond guy, Ted. When he sees you coming, he pats his friend's shoulder and steps past him, meeting you halfway.

"*That* is a great smile," he says, resting a hand on your hip as naturally as though he's done it a hundred times before.

"You like?"

"I do. It says, 'Why, I'd love to come with you. Let's get outta here.'"

Resist the Cavill bone structure.

"Actually, it says 'I do want to come with you. *A lot.* Which is exactly why I can't.'"

An exaggerated look of pain passes over his face and he grabs his chest. In a strained voice he says, "I'm hit. It's my heart."

You laugh. It's a bit cheesy, but he makes it work. "Shoot. I always forget to warn my suitors to wear Kevlar in my presence. I can give you the name of a *great* dry cleaner."

He tries another tack. "But... Who will protect me from the groupies?"

"Hopefully not the same guys who just watched you take a bullet."

Undeterred, he slides his arm around your waist and pulls you closer. You look up. Your faces are just inches apart, which certainly isn't making this easy. "But I ship out tomorrow," he says. His eyebrows knit together like a sad puppy. "What if I never see you again?"

You laugh and rest a palm on his chest, confirming the Man of Steel theory. "You feel...durable." *Hot damn.* "I have full faith you'll come home. Still, I'm not unpatriotic. We can see each other when you get back."

"All right. White flag," he says, waving a handkerchief he pulls from the inside pocket of his jacket. No doubt Val is swooning right now. "I surrender... For now. How do we set up a homecoming rendezvous?"

To give him your number, turn to section 87.
To take his number, turn to section 3.

16

From section 90...

Wrapped in a robe, you stare at your bedroom ceiling, chastising yourself for the way-to-soon sex you had with Nick last night.

Your phone rings and you grab it from the nightstand. It's Rachel.

Just don't tell her. It's her fault, anyway. She's the one who picked out the outfit that made you all irresistib-

Who are you kidding? He wasn't the only one not resisting. Still, no one needs to know you had amazing sex with the closest thing to perfection you've seen since Charlie Hunnam was on the cover of Details.

On the first date.

"I made a mistake," you blurt into the mouthpiece.

Well, you tried.

"Fuck." You hear Rachel hiss. "You got bangs again? They'll grow out."

You groan. "I slept with Nick."

"Bangs, banged. I was kind of right." She snorts. "And?"

"And that's bad."

"No, I meant was it any good?"

"Too good, which probably just makes me look sluttier."

"I think it's actually 'more slutty.'"

"That's helpful, thanks."

"What? I should console you? Don't get me wrong. You want sex, I say go for it. You want a relationship, let him down gently instead of letting him up. Easy. Or, not easy, as it were."

"Maybe he'll call."

"And maybe every other guy you regret sleeping with will send you flowers."

Continue to section 331.

17

From section 4...

"I'm sorry, I can't," you say, almost convincing yourself it's true.

Technically you can, and you want to, but you shouldn't, so for the purpose of this conversation, you couldn't possibly. Instead, you do what you do best: spin.

"The Evil Overlord dropped a huge RFP for a giant hotel chain in my lap this afternoon," you tell him, happily noting his small groan of disappointment. You aren't completely lying. This actually happened, two days ago, but you're already finished and set to hand it in tomorrow morning after a final proofread. "I'm looking at another two to three hours of spreadsheets."

Instead of two to three hours of spread sheets.

"Too bad," says Nick. He sounds genuinely disappointed. "Say...how about I just drop off some ice cream and then go. Help you to get through the night?"

"That's literally a sweet offer," you tell him as you wander into your kitchen. "Problem is, then I'll want you to stay."

"I'm willing to risk it if you are," he says in a low, suggestive tone. It's times like this you wish you didn't have perfect facial recall. Tempting as he is, you stand your ground. "How about Saturday?"

"For ice cream?"

"I like ice cream pretty much every day, so why not?"

"I know the perfect place. You'll love it. Pick you up at two?"

"Two it is." You'd feel worse than you already do if you weren't thrilled by how excited he sounds.

"Okay, I'll let you get back to it. Good luck."

On your way back to the couch, you grab a pint of Rocky Road-ish from the freezer and a spoon from the dish rack - because you eat when you feel guilty.

Yum. Ice cream was a really good idea.

Turn to section 61.

18

From section 6...

At first, you were mad at yourself for jumping into bed with Nick. Then Rachel came home and high-fived you, telling you listening to Val causes wrinkles before prying as many details out of you as possible.

That was Saturday.

This is Friday.

You haven't heard from Nick in six days. Between anxiety-induced insomnia and running to your phone every time it makes a noise, you're a zombie. A cute zombie, but walking dead nonetheless. You must fall asleep on the couch, because one minute you're watching Revenge and the next, a scrawny, hyperactive guy chopping everyday objects into tiny pieces with a tacky kitchen utensil.

You sit up and turn off the TV before dragging yourself to your bedroom. You crawl under the covers, deciding you will no longer pine after Nick. He didn't call. So what? You didn't call him either. Maybe you made a mistake, but if you did, it was a mistake with great sex.

You mercifully drift off into a blissful slumber only to be jolted awake by your phone on the bedside table, where it's been every night this week, set to maximum volume *and* vibrate. Just in case. Your alarm clock reads 2:00 a.m.

Hopefully no one's dead.

You don't bother to look at the caller ID. "Hello?"

"Hey," says Nick in total Nick voice. "I was with some friends and realized I'm nearby...so I thought I'd be a jerk and wake you up at two a.m. to see if I can tell you I miss you in person."

Talk about a wakeup call.

And you didn't sleep long enough for morning breath to set in.

To let him come over tonight, turn to section 23.
To make plans for tomorrow, turn to section 27.

19

From section 69...

You get comfortable on the couch and call Nick, smoothing your hand over a throw pillow as you listen to one, two, three rings go unanswered.

When the fourth ring comes and goes, you're surprised. As much as you've been thinking about Nick, and since you know he had a good time on Saturday, you figured he'd want to hear from you as much as you want to hear from him.

Of course, he may even be trying to play it cool to see if you'll call him first. (In which case, he wins.)

The machine picks up.

"You've reached Nick Wright," says his outgoing message. "I'm sorry I missed your call, but if you..."

Blah, blah, blah.

Okay, no big. Maybe he's working. Or on a date with another girl. Or watching sports with friends. Or on a date with another girl.

You leave a short and sweet message. "Hey, you. I had a really good time the other night and wanted to see if you were free for dinner Friday. Give me a call when you get a second. Bye."

Well done.

You set your phone on your belly and relax into the couch but your imagination continues to run wild. He could be grocery shopping, you may have been calling each other at the exact same moment (which would be so cute), he could be engrossed in an episode of Extreme Couponing and not paying attention to his phone.

Nearly twenty minutes later, your phone bleeps, tickling your stomach. You have a text from Nick suggesting you meet him for dinner at Perbacco on Friday.

Turn to section 5.

20

From section 33...

If this thing with Nick goes anywhere, you'll need to postpone introducing him to Rory indefinitely.

Still, you don't know how to downplay Rory. He's just about your favorite person. While your friends were locking their siblings in closets and banishing them from slumber parties, you were waiting for yours to come out of the closet and plotting together to scare Rachel during sleepovers. But here goes...

"Rory," you say, suddenly very interested in your wine glass. "Let's see. He's five years younger than me. He looks like me. I call him Golden Child because he's sort of perfect." Everything you say is factual. You have yet to tell a lie.

"Does he live nearby?"

Unfortunately not, though for tonight's purposes, it works out. "He's a 'citizen of the world,'" you tell Nick dramatically. "He's a painter. Got his art degree and has been travelling ever since. Says his passport is his muse."

"Are you close?"

Oh, sure. Make me lie to you.

"We could be closer. It's tougher the older we get, especially with so much distance. You miss all the little things."

You talk to Rory at least twice a week, even if just for ten minutes. You e-mail almost daily, but only because he can't text you every ten minutes like he would if you shared a time zone or if he had regular access to a data plan.

Your server arrives brandishing desert menus.

"Yes, please," you say, gladly accepting the change of subject and an opportunity to fill your mouth with something other than lies. You order a slice of apple pie. You don't deserve it, but you're livin' life pretty close to the edge these days.

Turn to section 48.

21

From section 44...

"Nick speaking," he says when you call for the second time that night.

"Hi," you say, too enthusiastically. "It's Elle. From Friday?"

"Sure. Hey, did you call about an hour ago?"

You smack your forehead.

Crap. Caller ID. Worst and best dating technology of all time. Think quick.

"I did. The phone slipped from my hand before I could leave a message. Figured I'd just call back. Sorry about that."

"No problem. How's the patient?"

"The patient?"

"Your phone. Any damage?"

"Oh. Investing in smart phone protectors was a shrewd move."

You hear him laugh quietly, followed by silence. Your mouth goes dry.

"Anyway," you say. "I wanted to see if you're free Saturday."

"Saturday? I think I'm booked. My whole week is kind of nuts, actually. Can I check my calendar and call you back?"

"Sure. I'll give you my number."

"No need. I've got in now."

"Right. Okay. Well, I'll talk to you soon."

Okay, so you momentarily forgot how cell phones work, but it's not like you called *repeatedly* without leaving a message. All in all, you think you handled that quite nicely. After all, you've got a date - sometime this week.

Turn to section 51.

22

From section 61...

Thirty minutes: the total time elapsed before the stain removal seduction played out more-or-less as you predicted. This has resulted in you and a very shirtless Nick entangled on his couch.

He does an incredibly convincing impression of an octopus, with what feels like an unnatural, but not at all unpleasant, number of toned, rippled arms and strong hands exploring the terrain that is you. Not that you aren't a rather convincing metaphorical octopus, too. The last time you spent this much time *just* kissing a guy was in college.

As Nick's hand transitions from over your sweater to under it, you a) enjoy it immensely, and b) recognize this as a slippery slope. Not that finding your way at the bottom of said slope would be such a bad thing.

You and Nick have been dating for a while now. You've passed the arbitrary third date mark. You've stopped analogizing him to a giant squid - in spite of that great suction thing he's doing to your neck right now.

To let him keep going, turn to section 142.
To tell him to hit the showers, turn to section 113.

23

From sections 66 and 18...

Nick arrives a little tipsy and a lot friendly. You barely manage a hello before his mouth finds yours. He walks you backward and shuts the door with his foot. As your hallway make out moves to the bedroom, you're thankful you changed out of your footie pajamas and into a cute short-and-camisole set.

An hour later, you lay side by side in your bed wearing sated smiles - that is until he gets up and begins dressing.

"You can't stay?" you ask.

"Sorry. I'm babysitting Monster tomorrow. She's a handful, so I've gotta get some shut-eye. If I stay here, I doubt I'll get much sleep," he says with a wink.

You're disappointed but you don't want to pout. You throw on the cute, silky robe you reserve for male company and follow him to the front door where he pulls on his shoes.

"Okay. How about when Monster leaves?" you ask. What an adorable nickname. "Maybe we could catch a movie?"

"I'm not sure what time Rory's planning on picking Lana up. Why don't I call you when I have a better idea?"

"Sounds good."

He pulls you in for one last kiss and then he's out the door.

You go to sleep, crawling out of bed at noon. You check your phone, which shows no missed calls or texts. You laze around until two and spend a few hours doing housework and catching up on bills. Five o'clock rolls around and there's still no word from Nick. You think of calling him but don't want to interrupt his time with his niece. Instead, you shower and pretty yourself up so you'll be ready when he calls.

At seven, you eat leftover pizza and order some books online. At eight, you clean out *all* of your handbags and begin to rationalize why he hasn't called yet. You decide he's curled up on the couch asleep with Lana.

At quarter to nine, you wonder if maybe you *were* supposed to call him, so you do, but there's no answer. Come ten o'clock, once you've finally clued into the fact last night was a booty call, you climb back into your footie PJ's and watch The Notebook, which is always a great cover for crying over something else.

-END-

24

From section 35...

You look at your watch for no other reason than it supports your upcoming fib.

"As tempted as I am to fall for the old 'wait out the rain at my place' line," you tell Nick. "I told Rachel and Valerie I'd meet them for a drink or three."

He looks disappointed but he's a good sport about it. "Pretty transparent?"

"Completely see-through," you say with an exaggerated nod.

"I'll work on that for next time." When you arch a brow, he continues. "Next time with you. Not the next gi- I'm going to stop now."

"Good idea." You balance on your toes to give him three quick kisses, squealing when the rain becomes a full on downpour, leaving you soaked in freezing cold water. Not wearing white was a decidedly good idea.

Nick grabs your hand and quickly guides you to the exit, bobbing and weaving through the crowd. When the car, thankfully parked under an alcove, comes into view, Nick makes a run for it. The trunk is open by the time you catch up. He pulls a clean white towel out of his gym bag. Perfect timing because you are shivering and suspect you look like a drowned rat.

All smiles, he towel-dries your hair and then gently rubs the soft cotton over your shoulders and down your arms. You finally get why Nicholas Sparks always goes for "in the rain" scenes. He lassos you with the towel and pulls you in for a kiss that warms you to your toes. After a comfortably quiet ride home, Nick stops in front of your building. He jumps out in a flash, opens your door and ushers you into the lobby.

"I had fun today," you say. Kiss. "Thank you."

"You're welcome." Kiss. "I did, too."

"So, I guess I'll see you sooner or later."

One last kiss. "Sooner."

Continue to section 4.

25

From section 46...

You pull your shirt over your head and move in for another kiss, upping the pace and intensity while he explores the newly exposed flesh on offer. *Fair's fair,* you think and untuck his shirt, slipping your hands underneath, pleasantly unsurprised by his toned stomach and chest.

Yep, shirt's gotta go.

You tug upward and Nick swiftly removes it before rolling you under him. Your legs automatically wrap around his waist and then it's all sighs, soft moans. Almost perfect.

When you reach for his belt, Nick pulls back to look at you. "Are you sure?" His voice is hoarse and, *had* you any reservations, would've obliterated them.

"I'm sure." You kiss him again.

"Because I'm okay if you-"

"I know." And again.

"- want to get to know each other better first."

"Isn't that what we were doing?" You reach for his buckle.

The familiar jingle of the door at That Great Greasy Spoon brings you out of your daydream. You hear Rachel behind you. "I can see today's journal entry now. 'Dear Diary. Today a woman with an eye patch gave me a bikini wax.'"

"I didn't want to be abelist," says Val, sitting down next to you in the booth. Rachel slides in across from you. "How do you get out of that?"

"How about, 'Listen lady, I'm pretty attached to my clitoris so, if it's all the same, I'm just gonna keep my sascrotch this month.'" When you don't laugh, Rachel looks at you. "What's with you?"

"Nothing," you say, your voice a touch high.

She studies you, squinting. "You've got that 'properly laid' look, but I'm also getting…regret and…yes, underlying panic."

"*You had sex!*" whispers-screams Val. "And if Rach is right, good-to-great sex, so…"

You sigh. "We had *great* sex, and everything was fine until he suddenly got *really* weird, saying he had to be up early and can't sleep in a bed with someone he doesn't know well."

Val's mouth drops open in shock.

"What. A. Dick," growls Rachel. "What a fucking cliché."

"*I'm* the cliché," you say. A sexually aggressive cliché, apparently.

"I take it you haven't talked to him." Valerie offers a sympathetic pout.

"Not yet."

"No way," says Rachel, padding her jacket pockets in search of something before moving on to her bag. "You are *not* calling him."

"I won't." *Will.*

"Shit. I forgot my phone." Rachel holds her hand out. "Can I borrow yours? Gotta tell Roma I'm running late." You give her your phone and she walks outside to call her grandmother.

"I'd call him, too," says Val.

She tries to distract you with her tale of the one-eyed bikini wax until Rachel returns. You order breakfast and half-listen to your friends until it's finally time to go. You exit the diner and Rachel heads one way while you and Val go the other. You feel a surge of hope when your phone bleeps a moment later. It's immediately quashed when you find a text from Rachel, not Nick.

Just as you're thinking she must have found her phone, you read: *Hate me now, thank me later.*

No! No! No!

"I'll kill her." You swipe quickly through your phone and learn Rachel not only erased Nick from your address book, but cleverly erased all incoming and outgoing texts and calls attached to his number. You're furious with her for the next few days, but it dulls to mild rage by midweek when you still haven't heard from him. Ten days later, you thank her.

Continue to section 45.

26

From section 50...

What a difference three years makes.

First, Rachel is celebrating her one-year anniversary with Jet, the musician. Second, Valerie's marrying Collin (the world's hottest ophthalmologist) in two months, following a whirlwind courtship. Third, you just got back from speed-dating.

Wait, third should probably be that you're single. Fourth is the speed-dating thing.

Let's back up.

Two years after you and Nick got not-married, everything went downhill. You never left the house unless it was for errands, cuddling on the couch became a thing of the past, and sex (if you can call it that) happened but once a season - if *you* initiated it.

At first, you figured it was normal: marriage without the rings, right? It was bound to happen eventually. But then he started working out more, buying new clothes *and* a car, and spending more time with the guys. He told you he was reinventing himself so you ignored your gut and left well enough alone.

Six months ago, you couldn't find your keys and went to grab his for a quick coffee run. You reached into his laptop bag pocket and there, next to his brand new car keys, was Saturday's newspaper - folded to apartment rentals. A handful of listings were circled in red ink with notes in his handwriting, including, *Make offer!!!*

Seriously - three exclamation points.

You searched for reasonable explanations, like he wanted to surprise you with a bigger apartment, or an old college buddy was moving from somewhere without internet and needed help apartment hunting; but your gut was like, *Oh, come on!*

Small, seemingly unrelated observations you'd made about Nick's recent behavior pieced together like a puzzle. Nick, your non-husband, was leaving you.

"I was going to tell you," he said from the bathroom doorway when he realized the jigsaw was up.

"When?" you asked, eyes glued to the paper and filling with tears.

"When I found a place. I knew it would be hard…afterwards."

"So you did what was easiest for you." A tear splashed the page and bled the ink. "And your new image is, what, training to re-enter the dating scene?"

"Not exactly," he said, uncomfortably crossing and uncrossing his arms.

"Already have your eye on someone?" you asked, surprised at your calm, even tone.

His silence said everything.

"Oh, my god!" you finally screamed, tossing the paper in his general direction. "You're *with* someone? How long?"

"Not long. Like two months."

"*Two months!*" You grabbed a throw pillow from the couch and did as its name suggested, narrowly missing his head. "*You asshole.*"

And so it went.

His excuses were typical: things were getting too serious, he was too young to settle down, and a bunch of other crap. He moved out that night and you only saw him once more when he picked up his things. Unfortunately for him, you'd already donated most of them to charity.

Oops.

Now, here you are again…on your own. No single girlfriends, and your only romantic prospect is Günter, the cream of the very sad crop at the speed-dating event - your birthday gift from Rachel and Valerie.

The best part? Nick's getting married! The announcement was right next to Val's in last week's paper. Not only that, but he and his fiancée, Polly (who is so cute you could puke - on her) are getting married the very same day as your best friend. So while watching Val say her vows, you'll be thinking about his.

Asshole.

-END-

27

From sections 18 and 66...

You tell Nick you're exhausted and ask if you can call him tomorrow to make plans. He tells you it's "all good" and that he's actually pretty tired, too.

It takes *forever* to fall asleep after you say goodnight, but you wake up feeling proud that the little angel on your shoulder kicked that tiny devil's ass in a fight over whether or not to let him come over. The devil's got a decent track record.

In a great mood, you change into yoga clothes you have no intention of doing yoga in and make some coffee. You wait until eleven to call Nick, but he doesn't answer. You figure he's asleep and leave a message. You spend the next hour making breakfast, drinking more coffee and reading the news on your tablet. Still no call, so you shower and dress, sort some laundry and... there it is! The phone! Hooray!

It's your mother.

You talk to her for an hour, listening carefully for a call-waiting beep that never comes. Five hours later, you have a clean and stocked fridge, fresh bedding and polished toes, but still nothing from Nick.

What is going on?

He sounded fine when you told him you were sleeping. Yeah, he got off the phone quickly, but you figured he was just embarrassed he woke you up. He must be really hungover or he would've called you by now. Unless...

Unless you've lost your ability to recognize a booty call when you answer it. How did you miss that? Are you not hearing from him because you gave him a glass of milk and then told him the cow was asleep?

Maybe.

Probably.

Jerk.

-END-

28

From section 10...

You open your eyes. It's bright. Way brighter than your bedroom usually is. And your head hurts. And your sheets are blue.

Wait. Since when are your sheets blue?

You hear a shower running and it suddenly hits you.

You aren't at home.

You don't remember leaving the bar last night, and you certainly don't remember coming here...wherever here might be.

Oh, crap. What have you done?

If you look as bad as you feel, you need to get out of here. Immediately. You lift the sheet covering your body and are confused. You're still wearing your clothes. Most of them, anyway - you're missing your top, but your bra and everything else are right where you left them. Which is a small relief.

You sit up quickly and regret it. Your head is pounding. Looking around the foreign room, you see a garbage bin beside the bed, as well as a glass of water and two aspirin on the nightstand.

The fuck?

You greedily drink the water and will your brain to work. Last night comes back to you in chunks. You were at a bar with Rachel, Nick and his friends. You were having a great time flirting and laughing. You even danced. *He* even danced.

And you kissed! Often. And well.

Between Ted and Rachel, you always had a drink in your hand. When Rachel's current boy-toy, Jessie, showed up, she left with him. *Some wing woman.* The bartender announced last call. And that's it. That's all you remember.

"What did I do?" you say, falling back onto the pillow. "Where *am* I?"

"My place." Nick's standing in the doorway, wearing a towel below his abs - or around his waist. Whatever.

Lord. Those abs.

"Feeling okay?" he asks.

"Mortified. You?"

"A little hungover when I woke up, but I'm good now."

"Did we…?"

"*No*," he says, a little too emphatically for your liking. Not that you're not relieved. "You were pretty smashed."

"And how did I get here?"

"I tried to take you home in a cab, but you kept telling me to take you to the brothel." There's a ghost of a smile on his lips.

"The brothel…"

"I think we ended up outside your office."

You hate yourself.

"I figured it was easier to bring you here," he says, adjusting the towel.

"The bucket? Please tell me it was just a precaution."

"I'd be lying."

"In the cab?"

He winces. "My mother's front hall rug."

You close your eyes. "I am *so* sorry."

"Don't be. I hated that thing."

"And my shirt?"

"Collateral damage."

Of course.

"You gave me your bed?" you ask.

"Guest room."

And then it's silent.

What do you say when the gorgeous guy you met last night tells you that you're a drunken menace who destroys carpeting with your bodily fluids?

Got an extra toothbrush?

He speaks first. "Listen, last night was fun, and I hate to rush you out when you're not feeling well, but… Well, I've gotta be somewhere in an hour, so…"

"For sure. No problem."

He leaves for a moment and comes back with a tee shirt and spare toothbrush for you. You retreat to the bathroom, horrified by the raccoon eyes and wild hair that greet you in the mirror. You take a couple of minutes to pull yourself together before your walk of shame. When you exit the bathroom, Nick's standing in the front hall where you assume the ill-fated rug once lay. You walk to the front door.

"Give me a call sometime?" he asks as you pull on your shoes.

"Yeah, sure," you say, more to your feet than to him.

He hands you your purse, and before you know it, you're alone in the hallway outside his apartment. The hideous floral print lining the walls amplifies your nausea. Then you realize he didn't give you his phone number. You wonder if he knows that.

You're not going back to ask him.

-END-

29

From section 41...

Earlier, Nick mentioned a sister - a twin sister, named Rory.

This *thrills* you, not just because your little brother is also named Rory (and you love little coincidences like that), but also because it means Nick will understand just how close you are to your baby bro, and not hold it against you or resent your for it as many have in the past.

He told you she runs a salon called Nailed It, which she took over from their mother when she retired, but that's really it. Perfect. You love talking about your Rory, and odds are he likes talking about his Rory, too.

"So, tell me about your sister," you say, setting down your fork and picking up your wine. "Do you look alike? Do you see each other often? Does she have any kids?"

Well, that was…enthusiastic.

Nick appears to be entering the early stages of rigor mortis. His once relaxed posture becomes stiff, and his mouth goes tight. After an eon, he clears his throat. "Yeah. She has a girl. Lana. She's two."

"That's great."

He's probably the sweetest uncle.

"Yeah. So," he says, returning his focus to his plate. "Seen any good movies lately?"

That may be a Guinness World Record for fastest change of subject in a romantic setting. Seen any good movies lately?

Why didn't you think of that?

You tell him you just re-watched The Avengers the night before, which sparks a conversation about your shared love of movies based on comic book franchises.

You're relieved when Nick's shoulders relax and his light mood and easy smile return. You also silently vow to revert back to your comfort zone and let him take the lead on questions for a while.

And definitely, *definitely*, never ask about his parents.

Turn to section 42.

30

From section 5...

You're folding laundry when Val calls you from Ohio where she's attending an optometry conference. She grills you about your date.

"What did you wear?" she asks.

"Dark blue jeans and my white V-neck sweater."

"Good choice. What did you order?"

"Scallops. White wine."

"Smart. There are two things you, and I mean you personally, should never eat in front of a man. Anything with red sauce-"

"And salad. I know. Oh," you say proudly. "And I paid."

"You paid?"

"That's a bad thing?"

"Girl power, I say, but guys still get weird about it."

"I don't think he's like that." You remember Nick's surprise when he returned to find you signing a credit card receipt, but he didn't look mad.

"Have you heard from him yet?"

"No. You really think he's not going to call me because I paid for dinner? That's ridiculous."

"On its own, sure, but don't forget you texted him to gush about how great your date was, he didn't respond, then he calls and asks you to *meet him* at a restaurant - which, by the way, I told you was a bad move - and *then* you paid."

"So now I look desperate?"

"I might think so if I had a penis."

Maybe she's right and a lot of guys would find your actions to be a turn off, but you really don't think Nick's one of them. However, it is Thursday and you haven't heard from him since your date. You could call him but, if Valerie's right, that could just make things worse.

To call him, turn to section 81.
To wait to hear from him, turn to section 71.

3 1

From section 42...

Who says you don't have willpower? Usually Valerie, but tonight you prove her wrong.

Despite the intoxicating effect of Nick's highly-capable mouth on yours, the silky feeling of his hair, and the urge to drag him upstairs and have your way with him, you gently pull back.

"I should get inside," you tell him. Though, you can't remember why.

"Five more minutes?" He rubs his thumb along your jaw. Combined with the prettiest set of puppy dog eyes you've ever seen, he almost destroys your resolve.

Well played, Mother Nature. Well played.

Now you remember why it is that you're going upstairs instead of reliving the nostalgia of high school in the front seat of his car. "The last time I played that game, I was interrupted by a knock on the car window from my dad."

He raises an eyebrow, playfully suspicious. "I thought you lived by yourself."

"I do, but I happen to be having brunch with my dad tomorrow and if I'm out here too long, he'll know it."

He smiles. "All right, I give up."

"So easily?"

He pulls you to him for another kiss. "Rain check?"

"Yes, if we go out again, we can make out in your car for as long as you want. Definitely."

"If?" Another kiss.

"All right." *Yes!* "The next time we go out, we can make out in front of my building for as long as you want."

He nods emphatically and you press one last smiling kiss to his lips before climbing as gracefully out of the car as you can manage.

Okay, so you fibbed about your dad, but you've also got another date.

Turn to section 69.

32

From section 283...

Nick leans forward, folding his arms on the table. "Well, that went by fast."

You know what he means: too fast. Dessert dishes are empty on the table and your server will be by any moment now to collect them and inquire about the check.

You push your wine glass aside and mirror Nick's posture. When his eyes flicker downward, you silently thank Valerie for helping you pick out something tight if not revealing.

"Busted," you say, laughing when he looks up.

He gives you an unapologetic smile. "So to speak."

Is it warm in here or is it just him?

Nick's surprise kiss from earlier has you feeling a little bolder, having taken nervousness out of the equation. "So, good fast or bad fast?" you ask him, sliding a hand forward on the table. He does the same, closing his over yours.

"Decidedly bad. I might have a solution, though."

"Try me."

"Well, we could go to a lounge a couple doors down that has loud music and *people,*" he says, rolling his eyes. "Or, we could go to my place, which is just a few blocks from here, has wine and *no* people. But there's a caveat."

"Caveat?"

"You need to promise to be on your best behavior. You know - keep control of yourself once you're alone with me."

And there's the magic word: *alone.* You'd love to be alone with Nick. Right now. And maybe run a hand through his hair or, you know, something.

To join him at his place, turn to section 46.
To make like Macaulay and go home alone, turn to section 42.

33

From section 2...

Okay, so there's a *minor,* unsubstantiated red flag about Nick's feelings on marriage. All he said was that you disproved an old wives' tale. He didn't say, *Hey, way to blow the lid off that whole institution of marriage thing.*

It's a first date. You're not on a biological countdown, nor do you need to know whether or not he ever plans to tie the knot. Still, even if he won't come out and say he *doesn't* think weddings are a cult-like cash grab, and marriage an outdated institution for those who fear dying alone or who haven't read divorce statistics, *some* indication that he's not Fear of Commitment Guy would be welcome.

"So you said your family is in Palo Alto," Nick says. "Tell me about them."

Okay, good. He's bringing up family. Him. Not you. You can work with this.

You start with your dad, a quality control manager for a custom kitchen cupboard manufacturer, who warns you never to trust a man who can't work with his hands - despite the fact his own home repair attempts usually result in many bandages. Next, your mother, the holistic nutritionist who always preferred homemade organic apple pie to apple slices for an after school snack, and who, unlike your father, can wield a hammer like nobody's business.

"And then there's my brother, Rory," you say.

Nick's bright eyes widen. "Did you say Rory?"

"Yes." You draw out the word.

Please don't be dating my brother, too. Once was more than enough.

"Weird, my twin sister's name is Rory."

"Twin?" He has a twin sister. At last, someone who'll understand your relationship with Rory! Who won't feel threatened that you're as similar as you are different, or by the fact you share a shorthand language few can understand. Who won't-

"Yeah," says Nick with sort of a sad smile. "We're not really that close, actually."

"Oh." Unexpected. "Can I ask why?"

He exhales deeply. This is clearly not a favorite topic. "We used to be close -inseparable, actually. Then she got married right out of college and was hoping I'd do the same. When she had a kid, our lives took separate paths and we just kind of grew apart. Don't get me wrong, I love Lana - that's my niece - and I see her all the time, but Rory and I just don't connect like we used to. Anyway," he says, forcing a soft laugh. "Downer. You were telling me about *your* Rory."

Oh, wow.

You feel horrible for him. You also hate the idea of your relationship with your brother changing like that. And now you're supposed to rub your brotherly love in his face? Maybe there's a middle ground, also known as the coward's way out.

To be honest with him, turn to section 7.
To finesse the truth, turn to section 20.

34

From section 11...

This is a nightmare, a living, breathing nightmare.

It's also your engagement party.

Yours and Nick's favorite people gathered in one room to celebrate your upcoming nuptials. And it was all Mrs. Wright's doing. She insisted she and Nick's father throw you a lavish party at a swanky hotel to kick things off "right."

It sounded pretty innocuous at first. Nick was dreading it, but no more than his parents' other parties, and as much as you don't love fan-fare, they postponed a trip to Europe specifically for this purpose, so you didn't want to be ungrateful.

Though, you're getting there.

It was going pretty well until you introduced your sweet but sassy, middle class mom to Nick's demure, well-travelled, well-styled mother. At first, they were mutually rapturous about the engagement, but it all went to hell when they shared their individual vision for *everything:* the dress, the location, the season, the number of guests, the food, the color scheme...all of it.

And they agree on exactly nothing.

These are not details you care about *at all.* You just want to marry Nick. You never really thought past that. But now you've got a terrible feeling you're witnessing a preview of Mom v. Mom with you and Nick in the middle. A domestic partnership looks pretty damned good right about now.

Nick squeezes your hand and you know he's feeling it, too. "This is bad," he whispers, pulling you away from your families.

"I know," you say back.

"You don't know my mother." He looks genuinely afraid. "This is 'elope to Vegas' bad."

"Not a bad idea," says Rachel, coming up behind you.

You turn to her. "You're not getting out of a maid of honor dress."

"*Co*-maid of honor dress, my best friend since high school. And I assure you I've never had a problem getting out of a bridesmaid dress." Nick chokes as Rachel catches Val's eye and waves her over.

"I just put money down on your mom," Val says. "She may wear jeans with a nine-inch zipper, but she's hardcore. What's up?"

"Okay." Rachel claps a hand on yours and Nick's shoulders. "Look around. Is there anyone missing from this room who you would want at your wedding?"

Confused, you humor her and do a scan of your guests. "No," you and Nick say simultaneously.

"Perfect. Now, you remember how I'm an ordained minister, right?"

Thirty minutes and some fancy footwork by Val and Rachel later, you and Nick stand behind a curtain, watching your guests assemble in front of the staging area in the ballroom.

You look up at him when he squeezes your hand. "This is *crazy,*" he says.

"Scared of your mommy?" you tease, not a single nervous feeling in your body.

"Seriously, she sprouts a second head - with Swarovski-"

"Testing, one, two…" comes Rachel's voice from the stage, immediately drowned out by hooting and hollering from the crowd as they lap up her strapless, blood-red cocktail dress and curly dark hair spilling around her shoulders.

"Hey there, cats and kittens," she says when they quiet down. "My name's Rachel Winters, your host for the evening and maid of honor." Val clears her throat. "*Co*-maid of honor. You're probably expecting a bunch of boring speeches that are really just first drafts of the ones you'll hear at the actual wedding but, tonight, we're gonna shake things up a bit."

Val and your brother walk forward and stop just before the stage. Russ and Ted, Nick's groomsmen, do the same to their right. Rachel motions for you and Nick to come out and stand with her and, all at once, the crowd begins to whisper. You also hear a *harsh* curse word from Mrs. Wright.

"Second head," Nick says out of the corner of his mouth. You squeeze his hand again.

"Most of you don't know me," Rachel says, holding the mic like a lounge singer. "But if you did, you'd know there's no bigger romantic on this planet than *me*." You hear a few guffaws as she hooks a thumb at you and Nick. "Except for these two. They took one look at you beautiful people, already celebrating their *epic* love, and said to themselves, 'Why wait? Why not pledge our undying commitment to each other *right now?*'"

The room erupts into cheers, your mom and dad being the loudest. "Nice try, gang, but you still have to buy them gifts," Rachel jokes and the crowd laughs. "Seriously. I know how much money she's spent on all of you."

She directs you and Nick to stand in front of her. "Okay, kids. By the powers vested in me by some website, let's get you hitched."

-END-

35

From sections 82, 111 and 43...

You're having a great time at the zoo, oohing and ahhing at the animals doing their thing. You and Nick are constantly attached; be it hand-in-hand, arm-in-arm, or a hand tucked in the back pocket of the others' jeans. And in between making faces at monkeys and feeding peanuts to elephants, there's been a whole lotta laughing and kid-friendly kissing.

You even let him take a photo of you wearing life-sized kangaroo ears, too excited that he wants a picture of you to worry about looking ridiculous.

When you make it to the reptiles, your skin crawls, but Nick *loves* them. All of them. So you muster as much enthusiasm as possible, only to turn into a jumpy girly-girl at the first snake. Nick gets a kick out of it. He also holds you even tighter to protect you from the monstrosities behind the glass.

Twenty minutes later, your fear is gone. Not because you're suddenly in love with geckos, but because you're being crushed by the mixture of humidity and foul smelling critters in an enclosed space. Nick reaches his limit, too, and leads you both outside where you gulp down fresh air. You feel two wet drops on your face and look up to find a sheet of dark grey clouds moving swiftly in your direction. Clearly Mother Nature wants to put a damper on your date.

Nick suggests you hightail it to his place to watch a movie, which sounds like fun. Of course, it might just bring out the animal in him. Or you.

If it's raining man, turn to section 59.
To take a rain check, turn to section 24.

36

From section 310...

You tell Nick you need to think and head to your parent's house in Palo Alto. They've been married for thirty years, so if anyone's going to have relevant insights in this arena, it's your mom.

When you called to give her a heads up you were coming, her intuition prompted her to send your father on some errands while she put a fresh batch of your favorite oatmeal raisin cookies in the oven.

Okay, that's not entirely true. She *did* send your father away but, instead of baking, she stuck a bottle of white wine in the fridge to chill for your arrival. By the time you finish your first glass of chardonnay, your mom's up to speed on your dilemma.

"Do you think Dad really wanted to get married?" you ask.

"Fat chance." She snorts into her glass.

"What?"

"Don't get me wrong, honey," she says, laying her hand over yours. "Your father and I are happy, but he wasn't exactly jumping for joy about the wedding."

"Are you...? Was I...unplanned?" She takes a long drink. *"I was!"*

"I'm kidding. Your brother was, but I'll deny saying so." She laughs heartily. "People did everything earlier back then. We'd graduated college, we had grown-up jobs, and we were in love. Marriage was just what you did next if you had someone."

The fact this is the exact argument you just used on Nick is not lost on you.

"I always wanted to get married, and I know your father's glad we did - especially now that he's gained in beer belly what he's lost in hair," she says with a pointed look. "But it was his parents who nudged him to propose - *not* with a shotgun. It was going to happen eventually, so why not be practical?"

"What would you have done if Dad said he never wanted to marry you?"

She answers without hesitation. "I'd have left him for Billy Parker next door.

He was getting ready to take over the family textile operation and *always* had a thing for me." She gets a faraway look in her eyes and you poke her shoulder. "But I probably would've regretted it for a long time - in really expensive shoes."

She stands and clears the table. "You can't go based on what I *might* have done, though," she says. "You have to think about what you're willing to live without in order to be with him *and* whether he's thinking as far ahead as you are."

To cut your losses, turn to section 68.
To lose your expectations, turn to section 243.

37

From section 137...

You decide your career is more important than a little casual conversation with the (awesome, incredibly funny and sexy) guy you're dating and get back to work.

You block out the little voice that keeps telling you, *One e-mail to tell him you're busy would be okay,* by plugging in your headphones and grooving to Lorde as you fly through each task. You're even a week early delivering a new business proposal the V.P. of the technology group, Sheri-Lee (call me Sheri) Campbell handpicked you to write.

You've been looking for opportunities to move into her department for a while. She's a great manager who's fun to work with, even though she rules with an iron fist. She's also down to Earth and covered in neat tattoos. She's a bit of a PR badass - your agency's Kelly Cutrone.

Sheri is so impressed with your ideas that she stops by your office. You're mortified when she finds you warbling Love Club. You yank out your ear buds. "Sheri. Hey! Sorry about that."

"No worries," she says, all smiles. "Lorde? Love her."

Phew! "She kind of owns me."

Sheri nods agreement and holds up your proposal. You hold your breath. "This is good stuff." Commence breathing. "You've got an instinct for tech. I think we could even expand on your ideas. Free to grab dinner and talk about it?"

"Absolutely," you reply, even though you can't remember if you have plans. You'd postpone life-saving surgery for this.

You float through the rest of the day on a high. At dinner, you and Sheri go through your proposal in detail, brainstorming enhancements. You've got a great rapport, and to say you like her better than your current boss would be the understatement to end all understatements.

"Ever thought about switching departments?" Sheri asks as she hands her company credit card to your server.

"I have, actually."

"Good. Let's see how this pitch goes and we'll talk about it."

At eight o'clock, you're in a cab en route to your apartment. You power up your phone, which immediately bleeps out message notifications. There's a *long* three-way text thread with Rachel and Valerie debating which of them you consider to be your best friend - and why each of them do or don't deserve the title. Knowing it's more about competition than you, you reply, *Cupcake bake-off tiebreaker.* Next is a voicemail from Nick.

Oh my!

You actually forgot about his e-mail. And thank goodness for that! You likely wouldn't have just had a potentially career-changing conversation if you'd gotten caught up in a flirt pro quo.

"Hey," his message says. "Sorry about earlier. I got pulled into a meeting literally the moment I pressed send on that e-mail. Looks like you had a busy one, too. Call me later. Oh, and Martha Stewart."

All around successful day.

Continue to section 104.

38

From section 44...

Beep!

You're on.

"Hi, Nick. This is Elle. Masters. From Friday. Which was fun, so I thought I'd see if you still wanted to hook up, I mean, get together. I'm pretty busy during the week, but I'm open Saturday night. Let me know if that works for you. Okay. Bye."

You're free every night this week, but he doesn't need to know that.

Exactly forty-six minutes later, not that you were counting (not that you weren't), your phone rings. You feel a mixture of relief and butterflies when Nick's name lights up the screen.

"Hey," he says when you answer. "You called."

You smile. "I said I would."

"You did, but I was starting to worry you'd changed your mind."

Seriously? "Guys do that?"

"No."

"But you do."

"Maybe."

You laugh. A few minutes later, you've got a time set for him to pick you up on Saturday for your first date!

Yay!

Turn to section 79.

39

From section 117...

Okay, so big deal. A couple of days ago, Nick wanted to defer buying *regular* tickets to The Broken Records for a couple of weeks. He didn't defer seeing *you* until then. Maybe he's got some kind of phobia.

Or a mysterious illness.

And these are amazing seats.

Front row seats.

With backstage passes.

This is a different story entirely.

"Can I assume I have Rachel to thank for this?" Nick asks. "With flowers, or...vodka?"

You laugh. "I'm sure the thanks would do, but if you feel compelled, she does like vodka. And rum. And rye."

"I'll tap into my stash of airline liquor bottles."

"Okay, so I guess it's a date then."

"Oh, this is more than a date," he says, his voice low and serious. "*This* will be the best date ever. This date will put dates on The Bachelor to shame."

You're still laughing, proving you were absolutely right not to read too much into the other day. Worst case scenario - if Rachel's right and Nick really isn't sure you'll still be dating by the time the concert rolls around - you'll just have her find you an appropriate rebound stud to go with you, and give *him* the date of *his* life.

Maybe the night of his life, too.

Continue to section 101.

40

From section 5...

It's Wednesday night. Your day at the office has been as long as it's been bad and you can't get out of there fast enough.

You zip home and change into yoga pants and your softest sweatshirt before walking to the kitchen to retrieve a chilled bottle of wine and a glass. You settle on the couch, fill 'er up and turn on the TV, feeling a surge of guilty pleasure as you press play on Monday's episode of The Bachelor.

A quarter of the way into the show, you're nearly finished with the bottle and feeling just fine. Your muscles have unclenched and the stress of the day is but a distant memory. You're typing out a snarcastic #TheBachelorette tweet on your phone when it rings in your hand, startling you.

You feel a little light-headed when you see Nick's name on the display and wonder if that - and the fact you're yelling at the people on TV like your dad does while watching sports - is a sign you shouldn't pick up the phone.

You also really want to talk to Nick.

If you'll accept this call, turn to section 67.
To decline the call, turn to section 82.

41

From section 134...

You successfully spin your job in PR, using broad speak about the opportunities for professional, interpersonal and personal growth at your company, careful to stay on message. When your meals arrive, you transition into a fluffy topic to avoid more questions. You're a pro.

The conversation loses steam and you realize Nick's been doing all the heavy lifting. It's your turn. Getting to know you questions are tricky, which is why you let guys do most of the asking. A harmless query can easily trigger a silent panic alarm only guys can hear, urging him to flee from Serious Girl.

Val once asked a date how long his parents were married and he actually stood up and yelled, *"Chicks!* We just met and you're talking about marriage?" Then he stormed out and stuck her with the check.

When Rachel asked a guy to share his Freebie List with her, he said it seemed like "jealousy trap." Rachel who broke into hives the first time someone called her his girlfriend!

You chew your salad and review tonight's subjects. You've talked about school (he was Prom King, you were…at your prom), work (he's fulfilled, you're not), close friends (yours are nuts, his sound great), where you were grew up (city boy, suburban girl), literary tastes (yours are good, his are questionable, but he reads, so you'll go with it), and you know he's tattoo free (a little disappointing). So what's next?

To ask him what happened with his last relationship, turn to section 2.
To learn more about his family, turn to section 29.

42

From sections 29, 7 and 32...

You're in Nick's car en route to your apartment. The closer you get, the more charged the air between you feels. You don't talk much, but it's a comfortable break from conversation.

You steal peripheral glances at him, hoping you're being subtle and not creepy. He even drives hot, his hands all masculine and hand-modely. *Oh, to be that steering wheel.* He's got a perfect profile - rugged and chiseled, with high cheekbones, a straight nose, square jaw and strong chin.

Can you date a guy with nicer cheekbones and longer lashes? Yes!

You bet he rolls out of bed looking like his hair was just styled - *by God.* When did you become so superficial? The day you met Nick.

You arrive at your building and he pulls into a visitor spot.

"Here we are." He smiles, almost shyly, an adorable contrast to his confident demeanor. His profile is great, but full frontal face is heaven, right down to the widow's peak and dimple in his chin. Not to mention the dusting of stubble that's grown in since he picked you up. You're a metaphorical puddle.

And here's the awkward moment you've been looking forward to all night. For what feels like forever, you alternate between looking in his eyes, at your lap, and at his stupidly generous mouth with its perfect Cupid's bow.

Finally, he leans in and kisses you softly. Your hand goes to his chest and his moves to your lower back, bringing you as close as the car's console will allow. When he deepens the kiss, you grab a fistful of his shirt.

The last thing you want to do is stop, but if you don't...

To put on the brakes, turn to section 31.
To keep on kissin', turn to section 84.

43

From section 9...

You'd be happy to talk to Nick until the sun comes up tomorrow, but you decide against it. Better to leave him wanting more and all those clichés.

"So," you say, standing up from the couch to stretch. "I should probably get going."

"Hot date?" he asks.

You make your way around your apartment, shutting off lights and powering down your computer as you go. "Wouldn't you like to know?"

"I would," he says wistfully. "But I'll settle for making plans for the weekend."

You're glad he can't see the silly grin on your face. "I'm free on Saturday. How about you?"

"Works for me. Any idea what you'd like to do?"

"I'd *love* to go to the zoo." You've always wanted to do a zoo date. "I don't think I've been since my sixth grade field trip."

"Lions and tigers and bears it is. I'll pick you up around one?"

"It's a date."

You hang up and connect your phone to its charger in the kitchen before heading to the bathroom to wash your face. You're about to settle into bed with a book when your phone bleeps. You pad back to the kitchen and swoon when you see Nick's text: *Sweet dreams.*

You count to sixty and type out a quick reply: *Same to you. X.*

Continue to section 35.

44

From section 3...

"Call him yet?" Rachel asks the moment you answer the phone. She's never beat around a bush in her entire existence.

You tuck the phone between your chin and shoulder. "Call who?" Thanks to the nervous energy you're directing into dusting, your voice sounds remarkably casual. Especially given it's Monday night, which means you can officially call Nick without looking desperate.

"Oh, I don't know... Nick? The reason you annoyed the fuck out of me all weekend with questions like, 'What if he met someone else?' and, 'What if I call him on Monday and he's away on a month-long business trip?' and, 'What if he eloped over the weekend?'"

"I never said that!"

"Not out loud."

Maybe.

You sigh. "No. I haven't called."

"After all that, what are you waiting for?"

"I'm in the middle of something." Yeah. In the middle of waiting until 7:12 p.m., which you've decided is the perfect, seemingly random, after work, after dinner, before whatever bachelors do at night, time to call. Calculated torture.

"6:57 or 7:08?"

"Shut up."

"I'm going with after seven."

"7:12." You rapidly rub at the tip of your itchy nose and fight the urge to sneeze.

"Fuck you, buddy!"

"Aw, that's sweet. You know, you're my best friend, too."

"Not you. Just some old broad who probably shouldn't have a licence."

"I've always loved that you never exclude the elderly from your road ragings.

It's very progressive."

"I'd be mayor if it weren't for my misspent youth."

"And adulthood. Where are you headed anyway?"

"Weekly stop at my dealer's. Just pulling up."

"Your grandmother's glaucoma is the greatest thing that ever happened to you."

"I know it. Call me later?"

"Sure. Kiss Roma for me."

You hang up and check the time. It's 7:02.

Screw it. Good enough.

You find Nick's name in your contact list, deciding you like how it looks there - like it belongs. You take a moment and loosely script some small talk before hitting send.

It's ringing.

Still ringing.

Damn. Voicemail.

You weren't expecting that. Recorded messages are not your forte.

To leave a message after the beep, turn to section 38.
To hang up and try again later, turn to section 21.

45

From section 25...

Rachel enlists you to pick up a bottle of rum on your way home. You note your good luck when you find a parking spot right out front the liquor store. Even better, the store is nearly empty instead of the Friday night mob you expected. *Everything's coming up you*!

And then you see him.

Standing by a vodka display, typing into his phone, is Nick. He's just as you remember him: tall, solid and loin girding good-looking. Warmness in your chest ripples outward - it's like your body's sighing. Then you remember the last time you saw him and the weeks you waited for him to call, and your stomach sinks.

You're about to walk away when he abruptly looks up. At you. You're easily fifteen feet away but can see his eyes clearly, all crystal blue and stupid. After a moment of awkwardly staring at each other, his mouth lifts in a half smile. Any anger Rachel tried to rouse in you since the last night you were together is gone.

So you might as well torture yourself.

You smile and approach him. "Hey."

"Hey yourself," says Nick, looking as relaxed as you feel.

"You look good."

"Um, thanks." He rakes a hand through his hair and you remember how soft it is. "You, too."

"Didn't think I'd see you again."

He laughs sharply. "Yeah. I picked up on that."

Huh? "I don't-"

"It's funny - maybe even karma - but I think I finally have an inkling of what it feels like to be a girl."

"I'm sorry?"

"I waited two, maybe three, weeks for you to call. Felt pretty dumb."

This makes no sense. "*I* waited weeks for you to call me. You-you practically threw me out of your apartment."

He blinks, his head jerking back slightly. "I thought that's what you wanted. You were…"

You wince. "Aggressive?"

"A little." He smiles wryly.

"I just didn't want you to think I was going to have expectations…after." You just assumed… He's a guy, and most guys would be good with that. Wouldn't they? Except him! He's not. And he's standing right in front of you. Divine intervention!

Praise something!

He opens his mouth to speak, but stops himself.

"Maybe we could try again," you say. "I mean, I'm game, if-."

"Nicky!" comes an excited, melodious voice behind you. *Nicky* cringes. "I found it!"

Appearing at his side, hand naturally molding into his, is a cartoon-like beauty with white-blonde hair, huge green eyes and a pert little nose. She smiles cheerfully at you. No subtext. No insecurity about her role in his life. Your PR self takes over and you extend your hand in introduction. She gives it a dainty shake.

"Sorry," Nick cuts in, clearly feeling tortured. "This is Polly. My girlfriend."

His girlfriend. Polly!

"Great to meet you!" says Polly Perfect.

He's coupled up, running errands with a girl he may never have met if you weren't a borderline-nympho blabbermouth who cavalierly gives her phone to someone who's almost *always* up to something.

Using your "You'd never know I secretly hate you" voice, you say a quick goodbye and flee, making it to the car before you realize you forgot Rachel's rum.

-END-

46

From section 32...

It turns out Nick's family is rich. At least that's the impression you get the moment you step onto the (hideous) Persian rug in the front hall of his Nob Hill condo.

This place is ginormous. You're in awe from the hardwood floors all the way up to the vaulted ceilings and chandeliers. The furniture is eclectic in many shades of brown and black, with different woods and metals thrown into the mix. Each doorframe is painted black in contrast to stark white walls.

You stand in front of a marble fireplace in the living room, hands clasped safely behind your back as you look at what appears to be a recent family photo. Nick's twin sister, Rory, has straight blonde hair and fine features like their mother, while Nick has the dark, wavy hair and angular features of his father. They share their mother's bright blue eyes. Those eyes could get a girl into serious trouble.

Nick returns from the kitchen with wine and hands you a glass. You smile your thanks and watch him walk to the stereo. Music fills the room and he sits on the couch, draping an arm across the back.

You walk over to join him. "No Sade?" you ask.

"Smooth Operator is for people who don't understand irony." You feel light-headed at the site of his killer smile, with those straight, but slightly uneven teeth, and perfect (like *perfect*) lips, which you should really stop staring at.

"Busted," he says, and your eyes dart up to his.

Hoping he can't see you blush, you set your glass on the coffee table and turn back to him. "How serious are you about that caveat?"

He places his glass next to yours, his mouth tugging up in one corner. "Not even a little."

You nod slowly. "Good to know." It's a challenge. A challenging challenge, because you really just want to-

Hello...

His perfect mouth is on yours! Your eyes flutter shut and you slide your hands up his back. When he pulls you against him, your stomach does a triple sow cow. His lips skim along your jaw to that spot on your neck that *does things* to you - like makes you push him against the backrest and straddle him. That kind of stuff.

He carefully pushes your hair back until his hands frame your face. You'd be uncomfortable under his gaze if you weren't hypnotized by it. "Beautiful," he says and kisses you again.

No kiddin'.

You press your fingertips into his shoulders as his hands slide along your neck, down your arms and over the thin fabric covering your ribs. They come to rest on your hips - or, half on your hips, half on the highly sensitized skin of your waist. You sigh against his mouth when he brings you closer.

This is all pretty innocent, but it feels so much better than that. You know where this could end up, but you're not sure if you should go, even though you really, *really* want to.

Really.

To see where this leads, turn to section 25.
To lead yourself to the door, turn to section 84.

47

From section 49...

The credits roll, the lights come up, and your fellow moviegoers rise from their seats, stretching, chatting, and throwing empty popcorn bags on the ground. When Nick stands to leave, you stay planted firmly in your seat.

He looks back at you and smiles. "All set?"

"In a minute," you tell him, zipping your purse closed. "I just need to say something first."

"Uh oh." He stuffs his hands in his jean pockets. "Sounds ominous."

"It's just that before the movie, at the concession, I guess I feel like you were a little hard on that kid."

His head jerks back, his brows raise. "How so?"

"Yes, he messed up our order and took a *really* long time, but he's obviously new and he felt terrible."

Nick leans back on his heels, surprised he's being chastised. "Are you heading up the union for movie theater concession guys or something?"

"I worked in a theater when I was in high school. It can be a crappy job."

His tone grows more defensive. "Do you expect me to go and apologize to him or something?"

"Listen, I don't want to fight, I just wanted to tell you what I thought."

"Well, you did that," he says. He looks down at his shoes for a moment. "Okay, maybe you're right. I may have overreacted a little."

"All I'm sayin'." You stand and kiss his cheek before grabbing your things and following him out of the auditorium, happy with yourself for speaking your mind.

Outside the theater, you suggest coffee in hopes of shaking off your little confrontation, but Nick tells you he's not feeling well. When he drops you off at home, you suggest getting together on Friday. He tells you it should be fine, but he'll call you during the week to confirm. You try to ignore the nagging feeling you may have gone too far.

Wednesday rolls around and your mom calls to tell you she and Uncle Lou are driving in from Palo Alto this weekend and want to take you to dinner on Friday. You'd love to spend time with your eccentric uncle, but you still haven't heard from Nick about your tentative plans for the same night.

To call Nick and see if you're still on, turn to section 76.
To carry on with your family, turn to section 86.

48

From section 20...

When your server clears your plates, you feel a kernel of nervousness in your stomach. Your date, which has been decidedly good, is almost over. You could get dessert, but your kernel warns against it. Still, not really wanting your date to be over is a good thing. You take advantage of a quiet moment to slip away and strategize your next move.

"I'm going to pop over to the ladies' and spare us both the fake grab for my wallet when the check comes," you tell Nick.

He nods. "And I'll be ducking out the front door the moment you're out of sight."

"I expect as much."

He stands when you do, very much a gentleman. You step into the busy foot traffic of the restaurant, gasping when Nick suddenly grabs your arms and pulls you to him. Behind you, a bus boy mumbles, "Coming through." You are now face-to-face with Nick's, you know, face.

You rule, bus boy!

Clear and present danger averted, Nick still holds your arms, a grin pulling at his lips. All you can do is stare dumbly.

"Saved your life," he says, not letting go.

The kernel in your stomach gets warmer. "So you did. Do I have to kill someone for you now?"

"Nah. I'm not that old fashioned."

"Too bad. I've got this monthly quota and there's a co-worker I've been meaning to off. Two birds."

Yep. He's still holding on to you. He's still gorgeous. Still has a mouth.

His eyes narrow slightly. "But since you're here, there is something you could help me with."

The kernel tumbles like it's in a tiny dryer. "Looking for a preferred rate on car insurance?"

He begins to shake his head and then stops. "Can you get me a preferred rate on car insurance?"

"Nope."

"In that case…"

You're lucky he hasn't released you because the moment your lips touch, he's the only thing holding you up. Your fingers grip the material of his shirt and the kernel goes *pop!* For a soft kiss, it sure sucks the air out of your lungs. He pulls away after a moment, ensuring you're safely upright before he lets go of you.

"Okay," you say. You can't remember why you're standing. What do you do now? You should excuse yourself to bathroom to… *Right.*

"So, of course, feel free to say no," he says. *Yes!* "But I live around the corner. We could go there. Have a drink. Talk some more…"

Kiss some more.

Well, this answers your question as to what to do next. It's early. You're clearly hitting it off, and giving up an opportunity to keep looking at his kind of perfect face would be like leaving the Louvre before you…saw some super beautiful painting.

Of course, being alone with him could lead to being *with him…*

To avoid a roll in the hay, turn to section 328.
To roll the dice, turn to section 57.

49

From sections 83 and 84...

You and Nick agree on the newest Channing Tatum movie. It's the fairest compromise: action and foul language for him, action, foul language and bulging biceps for you. He buys the tickets and you walk hand-in-hand to the concessions stand to purchase the essentials: popcorn, Twizzlers, Peanut M&Ms and soda.

The kid behind the counter lays your order out in front of you and you notice he's given you two regular sodas instead of one regular and one diet (Nick's. Go figure.), as well as chocolate M&Ms. You kindly point out the errors, which he quickly fixes before ringing up your order.

You watch him unsuccessfully hit multiple combinations of buttons on the cash register, the machine bleeping loudly each time he makes an error. His face is turning redder by the second, and...yep, that's sweat on his brow. Nearly two minutes later, you still don't have your total. You're cringing for this poor kid. Nick's, well...

"Dude," says Nick, head raised to the ceiling. "Can we hurry this up?"

Maybe he just really likes previews.

The kid apologizes, takes a deep breath, and attacks the buttons again, with no luck. Nick sighs loudly.

You suggest he grab your seats while you pay. After a moment's hesitation, he hands you your ticket and says he'll see you inside. You look at the kid behind the counter who is now sweating bullets. According to his employee badge, his name is Justin.

"Sorry about that, Justin" you say sympathetically. He looks up, surprised. "New to the job, huh?"

He tells you it's his first day working alone and thanks you for being patient. He also looks at your chest more than once, but you remind yourself he's a horny teenager. A minute later, you're on your way with your snacks.

You find Nick and sit down just as the previews end. Though slightly improved, he's definitely still in a mood. You try to focus on appreciating Channing, but can't help thinking about how unnecessarily rude Nick was to that poor, horny kid

To let it go, turn to section 73.
To tell him what you think, turn to section 47.

50

From section 310...

Though you've pretty much got your mind made up, you figure it couldn't hurt to take a walk and clear your head. It also doesn't hurt that it's probably freaking Nick out just a little.

Over two hours and two Chai lattes, you reflect on why it is that marriage has suddenly become so important to you. Growing up, you never dreamt about it the way your girlfriends did, but now that you're older, you've conformed - a little.

You just don't know when it happened.

You like the idea of celebrating your commitment to one person in front of friends and family, the professionally retouched pictures that will eventually prove how hot you once were, and even (maybe mostly, as ashamed as you are to admit it to yourself) the beautiful, unjustifiably expensive dress you'll only wear once. That's really it, though. Oh, and presents. At the very least, it would be nice to see ROI on the gifts you've shelled out for over the years.

But that's a wedding.

Not a marriage.

Sure, there's the whole "security" thing that comes from signing a paper and committing to another person forever, but is that realistic? Don't something like ninety percent of marriages end in divorce these days? And how many of those couples would've stayed together if they *hadn't* gotten married?

You could break up with Nick and spend the next twenty years looking for the Mr. to your Mrs. and still never find him. No. You know a good thing when you've got it and Nick is more important than a single day everyone but you will ultimately forget anyway, and which will likely put you into debt. Plus, with all the money you'll save on a wedding, you can buy all of the monogrammed towels and crystal champagne flutes your heart desires.

You return to the apartment and wake Nick, who's asleep on the couch next to the same pile of unfolded clothes. You sit beside him and he rouses with a sleepy smile as you brush the hair off his forehead.

"I'm okay with not getting married," you say.

He looks at you cautiously and then closes his eyes again. "For a second I thought I was awake."

"You are." You laugh softly. "I thought about it and you're right. I don't want to give up everything we have for a single day that won't change anything."

"You're sure? You're not saying this today and then a year from now you go and hatch some clever ruse to get me to marry you?"

"Ruseless, I promise," you say, raising your right hand. "But I have a condition."

"Does it involve tattoos?"

"Nope."

"Then I'm listening."

"You have to buy me a really expensive dress and sit for professional photos that will capture my eternal beauty and our undying love."

"Um, okay," he says, still unsure of what exactly just happened. "Is that all?"

"That's all."

"Awesome."

It *is* awesome.

Turn to section 26.

5 1

From section 21...

As Tuesday's workday draws to a close, you feel butterflies multiply in your stomach in anticipation of Nick's call confirming your first date. The day turns to evening, and then into night. When you still haven't heard from him after reorganizing your dresser drawers, the anticipation morphs into disappointment.

The next day you wake with renewed enthusiasm. You're sure you'll hear from Nick by the end of the day. You feel great all morning at work, through tedious afternoon client meetings and a particularly crowded BART ride home. But when it comes time to get ready for bed, the only action your phone has seen is a text from Val saying her blind date's outfit nearly blinded her. The underlying feeling of disappointment gives way to dread.

By Thursday, against both Rachel and Valerie's advice, you call Nick once more. You tell yourself it would be silly not to, given the obvious chemistry between you. And besides, with your luck, he probably accidentally deleted your number instead of saving it and is currently panicking over the notion he'll never hear from you again, or worrying you've found someone else.

When his machine picks up after the third ring, you leave him a short and sweet message with your number and availability over the weekend.

Now it's Sunday afternoon and, not only are all of your scarves sorted by color and neatly folded, but you're finally ready to accept that you won't be hearing from Nick.

You scroll to his number in your phone and stare at it. For a split second, you consider hitting call but hit "Delete Contact" instead. The screen asks if you're sure. You hit "Yes."

Easy come, easy...sigh.

-END-

52

From section 293...

You go for a walk after breakfast to digest your friends' advice. You know Nick appreciates your support of how hard he works - even if it's murder on your time together - but today is today, and tomorrow is tomorrow.

What if this busy period drags on until he eventually decides he's bored with you? Or worse, what if it's just a preview of your future with a workaholic husband, minus the kids? Are you just setting yourself up for disaster?

You make a decision to get your cute little butt in motion and, well, get a life.

For the next two weeks, you're barely home. Even less than Nick is. You add a couple of classes at the gym, reach out to friends you haven't seen in a while, and even volunteer at an after-school program.

You're the best kind of tired, barely managing to keep on top of your own chores, let alone Nick's. And screw cooking - you've got plenty of time to master sautéing.

You feel great! You almost forgot what you were like before Nick: Fun. Spontaneous. A little needy, but still fun and spontaneous.

Your resurgence as a social butterfly throws Nick for a loop. He's never said anything outright - What could he say? *Hey, babe. Could you get around to my laundry after you make dinner?* - but his behavior has changed.

He calls you when you're not together - like he *misses* you or something. He hasn't done that since before you moved in together. He's scaled his weekly poker game back to monthly so you can "go out together" more often and even made dinner for you last night.

Maybe you should listen to your friends more often - you know they think you should.

Turn to section 297.

53

From section 77...

The week after you met Nick, you were all the clichés wrapped into one. You were walking on air, then on sunshine, all the way up to Cloud 9.

When a week passed and you hadn't heard from him, you had the blues, were down in the dumps, and looked like you'd just lost your best friend.

By week three you were seeing red, mad as a hatter, and fit to be tied over the fact adults *still* take a person's number with no intention of calling them.

Friday rolled around and you jumped at Rachel and Val's invite to Mix after work, ready to pick yourself up and dust yourself off. You had no intention of meeting someone new, but Rachel still shoved a couple of condoms (one regular, one large) in your purse, insisting that if you *do* decide to get back on the horse, you won't be going bareback.

And now here you are.

"How about him?" asks Rachel, nodding toward a spiky-haired guy across the bar. He's cute - light brown hair, tall, dressed in black. The studded leather bracelet on his wrist isn't really your thing.

"Nah," you tell her and sip your drink. "Not my type."

"Not for you, selfish - for me."

"Oh. In that case, absolutely."

She's considering making her move - of standing there and waiting for him to come to her - when you spot Valerie on her way back from the ladies room. You know something's off from her hurried pace and wide eyes.

"What's eating you?" Rachel asks when she reaches you.

Val speaks quickly. "Nothing. Just bored. Hate the music. Should we go somewhere else? Let's go somewhere else. Cab's on me."

"I was about to set a trap," says Rachel. "Can you keep your panties on long enough for me to figure out if I want to take mine off?"

Val adjusts her glasses and steals a sidelong glance to her left. "We'll get stuck in a line. Now's a perfect time to go."

"You're extra weird right now," you say. Rachel curses under her breath and you notice her eyes locked in the same direction Valerie keeps looking. You turn your head and curse, too - but not under your breath. *"Mother fucker."*

Nick. Right there in living color. And he's walking toward you. You're torn between meeting him halfway and cursing him a blue streak or getting the hell out of Dodge, but you can't move. Before you know it, he's in front of you. Looking sheepish. And gorgeous. Mostly gorgeous.

"Ladies," he says with a half-smile, looking only at you. He rubs a hand over the back of his neck.

"Hey, jerk," says Rachel, earning an elbow from Valerie.

Nick winces, but doesn't waver. "Can I talk to you in private for a minute?" he asks you, clearly uncomfortable. *Good.* "Please. Just for a minute."

"Here's an idea," says Valerie, always one for the benefit of the doubt. "I'm going to buy Rachel a strong drink and you two can chat."

And then they're gone. You don't know if you want to kiss Valerie or kill her.

"Hey," he says softly, resting a hand on your arm.

You exhale. "Hey."

"I'm so glad you're here."

"And here I was worried you were using the 'wait three weeks to call' rule."

He drops his hand to his side. "I went to call you the next day, but your number was incomplete."

You roll your eyes. You entered your number in his phone yourself. He pulls it from the inside pocket of his suit jacket, hits a few buttons and holds it up to you. There's your name and *most* of your number - it's missing the sixth digit. You feel a flutter of hope, but there's also a voice telling you to tread carefully.

"You could have *just* deleted a digit."

He shakes his head. "I didn't. I swear. I called eighteen people hoping the missing number was either the first or last one."

You study his face hoping for a clue: a twitch, lack of eye contact - something. But this is the same confident guy you met a few weeks ago. He could be telling the truth, but how would you know? This could be a routine he and his buddies use on girls all the time.

"Look, you hardly know me, and you've got no reason to believe me, but I've been here every week hoping you'd show up." He's got the eye contact thing down, you'll give him that. "We had a good time, right? I really want to see you again. Please?"

You're torn.

You don't know if you want to kiss him or kill him.

If you want to give him the benefit of the doubt, turn to section 314.
If you doubt he's telling the truth, turn to section 259.

54

From section 73...

"Thanks, but I've reached my limit unless you want to carry me home," you say, setting down your purse.

"More for me." Nick quickly downs both shots and firmly sets the glasses back on the table before signaling for the check. Ten minutes later, you're still waiting for the bill and Nick is increasingly agitated - his cheeks are red, he sighs loudly and often, scrubbing his face with his hand. When he spots your harried server doling out drinks to a table ten feet away, he shouts, "Miss. Could we get our check sometime tonight? Please."

Blushing, your server tucks her now empty tray under her arm and hurries to the register at the back. A dozen or so customers turn to see what all the fuss is about and you are mortified. And shell-shocked.

He's just having a bad day. He isn't normally this cantankerous. At least not from what you've seen during the time you've spent together. He's probably just amped a little because of the extra shots.

"Finally," Nick says when the server sets the bill on the table.

"I'm really sorry," she says. Her nametag says Bonnie. Her hair is pulled back in what was probably a perfectly smooth bun when she began her shift, but now has tiny wisps of hair sprouting from of it. "We got slammed with game night traffic."

"Hard to foresee for a sports bar," Nick replies as she walks away. You're glad to see he gave her a good tip. Still, having hoisted your fair share of trays, you're increasingly furious at his treatment of the serving staff you've encountered tonight. Once outside of the restaurant, you decide you can't hold your tongue anymore.

"Feel good now?" you ask him.

"Whad'ya mean?" He tilts his head. You look at him until he points back at the bar. "*That?* If she can't keep up, she's in the wrong business."

"It was *maybe* ten minutes! She was doing the best she could." *And since you're on the subject...* "Just like that poor kid at the theater."

"What, so you're the defender of minimum wage workers now? Maybe you could start a union."

"You know what? *I am,*" you yell as dozens of people walk by. "And on behalf of all of us, you're an asshole!"

You leave Nick dumbfounded on the sidewalk and walk back into the bar where you find Bonnie, double her tip and apologize for his behavior for the second time that night.

-END-

55

From section 86...

On Saturday night, you doll yourself up in your best house-party attire: tight jeans, a thin oatmeal-colored sweater with a deep V-neck, and flat, black knee-high boots. You drag Rachel along to support your morals when you try to get things back on track with Nick.

You take the subway to a house in the Sunset District, arriving to find it packed with twenty-somethings. Notably, while there are a handful of people closer to your age, most look like they're barely out of college. Even more notably, the majority of partygoers are female.

"Tell me we're not at a fucking frat party," says Rachel, stopping at a keg in the center of the living room.

You look around. "I don't think so. They're young, but not that young."

"Even worse, guys who don't realize they've graduated," she says, pointing to a bearded man standing in the corner who's shot-gunning a beer.

You watch a guy pump the keg and accept the red plastic cups of frothy beer he hands you. Then you make your way through the rowdy crowd in search of Nick, barely able to hear Rachel over the blaring, mediocre hip hop beats.

You reach the back of the house and finally spot Nick. It's hard to miss him, given he's surrounded by a group of girls with bare midriffs and fake tans, laughing hysterically at something he said. The sight of him holding court for a group of wide-eyed Hooters girls leaves a bad taste in your mouth, though that could also be the cheap beer. You take a sip of liquid courage and make your approach.

Nick's spine stiffens. He looks genuinely surprised to see you. "Hey," he says.

His new gal-pals are quick to size you and Rachel up for competition. When you reintroduce Rachel to Nick, he says hello and shakes her hand, but immediately turns his attention back to his new harem, paying special attention to the buoyant blonde on his right. After a couple of uncomfortable moments, Rachel drags you into the kitchen.

"Ready to go?" she asks.

"We just got here," you tell her.

And it already sucks.

"If you haven't noticed," she says, pointing to Nick, who apparently just said something that has Alpha Blonde doubled over with laughter. "He doesn't seem to care."

"He was mid-conversation! It would be rude to cut them off just because we showed up."

Rachel gives you her you've-got-to-be-fucking-kidding-me face.

To leave, turn to section 103.
To stay, turn to section 92.

56

From section 3...

You're perched on the edge of the couch, tapping your foot on the floor at hummingbird-speed and meditating on your upcoming call to Nick.

Last night's conversation was so easy and your mutual attraction was palpable, but today... Today you're the nervous, insecure girl you were in high school. And college. Will he remember you? Did his friends tell him he had a serious case of gin goggles and urge him to cease and desist? Did he meet someone else who's sharing his bed at this very moment? Will she answer the phone?

Get a grip, woman. You've long outgrown your embarrassing adolescence. You're an engaging, intelligent, beautiful woman. No more over-thinking it. Just call him. Keep it casual, enthusiastic - but not overly so - make a date, and get off the phone.

You find Nick's number and hit enter. No turning back now.

It's ringing.

Still ringing.

And...ringing.

You're more than a little disappointed when you get his voicemail. Isn't he waiting by the phone? Ah! You bet he's in the shower, soaping away, smiling, and thinking about meeting you.

There's the beep! Go!

"Hey Nick. It's your friendly alleged neighborhood brothel owner calling. I hope you guys enjoyed the rest of your night. Just touching base to see if you want to get dinner or something."

You leave your number and hang up. Now you wait for him to call back. That's the easy part, right?

Turn to section 70.

57

From section 48...

Fifteen minutes later, you walk through the massive front doors of Nick's building. You try to keep your jaw from hitting the perfectly polished marble floors of the lobby - a lobby that makes your apartment look like a broom closet. By Ikea.

You smile at the concierge, who Nick calls Jerome. Little hat and gloves and everything. Your building comes with a closed circuit security feed broadcast to all units (which you and the girls use to spy on each other), and the guy camped outside of Starbucks every morning who wears a paper bag on his head and insists it's a carrot.

The guest lounge is posh, with beautiful sofas, and ornately carved tables and lamps. Fresh flowers and plants sit on every surface. The elevator is the size of your bedroom, and when you step out into a page from Heavenly Hallways Monthly, you can't help but wonder if Nick's slumming it.

Nick lets you in and turns on the foyer (*foyer!*) light. You inhale the scent of, well, money. This is easily the nicest home you've ever been in. Like something scouted for a film shoot location. You fold your arms, hearing your Aunt Pauline's shrill reminders to keep your hands off the walls.

"I feel underdressed," you say, taking in the cathedral ceiling, light and dark woods and...is that a *second story?* There may even be a library up there - with a bookshelf that gives way to a secret room.

"I think you mean *over*dressed, and by I think, I mean *I'm hoping* you mean overdressed, though I'm neither encouraging nor discouraging any particular state of dress. Or undress."

You laugh and he stands behind you, resting his hands gently on your hips and his chin on your shoulder. "Seriously." You cover his hands with yours. "I make pretty good money by chick standards, any standards, really, but this-"

"-is totally above my pay-grade," Nicks says with a gentle laugh. You remember this is his parents' place, which he stays in while they're away. "Before you think I'm spoiled, know that I pay rent *and* take care of all the cleaning and grown up stuff."

"Nice work if you can get it." He breathes in the scent of your hair.

You tilt your head back and kiss him, once, twice, thrice.

Time passes and you find yourself lying beneath him on a soft, chocolate colored sofa. You're both fully clothed, but any parts of each other's bodies yet to be touched are simply a matter of ease and access. He drags his mouth from your neck and pulls back to look at you, wordlessly indicating the staircase beyond the couch. "Wanna see my baseball card collection?"

For a home run, turn to section 75.
To run home, turn to section 69.

58

From section 62...

You set your curling iron down and unplug it from the wall. You examine your reflection in the mirror and use a cotton swab to remove smudged mascara around your eyes. You quickly run a blending brush over your face, swipe some gloss over your lips and you're ready to go.

To meet Rachel and Valerie, that is. Not Nick. That ship appears to have sailed, and you weren't on it.

It's been a full two weeks since your horizontal no-no and you haven't heard from him. You're probably more disappointed than is reasonable. You've only known him for a month, but you were *really* starting to like him. You thought you'd be good together.

Now you're disappointed in yourself for taking that step, but memory confirms you were not only a willing participant, but also a spirited initiator. You're still finding charcoal-colored buttons around your apartment, from the shirt Nick wore that night. Until you tore it. Off. Who doesn't call that girl back?

With a heavy sigh - and the blessed arrival of your period - you decide to chalk this one up to an unfortunate alcohol-induced mistake and file it away under T for Tequila. You do a last minute purse check for keys, ID, credit card, emergency cash, lip gloss, etc., and head out. Rachel and Valerie meet you in the elevator, bickering over whose turn it is to pay for the cab. Sounds and feels just like the last time they took you to Mix. Only this time, you're hopefully a little wiser for it.

Though - let's be reasonable – you're probably not.

-END-

59

From sections 84, 35 and 83...

The other night, you and Nick talked about your favorite actors. You were glad to see you have similar tastes, and he looked relieved to learn you like action flicks as much as you do rom-coms.

When you told him you hadn't seen Warrior, he had an attack of enthusiasm, evangelizing the movie as one of Tom Hardy's best roles and the best sports film since Rocky. When you said, "Oh, I love Rocky!" he nearly fainted.

So here you are in Nick's gigantic Nob Hill condo. You don't need a tour to know it's bigger than your place and Rachel and Valerie's combined. You settle on the sofa and look around. The very grown-up feel of his apartment contrasts the feeling in your stomach.

"Come over and watch a movie" hasn't had a literal interpretation since sophomore year of high school when you'd tell your parents you were going to Rachel's when you were actually going over to Brian Pompano's parent-free house. To make out.

Nick joins you and wraps a solid arm around your shoulder. And so the dance begins. You lean into him and he plays with your hair. You lay a hand on his chest and his slides from your hair down the length of your arm. You do that thing cats do, sort of nuzzling, rubbing your head gently against his shoulder - the universal sign to *just kiss you already!*

And then he does, softly and sweetly at first, but the pace quickly increases and you turn into each other. His hands find your hair and you plant yours firmly against the firmness of his firm chest. You feel his heart thudding under your palm as he eases you back until you're half-lying on the couch. Your breathing becomes ragged, your body temperature spikes, your head spins a little.

Nick's lips trail from your earlobe down your neck until they reach the high collar of your shirt. You don't object when he undoes the top buttons to gain access to your collarbone.

"How rude of me," Nick murmurs against your hair. "You've been here an hour and I haven't shown you the apartment."

So, maybe you *do* need that tour after all.

To proceed to the bedroom, turn to section 6.
To head home, turn to section 4.

60

From section 75...

You keep your composure, casually saying, "Cool" before rolling into him for another sex-spurred oxytocin rush. You don't ask for details about *her*, and he doesn't ask what you're thinking.

You see each other at least twice a week for dinner or drinks, and then wind up in his or your bed until you fall asleep. It's relatively easy at first. You rationalize it by telling yourself that, since you're the one he's having monogamous sex with, he sort of already *has* chosen you.

Two weeks pass and you're haunted by this nameless, faceless ~~back-up plan~~ girl, wondering why he still sees her, what she's like, if she's like you, and even whether she's a better kisser. On nights you're not together, you assume he's with her.

You hide your worries from Nick, but it's hard during pillow talk when you feel all girly and vulnerable.

"You okay?" He threads his fingers in your hair and lets the strands fall.

"Right as rain." Lie.

"I call bullshit."

"You'll think I'm a silly girl."

"I doubt that."

"Well, I feel like one." You try to hide your face from him. "I honestly thought I was cool with it, but I can't stop thinking about the girl you're seeing."

He laughs softly. "I broke things off with her last week." *For you!* "I only saw her once after you and I were...together, and I've been so busy that I hadn't thought to call her. When she called, I told her I met someone."

"Why didn't you tell me?'

"Didn't think you'd want details."

"Really?" You raise a brow.

He shrugs. "That and I wasn't sure if you'd started seeing someone, so I didn't want to make you uncomfortable."

Why not? "That's it?"

He scrubs a hand over his face. "It would complicate things. Would you think I ended it with her for you? Would it mean automatic exclusivity?"

"Guys really do think like girls sometimes."

"We try to hide it."

"Okay, so what now?"

He stiffens. "What do you mean?"

"Are we still seeing other people? Do you want to have The Talk? Those other things you mentioned?"

"Well, I'm not *looking* for other people, but it's only been a few weeks, so I don't know about the other thing. You?"

You picture yourself, past, present and future. A girl who has rooted through e-mail boxes, scoured Facebook walls for hidden meanings, and who once hid behind a tall fern to spy on a guy you *thought* was your guy when you saw him with a pretty redhead.

"You really think it's too soon?" you ask. He shrugs and your shoulders drop. "Got it."

"You disagree?"

"I just don't want to be worrying you'll meet someone you like more."

"Yeah, but it's the same for me."

"I guess, but it doesn't seem to worry you. And that's fine, but maybe it tells us something. You know?"

You finally agree that if you're not in sync, it's better to end things now. And then you break the cardinal rule and have sex one last time, not because you think it will change his mind, but because it's great sex and you're not stupid.

-END-

61

From section 17...

Nick is indeed still craving ice cream on Saturday. He takes you to an old diner you've never heard of that looks just like Pop's Chock'lit Shoppe from the Archie comics. You'd swear it jumped right out of a comic book panel. You could live here.

"Nicky!" exclaims an older man behind the counter. He has a warm, happy face with a smile that makes his impressive moustache fan like an accordion. He wears a paper cap and a colorful apron. "Give us a hug, son. We never see you anymore."

Nick embraces the older man before introducing you. "Meet Rudy. This is his shop. I worked summers here in high school."

Rudy smiles at you. "Terrible with a scoop, but look at that face." He grabs Nick's chin. "Always had the place crawling with girls."

Nick shakes his head. "Sexist."

Rudy waves him off with a hand towel and takes a better look at you. "Can I assume this lovely lady is the reason for your long-overdue visit?"

"I told I'd take her to the best place in the city," Nick says. "They were closed, so I brought her here."

Rudy playfully smacks Nick upside the head and takes your orders. You keep your date with Ben & Jerry to yourself, ordering a French vanilla cone. Nick opts for a triple chocolate fudge waffle cone with chopped nuts. You find a sunny table out front and watch him inhale his cone - and splatter chocolate all over his shirt.

"Fantastic," he says with a low laugh. "Well, unless you want to walk around with a giant toddler, I'm gonna need to change." He dabs at his chest with a napkin. "Is it cool if we go to my place? We could hang out there for a while."

The truth is, you're dying to go *make* out at his place for a while, all day even, but you aren't sure if you've got the willpower to leave it at that.

You've watched this scene in movies dozens of times. Guy spills something on shirt, guy and girl go back to guy's apartment where he frets over the fate of said shirt, and she offers to help him because she has that innate, god-given female ability to remove stains. He takes off the shirt - in front of her, naturally - and she turns to jelly at the sight of his perfect abs. Within seconds, they can't keep their hands off each other. What shirt?

In reality, it's far more likely he'll toss it on his bedroom floor and put on a clean one before you sit on the couch together under the guise of watching a movie, only to start making out twenty or so minutes later. Either way would be fine, really.

To be led into temptation, turn to section 22.
To deliver yourself from evil, turn to section 64.

62

From section 73...

You awake to the painfully loud sound of sirens. In your bedroom. Which makes no sense. You struggle to open your eyes. It's 7:01 according to the alarm clock you forgot to shut off last night, which is also responsible for the excruciating assault on your brain.

You clumsily find the blessed "off" switch. The silence is heaven, but the painful vibrations you feel from head-to-toe tell you a wicked hangover is coming. It takes longer than you'd like to remember exactly how you wound up in bed, but you eventually recall multiple Jaeger bombs and your insistence Nick come home with you.

You remember you had sex, you *think* you enjoyed it, and, spotting the empty condom wrapper on the floor next to your bed, are relieved to know you were safe. You're even more grateful there's no sign of Nick, affording you the freedom to crawl to the bathroom like a very hungover caterpillar and vomit up your dignity.

Dehydrated enough to wish you kept IV bags on hand, you situate yourself on the couch with a bottle of coconut water and your phone, waiting until it's late enough to call Rachel.

"You sound hungover," Rachel says unnecessarily loudly when you greet her.

"I am," you whisper.

"And regretful. You had sex."

"Yes." You'd hit yourself over the head but it would hurt too much.

"Tsk, tsk." She's undoubtedly enjoying this.

"I couldn't help it," you say. "I was having such a good time and he was really sweet and I can tell he really likes me and he's *so gorgeous* and it's not like it was our first date and who cares if I had sex with him - I'm a grown woman."

Rachel whistles, long and low. "I see you've been using the Rationalization of the Day calendar I gave you for Christmas. You should hear yourself."

You groan. "I can barely remember enough of last night to know if most of that's even true. I doubt he remembers either."

"Perfect! Maybe Nick won't remember either. Born-again relationship virginity!"

You drop the phone and race to the bathroom to empty your stomach.

Come Wednesday night, you're about ready to give up hope that Nick's suffering from sex amnesia. You haven't heard from him since you cashed in your relationship V-card - not even the courtesy of a booty-call text. Sprawled on your couch like a sloth, you run through the list of potential reasons he hasn't called.

a. He's busy with work.

b. Sex with you made him realize he's falling in love and now he's scared.

c. He's running around San Francisco scrawling "For a good time call 555-ELLE" on bathroom stalls.

Not knowing what he's thinking is killing you. You stare at your phone. There is a way to find out.

To call him, turn to section 65.
To not call him turn to section 58.

63

From section 86...

There's a pretty big difference between a date where a guy picks you up and takes you somewhere, demonstrating gentlemanly behavior and...whatever this is.

Nick might as well have added "or whatever" to the end of his text. How did things go from bright, shiny and hopeful to indifferent and chilly in under two weeks?

Your mind regularly revisits the awkward conversation you and Nick had about the kid at the movie theater. He said he was fine, but you can't help feeling like he must still be pissed about it.

On one hand, you can imagine being in his shoes and none-too-thrilled when someone you barely know lectures you in public. On the other hand, you weren't wrong, and if Nick is going to act like a child, or push you away every time you speak your mind, then there's a bullet to dodge.

And even if he isn't mad, he hasn't even acknowledged the fact he was supposed to call you to confirm plans last week. He just glossed over it with an invite to a house party with god-knows-who, god-knows-where. Is that any way to treat a girl you respect?

Screw this!

No matter how good-looking - okay, gorgeous - no matter how tall, how well-sculpted, how funny, or how great of a kisser Nick is, you're not going to waste your time with stuff like this. You're just getting to know him and you already feel neurotic.

You hit reply on his text, pausing in search of the right words to turn him down, wondering if it's worth bringing up the theater conversation again, if only to satisfy your curiosity as to why he suddenly started acting aloof. You type out a quick "Thanks, but no thanks" and hit send.

Why spend any more time on someone who obviously wouldn't do the same for you?

-END-

64

From section 61...

You look around, scrambling for a way to reject another invitation to be alone with Nick at his place. You also try to come up with a good reason for yourself as to why you're avoiding it.

Your gaze settles on a novelty shop directly across the street. "I have a better idea!" you proclaim. You grab his hand and jaywalk him across four lanes of traffic, stopping in front of the store's display window. You take in the oddly impressive array of cheesy gag items, from whoopee cushions to bumper stickers to tee shirts with clever and crude slogans.

That's it!

You were hoping for a giant button, or sticker, or *anything* to cover the stain at the center of his chest, but...

This is so much better.

"Let's get a new one!" you say.

He's skeptical. "Both of us?"

Sure. Take one for the team. Or don't, as it were. "Yep. I'll pick one for you and you pick one for me."

He raises a wicked eyebrow. "Anything I want?"

"Yes." You bat your lashes at him. "But in making your selection, I advise careful consideration as to whether or not you'd like me to go on another date with you in the future."

You enter the store together and soon reemerge sporting your new tees.

The silver lettering of his fitted, pink "*GIRL POWER!*" shirt really brings out the blue in his eyes, while the red lettering of your white, "Honk if you want it!" tee really brings out the big in your chest.

You're quite pleased with yourself as you walk arm-in-arm down Market Street - partly because way more people are honking than you would've anticipated, but mostly because your new relationship virtue remains intact.

Turn to section 113.

65

From section 62...

You can call him. Of course you can. You just had sex with him, after all.

You dial Nick and wince each time a ring goes unanswered. You're full out cringing when his voicemail picks up, but you clear your throat and leave him a message.

"Hi, Nick. It's me. So, were you as hungover as I was on Saturday? Wow. Anyway. I just wanted to call and say hi and see about making plans for this weekend. If you're free. Give me a call? Bye."

Hoping you didn't sound too desperate, you settle in for another round of waiting for him to call. And wait you do - for another week. So much time passes that you're genuinely surprised tonight when his name appears on your caller ID. Surprised, but not giddy surprised. You actually feel a bit of dread in your tummy.

"Hey," Nick says when you answer. "Sorry it took me so long to get back to you."

"No problem," you say, not that you mean it. "Been busy?"

"You could say that."

Not loving the weird undertone in his voice.

"So...did you want to grab dinner tomorrow night?" you ask. "Valerie told me about a great place down the street I'd love to try."

"I'm sorry," he says, and you hear him sigh. You picture him pinching the bridge of his nose. "I can't tomorrow."

"That's okay. What's a good night for you?" After a stretch of silence, you ask, "Are you still there?"

"Yeah. Listen. This is awkward, 'cause I think you're a really cool girl, and I had a good time last weekend..."

Here it comes.

What'll it be? He's just not ready to be exclusive? Needs to spend more time on work? Doesn't want to get too serious?

Drum roll please…

"I actually just became exclusive with someone…else I've been dating. It just happened this past Monday and I've been pretty wrapped up in that…" Really, buddy? You had to add in how wrapped up you've been *in her?* "So I haven't had a chance to call you, but I didn't want to leave you hanging anymore. Um. I'm sorry."

You blather something about how you get it and appreciate the call and blah, blah, blah, but you don't mean a word of it.

-END-

66

From section 67...

You've never been happier to see a workweek come to an end. You're physically and mentally exhausted from your job, and you haven't heard from Nick post-romp.

You leave the office around eight, ordering a pizza before you go. Then you stop at a corner store to load up on sugary supplies. You'll regret it tomorrow, but tonight, you wallow!

At home, you head straight to your bedroom and shuck your business attire in favor of your kitten-covered footie PJs, which get a snicker from the pizza guy. A few hours later you're curled up on the couch, watching the credits roll on Mr. and Mrs. Smith for the hundredth time and wondering how a nice girl like you goes about finding a sexy assassin to take care of that nasty little problem called your boss. And maybe do some recon on Nick, who has apparently gone AWOL.

You clean up your mess and go through your pre-bed washing and brushing routine, convincing yourself it'll ward off the impending breakouts and cavities from your snacks. You're about to hit the hay when your phone rings.

It's Nick!

You answer.

"Hey, gorgeous!" he says. It sounds like he's in a great mood.

"Hey yourself," you reply in the voice of a girl who has *not* been waiting for this call for nearly forty-eight hours.

"I was just with some buddies in your neighborhood and I thought I'd say goodnight. In person."

You feel a rush of relief, excitement stirring in your stomach at the prospect of seeing him in just a few minutes.

To go back to bed alone, turn to section 27.
To let him come over, turn to section 23.

67

From section 40...

You pick up the phone and learn Nick had just as crummy a day at work as you did. You let him know what you're up to (leaving out the part about The Bachelor) and suggest he come over and unwind with you.

In less than twenty minutes, Nick is at your door. His suit is rumpled and his hair looks like he's been raking his fingers through it all day. He's also got a chilled bottle of pinot grigio in hand.

You kiss him hello and grab a bottle opener and another glass from the kitchen. When you return to the living room, Nick has shed his jacket and tie, both of which now hang over a chair.

He is adorable.

He fills your glasses and you sit together and talk about your days before moving on to lighter subjects, teasing each other and laughing. You inch closer to each other until your legs are eventually draped over his. One kiss turns into two, and then three, and then you lose count. Before long, touching each other through clothes is no longer enough and they start coming off, leaving a trail en route to your bedroom.

When you wake up alone in the morning, you initially hope the clumsy - but still quality - sex you had last night was just a blurry dream. The empty condom wrapper on the nightstand says otherwise.

You sigh. This is not how you planned it. In fact, you hadn't really planned anything.

Turn to section 66.

68

From sections 68 and 310...

The next morning, you arrive at home well-rehearsed and chalked full of resolve.

"You're back," Nick says when you open the door. He crosses the room and kisses you hard before enveloping you in a hug. "How was your visit? Did your mom bring out the good stuff?"

"She did." You feel your nerve slip just a little, but rein it in. "Can we sit?"

"Uh-oh," he says warily, his earlier cheer at seeing you all but a memory. He lowers himself onto one of the kitchen chairs. "What's up?"

Breathe in through your nose...

"After talking to you, and to my mother, I realized you're both right."

"Your mom agreed with me?" He raises an eyebrow.

"Sort of. You both pointed out that it all came down to whether or not I could live without getting married if it meant being with you and...I don't think I can."

The confused look on his face tells you this is not the outcome he was expecting. "Wait," he finally says. "You want to get married *so* badly you would rather break up with me than be with me?"

"You want *not* to get married so badly that you'd let me walk away?"

He considers this for a moment. "Okay, I see your point. But why break up now? Shouldn't we give it some time?"

"What's the point? You're not going to change your mind, and I'm not getting any younger. Why drag it out? It would just get ugly and we'd resent each other."

There's nothing worse than the break up nobody saw coming. One day, you're happy, with a future hazily forming in your mind, and the next you're worried about whether you've got muffin top again.

You did the right thing, though, and Nick knows it, too.

-END-

69

From sections 328, 31 and 57...

On Monday morning, your alarm clock lets out a screech during a pivotal moment in a dream. A dream about Nick. And a bed shaped like a star.

Despite the interruption, you smile, sit up, stretch, and start your morning routine. You sing in the shower and dance naked while setting out the day's clothes, all while thinking about Nick. You even decide to walk to work despite a downpour, which you meet with an umbrella and good cheer, making passersby give you funny looks.

You stop for coffee but are so distracted reliving your first date that you pay for your overly expensive, overly complicated beverage only to forget it on the counter before you leave. You don't even realize it until you sit down at your desk and automatically reach for the cup as your open your e-mail. Normally you'd curse a steady stream of expletives reserved for Mondays and sneak downstairs for another coffee, but today you just shrug and walk to the kitchen for a glass of water.

Your annoyingly sunny disposition and erratic attention span sends your office neighbour, Laura Bauslaugh into interrogation mode over lunch. You share just enough detail about your date with Nick to satisfy her curiosity - and brag a little. Not too much, though. You don't want to jinx it.

Nick still preoccupies your thoughts after work. This results in burning the rice to accompany the stir fry you *were* making for dinner, and the failure to notice that your apartment door is slightly open with your keys still in the lock (*Come and get it, serial killers!*). It's another hour before you realize the TV is set to an all-Italian station, which wouldn't be odd if you understood Italian.

Standing in the kitchen, you set a freshly scrubbed, rice-free pot in the drying rack before looking at your phone on the counter and wondering why it hasn't rung yet. Up to now, you've just assumed Nick would call, and sooner than this.

You walk over and pick up the handset. You sent him a text after your date to tell him you had a good time, but should you call him? He called you last time. Maybe it's your turn.

Call him, he's alive, turn to section 19.
Let his people call your people, turn to section 12.

70

From section 56...

Four long days since you called Nick and...nothing. You've spent as many days pacing, checking your phone, and trying to get the girls to approve *just one last call.*

To distract yourself, you're helping Valerie decorate for a small gathering at her place. You're celebrating Rachel's last minute gig doing the music for a teen drama pilot filmed in Toronto where she was born. Her American dad met her mom while his band toured Canada. Her parents were never "together," but she got dual citizenship (and life) out of the deal.

Long story short, when things got rocky at home, Rachel jumped at the chance to live with her grandmother in Palo Alto at the start of freshman year - or "Grade 9" as she called it. Having just moved from Chicago, you didn't know anyone either and the two of you became instant friends. "Finally, eh?" she said when you met. "Somebody else who knows *actual* fucking cold."

"My arm's falling off up here," says Valerie, snapping you out of a daze. You look up to where she holds the corner of a paper banner against the wall.

"I didn't think giraffes had arms," you say, noting she barely has to stretch to reach above the window frame.

"Just big ol' hooves," she says, kicking out at you with a wedge heel.

Pinching the opposite corner between your thumb and forefinger, you use the stepladder and stretch until your side is level with hers.

Val leans back slightly. "I think we're good. Smooth down the tape."

You climb down and take a few steps back to look at the banner, which reads "GO AWAY" in bold, black letters that match the helium balloons scattered around the apartment.

You smirk. "Might this be a misprint?"

Val squints to make sure it hangs evenly. "Hmm?"

You shrug. "It seems to be missing a word. And maybe some letters."

Val reads it again. "Nope. It's right. Besides, she's barely leaving."

Valerie and Rachel have never been apart longer than two weeks for as long as you can remember. Neither will admit it, but they're acting out their separation anxiety as part of their routine shenanigans.

"I'm sure she'll love it."

"That and the 'Everything Must Go' sign on her bedroom door."

You sit down next to Valerie on the couch. She hands you your wine and you check your phone. Again.

"Three days?"

"Four."

"Wanna play *Maybe*?"

You give a small smile. "Okay, I'll go first. *Maybe* at the next bar, Nick met a super model - which she would have to be to top *this*." You gesture along the length of your body. "And now he lives in Hollywood and gets photographed by TMZ for being an entitled douchebag."

"*Maybe* he was already seeing someone who just found out she's pregnant, so he's tied up at the moment, what with waiting for paternity tests and all the, 'Well, you're already pregnant so we might as well have sex,' sex."

"Went the distance on that one." Your face scrunches up in contemplation. "*Maybe* he's got a six-day hangover. They happen, right? *Maybe* he had to get his stomach pumped and he's too sore to talk."

"I can see why you'd be disappointed not to hear from that guy."

You brighten, hit with an actual, plausible reason why he hasn't called. "*Maybe* he left his phone at the bar, and they found it, but he's been so busy he hasn't had a chance to pick it up before today, so I should be hearing from him right about…"

You both stare at your phone.

Val grabs the bottle. "Or *maybe* you should've waited three days to call."

-END-

71

From section 30...

It's been one week since you heard from Nick. You still have hope he'll contact you, but imagine reasons he hasn't. Like he was framed for murder and is awaiting bail; or he decided to give up electronics; or he was attacked by wild raccoons and is unconscious from the medication and rabies shots.

Impressively, you listen to Rachel and Valerie when they tell you not to call him, but you *do* email him on Tuesday, which is totally not the same as a phone call.

You're standing in line for coffee this morning when your phone alerts you to a new e-mail. Your heart leaps when you see Nick's name as the sender. Then you open the message and your heart promptly crumples into itself like a week-old 'Get Well Soon' helium balloon.

It reads: *Hey. I've been meaning to call, but I've been swamped with work. I'm not really sure how to say this - I guess there's never a good way - but as much as I think you're great, I'm just not sure this is working. I think it's better we call it quits now rather than wait it out. I hope you understand. -N*

You begin to reply, but stop yourself. He's said what he has to say. You're not going to change his mind. You'll just embarrass yourself. You delete the draft and his message.

It sucks, but fortunately you aren't too emotionally attached yet. For good measure, and a bit of a safety net, you erase all traces of him from your email and phone so you won't be tempted to drunk dial him.

-END-

72

From section 14...

It's Thursday night and you're searching drawers for the battered T-shirt and hospital pants you and the girls have used for hair dying since you lived in the dorms. You'll need them tonight when Rachel plies you with pizza and wine in exchange for fixing her roots and highlights.

"Shazam!" you exclaim when you find them in the bottom drawer, spattered in countless shades of black, red, blonde, orange, and even green. Each splotch of color carries its own memories, bringing a smile to your face.

You're shedding your work clothes when Nick calls.

"Hey!" he says, and you can picture his mega-watt smile. "Are you busy tonight?"

"Actually, I am." *Damn!* "I've got plans with Rachel."

"Any chance you could reschedule? I've got a surprise."

You listen with glee as he explains that a buddy just cancelled, leaving him with an extra, much-coveted ticket for an NBA playoff game.

"And you thought of me?" *He thought of you!* "I don't even watch baseball."

"Hockey," he says, on to your joke. "I know you've never been to a game, so you were my first call. Are you at home? I can pick you up in five minutes."

It's so sweet that he wants to share something important to him with *you* instead of calling a friend. Rachel would *probably* understand if you rescheduled.

If you think Rachel and her roots will forgive you, turn to section 74.
To be the highlight of Rachel's day, turn to section 80.

73

From section 49...

The lights come up and the auditorium fills with the usual hustle and bustle of moviegoers talking about the film as they shuffle out of the aisles. You take Nick's hand and follow him out to the street where you suggest getting a drink at the pub next door.

Two hours later, you're having such a good time laughing and lobbing flirty banter back and forth, you don't even remember what happened earlier. You also can't remember how to play pool, much to Nick's delight.

His mood has improved, though it could be due to his blood alcohol level. As you play, he regularly finds reasons to touch or tickle you, occasionally planting a spectacle of a kiss on you for all to see.

You excuse yourself to the ladies room, leaving Nick to rack the balls. You find yourself smiling, with a thrilling sensation in your stomach at how well things are going, especially now that you're past that awkward phase where you're unsure if it's okay to touch each other. Oh, how you've missed the PG PDAs and flirtation that come with new relationships.

You wash your hands and reapply your berry-stain lip-gloss before returning to your table, seeing the waitress drop off two fresh drinks and a couple of shots. Nick kisses your cheek and hands you a shot of tequila.

To shoot'er up, turn to section 62.
To shoot it down, turn to section 54.

74

From section 72...

After changing into a pair of jeans and button-down shirt, you dial Rachel.

"Reschedule?" she shrieks. "I have a date tomorrow. *I fucking look like 2004 Shakira!* Tell him you can't go."

You wince. "It's a little late for that. He's kind of downstairs."

"*Dude.* You don't even *like* baseball!"

"It's basketball."

"I don't care if it's naked 4-man Olympic bobsleigh," she yells, clearly caring. "I can't believe you'd just ditch me for a guy."

"I'm sorry. I'm sorry." You forgot how great she is with guilt trips. "I'll come by after the game and we'll get it done. I promise."

"Don't bother. I'll ask Valerie. Leave the sweats out. I'll get them when you're gone." Then she hangs up.

You pull the last of your things together and race downstairs to where Nick's waiting in the car. You get in and kiss him hello.

"Is she mad?" he asks as you exit the parking lot.

"Yeah." You sigh.

"She'll get over it." He puts his hand on your knee. "This is going to be awesome!"

Rachel *will* get over it - probably at a price - but you feel terrible.

Nick's paying the parking attendant at the stadium when you get a text from Val. *Hoes before bros*, it reads. *Hoes before bros.*

Continue to section 89.

75

From section 57...

Okay, so the fact you slept with Nick was kind of predictable, but the actual sex? Nothing predictable about it. You silently thank Denise, your yoga instructor, for giving you the flexibility of a high school gymnast.

You and Nick lay face-to-face, wrapped in grey sheets and each other, breathing raggedly. Your body feels liquid. If you tried to get up, you'd pool into a puddle of flesh that looks like you. It turns out Nick's a pleaser - who gave you the first orgasm you didn't...have a hand in. More than once, so you know it's no fluke.

If you heard this from a girlfriend, you'd congratulate her while silently calling her a liar. But nope. You were there. Both times. And this wasn't awkward-first-time-together sex, either. If practice makes perfect, then Nick...

There it is.

The fuzzy, floaty post-coital cloud dissipates. With one arm wrapped around your waist and the other resting above his head, he feels the tension build in your body.

"You okay?" he asks, kissing your shoulder.

"Good," you say. "I feel great."

"Good," he says. "Me, too. *But...*"

You wish you weren't facing him. "I don't want to make a big deal out of it, and I should have mentioned it before, but I'm a sexually monogamous person."

You say this knowing it's kind of a trap, though you don't mean it to be. It's like saying, "I'll date other people, but I only want to mattress tango with you." If he says he's okay with the same arrangement, you'll feel crushed that he wants to see other people, even if you're the only he wants to have sex with.

Nick buries his face in your neck. "Well, that works out, because so am I."

"Oh." You feel relieved. "All right then."

"But I'm seeing someone else, too."

"Oh." Less relieved.

"You're not?"

"No." But now you really wish you were.

He seems slightly relieved. "I'm not sleeping with her."

You don't ask for more details, but you wonder how long he's been seeing her, how often he sees her, why he slept with you and not her, and if he'll eventually decide he's bored with you and move up your understudy, giving her two unassisted orgasms.

Your brain hurts. Still, you're a modern woman, and the fact you really like this incredibly sexy, magically sculpted man in the bed next to you shouldn't change the approach you take to relationships. You're not exclusive, no one's cheating, but can you handle waiting to see if you'll maintain your number one spot until he decides he's ready for exclusivity, or will it make you crazy?

Take it as a win and keep going, turn to section 60.
Cut your losses now, turn to section 326.

76

From section 47...

Your mother, the unabashed romantic, completely understands when you explain that you have tentative plans with Nick, promising to let her know if anything changes.

You say goodbye to her and call Nick. The phone rings four times before his machine picks up and the sound of his voice, which you're growing to love, fills your ear. You leave a short and sweet message asking if you're on for Friday and suggest bowling, which is almost always a fun date option. You figure that after your gentle dressing down at the theater, you could both use just that - fun.

When you don't hear back from him by Thursday, the sinking feeling that's taken root in your stomach continues to grow. Determined not to focus on it, you call your mother back and explain your dilemma, right down to the drama at the movies.

"Oh, honey," says your mom. "That's men for ya. You point out their shortcomings and they pout for days. Your father does that every time I stop him from taking on a home repair project. This fella of yours, Nick is it? He'll come around. In the meantime, you're welcome to join us either way."

Friday night arrives and you *still* haven't heard a word from Nick. No text, no e-mail, and no voicemail you accidentally missed. Your sense of foreboding reaches a new peak. You try to put it out of your mind and meet up with your family for dinner. It's great to see them and catch up, but you're majorly distracted.

No matter how many times you remind yourself that Nick agreed he may have overreacted, or that he didn't seem mad when he dropped you off, it's increasingly hard to ignore the fact he did cut the date short (with an excuse you've used *many* times) and hasn't returned your message. You wonder if your mom's right and he's just sulking, or if you'll never hear from him again.

Turn to section 86.

77

From section 10...

"Thanks," you tell Ted. "But we really should get going." You take hold of Rachel's arm. She's long past tipsy. Leaving is definitely the right idea.

"Yeah?" asks Nick. He's disappointed, but when he sees Rachel's glassy eyes, he says, "Yeah, you should probably get her to bed. I'll walk you out."

Outside on the sidewalk, you pour Rachel into a waiting cab and turn back to Nick. He hands you his phone. "How about you save your number in here and I'll call you this week?"

Working to keep the smile on your face from spreading, you key in your info and hand it back to him. You plant a kiss on his cheek and climb in beside Rachel. Nick shuts your door and moves to the driver's window where he hands him some cash and asks him to get you to the Marina District safely. As the cab pulls away from the curb, you glance back through the rear windshield. Nick waves. You wave back.

From her crumpled position beside you, Rachel says, "That was so romant-*hic*...romantic...*hic*."

From the front seat, the cabbie nods in agreement.

You can't help but concur.

Turn to section 53.

78

From section 88...

When Nick isn't nudged into nuptials, you have no choice but to make it look good.

You dad looks over your finances and you actually *can* buy! And why not? You work hard and, thanks mostly to your shopping aversion, you've saved some money. You deserve it!

And since you've already done so much of the groundwork, the rest is easy. Sexy Realtor? Check. Pre-approved mortgage? Check. List of one-bedroom condos with dishwasher, laundry and two bathrooms? Check. Not too far from Val and Rachel? *Check!*

The next month is surreal. You bring Nick or the girls to see the first couple of listings, but eventually decide it's better to go alone. No distractions, just you and the condo seeing if you've got chemistry.

This morning, you meet Sexy Realtor outside of a gorgeous building near your current address. It's a charming low-rise with immaculate lawns and a cute little gate at the entranceway.

You've always assumed this place was above your pay grade but you sure as hell want to look inside. You step into the lobby and fall in love with the marble floors, elegant furnishings and remarkable natural light spilling in from huge windows.

"We both know I can't afford this," you say on the ride up to the fifth floor.

"You'd be surprised," Sexy Realtor says as he flips through his folio. "It's a buyers' market."

You exit the elevator and he stops short. "Damn. I left the listing in my car. Why don't you look around while I run downstairs? It's vacant, so it's fine."

He lets you into Suite 507 and jogs back to the elevator.

It's *beautiful.* Cream-colored walls, high ceilings, hardwood floors, and French doors leading out to a balcony. Your jaw drops, dragging along the ground as you wander. In the hallway there are four doors, one of which is closed. You expected a bathroom, bedroom and a closet, but where does the fourth door lead?

You open it and a barely audible gasp passes your lips.

What on earth?

It's Nick, standing with his back to a bay window, the city skyline behind him and a huge smile on his face.

"What are you doing here?" you ask incredulously.

"Well, I saw the kind of places you're looking at - and they're great - but I thought if you had a roommate, we could live in an even better place."

"We talked about the whole living in sin thing," you say, feeling the corner of your mouth tug upward.

"I remember. But I was thinking maybe we could bend the rules. Just a little."

"How?"

"A show of good faith," he says, walking toward you. You're about to ask him what he means when you're blinded by bright light. Squinting, you follow the beam to the window ledge. And nearly pass out.

A ring!

You approach carefully to avoid spooking it. Upon closer inspection, you see it's a cushion cut stone with a diamond band – the ring you saw while memorizing inventory for a jewelry store opening you handled. You had a visceral reaction to it - and you never told a soul.

"Go ahead," says Nick, grinning like a fool. "Pick it up."

"I'll drop it," you say softly.

"Then allow me." He walks back to the window. "I'd been waiting for the right time to give this to you, but then you up and threw a wrench in my plans."

"Oh." You forgot about the part where you lied, setting this whole thing in motion. You choose to forget about it again.

He picks up the ring with one hand and takes your left hand in the other. Then he leans in until his lips graze your ear. "I love you," he whispers. "Marry me."

No words come out when you open your mouth, so you close it again, nodding your head only slightly slower than a paint-mixing machine as Nick slides the perfectly sized ring onto your finger.

"Still speechless?" he asks and you nod again. "Perfect."

And then he kisses you until you're dizzy. It isn't until you're unbuttoning his shirt that your mind snaps back to reality.

"The agent," you say, out of breath. "He's coming back."

"Nope," Nick says, ridding you of your sweater. "I bought this place yesterday." He pulls two sets of keys from his pocket.

"Seriously?" He nods smugly. "Then we should probably christen it."

-END-

79

From sections 87 and 38...

The first date is both your most and least favorite social occasion. Depending on the guy, it can induce nervousness, excitement and nausea. You figure it's kind of like pregnancy.

Your favorite part of a first date, however, is the excuse to buy a new outfit. If things go right, it's an investment in your new relationship; if they go poorly, it's a pretty, color-coordinated consolation prize.

Still, you're not known for your style prowess. Rachel says you're more Fashion *Weak* than Fashion Week, so you let your friends tag along to help you find the perfect something for tonight.

"This is torture," you say as you walk into the fourth store.

"It'll be worth it," says Val. "Trust us. At least, trust me."

"I hate that you have to pick out my clothes."

"Lots of people have interior decorators, so just think of us as your exterior decorators."

"Yeah," says Rachel, poking your side. "Your insides can't be helped."

Thirty minutes later, you're shivering in your skivvies in a dressing room while they bring you outfit after outfit, plastic hangers clattering in their hands, their shoes clacking against the linoleum.

They let themselves into the room and hold out their latest picks, smiling at you but rolling their eyes at each other.

Valerie is first: a long-sleeved, black mini-dress with a high neckline, paired with black tights. It's very pretty and will show off your figure while still leaving *a lot* to the imagination.

Rachel's selection is bolder: a deep red tube top and tight-fitting low-rise jeans - very sexy while leaving, well, *not* nothing to the imagination.

"Are you kidding me?" exclaims Valerie as she examines Rachel's pick. "Why don't you just print the words 'Dinner first. Sex later' on the front? Could it be for lack of fabric?"

"You're right," Rachel fires back. "Better to write 'Your parents would love me' or, even better, 'Bad in bed.' Actually, with all that material, you can use both!"

You only get one chance to make a second impression, so whose fashion advice should you take?

For Valerie's pretty pick, turn to section 134.
For Rachel's sexy selection, turn to section 123.

80

From section 72...

Of course.

Of course Nick would call with a spontaneous invite to an event he's been looking forward to for months on the very same night you've committed to help Rachel exterminate the skunk living on her head.

You want to cancel on her. *So, so badly.* You even run through all the times she's bailed on you for last minute plans with a guy, only you can't think of any.

Sigh.

You must decline his invitation.

"It's *so* great that you'd think of me," you tell Nick. "And on any other night, I'd love to go."

"But?" he asks slowly.

"I can't cancel on Rachel with such short notice. She needs my help with something."

"No worries," he says, his voice its usual casual tone. "I can find another girl to convert into a basketball fan."

You blink. "Seriously?"

"No." He laughs. "I've got a few buddies who would ditch their grandmother's funeral for this game. Don't worry. The ticket won't go to waste."

"You're not mad?"

"Of course not. Truly. Says a lot about you. I'll call you after the game."

An hour later, you're outfitted in your sweats and laying down newspaper to protect your kitchen floor from wayward dye. Rachel arrives with a bottle of wine and a bag of supplies. You tell her about your call with Nick.

She looks at you, surprised. "You totally should have gone."

"Really?" you ask, simultaneously shocked and disappointed.

"Of course not. I'd have *fucking* killed you."

You smirk. "That's what I figured."

You mix the dye and organize your tools while Rachel fills wine glasses. Yes, it's disappointing you aren't with Nick right now, but he invited *you* to a big event over many enthusiastic parties. And you didn't ditch Rachel for him, showing both of them what a good friend you are. Plus, you get wine and pizza.

Life could be a lot worse.

Turn to section 91.

81

From section 30...

Following your call with Valerie, you pace around your apartment for a few minutes to mull things over.

You finally decide you have no intention of wasting any more of your time or energy worrying about whether or not you're making mistakes with Nick. There's only one way to know for sure, and that's to call him. So you do.

Of course, the courage of that conviction evaporates the moment you dial his number. Nervousness takes over and you feel a little nauseated. Still, there's no turning back now. You sit next to the stack of freshly folded laundry and wait for Nick to answer, sort of hoping he won't. He picks up on the third ring.

"Hey there," he says. He sounds neither happy nor unhappy to hear from you. "Sorry. I've been meaning to call since I got your text."

You brighten a little. "No worries. Busy week at work?"

He exhales loudly and you hear the unmistakable sound of fingers clacking on a keyboard in the background. "That's a gross understatement."

"Me, too." That's not true. Your boss is away at a client trade show, so you've enjoyed a heavenly, relatively light week with few fires to put out and even fewer unnecessary, time-wasting meetings. "What do you say we empty our brains with a movie on Friday night?"

"Yeah, that sounds good. Why don't you choose the flick and I'll pick you up around seven?"

"Perfect," you say. "One cheesy rom-com coming up."

"My absolute favorite."

You say goodbye and hang up. Relieved, you sink into the couch. Valerie really had you worried for a second.

Continue to section 85.

82

From section 40...

You empty the last of the wine into your glass as Chris Harrison announces the final rose of the night. At the same time, your phone alerts you to a voicemail from Nick.

You briefly consider waiting until after the obligatory back-of-the-limo cry by whichever devastated gal The Bachelor sends packing, but who's kidding who? Not answering the phone is one thing, waiting to find out why he called? Totally another.

You pause the TV and pick up your phone. After a couple of fumbled password attempts, you finally play Nick's message.

"Hey, it's me," he says. He sounds exhausted. "Hope you had a better day than I did. Just calling to see what you're doing on Sunday. I thought maybe we could do a daytime thing. You pick the place - anywhere you want to go. Give me a call when you get a chance and we'll sort out the details. I'm rambling now. Okay. Sweet dreams, which is a lock given I'll be in them."

You replay his message - twice - with a happy, tipsy grin on your face. Nick had a bad day, he's exhausted and, still, he calls to ask you out.

You set the phone back on the coffee table and reach for the remote, knocking over your glass and spilling wine everywhere. You scurry to the kitchen for paper towels.

Yeah, good call not answering the phone.

Continue to section 35.

83

From section 325...

You wake to the sound of a... Is that a chicken?

"Buk, buk, bukka!"

It won't stop, forcing you to stagger from your bed toward the noise. You wind up at the couch where you tossed your purse earlier. You reach inside for your phone, which is lit up with Valerie's name. Rachel's been programming ringtones again. You answer with a grunt.

"If you're picking up the phone during sex, he's not doing it right," Rachel says.

"*Wha?* Val?"

"I'm here, too," she says, and you realize you're on speaker. "Are we having a four way?"

"I'm alone."

"And still asleep at noon," says Rachel. "Telling."

"Not much to tell."

"Really?" asks Val cheerfully. "What time did you get home last night?"

"Home? Around 10:30? Ish."

"Funny, your lights weren't on."

"Maybe a little later." You yawn.

"I'll say," says Rachel. "Unless you weren't the bright red spot in the foggy-windowed Camaro out front when we pulled in at three a.m."

Of course.

"So *a lot* later. What do you want from me?"

"Details!" they say at once.

"Did your upper half stay above his lower half?" Val asks eagerly. Anyone who thinks your dainty friend is a prude is sorely mistaken.

"Yes!"

"All right. Sheesh." After a beat she says, "Did his?"

"Well- That's a trick question."

"How many bases?" ask Rachel.

"Not answering."

Maybe two. Or three. What's the difference between second and third base again?

"I warned you about wearing a fire engine red tube top and eff-me pumps on your first date," says Val.

When your phone moos, Rachel exclaims, "Oh, you've got a text!"

It's a message from Nick. "He's inviting me over for a movie later."

"Ooh, sticky situation," teases Valerie. "You're clearly warm for each other's forms. What if his parents aren't home to chaperone?"

"If you go, you'll have to yay or nay a roll in the hay," says Rachel.

"Dirty Dr. Seuss. I'd pay to read that."

"I'd pay you to read it to me." They laugh.

"Stop weirding me out. What do I do?" you ask.

"Like what we think matters," snorts Val.

"Just listen to your vagina," says Rachel, in a singsong voice. "It'll tell you what to do."

You hang up and think back to last night in Nick's car. With Nick. And his mouth. And his manly man hands. And the sunrise. Instead of waiting around and wondering if he's going to call, you could be with him again in just a few hours - with a couch between you instead of a gearshift. And no audience.

If you think coming attractions are safer in a theater, turn to section 49.
If you're willing to risk giving into your attraction, turn to section 59.

84

From sections 46 and 42...

It's Tuesday and you're still feeling the effects of your great first date with Nick.

From the moment you said goodbye, you've been daydreaming about him, replaying each of the night's highlights in your head on loop - with special emphasis on the game of Twenty Minutes in Heaven you played in the front seat of his car before finally pulling away and forcing yourself upstairs.

You're the kind of cheerful you usually hate in people. You're a confetti cannon. You're also unusually enthusiastic about *everything,* including yesterday's three hour car ride with your boss and her collection of Broadway musical soundtracks. Mostly, you feel awake - wide-awake.

"I hate it when you're this happy," says Rachel, pretending to jab a pen in her eye.

"I value your friendship, too." Your friend has been a good sport about your repeated recaps of My Date with Nick. She's only threatened to kill you in your sleep once.

"Don't get me wrong. I don't want you to be *un*happy, but right now, you're at a nine, and I could use you around a six. Maybe a seven, but with a healthy balance of paranoid insecurity. Try it for me?"

"Okay." You arrange your features into a slightly pensive expression. "How's this?"

"Better."

Your phone rings. It's Nick! "Hooray!" you yell. "It's him."

"*Yay!*" Rachel squeals back with mock-excitement. "Hopefully he'll ask you out again so you'll have a captivating *new* story to tell me until I drink bleach."

"Go ahead, hide your jealousy behind sarcasm." You clear your throat and answer the phone casually. "Hey."

Rachel gags.

"Don't want to pretend you didn't know it was me?" he asks, and you feel goose bumps sprout up at the sound of his husky laugh.

"Oh, Chris. You're so funny."

He sighs. "You know I prefer Christopher." You giggle.

"I'm going to wait until you're asleep, sneak into your room with a cage of rabid vampire bats, release them and then slink back into the night," Rachel whispers.

You stick your tongue out and listen to Nick. He invites you over to his place on Saturday to watch a movie he told you about the other night.

Hmm.

Is it a good idea to be alone with Cute Great Kisser Guy and a couch? A bad idea? A good bad idea?

To suggest a movie at a theater instead, turn to section 49.
To offer to bring the popcorn, turn to section 59.

85

From section 81...

Your light workweek dragged on as you anxiously awaited tonight's movie date with Nick. When you hung up with him the other night, you immediately picked a 7:45 showing of Christian Bale's new movie. And your outfit.

At seven on the dot, you ride the elevator downstairs with your neighbour, Ida Splenta and her dog, Smacks. Nosy as ever, Ida asks you what your plans are and you tell her you have a date. In the lobby, you say goodnight to Ida and watch for Nick's black Camaro to pull into the parking lot.

For the next fifteen minutes, you watch people walk in and out of the double doors, including Rachel. She offers to wait with you, but you quickly shoo her away with a reminder Valerie's waiting for her to start a Ryan Gosling marathon.

Then you begin to worry you'll miss the movie, but remember there's a later showing, so you and Nick could grab a drink first and still salvage the night. At 7:20, you get the sinking feeling you're being stood up. At 7:30, Ida and Smacks reappear. When she sees you're still standing there, she gives you a knowing look that says, "Poor thing. Stood up for a date." You want to trip her but, fortunately for her, your phone rings.

It's Nick.

Phew.

"Hey," you say cheerfully into the receiver. "Traffic?"

"Not exactly," Nick says. His voice is hollow. "I'm still at home."

"Are you sick?" 'Cause you're starting to feel sick.

"No, I just… Listen, I never know how to say this, but I don't think this is going to work. I'm just not, you know, feeling the spark - or whatever."

You're crushed. And a little disappointed he couldn't come up with a better (and more enthusiastic) cliché to dump you with. Still, you maintain your dignity. You tell him you're relieved to hear him say it because you'd planned to tell him the same thing tonight. You both know you're lying, but fuck it.

A couple of minutes later, you're knocking on Rachel and Valerie's door.

Valerie opens it, instantly sympathetic. "Aw, sweetie," she says, and gives you a tight hug that *almost* softens the "I told you so" that immediately follows.

"*Hey, girl*," calls Rachel from a mountain of pillows on the living room floor, a joint in hand and Crazy, Stupid, Love cued up on the TV. "Ryan wants to turn that frown upside down. Come, let the Canadian magic that is Gosling soothe you."

And it does.

-END-

86

From sections 47 and 76...

Tuesday arrives and you're emptying your fridge of expired food and listening to Valerie talk about her upcoming date with Todd, a fellow optometrist she met online.

She made the mistake of telling her over-protective older brother, also an optometrist, who in turn told their father, yet another optometrist, who immediately called to insist he didn't want his only daughter going out with some creep she met online who could be planning to lock her in a well in his basement and turn her into a second skin.

"Just once," says Val, perched on a stool on the other side of your kitchen counter. "*Once*, I'd like to be able to go out with a guy I met online-"

"Without getting a Hannibal lecture?" you finish for her.

"I see what you did there."

You sneer when you peel the lid off a container of what used to be your mother's chicken broccoli divan, but which now smells - and looks - like the inside of a coffin. At least, that's how you imagine a rotting corpse to look and smell. You both dry heave as you empty the contents into a garbage bin.

With a contorted look of disgust on her face, Val says, "Moments like this make me glad I moved in with Rachel instead of you. The nice thing about a roommate who doesn't cook, or even shop for that matter, is a blissfully Type A fridge."

"You remember you never had the option of living with me, right?"

"Semantics." She waves you off. "Heard from Nick?"

"Nope." You tie off the top of the garbage bag. You're pretty sure Nick is officially out of the picture, what with more than a week gone by since your last date and six days since you left him that message. Hence the symbolic purging of the fridge.

"Maybe he's busy making a skin suit."

"Hadn't thought of that. Could be."

Just then, you get a text. You're genuinely surprised to see it's from Nick.

Hey. Last couple weeks have been crazy, It reads. *Going to a house party Saturday if you want to meet me there."*

As glad as you are to hear from him, you're also confused. His invitation sounds kind of indifferent - like he's inviting a guy from work instead of the girl he's dating. Still, he must want to see you, right? Otherwise why ask you at all?

You show the text to Val. "Huh," she says. "Do you want to go?"

To meet him there, turn to section 55.
To decline, turn to section 63.

87

From section 15...

You sit on the couch with your legs tucked beneath you as you absently change channels on the TV. You still haven't heard from Nick.

Over the last six days, you've run a gamut of emotions, starting at happy and hopeful, devolving to somewhere between anxious and depressed.

Just as you begin your descent into anger that he'd make such a fuss about seeing you again only to blow you off, your phone rings. It's a number you don't recognize.

It might be Nick!

It could also just be your bank calling to offer you life insurance. Again.

You clear your throat, warming up for your best casual voice.

"Hello," you breathe into the mouthpiece.

"Hey. How's it going?" Nick says. It sounds like he's smiling.

"Great. Um, sorry. Who is this?" you ask - your attempt at redemption for nearly breaking down moments earlier.

"It's Nick." He pauses for a moment. "Friday night?"

"Friday ni- right, of course. Sorry. How's it going, Nick?"

"I'm good, thanks. Listen, I know it's late notice, but I was hoping you're free on Saturday night."

Anxiety and depression subside. Happiness and anticipation return. You are *so* free on Saturday. He's right though, it *is* kind of late notice.

To see him sooner, turn to section 79.
To see him later, turn to section 159.

88

From section 258...

Twenty minutes and a call to Colleen later, Valerie presents you with a list of real-estate-ruse how-tos, which she's improved upon, and the three of you set the plan in motion.

"For the record," says Rachel. "This is a horrible idea, which will backfire. That said, I support it based purely on caper potential."

Five minutes later, Rachel has created a soundtrack for the evening - appropriately starting with A little Less Conversation, A Little More Action - and you spend the night executing Val's plan - and starting to fear her potential capacity for evil.

You go online and find the best looking male realtors in the city, printing out their homepages, followed by a pre-approved mortgage application from your bank. And finally, a stack of real estate listings in your neighborhood that fall within your imaginary price range.

You tear through the documents with pink highlighters and circle pertinent details, and then stack everything in three neat little piles on your dining room table. After a good night's sleep, you do an hour of practice Q&A with the girls to prepare for all potential eventualities. Now you know how your clients must feel after media training. More importantly, you feel ready.

When Nick arrives, you let him in and walk straight to the kitchen to pour wine, letting him hang his coat in its usual spot - the back of a dining room chair.

"Hey, what's all this?" he asks casually.

As if on cue...

You join him at the table and hand him a glass of wine.

"Are you ready for this?" you ask, hoping you're believably gleeful. "You're looking at a soon-to-be home owner!"

"What?" He blinks rapidly. His eyebrows furrow. He looks like you just told him you're really Batman.

You hear Val's voice in your head: *Keep going!*

"I know! I almost don't believe it myself. Remember when I was at my parents' place last week? Well, my dad asked me to bring my financial stuff to look at and yesterday he called to say I can actually afford to buy! I was up half the night getting organized."

"Wow," he says, still shell-shocked.

"It'll be hard to live away from Rach and Val, but still… Feelin' *pretty* grown up."

"I'm happy for you," he says, but his voice comes out flat.

"What's wrong?"

"Nothing. I am happy for you. It's just… Well, it seems really fast. I mean, you don't think you should wait a while?"

"I guess it's a little sudden, but what am I waiting for? My dad showed me how much money I'm wasting on rent and it's crazy!"

"Well then, *congratulations*!" He touches his glass to yours and gives you a lop-sided smile.

Wait.

This is not how this was supposed to go.

Turn to section 78.

89

From sections 109, 133, 128 and 74...

You're running around your apartment, short on time before a movie date with Nick. Your phone rings and you see his name. A few weeks ago, you'd worry he was bailing on you, but today you figure he's running late.

No such luck.

"Proving miracles do happen," he says. "I'm early."

"Why do miracles always have the worst timing?" you ask. "I'm a little behind."

"No worries. I'm on my way up thanks to a rather unsuspecting woman in the lobby."

"Great!" *Crap.* "See you in a minute!"

You quickly slide your arms into your shirt and fasten the buttons, finishing just as Nick knocks. You open the door and are immediately overwhelmed with the smell of...apple pie.

Nick smells like apple pie.

Apple pie sprinkled with cinnamon and laced with icing sugar.

Nick smells edible.

Delicious.

You *hate* the word "delicious" like most women hate "panties," but the way Nick smells is having a delicious effect on your, well, panties.

"Why do you smell like my birthday?" You sink against his chest and inhale.

"You wouldn't believe me."

"Try me."

"Baking pies with Nana."

"You're right." Inhale. "I don't believe you."

"Proof." He produces a pie from behind his back - in a glass baking dish. You happily take it from him and he follows you to the kitchen where you set it on the counter. You turn and walk right into his chest. Electricity lashes through your body, convincing you his pheromones are comprised mostly of apple pie.

He looks down at your shirt and a slow grin spreads across his face. "You're adorable."

"I am, but why?" He points to your woefully misaligned shirt buttons. "Oh, that."

"I happen to be *great* with buttons." You watch him slowly and skillfully unfasten each one, occasionally grazing your skin as he works his way down, which provokes shivers from you and husky laughter from him. As he reaches the last one, you look up, grab his face with both hands and kiss him full on the mouth. Before you know it, you're sitting on the counter next to the pie, with your fingers twisted in Nick's hair and his warm hands on your bare skin. You can't breathe. You don't care. You lock your legs around his waist and bring him closer.

"We're going to miss the movie," he murmurs against your mouth.

"Yeah."

"Care?"

"Nuh uh. You?"

"Nope. Bedroom?"

Yes! Or, at least, why not? You've lost count of how many dates you've been on, you *really* like him, and you haven't had sex in - six weeks, plus the time since your break-up with James, carry the one – a long time. Still, if you've held out this long, what's a little while longer gonna hurt?

To ask him to wait, turn to section 135.
To wait no more, turn to section 142.

90

From section 123...

"Nipple?" you say, choking on a mouthful of wine and turning heads at Aziza, the Moroccan restaurant Nick picked for dinner.

"Nipple," he says, cringing as he rubs the back of his neck. "I already regret telling you that."

"As well you should." You laugh and set down your glass. As part of getting-to-know-you questions, you asked Nick what his first word was. "I expected something endearing, like 'truck' or 'kitty,' but 'nipple'... Well, that's an unexpected delight."

He waves you off good-naturedly, picking up his beer. "Okay. Now you. Please let yours be something equally humiliating."

You fold your arms on the table, inadvertently elevating your cleavage, which doesn't escape Nick's notice. "Nah. Adorable, really. My dad came home to find me running around my playpen like a maniac, squealing, "Lordy, lordy, lordy." On loop. It was my nanny's catchphrase."

Nick crosses his hands over his chest, eyes closed as he shakes with silent laughter. "Tell me there were pigtails."

You nod. "Nipples, too. I was only wearing a diaper."

"That's hard to beat."

"Unless you're my younger brother, Golden Child. He went so long without speaking, my parents were worried he never would. Then one night, my mother's cleaning up after dinner and Rory says, "Mommy, may I have a cookie please?""

Nick's eyes widen with amusement. "And?"

"Gave him the whole box."

"It's the 'please' that makes it art."

You shake your head, smirking. "Golden Child."

And then it's quiet. Not uncomfortably so. In fact, it's just the opposite. You feel happy. Warmed from the inside with anticipation. Like something good might be happening.

Your server discreetly places a credit card receipt in front of Nick for his signature and then disappears just as quietly. You watch as he reaches across the table and takes your hand, tracing small circles on your palm. The tiny hairs on your neck and shoulders stand up and do the wave. You raise your eyes and they lock with his.

Oh my.

"Shall we go?" he asks after a beat.

You give a quick nod. "Let's."

On the drive to your apartment, Nick keeps one hand on the wheel and the fingers of the other entwined with yours. You try, unsuccessfully, to avoid stealing looks at his profile. The only sound is the music from the car stereo.

You reach your parking lot where he pulls into a visitor spot and shuts off the car. You start to thank him for dinner when he leans across the console and kisses you, softly at first, then intensely. Your fingers slide up the back of his neck, spearing into his hair when you feel the pressure of his hand on your lower back.

Not bad at- Hey now. Easy there, Handsy McGroperson, where's that... My, what nicely-developed biceps you have there. As you were.

You don't know how much time has passed when he pulls back and rests his forehead against yours. You watch his chest heavily rising and falling and place your hand on it, feeling his heart beating as rapidly as your own. You can't help but imagine things without his shirt in the way.

Your mouth goes dry when he whispers in your ear, "May I escort you to your door, please?"

Lordy, Lordy, Lordy.

To let him walk you up, turn to section 16.
To let him down gently, turn to section 325.

91

From sections 80 and 96...

You and Nick have been dating for six weeks and it's been wonderful. You can't remember the last time you had this much fun with someone. You're never bored when you're together, never at a loss for conversation, and when it is quiet, it's a good quiet.

You are happy!

During your Friday night dinner date at your favorite Thai restaurant, you're hard at work trying to convince Nick of his completely wrong, unjustified and undeserved preconceived notions of Jane The Virgin, and that he should really give the show a chance - if not for himself, then for you.

"I'll hate it." He shakes his head rapidly.

"You don't think I know what you'll like?" you ask with a wriggle of your eyebrows. He coughs.

And that's when you hear it.

"Oh, myyyyyyyyy god! Nick!"

If it's possible to be allergic to a particular audio frequency, then you are allergic to this one. Wincing, you rub your ears and follow the shriek to its source - a tall, curvy, dark-haired beauty whose face must prevent heterosexual men from hearing her voice. Yes, she's hot enough to make men to ignore her voice and make you incredibly catty. "What are you doing here?"

Seriously - like acrylic nails on a chalkboard.

Hottie McHotterson, as you've named her, invades your table. She flaps her glossy lips and you try really, really hard to listen to what she says so you can report (and mock) her every word to Rachel and Valerie. Unfortunately, you're powerless against staring at her spectacular breasts. It's fine, they're staring at you, too. And, anyway, you're not sure she's even noticed you yet.

A few awkward moments later, she squeals goodbye to Nick and leaves a big, shiny mouth-print on his already crimson cheek before she struts off.

Nice to meet your breasts, too.

You look at Nick, who wears a thoroughly pained expression. He starts to babble an explanation of how he and Hottie know each other, which, of course, you're dying - *dying* - to hear.

At the same time, it's not really your business, is it?

Give him some rope to hang himself, turn to section 108.
Give him a stay of execution, turn to section 120.

92

From section 55...

"What's *with* him?" Rachel asks, pausing to glare at a short little thing who drunkenly stumbles into her. "It's like he trying to get dumped."

"I dunno." You still haven't told her about the tiny argument you had at the movies, which is probably a good thing.

"Then why invite you to Frat House of Whores?"

You survey the people around you. "They're not whores."

"Statistics suggest at least a handful of them are. Male and female."

"They have statistics on this?"

"I do."

Undoubtedly.

"Can we just give it a little more time and see what happens?"

She sighs dramatically. "Fine. But I'll be damned if I let you stand around like a groupie waiting your turn."

She looks around and leads you back to the room where Nick is still the center of attention. You walk right past him, stopping beside two adorable guys directly in his eye line. They both introduce themselves as Mike and immediately strike up a conversation with Rachel about the poor quality of the party's music.

Forty-five minutes later, Rachel and Mike Sandwich are having fun, but you're not. You chime in now and then, but you're mostly preoccupied with stealing peripheral glances at Nick, hoping he'll break away from his ladies in waiting to talk to you. You're growing more irritated by the second, and given you didn't eat much prior to the party, the beer is going straight to your head.

Finally, Nick walks toward you. "Hey," he says. He looks at you briefly before turning his attention to the foam topping his beer. "Having a good time?"

"Not as good as you are," you reply, surprising yourself.

He flinches. "What's that supposed to mean?"

"Had I known you'd spend the entire night flirting with the Sigma Cum Often girls, I wouldn't have wasted the subway fare."

"What?" He shakes his head almost imperceptibly. "Listen, no offense, but I'm not really looking to-"

Before he can finish, Alpha Blonde walks up and grabs his arm, completely ignoring you.

It really is just like college.

"*Nick!* We're doing body shots. Coming?" she asks, batting her eyelashes frantically. Remembering you're there, she offers an insincere, "Oh. Do you want one?"

"Thanks, but I shouldn't." You look at Nick. "Last time I did shots with this guy, I had to take antibiotics for three months."

Before he can protest, you turn to an eavesdropping Rachel, who is barely containing her laughter. "Sorry, Mikes," she says. "Gotta jet."

As the two of you flee the scene, you look over your shoulder, pleased to see Nick trying to assure his new friend that you're lying.

-*END*-

93

From section 12...

When you get a text from Nick letting you know he's in the parking lot, you all but run out the door, pausing briefly for one last inspection of your reflection in the hall mirror. Not bad, if you do say so yourself.

You ride the elevator to the lobby and spot him typing into his phone. When he sees you, he gives you a huge grin and shoves the phone into his back pocket. You walk toward him, carefully putting one semi-wobbly foot in front of the other. As you near him, he leans forward slightly. While deciding whether he's going for a hug or a kiss on the cheek, you lose your concentration and stumble in your too-high heels, reminding you why you never wear them. You pitch forward, giving Nick a chest-bump.

Perfect.

Fortunately, he has a sense of humor and puts you at ease with an easy laugh and a high-five followed by a graze of his lips over your cheek. He holds your hand on the drive to the restaurant while the two of you make pleasant small talk and do a little innocent flirting.

In your experience, it's usually the second date - when conversation slows and the novelty begins to wear off - where things go off the rails, but tonight's date is going just as well as your first.

Following an amazing dinner, complete with a shared desert of mint chocolate chip gelato, the two of you leave the restaurant and walk a few blocks to a tiny jazz bar. The hostess unsubtly (and unsuccessfully) flirts with Nick before seating you at the last available table - a private booth in the back. Your heart rate speeds up a little when Nick slides in next to you rather than across from you.

You order wine and sip away as he tries to explain jazz to you. It's futile

(Rachel's tried) but you happily listen to him anyway, loving the sound of his voice and the very unique scent that is him. There's about a five-inch gap separating you on the leather bench.

To stay where you are, turn to section 8.
To get a little closer, turn to section 13.

94

From section 13...

More feline than canine is right.

When you enter Nick's ginormous apartment, you expect to be greeted by a bounding, wiggling ball of energy and affection. Instead, you see what looks more like a baby lion, slowly strutting toward you like she's working a runway.

Cat scrutinizes you for a moment and then, apparently deciding you're worthy, rubs her body against your leg. Fascinated, you bend down to pet her, complying when she raises her chin for you to scratch. You swear she's actually purring. After a moment, she walks over to Nick and sits prettily in front of him, her tail wagging rapidly, reminding you she's actually a dog.

"Okay, beauty," he says, scooping her up in his arms and stroking her silky coat. "Let's get you fed so you can get back to sleeping."

Twenty minutes later, a satisfied Cat jumps onto an armchair and turns three times before curling up in a ball and falling fast asleep. Nick takes the opportunity to give a quick tour of his parents' apartment, which is incredible - two levels, high-ceilings and a view of the city you rarely see. When he breezes through the upstairs level, you figure he wants to avoid making you uncomfortable.

Once downstairs again, you follow Nick to the family room where Cat is still napping. You lean down to pet the top of her head and she unconsciously unfurls, exposing her belly for a rub before she coils up again.

You stand up and turn to face Nick. "I'm not sure which is better, the apartment or the dog."

He steps closer and places his hands on your hips. "I'm not even in the running?" he asks with a raised eyebrow.

You rest your hands on his biceps, which are *substantial*. "Third place is very respectable."

He looks at your mouth, which makes you look at his mouth. Taking a page from Cat's playbook, you raise your chin toward him. He takes the hint and lowers his mouth to yours.

You go all melty against him. He pulls you down to the couch and you go to that place where time doesn't really exist and breathing doesn't really matter - a bona fide make out session. Your hands find their way under his shirt and over the smooth, taut muscles of his back. He slides a hand to your lower back and pulls you close, causing you to arch into him, kissing him more intensely. Your heart beats loudly in your ears.

Nick leans back and looks at you with heavy-lidded eyes. "Did you get a good enough look at the bedroom?" he asks.

Between the tight feeling low in your belly and the goose bumps on your skin, your body is working very hard to communicate that it would very much like to revisit his bedroom.

To go upstairs, turn to section 16.
To turn him down, turn to section 9.

95

From section 111...

Three short beeps of a horn startle you out of your daze. You've been sitting in your parked car, moping because it's been three days since you sent Nick that desperate, presumptuous e-mail, which may or may not have sounded like you were comparing him to a Disney princess.

The honks belong to Valerie, who pulls into the parking spot next to yours. You grab your purse and exit the car. "Still nothing?" she asks, hip-checking her door shut.

"Nope."

"Sigh," she says. "I'm roommate-less for a week. Keep me company? I'll get you drunk."

"Absolutely."

There's a medium-sized shipping box at the foot of her apartment door. She picks it up. "Ooh! Mystery package. For me."

Once inside, your phone blips to notify you of a new e-mail. You take it out of your purse and perk up immediately. "E-mail from Nick."

"Let's hear it," says Val as she neatly and systematically puts her things away.

"Sorry. Plans. Call you next week."

"That wasn't a text?"

You blink at the screen. "E-mail."

Valerie sets the box on the kitchen counter. "Maybe he's starting an eco-friendly trend of digital word conservation. Or..."

"He's blowing me off."

"Or that. What did you do?"

"What makes you think I did something? Things have been going really well. We've had two great dates...we even talked on the phone for an hour the other night."

"Ah," she says, pulling a pair of scissors from a drawer. "Now it all makes sense."

"What? *He* called me."

"Right - and you gabbed to him for an hour like a gal pal. Have you ever met a guy who liked talking on the phone who wasn't your brother?" She slices through the packing tape. "Then *you* e-mailed him *and* asked him out. One word: needy."

"Oh, come on! I am not."

"I'm just saying that when it's the other way around, you usually call the guy needy."

She's right. *Eff her.* "So he blows me off. *By e-mail?*"

She shrugs. "Could be worse."

Val raises the lid on the box and it opens with a loud pop, followed by an eruption of color in her face. It's confetti. And it's *everywhere*. Especially in Val's long, red hair. And in her mouth.

Your initial shock gives way to amusement when Val's face turns from pale white to bright red. This was clearly Rachel's doing. When you step closer and find tiny yellow, red and blue F's and U's, you immediately double over with laughter.

"You're right," you wheeze. "He could've sent me a letter bomb."

-END-

96

From section 116...

After yoga in the park, your usually quick stop for coffee is taking longer than corpse pose. You near the head of the world's slowest moving line when what little momentum it had stops. A barista works to keep a smile on her face as the man at the counter casually scans the gigantic, colorfully hand-chalked menus mounted on the wall ahead, whistling while he decides what to order.

You try to keep the inner calm you worked for through many a downward dog, pretending the people in line are a chain of dominos, snaking around a display case of chocolate croissants and fruit cups, and past the easy listening CDs.

Who is still buying CDs?

You silently chant, *Ommmmygod would you hurry up so I can get home and watch a week's worth of TV.*

That's when one of the dominos yells out in a delightfully agitated Scottish accent you'd know anywhere. "Cannae we get the gent a caramel macchiato? It's Sunday in Beijing, ay."

You scan the line until you find the face you're looking for and exclaim, "You!"

Wide-eyed, he shouts back, "Me!"

It's Scott! Scott the Scot. You were madly infatuated with him from the moment you stood in line together for the dorm's co-ed showers back in school. Tall and brawny with that incredible accent and wrapped in a towel? What's not to love?

Then one night you threw yourself at him during a pub-crawl and he gently straightened things out - so to speak. Once thick as thieves, you've grown apart since his consulting firm sent him to Mexico for an assignment. It was only supposed to last six months, but when it turned into two years, Scott's fiancé, Curt, followed him out there.

"Pardon me, folks. Thank you," he says, barely looking at those he bypasses to get to you. He envelops you in a warm hug (of steel) and you smell his familiar cologne. "Reunited with my true love!" he tells everyone, earning sparse applause. He looks down at himself and you note his biceps strain against his polo shirt.

What? He's gay. You're not.

"Am I no longer butch enough to be the presumptive boyfriend?" Scott asks.

"Lesbian girlfriend, maybe."

"Oh, I've missed you, luv."

"Speaking of…*what* are you doing here?"

"I've just got back!"

"Visit?"

"Permanent! It was all very sudden."

"*Yay!*" you squeal and hug him again. "We need to catch up. *Yesterday.*"

"Absolutely."

"My phone's in the car, but you've got my number."

"I don't actually! Someone nicked my mobile. Lost all my contacts," he says as you reach the front of the line. "We'll do it the old fashioned way."

"Carrier pigeons?"

Orders placed, Scott charms a pen from the busy barista and writes his number on a napkin, which you stuff in your pocket.

Turn to section 91.

97

From section 236...

"This is too ironic even for me," you say, pouring yourself a glass of beer from a plastic jug.

Rachel takes it from you. "Maybe you'll think of that next time you lie to your boyfriend and tell him you're out getting a manicure to get out of watching football with him."

Around you, there are easily one hundred men, most of them wearing sports paraphernalia, especially for The Patriots, who you're watching on seven gigantic HD screens, sitting on stools taller than Val's legs.

"Why are we here again?"

"Because Valerie did a crash course on 'football for girls' on YouTube and I couldn't wait to see her try it out, so I brought her to the only place I knew would be filled with mostly hetero penises on a Sunday."

"And I haven't seen her since I walked in, so that backfired."

"On me." She gestures to Valerie across the room. You see her back, smack dab in the middle of nearly a dozen guys fawning over her. Like she senses you, she turns around - and winks.

"Holy shit," Rachel says suddenly. "I'm guessing Nick didn't mention he was coming here."

You whip your head around to the door but there's no one. Rachel slaps your back and laughs. "Val's idea," she says. "My day just got a little brighter."

You look back to Valerie and flip her off with a non-manicured finger.

Turn to section 268.

98

From section 320...

People-pleaser that you are, it takes everything you have not to offer up your cottage, but you manage to keep your mouth shut.

When it's time to go, you say goodbye to Nick's friends and wait for him by the front door, while he makes the rounds. Adjusting your jacket in the hallway mirror, you stealthily watch the background reflection and are pleased to catch one of his buddies giving him a thumbs-up, presumably for you, even if no one uses a thumbs-up anymore.

On the drive home, you're reveling in a job well done when Nick puts a hand on your leg. "Did you have a good time?" he asks.

"I had a great time," you tell him. And you did.

"Good. I think everyone really liked you. And how much fun would a cottage weekend be?"

"So much fun."

Turn to section 252.

99

From section 327...

Not telling Nick just yet is one thing, but you need to get to a doctor - STAT.

Rachel and Val drive you to the nearest walk-in clinic and sit quietly with you. You notice all of the other chairs occupied by watery-eyed girls and their own concerned chaperones.

You hear your name called and follow a surly nurse down a grimy hallway.

Well, honey. Mommy found out she was pregnant while filing a complaint with the Health Department.

You follow her to an exam room where the cup of urine you provided earlier sits on a counter. You watch her dip two strips into it and lay them on a paper towel before leaving.

You wring your hands until, *finally*, a haggard man walks in. You hope the stethoscope around his hoodie means he's a doctor. He looks at his clipboard and...*chuckles?* You're about to torpedo your and Nick's lives with a baby, and this guy thinks it's funny?

"Let me guess," says Dr. Eminem. "Sure Thing*?*"

You grit your teeth. "Excuse me?"

He laughs again. "I mean the brand of the tests. Sure Thing*?*"

You peek at the tests in your purse and see the name embossed on both handles. "Is that a good thing?"

He looks at the urine-soaked strips on the counter. "Judging by your ghostly pallor, I'd say so. It's been happening all day. Women coming in after two 'Sure Thing' tests. Must be on sale. These two here are negative."

Two for One. Save ten bucks, lose twenty years off your life.

You've never felt such pure, weightless relief. You throw your arms around Slim Shady M.D. "Thank you!"

You drop the faulty tests in the trash and collect your friends, who are almost as relieved as you are. At home, you step off the elevator in good spirits. Now you can call Nick, who you've decided not to tell for fear it would change things between you.

You round the corner and find a smiling Nick sitting outside your door. "Security in this building is atrocious," he says, rising to his feet.

"Hey," you say, closing your arms around his neck. "This is a surprise."

"Lucky you." He lifts you for a slow, stomach tightening kiss and sets you back down.

You fish your keys out of your bag, grateful you ditched the tests. Once inside, Nick tells you about his golf game, and you notice a tinge of sunburn on his nose.

"How about you?" he asks. "Fun day with the girls? Tell me *everything*!"

You're as truthful as possible: lazy Sunday movie with Valerie, errands, Rachel found a great sale.

Nick heads to the bathroom and you close your eyes. You hate lying, but it's not like you're hiding a pregnancy. If you were him, you'd rather not-

"I'm guessing the odds are one-in-three this is yours?" Nick asks. You open your eyes to find him holding an empty Sure Thing box.

Shit. You consider another lie. A false alarm with Rachel, but no baby on board. Dinner? But, by the time you decide to come clean, he's already read it on your face.

"So, just a lazy Sunday pregnancy scare? Assuming you're not pregnant." His face reddens and your stomach falls through the floor. You tell him everything. "And you decided I didn't need to know?"

"If we were together when I realized I was late, I'd have told you, but I wanted to spare *you* the agony *I* was feeling until I knew for sure."

"And when *both* tests were positive?"

"I wanted a blood test before I told you."

He's silent. His jaw is rigid.

"When it *thankfully* turned out I'm not pregnant - an hour ago - I didn't see the need to tell you. I wouldn't want to know."

"Bullshit!"

You blink. "What?"

"Of course you'd want to know. Either way, you don't decide for me."

"I was worried you'd overreact. So glad I was wrong."

"Overreact? That's just-"

"I'm sorry. Next time I'm worried I'm carrying your child in *my* womb, you'll be the first to know."

"Do you hear yourself? You know what? Forget it. This is good. Good you're not pregnant, good I found this box, and good I saw this side of you."

Well, you undershot when you worried that Nick finding out would change your relationship. Turns out it ends it.

-END-

100

From section 157...

"Yeah, of course it's cool," you tell Nick, hoping you sound convincing. "I just didn't want to make assumptions one way or the other."

"We're on the same page?" he asks.

"Same paragraph even."

"Okay. I should get back to this, but I'll call you about the weekend?"

"Sure. Talk to you soon."

Ten minutes later, you're shaken from a daze when Maxwell calls. You consider changing your mind, suggesting the two of you meet tonight, but then remind yourself of the drama that accompanies new relationships - and the fact you've already got enough of it in your non-exclusive relationship to even think of starting another. Even if he is gorgeous.

"I'm really sorry, Max," you tell him when he suggests dinner on the weekend. And you are, especially after he tells you he doesn't go by Max, just Maxwell, which intrigues you all the more. "I probably shouldn't have given out my number."

"You're seeing someone?" he asks. To your ego's delight, he sounds disappointed.

"We're kind of at the tipping point of exclusivity," you explain. "It would be unfair to start seeing you."

"To him or to you?" he asks, with a trace of a challenge in that incredible deep voice of his.

"To me, but to you, too."

You say goodbye to Maxwell and dial Rachel. You fill her in on your day, but don't get past the call with Nick.

"*You* asked him if you're exclusive?" she asks.

"Yeah," you say with a flat voice, still bummed. "Aren't you proud of me?"

"For what?"

"Asserting myself and asking Nick outright instead of waiting around and wondering like a helpless woman?"

Rachel's quiet for a moment. "Assertive's good," she says. "But... Aw, fuck. If you knew the answer, why'd you have to ask?"

"I'd rather be certain." *And now you are.*

"Who wouldn't? But you probably spooked him. Men are like deer."

"You're comparing my clarifying couple status with Nick to *hunting* him?"

"And mounting his stuffed head on your wall, yeah. I'm not saying it's not stupid - it's plenty stupid."

Your stomach drops. You were *sure* you were doing the right thing - the grown up thing.

"Don't beat yourself up," she says. "Go out with Mmm. It'll cushion the blow if Nick drops slowly out of your life."

"Yeah, about that..."

"What is *wrong* with you today?"

Turn to section 162.

IOI

From sections 39 and 164...

Wednesday night brings yet another "mandatory fun" work function at a pub down the street from your office. After six cocktails on the executive tab, you accept your favorite co-worker, Laura's challenge of a best-two-out-of-three darts match despite having never played the game before.

As you walk to the billiards area at the back of the bar, you could almost swear you see Nick - or his doppelganger - with his arm around a petite brunette as they watch the live band.

You give your head a shake and begin to doubt the wisdom of throwing sharp objects when you're clearly hallucinating. Then you realize you're seeing things with perfect clarity and that it really is Nick – *with some hussy!* Okay, she doesn't actually look like a hussy - from what you can tell from the back of her head - but you're free to think what you like in this situation.

Horrified, you abruptly stop and turn to Laura, telling her you've got to go before doubling back through the crowd to your table. You grab your things and tell your colleagues you're watching your neighbor's dog and need to walk him before he makes a mess of your apartment. Whatever. You just need to get out of there before Nick spots you.

You quickly find a cab and sink into the seat as the car merges with traffic. You're a little bit heartbroken and a lot embarrassed after seeing him with someone else. Last week, you told yourself you were okay with it, so you shouldn't freak out now. Right? You really like him and you're pretty sure he really likes you, too, so he'll probably end up picking you anyway.

Right?

To ditch him, turn to section 125.
To date him, turn to section 114.

102

From section 152...

Sometimes you're so clever you amaze yourself. To reduce your chances of being a Stupid Cupid, you masterminded a plan called Operation V-Day.

Phase One included buying *two* cards. The cover of the first one has an adorable chipmunk couple standing on a pile of acorns. Inside are the words, *I'm nuts about you!* Whatever, you panicked. The front of the second card is bright and colorful with "Love" written all over it in different fonts. Inside, it simply reads, *Happy Valentine's Day.*

Phase Two started before your date tonight, leaving your gift for him, sans card, on your dining room table, knowing that's where he'd put your gift when he picked you up for dinner, laying the foundation for...

Phase Three. This is where you invoke the "ladies first" rule to make sure you get to read his card first. Then, you run to your bedroom and grab the card that most closely matches the sentiment of his. Pure genius.

Phases One and Two complete when you return from dinner, you immediately lead Nick to the table to commence Phase Three.

"Ladies first," he says and hands you a small rectangular box tied to an envelope with a bow. Sliding the card out, you see a colorful basket of strawberries, blueberries and raspberries on the front. Not promising.

You open the flap and read, *Hope your Valentine's Day is Berry-Happy, Nick.* You try to keep smiling as you set down the card and pick up the white leather box. You're surprised to find a pretty, silver heart-shaped locket. Things are looking up. You carefully open the clasp and see a tiny piece of paper. It reads, *I love you.*

Nick laughs. "You should have seen your face when you opened that card."

You wrap you arms around his neck and kiss him. "Love you, too. Jerk."

Turn to section 191.

103

From section 55...

You drink your beer and think.

Rachel's right. It's totally uncool for a grown man to blow you off for a week and then suddenly invite you to a party, only to brush you off in favor of girls who are blatantly cruising him. You're not exclusive, but that doesn't mean it's okay to flaunt the flirts in front of you. It's also totally embarrassing.

"Okay," you tell Rachel, who looks instantly gratified. "Can we ghost, though? I don't want to say anything and risk causing a scene or, say, punching the blonde dye out of that girl's hair."

Rachel nods. "Good call. Speaking of hitting the head, I've gotta pee. Why don't you wait outside so you're not tempted to spy on Nick and I'll meet you out there?" You take her advice, knowing she's exactly right and that you would torture yourself by watching him with Alpha Blonde and her troupe.

Rachel climbs the stairs toward the lineup for the bathroom and you step outside. You stand on the lawn and finish your beer, politely declining a cigarette from a friendly guy who introduces himself as Randy. Less than two minutes later Rachel walks out, grinning from ear to ear in that way that tells you she's proud of herself.

Now you're nervous.

She bounds down the stairs to you and introduces herself to Randy, who offers her the joint he's now toking away at.

"Right on," she says, taking it from him. "Cheers."

"Line up too long?" you ask.

"Something like that," she says, exhaling a plume of smoke before handing back the joint. "Thanks, mate." Randy, apparently speechless now, just nods at her emphatically.

"Nice try," you say. "What does 'something like that' mean?"

"It means I got upstairs and realized I didn't actually have to pee, *but* interestingly enough, Alpha Blonde was in line, too. So I says to myself, I says, what kind of person would I be if I didn't warn a fellow sister that Nick once gave me the worst case of crabs my doctor's ever seen?"

"*You didn't!*"

"I did. Poor thing. Face turned all ashen. Which says a lot given how many layers of spray tan are on there."

"You're evil," you tell your loyal friend with a smile.

"I know it. Now, let's get out of here. Randy's weed is shit." She turns to him. "No offense, Randy."

"None taken," he croaks.

Rachel links her arm through yours and leads you toward the subway. "Come on. I've got way better stuff at home. We'll pick up some Pecan Butter Tart ice cream on the way."

Rachel is your She-ro.

-*END*-

104

From sections 120 and 37...

Having somehow found yourself in another marathon make-out session on Nick's couch, you jump up and suggest the two of you take an evening stroll before things get out of hand. He agrees and you grab your coats and head downstairs.

The sun is setting as you walk hand-in-hand down the street. You occasionally stop to look in display windows and then pop into your favorite pet store to visit the kittens. You give the puppies their fair share of attention and leave the store, turning back the way you came.

Your lips could use a little TLC after all that kissing earlier, so you reach into your pocket for your lip balm. It catches on the napkin Scott gave you, which falls at Nick's feet. He picks it up, undoubtedly seeing your friend's name and number written in capital letters in bright blue ink. Underlined. Twice.

He straightens up and holds the napkin out to you, a confused (and maybe even jealous?) look on his face. It takes a moment to remember he doesn't know that not only is Scott part of a couple, but that the other half of that couple is a man - making you the furthest possible thing from his type. Nick doesn't ask you any questions, he's just quiet. And tense. A tiny muscle pulses in his jaw. It definitely looks like Nick may have the wrong idea about Scott.

Hmm.

Should you let his imagination run wild for a while longer? A little jealousy can be good. What's that old saying? You don't know what you've got until some Scottish dude's phone number falls out of the pocket of the girl you're dating?

Something like that.

To let Nick's mind run in circles, turn to section 112.
To set Nick straight about Scott, turn to section 121.

105

From section 157...

You're sprawled out on your couch when your front door flies open. Rachel walks in with Val in tow, carrying break-up gear: wine, whiskey, ice cream and tissues.

"I made Val empty her bra," Rachel says as she shakes the floral print box.

Val raises her stubborn chin. "You know," she says in a haughty voice. "I may not have hooters, but I'm a hoot."

In spite of yourself, this makes you laugh. Hard. You fold at the waist and wheeze, tears eventually streaming down your face. It takes a moment and Val's hand on your shoulder for you to realize these are no longer happy tears.

"I don't know why I'm crying," you say. "I barely even know him."

"Didn't you break it off with him?" Rachel asks, setting everything out on your kitchen table. "I'm lost."

After a recap, your friends assure you that you did the right thing.

You take a glass of wine from Rachel. "You guys don't think I overreacted?"

"No way! It's been weeks. If he's not into it by now..."

"Yeah," adds Rachel, sitting next to you on the couch. "Were you supposed to keep just having fun with him until he finds someone he does want to be exclusive with and dumps you? Fuck that."

"That is so not making me feel better," you say, and drain your glass, which actually does help a little.

"If you want to feel better, call Mmm back and make a date," Val says with a flash of excitement in her green eyes.

"Yes!" agrees Rachel. "What did Roma teach us? The best way to get over the last one..." You and Val join in. "*Is to get under the next one!*"

-END-

106

From section 199...

You know there's a fine line between self-respect and being a nag, you just aren't sure where that line is. What you do know is that Val will never let you hear the end of it if you tell her you passed up the chance to set a relationship precedent.

"For sure. I just wish you'd mentioned it sooner," you tell Nick. You work to keep the annoyance out of your voice, but you hear a trace of it. You wonder if he recognizes it yet.

"But...we didn't have plans." He sounds confused. "Did we?"

"No." And that really is the operative word here, yet you proceed. "But we've spent that last three or four weekends together, so I just assumed..."

"I didn't realize I needed to run this kind of stuff by you." Now *he* sounds annoyed.

"That's not at all what I mean. I just would have made other plans. That's all."

The line goes quiet.

"Hello?" you ask. *Did he hang up?*

"I'm here," he says. "Listen, I gotta jet. My ride's here."

"Okay, so I'll see you tomorrow?"

"I'll call you."

"Have a g-" He hangs up.

Maybe you should have just let it go.

Turn to section 207.

107

From section 296...

Tick - tick - tick - tick goes the sound of your matrimonial clock, reminding you of Christmas Eves you spent on your Aunt Pauline's couch, unable to sleep because of the relentless noise from the grandfather clock. You're also reminded that not only does Aunt Pauline still have that clock, and the couch, but she's as much a spinster now as she was then.

And you're well on your way to following in her sensible footwear steps.

Just a year ago, you and Nick were happy. You chose to keep quiet about his aversion to marriage, positive that he'd eventually come around if you didn't press the issue. You're still not sure you if you were naïve or in denial.

And Rachel got engaged!

One day she was her glorious cynical and jaded self, and the next she was fused to Jet (name verified on original birth certificate), a musician she began dating following a confrontation on a subway platform when his guitar case literally knocked her head over heels. Just eleven months later, he proposed. He said he couldn't live the rest of his life without her and didn't want to wait another day to start the rest of his life. In a song.

Right?

Of course, you were thrilled for her - and for irony, for pulling off a feat of such magnitude - but as maid of honor, when it came time to plan her engagement party, something in you snapped - like a *really* taut rubber band.

At Nick.

You're not quite sure how it happened. You were quietly folding laundry together one minute, and the next you (politely) demanded to know when he was going to propose. He reminded you that you'd already talked about it and you knew where he stood, but you kept at it. It sparked an argument, which escalated until he finally broke up with you, not wanting to fight every time someone got married.

He also called you scary, and you kind of were.

You're not exactly counting your genetic material, but you're practical enough to know you've wasted some seriously viable eggs, waiting for them to hatch while you sat on your marriage doubts.

If you hadn't chickened out, you could've moved on long ago, with a new cock in your henhouse to escort you to Rachel's wedding. Instead, you're scouring the guest list and making mental notes of any of the bride and groom's friends who RSVP'd without a Plus One.

Sigh.

Here we go again.

-END-

108

From section 91...

Rachel passes you a bowl of potato chips in the middle of a stoned rant. "I'm just saying, gun silencers *aren't* silent, so to call them that is false advertising."

"Maybe Don Draper thought calling them Pew Pews would discourage assassins and snipers from buying them." Val says and makes a finger gun. *"Pew Pew."*

"Yeah," you say through a mouthful of salt, vinegar and sarcasm. "Imagine how hesitant people would be to call 911 and say, 'Um, I think I heard Pew Pew shots next door?'"

Rachel nods thoughtfully. "Fair points. Slightly douchey delivery, but fair points."

"Our friend is in crisis and you're asking her opinion on brand management for deadly weapons."

"Douché," says Rachel, laughing at her joke. "I seriously kill me."

"Good. It'll save me the hassle of going to the Tenderloin to buy a Pew Pew." Val turns back to you. "You were panicking?"

You give them a quick recap of last night's date crasher, hoping they can help analyze Nick's explanation of how he knows Hottie.

"And I quote," you begin. "'We, uh- She was in my Intro to Psych class in college. I, uh, ran into her last year and we hang out...once in awhile.' What does *that* mean?"

"He's fucking her," Rachel says, taking back the potato chips and popping one in her mouth. "Present tense."

That's what I thought. "You think?"

She nods. "Not regularly, though. Booty buddy."

"Ooh. Yeah, yeah," agrees Valerie. *"That."*

"So what do I do?" you ask.

"What you should do," says Rachel, "Is remember you're not in an exclusive relationship and forget about it. What you will do is obsess about it anyway, so just try not to get passive aggressive about it."

"That should be easy," you say, and slump down further into their couch.

"Do you think I could sue a manufacturer if I got arrested and convicted solely because someone heard a supposedly silenced shot?" Rachel asks.

She's already moved on in her head. If only it were that easy for you.

Turn to section 137.

109

From section 137...

Oh, why the heck not?

It's your lunch hour and you can do what you want with it. And what you want to do is not waste an opportunity to talk to Nick, especially when *he* initiated it.

That would be silly.

You reply to his e-mail and tell him you're bored, too. That's not true, of course - you'd hit a dorky organizational groove, but whatever. You suggest a classic game of Ultimatum, where you take turns suggesting pairs of famous people so the other can decide which of the two they'd rather sleep with. It's a never-fail fun way to pass time, and you can tell a lot about a person by their answers.

You offer Nick his first pairing of Martha Stewart and Hillary Clinton and hit send. Your money's on Martha, though you'd probably choose Hillary yourself.

You make sure your computer speakers are on and return to the stack of files on your desk, figuring you can still get a little something done while you wait.

And wait you do.

Five minutes pass and nothing.

Another ten go by and...nothing.

Twenty more minutes. No ding from your inbox.

Half an hour later, you've accomplished about two percent of what you could have if you'd given your work your full attention.

Still, you wait some more.

Before long, you're compulsively checking your inbox. You tell yourself Nick probably received an important phone call. Or he was pulled into a meeting. It's also entirely possible he's taking the decision between Hillary and Martha really seriously. Like Archie with Betty and Veronica. You get it. It took you ages to decide between Al Roker and Gordon Ramsay. (Al For the Win!)

And that's how the afternoon goes. Organize files for a few minutes, check your inbox. Answer a time sensitive e-mail, refresh inbox. Clean your keyboard with that compressed air thingy, check e-mail. You even check your cell in case he wanted to take things offline because his company has a weird policy about playing Ultimatum on company equipment. No go.

Yep, it goes like this right up to five o'clock, at which point you realize you've gotten so little done this afternoon that you're actually going to have to stay late to catch up.

Good times.

And so Betty Cooper.

Turn to section 89.

110

From section 323...

"Wakey, wakey." You clap your hands together, wishing you had a megaphone. "Time to get up."

Startled, Nick sits up and rubs at his eyes. "What's happening?"

"Time to go." Still in lingerie, you hold the bedroom door open - like a sexy, angry game show hostess.

Taking in your outfit, he asks, "Where exactly are we going?"

"*We* aren't going anywhere. You're obviously tired and should get home."

"What the hell did I do?"

"You have to ask? I spent *all day* preparing a nice evening for us and you pass out – twice."

"I'm sorry." He puts his hands up in surrender. "I'm so tired. You know I worked late all week. I'm a zombie."

"Oh, save it," you tell him, not budging an inch.

"You know you're acting crazy, right? And completely unreasonable? I didn't even know you had something planned. If I had, I'd have told you it wasn't a good night."

"So now I need to *warn* you when I want to do something nice?"

"That's not what I said. Forget it. You win. I'm out." Now wide-awake, he walks past you and out of the room. A moment later, the front door slams behind him.

Not done venting, you throw on a robe and call Valerie, knowing she'll empathize with your linge-rage.

"You kicked him out?" she asks when you tell her about the fight.

"Yes," you say proudly, picking up a glass of wine from the table. "Inconsiderate jerk."

"Oy." You hear her slap her forehead. "Let me get this straight. You completely surprised him with a romantic evening – knowing he had a long work week

– stuffed him full of food and wine and then, when he collapsed into a coma from exhaustion and overeating, you woke him up, yelled at him - in your underwear - and kicked him out of your apartment for being *inconsiderate*?"

You pause. "When you say it like that, I sound like a crazy bitch."

"I was going to say spoiled brat, but yours is good, too. Either way, you had better figure out a pretty spectacular apology if you don't want to end up single."

Ten hours later, you're in Nick's kitchen. *Thanks for the key!* You make breakfast quietly so as not to wake him upstairs. You were up for hours deciding how to make up for your "moment" and settled on more food. It's what your mom would do.

As a twist, though, you redressed in your sexy skivvies and an apron to prepare breakfast. You really hope she wouldn't do *that*. With bacon, eggs and sour dough toast keeping warm in the oven, you're setting the table when you hear Nick behind you.

"Well if it isn't the Half-Naked Chef," he grumbles at you. He's doing his best to look mad but isn't having much luck, mostly thanks to the lacy distraction. "What are you doing here?"

"Good morning," you say cheerfully. "Before you get mad, let me say that I am fully aware I was acting like a selfish child last night and I'm sorry."

"Go on," he says, amused but not satisfied.

"And I'll wear only underwear for the remainder of the weekend."

"Apology accepted."

Turn to section 298.

III

From section 9...

You spend nearly two hours on the phone with Nick.

You top his "trapped in the trunk of a Volvo" story with the time you toppled your school's cheerleading pyramid - in a mascot costume. He tells you about the phase in college where he wore black nail polish and worshipped Chris "Birdman" Anderson. You share your first office Christmas party, where each of your co-workers - including you - passed around the gel insert from your water bra, everyone guessing at what it could be - and why it was so warm.

A little before eleven, you notice Nick's not really responding anymore. If it weren't for the deep, even breathing indicating he's asleep (and a non-snorer), you'd have thought you'd been talking to air for god knows how long. You're not sure if it's weird or not, and you'd deny it if asked, but you listen for a moment before you whisper goodnight and hang up the phone.

You sleep and dream of Nick, a large otter, and The World's Biggest Ball of String, whatever that means. You wake before your alarm, bright-eyed and bushy-tailed as you remember you and Nick have reached the unspoken milestone of casual phone conversations.

You can barely concentrate during your two-hour managerial meeting, your mind constantly floating back to Nick and the strides you're making toward coupledom. You also realize you're more excited about the prospect of being "off-the-market" than you've been in a long time. Back at your computer, the mouse hovers over the send button on an e-mail you've drafted to him.

It reads: Hey Sleeping Beauty! It was good talking to you last night. My Saturday's open at the moment if you want to do something. Let me know when you get a minute. From, Me.

It's good. Cute, casual, familiar but not presumptive.

To send, turn to section 95.
To trash, turn to section 35.

112

From section 104...

"Thanks," you tell Nick when you take the napkin from him. You shove it back into your pocket quickly, careful not to offer any more information than necessary.

As you walk back to his place, you try re-stoking your earlier conversation about the adorable little critters from the pet store, but it quickly becomes clear he's distracted.

You see a small group of protestors walking down a connecting street and tell him the story of Valerie's near suspension from school for organizing a protest on the university administration building. More specifically, that she wore a sandwich board that read *Hell No, We Won't Blow!* in response to the school's consideration of an "everything but" system for student sexual relations, which most guys interpreted as "free blow jobs." She talked her way out of a suspension but was banned from sandwich boards and art supplies for the remainder of the year.

That's usually a story guaranteed to have 'em laughing, but Nick remains lost in thought. You ball one hand into a fist and tap it a few times with the other. "Is this thing on?" you ask into your mime-mic.

"I'm sorry, what?" His attention snaps back to the present.

"Everything okay?"

"Fine. Yeah. Sorry." He rakes a hand through his hair. "I just got a feeling I didn't finish something at work. It's all good."

You come to a stop at a streetlight and Nick folds your hand snugly into his, giving it a gentle squeeze.

All good, indeed, you think when the "Walk" signal appears.

Even if you feel *a little* bad about the subterfuge.

Turn to section 117.

113

From sections 64 and 22...

No matter how many times you remind Nick that you both hate That Pizza Place and love It's Been a Pie, he never gets it right. Except that one time you showed up after an office gathering and immediately passed out drunk on his couch, laptop bag still gripped in your hand. The next morning you woke up to an empty pizza box, propped open, with a note written on a napkin inside: *You snooze, you lose.*

Tonight is no exception - the pizza tastes like dirty gym socks smell. Too hungry to do anything about it, you alternate between taking large bites, chewing quickly, and washing it down with soda. Your bouche is far from amused, but you're still delighted because Nick is sharing gossip with you.

A milestone!

Sure, guys put on a good show of pretending they don't talk about (or listen to talk about) others, but *that's* why they always have the best information. They're flies on walls. And when a guy dishes more than small talk about his friends and/or their lives, he's into you.

Nick's best friend, Russ, has been with his girlfriend, Sally for around six weeks. You like this for many reasons, but mainly because a) you love the name Sally, and b) it's roughly the length of time you've been dating Nick, so it's probably better for you if his buddy's all-a-glow over a gal rather than the alternative. Girls can sour their friends on the opposite sex, true, but a man can do it in half the time and with less effort. It's probably connected to men's rooms never having line ups.

According to Nick, Russ feels pressured because Sally gets irritated when they're not in daily contact the way, she says, "normal" couples are. He really likes Sally but doesn't want to feel like he *must* check in with her.

Nick shakes his head. "Big red flag that says: *Red Flag.* In capital letters."

You've only gotten one out of four sides to this story (Nick's, Russ', Sally's, and the truth) but, in general, you don't think it's unreasonable for a girl to hope her *boyfriend* would want some daily contact with her. Even if it's just a quick text to say, "*Hey. Had a great beagle today.*" Followed by, "*Fucking autocorrect. Had a great BAGEL today.*"

To rally around Russ, turn to section 116.
To side with Sally, turn to section 133.

114

From section 101...

Two days after The Broken Records concert with Nick, you're still on Cloud 9.

The band was phenomenal, but being there with him was even better. You danced together, drank together and sang off-key together. You even shook rock stars' hands together backstage. You were totally in sync. So much so that you're now positive your relationship is about to make the leap from Gold to Platinum, making you an exclusive couple.

When Nick calls to confirm tonight's date, he asks if he can come upstairs first to talk to you about something. Finally! You're positively bubbly over the idea of *"our-ing"* and *"we-ing."*

When he shows up at your door, you have to manage the smile on your face so he can't tell you know what's coming. You invite him in and give him a quick kiss before offering him wine.

"No thanks," he tells you and sits on the couch. "But you go ahead."

You pour yourself a glass and sit down, turning toward him. He looks at his hands, which are clasped in his lap.

He's nervous. That's so sweet!

"So what did you want to talk to me about?" you ask, reassuringly touching his arm.

He tenses. "I've been struggling to find the best way to do this," he says. "And there isn't one, so I'll just say it."

Here it comes.

"I don't think we should see keep seeing each other." He spits the words out without looking up. When you're too shocked to speak, he continues. "I think you're awesome, and hilarious, but when we were at the concert... Well, I can't help but think you're starting to feel more than casual about this. And I'm really not looking for anything too serious right now, so I feel like it would be a lot of pressure if..."

You're so dizzy now that you wonder if this break-up blind-side gave you a concussion. Nick continues to ramble on, but you barely hear him. You just flit back and forth between feelings of sadness that you're being dumped and embarrassment because you didn't see it coming.

Even though it was right in front of you.

-END-

115

From section 185...

There are many advantages to finally being able to call someone your boyfriend.

For one, there's the sex - which was pretty damn great, and you're glad you waited as long as you did. As cliché as it sounds, you really do feel more connected to Nick as a result.

For another, there's the decrease in mixed signals that usually pile up because you're too much of a chicken shit to ask the guy you're dating for clarification, spending hours analyzing what he *may* have meant instead.

And, of course, there's knowing you're the only girl he's with and vice versa. No more nights wondering who he might be with when he's not with you. No more letting him think that when you're not with him, you're with his competition, even when his competition is a fictional character from a book you're reading in your pajamas.

If all of the above is true, you can sure as hell be honest with Nick when he asks why you're in a good mood.

"Just thinking about the weekend," you tell him, figuring you'll ease into it.

"I've been thinking about the weekend quite a bit myself," he says. "I've had a stupid grin on my face since I left your place. Made for a rather embarrassing staff meeting this morning."

His words give you a body buzz. "So, you're happy, too, then?"

"You could say that. Probably easier if I show you, though."

"Is that so?"

"Be there in fifteen."

Yup. Everything is better.

Continue to section 177.

116

From section 113...

This is a very crucial time in your relationship with Nick, partly because you're not exactly sure what type of relationship you're in.

Are you casually dating?

Are you an unspoken (imaginary) couple?

Is he seeing anyone else?

Does he think you're seeing other people and, if so, is he okay with it?

Could the answers to any of these questions dramatically and negatively impact whatever you have going on with Nick?

Yes!

Of course they could. All of them could. And *that* is precisely why you're about to throw Sally under that proverbial bus. You've never met her, which makes it a little easier when your mind conjures the image of a cartoon-like, dark-haired girl with big doe eyes behind giant glasses who tears up when you say, "Come on, Nick. You know as well as I do that the only way to be a perfect couple is to talk *everyday*."

"Right?" Nick laughs. And, if you're not mistaken, looks the tiniest bit relieved. "I just don't get women. *Some* women… You know what I mean. Or don't mean."

Behind your reassuring smile is a little bit of shame - you just sold out the sisterhood, after all – but not as much shame as you anticipated. And anyway, it probably works like heaven. When you get there, everyone finds out all the bad shit everyone else did and calls it a draw before they party like it's 1999. And if The Sisterhood of Traveling Grumpy Pants insist on being wet blankets about the whole thing, screw 'em.

All's fair in love and war, so save your perfect tear, Cartoon Sally.

Turn to section 96.

117

From section 112...

Earlier this week, you found out your favorite band--which also happens to be Nick's favorite band--The Broken Records, are coming to town for a concert in three weeks. You immediately e-mail him.

You: *Hoorary! TBR tickets go on sale tomorrow. Were we not just talking about how awesome it would be to see them live? We must get seats. Are you free on the 10th? If not, you are now.*

Nick: *Sounds fun, for sure, but I'm not much of an advance planner. Why don't we wait a couple of weeks and see if we can still get tickets then?*

You know the concert will sell out in under an hour, and you know how much he loves the band, so this makes no sense. Deflated and confused, you forward his e-mail to Rachel.

You: *WTF does that mean?*

Rachel: *Male-onics translation - 'Listen, I don't know if we'll still be dating a few weeks from now, so I don't want to buy tickets just yet.' Don't take it personally - all guys are like that. P.S. Your taste in music sucks.*

Two days later, you come home to find Rachel waiting outside your apartment door with a Cheshire grin and a hand behind her back.

"What are you up to?" you ask.

"It's what *you* are up to, pal o'mine!" She presents you with two tickets, and two *backstage passes* to the concert. "Work hook up."

You throw your arms around her. "You're amazing! I don't know how to thank you."

"That's easy. Don't invite me."

"Deal."

When Nick calls tonight, you excitedly share your news.

"Are you serious?" he asks. "This is going to be amazing! I can't wait."

Say what?

Now he wants to go to an event that's three weeks away?

Half of you is excited and already imagining an amazingly perfect night together. The other half, however, can't help but suspect his motives.

Tell him you invited someone else, turn to section 119.
Start planning your outfit, turn to section 39.

118

From section 119...

Thursday gives you a major case of The Blahs.

This morning's blow dry came out *blah*, your coffee was *blah*, your morning meeting was *blah*, lunch was *blah* - actually, more *meh* than *blah*, but still - and your commute was *blah*. The take-out you got for dinner was *blah*, as is the stack of bills you're now sorting through due to a lack of new content on your Tivo,

Blah.

And then your phone rings and The Blahs take a hike. It's Rachel calling you from downstairs.

"Get down here, Baby!" she hollers into the mouthpiece. "And get ready to have the time of your life!"

"On a Thursday?" you ask. "I always thought you could only have the time of your life on a weekend. Probably a Saturday."

"Who's your best friend?"

"Val." You can almost hear her rolling her eyes.

"Try again."

"Rory."

"Last try."

"Well, golly, Rachel. I guess it's you."

"In spite of your underwhelming appreciation for our friendship, I'm *still* going to let you be my date to..." She pauses for dramatic effect, and it works. "Dirty Dancing: The Musical.*"

"You *lie*."

"All the time, but not about something this important. You know I'm crazy for Swayze."

"Bless his soul," you say in unison.

You hang up, grab your things and are out the door, making it down to the lobby in record time. Unsurprisingly, Rachel is creating a spectacle out front, hanging out of her window with the Dirty Dancing soundtrack blasting from the speakers as she sings along.

As you buckle your seat belt, you remember for the first time today that Nick said he would call if he was free tonight. It wasn't a definite thing but, still, it would just be good manners to let him know you made other plans so he can, too.

That's what you'd want.

To give him a call 122.
To focus on curtain call, 126.

119

From 117...

"Oh," you say, playing with a loose thread on your sweater. "Sorry, but when I mentioned the concert before... Well, I didn't think you wanted to make plans so far in advance, so I invited someone else."

"So who's it going to be?" Nick asks, definitely disappointed but being cool about it. "Rachel or Valerie? My money's on Rachel, since she gave you the seats, yeah?"

You are suddenly, and out of nowhere, overcome with exasperation that Nick would assume that if you didn't bring *him* to the concert, your only other options would be the girls.

That's partly true. Of course they'd be the first people you'd ask, but you could invite other people, like that new guy at work who's always hitting on you. You could invite Laura or Sheri. Or Scott.

Yes!

Scott who you haven't seen in ages!

Scott who loves The Broken Records as much as you do!

Scott will be your date.

Hopefully.

Once you ask him.

"Neither, actually," you say, careful not to offer more details than necessary.

"*Oh.*" You love the tone in his voice right now. It's somewhere between surprise and, yes - jealousy! "Is your brother in town?"

"No." You should *not* be enjoying this that much. And yet you are!

"So...who?"

You can tell what he's thinking from the edge creeping into his voice. "Scott."

"Right. Well, I guess that's my fault. No worries. You'll have a great time."

As soon as you hang up with Nick, you call Scott who gladly accepts your invitation - without hesitation.

Turn to section 118.

120

From section 91...

Nick clears his throat. "That's Hottie," he says into his plate. He actually called her Holly, but whatever. "We, uh…"

You quickly hold up a hand. "Don't explain," you say. "It's cool." To drive home your lie (because it is so *not* cool), you give him your best fake PR smile.

Relief, gratitude, and a little confusion wash over Nick's face and you resume your pre-random hot chick discussion. Excellent. Nick now thinks you're Cool Girl. Maybe even Cool, Easy-Going, Happy-Go-Lucky Girl. And maybe he's also wondering if you're getting your jollies with any Hollys of your own.

You wake up early the next morning with bed-head that would make Tina Tuner jealous, dressed in a tank top and the granny panties you used as birth control last night. You're en route to the kitchen when your apartment door flies opens and Rachel storms in holding a water machine gun, kicking the door shut behind her.

Holding the gun by her side like it's the most natural thing in the world, Rachel looks you up and down. "Laundry day?"

"Offensive measures." You retrieve your mug from the one-cup coffee maker.

"Well, they're effective. They've put me off sex forever."

You motion to her weapon. "Do I want to know why you're packing heat so early in the morning?"

A maniacal laugh escapes her as she raises the gun toward the ceiling. "Because for the first time in months, Valerie is still asleep before eleven a.m. I'm *finally* getting revenge for her spring cleaning to the Sound of Music during the second worst hangover of my life. How, you ask? By waking her with a blast to the face with all the power this bad boy'll dish out."

"Isn't that misogynistic?"

"Nah." She shakes her head. "Not if a chick does it. We'll ask her afterward."

Rachel loads up on ammo in the kitchen sink while you fill her in on last night.

"So, how do you think he knows her?" she asks as she goes to leave.

"I've decided she's his harmless lesbian neighbor - who is also a nun."

"Really? 'Cause I figure she's his fuck buddy."

"That's helpful, thanks."

She starts to open the door, but pauses to look over her shoulder. "Could be worse," she says.

"How?"

"We could both be right." She gives you a wicked look and opens the door - to a stream of high-pressure water in the face.

In the doorway stands Val with a shit-eating grin and water pistol, taking advantage of Rachel's shell-shocked state to disarm her before spinning her own gun around on her finger and holstering it in the waistband of her yoga pants.

And then she hauls ass down the hall.

Turn to 104.

121

From 104...

Holy crap!

You know it's *so wrong,* but you can't help being a little bit thrilled by the jealously radiating from Nick right now. Still, it would be kind of cruel to let him get the wrong idea about your relationship with Scott. You'd hate it if he did…whatever the inverse of that is to you.

"Thanks," you tell him, taking the napkin and returning it to your pocket.

"No problem," he says. You start walking again, but he doesn't take your hand like he did before. Evenly, he says, "Wouldn't want you to lose Scott's number."

Passive aggressive. Normally you'd hate that, but in this instance you don't mind, it being good for your ego and all.

"Definitely not," you say. "If we did, I'd have to spend all my time in the Castro, downing martini after martini while scouting a new, not-so-stereotypical, token gay friend. Sounds like fun but, alas, too many calories."

Nick's brows knit together in confusion, so you fill him in on your relationship with Scott. Once he understands your friend isn't a rival for your affections, you can actually see the tension leave his body before he wraps an arm around your shoulders. "For a minute there, I was almost jealous."

He was *jealous!*

He was!

You saw it!

You want to tell him so, but think better of it. As you continue your walk back to his place, half-listening to him talk about something sports related (or possibly about tigers), you can't help but wish you'd let Nick's mind wander *just* a while longer.

Turn to 128.

122

From section 118...

Being the considerate woman you are, you type out a quick text to Nick. "Hey, I know we said 'maybe' for tonight, but I'm at a show with Rachel. Call you later."

The performance is incredible, but your mind wanders occasionally, worried he'll think you bailed on him if it turns out he is indeed free tonight. You power up your phone the moment the curtain falls, an unpleasant feeling settling in your stomach when you don't see a response to your text from earlier.

He *is* mad.

Damn.

During the twenty minute drive home, you're half-listening to Rachel recount her favorite parts of the production, and half-silently willing her to speed - more so than usual - so you can get home and apologize to Nick as quickly as possible.

When you finally pull into your parking lot, you ask Rachel to let you out at the lobby so you can pee, barely waiting for the car to come to a stop before you hurriedly thank her, say goodbye and jump out. You rush across the lot, through the lobby and into an elevator, pushing the button for your floor five or six times as if it will quicken the trip.

As soon as your front door closes behind you, you dial Nick's number. He picks up on the last ring. There's an awful lot of commotion in the background.

"I'm *so* sorry," you say by way of greeting. "Are you mad?"

"Mad about what?" *Is he drunk?* You couldn't have upset him that much. Could you?

"Didn't you get my text?"

"Sorry, I haven't looked at my phone in a while. Hang on. I'll check it now."

He pulls the phone away from his ear and you hear the distinct sounds of people having a good time: cheering, laughing and lots of testosterone. You're guessing he's at a sports bar.

"Oh, no worries, babe. I actually forgot we said we might do something. I'm watching the game with Russ."

He called you babe, which is a first, and he forgot about you - also a first.

Continue to section 127.

123

From section 79...

You take your time getting ready, starting with a long, hot shower, followed by a glass of wine and some music while you carefully apply your makeup and blow dry your hair. You dress in your new jeans and tube top, the diamond studs your parents gave you for graduation, and the finishing touch - a pair of red heels Rachel loaned you to complete your outfit.

How the hell does she wear these things?

You spend twenty minutes walking around your apartment trying to adjust to your new altitude. At least if your nose bleeds, you'll still match. Your feet already hurt, but you hear Rachel's voice insisting it's a small price to pay for how good you look.

At 7:58, you make sure your purse has everything you need, do one last hair check, and ride the elevator downstairs to wait for Nick. You reach the lobby and immediately spot him outside, leaning against a late model black Camaro.

Muscle car. Appropriate.

He's looking down at his phone, so you take the opportunity to ogle. He looks like heaven in dark jeans and a greyish blue shirt with the top buttons undone and sleeves rolled up to the elbow. Proof that if god exists, he's a gay man.

You take a breath and exit the lobby, focused on not falling face-first in your ruby red slippers. When Nick sees you, he straightens immediately and you can actually feel his eyes run down your body and up again. He walks over and places a hand on your hip and a kiss on your cheek.

"So," he says. "You look... Well, you look really good."

"Thank you," you say. You're sure your face is now the same shade as your shirt. That was the reaction you were going for, right?

He rests a hand on your back and leads you around to the passenger side of the car. You climb in carefully and smile up at Nick, who is either staring at you or being incredibly cautious that your limbs are tucked safely inside the vehicle before he closes the door. Once he's settled behind the wheel, he turns to face you. "Ready, beautiful?"

"Ready."

On the ride to the restaurant, you point out your favorite Thai place, the diner you and the girls frequent for brunch, the bar that makes the best gin and tonic and the one that makes the worst, and even the dry cleaner who always has porn playing on the TV behind the counter. All the while, Nick's attention is split evenly between the road ahead of him and the view beside him.

You'll have to remember to thank Rachel.

Turn to section 90.

124

From section 127...

Before the play, you meet Rachel and Valerie down the street for Bellinis and appetizers. You'd only planned on having one drink, but the delicious, slushy, rainbow concoctions topped with adorable plastic giraffes and frogs sucked you in. As usual.

Before long, you and Rachel have the beginnings of an ark manifest in front of you: two plastic monkeys lead two giraffes and frogs, with a pair of teeny hot pink pumps bringing up the rear. (They could need heels in the new world.)

As you devour a plate of breaded shrimp, Rachel hammers you with details of her new prospect, the construction foreman in charge of the building renovation next door. She's wanted to screw him since they met, but managed to leave his tool belt alone for four whole dates. You know that your friend giving Blue Collar a set of blue balls means she's laying the foundation for something serious - at least, Rachel-serious.

"Christ. I'm one step away from becoming a chick who watches super couple fan vids on YouTube," says Rachel, tilting her head and directing her eyes at Valerie.

"Oh, shut up." Valerie shoots her a dirty look through purple specs perfectly matched to her clutch. "It's emotional porn for women. Also, Olicity forever."

"I'd take Stephen Amell forever."

"Speaking of serious." You redirect the conversation to you. "How great is it that Nick's coming to a *family* event with me?"

"Pretty great. So, are you a couple now?" Valerie spoons a heap of spinach and artichoke dip onto a chip. You watch in amazement as she daintily fits it all in her mouth without disturbing her lip-gloss.

"How do you *do* that?" you ask.

She shrugs and chews. "Don't change the subject. Coupledom?"

Before you can answer, your phone rings and you dig it out of your purse.

"Do you do that in front of the guys you date?" Rachel asks Valerie. "'Cause if you don't, you should. *I'm* kind of turned on."

"Guess I'll be locking my bedroom door tonight," Val says.

"Everything okay?" you ask Nick, who just cancelled your date.

"I've got the flu," he says. His voice is weak. "Came out of nowhere. Sorry to bail, but can anyone else go with you?"

In the background, you're positive you hear a woman say his name. He covers the mouthpiece, but you hear his muffled voice say he'll be there in a minute.

"Yeah. Sure," you say, hoping he doesn't hear your suspicion. "Feel better, okay?"

"Thanks. You're the greatest. Have fun without me. As if that were possible."

You sink into the cushion of the backrest and relay the conversation to your friends.

Rachel brings both hands down on the table, knocking over your ark procession. "Drive-by," she says.

"That seems a little extreme," says Valerie. "Besides, you know my Glock doesn't fit in this purse."

"Last minute sick-excuse? Mystery voice? It's got drive-by written all over it - in lip-liner."

To buckle up, turn to section 138.
To buck up and order another round, turn to section 132.

125

From section 101...

In the morning, now sober and with a few hours of shuteye, you finalize plans for Operation Dignity. It basically involves breaking up with Nick over the phone rather than risk chickening out when you see his stupidly good-looking face in person.

You stare at the ceiling above your bed and ask yourself, for the thirtieth time, *Are you sure you want to do this?*

And for the twentieth time, you answer, *yes.*

At eleven o'clock on the dot, you dial Nick. He answers on the third ring. His voice, sexily rough with sleep, instantly makes you question your decision. Again.

"I'm sorry," you say. "I didn't mean to wake you." You suddenly worry he may not be alone.

"S'okay," he says. "Good way to wake up."

Why? Why must he be adorable?

"So, what did you do last night?" You keep your voice as innocent as possible.

"What did I do last night?" he repeats, and you know he's buying time to think. "Babysat for Lana until pretty late. Got to live out my dreams of being a human pony."

"Right," you reply, saying the word really slowly. You'd hoped he'd say he took his favorite cousin out, proving you misinterpreted what you saw, but this outright lie (that came far too easily) is a big red flag with a bow on it.

"So listen." You clear your throat. "I was calling to tell you we can't see each other anymore."

"Really?" He sounds genuinely surprised and you're not sure if that makes you angry or regretful. "Okay, but can I ask why?"

Because I hate that you're seeing other people and now I know you're a big fat liar.

"I've actually been seeing somebody else and last night we made it exclusive," you tell him as planned. "Probably works out best for both of us, right?" Your voice is purposefully cheery to sell him on how happy you are with Make Believe Boyfriend.

He's quiet for a moment but finally says, "Sure."

Okay, so you lied. You're not going to hell. Two wrongs may not make a right, but you're willing to risk karmic retribution for the sake of dumping him before he dumps you.

Operation Dignity successful.

-END-

126

From sections 118...

After nearly three hours of singing along, cheering and chair dancing in an auditorium with rapturous strangers, the show has come to a close, complete with The Lift.

Rachel throws an arm around your neck. "Time of your life verdict?"

"And then some!" You fish your phone out your purse and power it up. "Thanks for taking me. Wait. Where's Val?"

"I thought she was your best friend," she teases. "She's got a date. We're in the clear."

"Oh, I don't know about that," you say when your phone alerts you to a new voicemail and a text from Valerie. You read the text aloud. "'He's got breath like Gandhi's flip flops. I hate you both.' Okay, so you're definitely my best friend."

"Back at ya. The bitch stole my joke!"

Standing in line for your *I carried a watermelon* tee shirt, you play the voicemail. It's from Nick, which makes you a little nervous even though you're sure you didn't stand him up for Johnny Castle.

"Hey," he says. "Just calling about getting together tonight. Gimme a call."

You look at your watch and see it's only ten o'clock. You decide it's not too late to call him back.

"Sorry I couldn't call you earlier," you say when he answers. "I just got out of the theater with Rachel."

"No problem," Nick says casually. "Only, did I mess up? I thought we made plans for tonight."

"You said you *might* be able to do something, but when I didn't hear from you, I took Rachel up on the show." Truthful, you just spun it a little.

"Right. That's my bad. Did you ladies have a good time?"

You give him a quick recap of the evening, and he laughs when Rachel grabs the phone to tell him you can shake your maracas with the best of them. By the time you get to the car, you've got a date for the weekend and a huge grin on your face.

Nobody leaves Baby with ambiguous plans!

Turn to section 145.

127

From section 122...

Your cousin Bex is without a doubt the most overly dramatic person you've ever met. Whether about the length of the line at the grocery store, or how much interest a guy shows in her, or how sore she is from a workout, she *always* exaggerates. Like, all the time.

In regular life, this is annoying. But you have to admit it does give her a unique talent for theater. Community theater, that is - she's not *that* good. You dread her annual performances, always tempted to make up an excuse as to why you can't go, in the end deciding that two and a half hours of torture is better than the two and a half years of torture you'll endure if you don't show up. It's also a great way to get your parents off your back about 'supporting your cousin.'

Two birds, one ticket.

You've been so busy between work, Nick and, well, your life, that you would've forgotten her lead part in a production of *The Last Picture Show* ends this weekend if she hadn't sent you an e-mail reminder and a whiny voicemail earlier today, nagging you to show up.

You have to go. The question is who do you drag along with you to endure Bex's pre-show nerves *and* give you the excuse you need to leave afterward and avoid her post-show bravado? Valerie hates live theater, so she's out. Rachel loathes Bex, and vice versa, so you'd spend the whole night pretending to be mad at her when she lobs insults your cousin's way.

You could invite Nick. It's obviously a little early for the family thing, but it's not like it's your immediate family, and you don't hate the idea of showing him off to Bex. In fact, you kind of adore it. Your parents already went, Rory's still out of town, so...

To invite Nick, turn to section 124.
To invite Rachel, turn to section 129.

128

From 121...

A few days later, you're in dire need of some new duds for the awards dinner your office is attending next week. You're up for three awards on three accounts, which means you can't just wear the same old wraparound dress and heels you've worn to the last three years' ceremonies. With the promise of a beer afterward, you convince Nick to accompany you to the mall to pick something out.

Despite the fact you're now on your third store, Nick's being an incredibly good sport. It may have something to do with the fact you've given him the occasional glimpse of you and your strategically sexy underwear through the changing room curtains. Given he hasn't yet tried to off himself with a clothes hanger and still wears a smile on his face, you figure he must have stolen a glance here and there.

You're dressed in a high-waisted, charcoal grey pin-stripe pantsuit with a long-sleeved blouse the color of Nick's eyes. For a moment, you wish you could bring him to the dinner so you can hear all of your co-workers remark on exactly that fact, but back to the matter at hand. This is just your style and you think you look pretty damn good.

"What do you think?" you ask Nick, who is now leaning against the wall across from the change room.

He gives you a thorough onceover and nods. "It's nice, but how about that?" He points outside the changing area to a womannequin (God, now Valerie's even got you saying it), modeling a gorgeous, silky, fuchsia-colored strapless dress that would probably sit a few inches above your knees.

Beautiful, yes, but so *not* your usual style. You can picture yourself constantly straightening the fabric and pulling up the bodice. Not to mention the gawking from your colleagues, which isn't a *totally* horrifying prospect. "For a work function?" you ask. "I dunno."

"The girls at my office wear stuff like this all the time."

Hmm. Maybe with a cardigan?

And what did he just say?

To try something new, turn to section 156.

To pantsuit yourself, turn to 89.

129

From sections 132 and 127...

It's Friday night and you are positively energized. You've haven't seen Nick in a week, which is way too long, and your anticipation over tonight's date has reached a fever pitch.

You leave work at exactly five o'clock, head home, shower, dress (three times), painstakingly - and painfully - blow dry your hair with a round brush, and carefully apply your make up without so much as a single smudge of mascara.

You've got an impressive hour to spare before Nick picks you up. You try calling Rachel and Val to kill some time but can't reach them, so you pour yourself a glass of wine and grab your tablet to see what's happening on Facebook and check your e-mail. Your phone rings. It's Nick. You pick up.

"Hey," you say cheerfully. "How are you?"

"Exhausted," he says, and you don't doubt it. His voice is low and gruff, which is kind of adorable. "I just had a shower hoping it would wake me up, but that was a pipe dream. Would you hate me if I bailed on dinner? I'll make it up to you next weekend."

The only thing more disappointing than your date canceling on you when you're already primped to perfection is when it means you'll have to wait another full week before you can see him again.

You're pouting in silence when you're struck by the idea of bringing the date to Nick. Something simple and relaxing. A win/win. You perk up a little at the thought…

To take the date to him, turn to 130.
To take one for the team, turn to 144.

130

From section 129...

It didn't take much to change Nick's mind about canceling your date - just the promise of a pizza and his favorite beer delivered to his door by yours truly. Your primping shall not go to waste.

You grab your things and drive to the liquor store to buy a six-pack for him and a bottle of wine for you. Next you hit up It's Been a Pie to pick up a large pepperoni with double cheese. Before long, you're knocking on Nick's door.

He greets you in loose grey sweatpants and an old tee shirt. He's got at least two days worth of scruff on his face and his hair stands up in half a dozen adorable directions. He kisses you hello.

"You smell like heaven," he says, taking the pizza from your hands.

You follow him to the couch and he tells you to pick a movie - anything but a rom-com. Thirty minutes later, the pizza is gone and you're snuggled together watching Man of Steel. At least, you're watching Man of Steel. Nick is out cold.

Now that you think about it, bringing the exhausted guy beer may not have been the greatest idea. You give him a less than gentle nudge and he opens his eyes, blurting, "I'm awake, I'm awake."

He's asleep again within ten minutes and after a few more unsuccessful attempts to wake him, you give up and turn down the volume a little. Then you focus on Henry Cavill, agreeing with Rachel that he wears entirely too much pants in the film. You're not spending the night alone - you're sandwiched between two hot men. There are worse things. And at least you know he doesn't snore.

That's something.

Turn to section 131.

131

From sections 155 and 130...

Joel, a good friend from college, calls to invite you and a plus one to an unofficial reunion party he's having. You RSVP *Yes* and race to Val and Rachel's to see if they're as excited as you are to catch up with old friends and show off to old frenemies.

You hear AC/DC blaring through the door, a sure sign Rachel is indeed excited. You let yourself in and are hit with the potent aroma of grass, finding Rachel teaching Valerie the proper technique for air guitar - and taking it very seriously.

You shout hello and Rachel turns down the volume.

"You realize AC/DC was a thing *way* before we were in college, right?" you ask.

"You realize AC/DC is *always* a thing, right?" she mocks back. "And two words: Liam Starr."

At that, you both sigh. It's all coming together. Liam Starr was Rachel's favorite college "relationship," and in an AC/DC cover band. The consummate bad boy, Liam was tall and broad-shouldered, with longish dark hair, a leather jacket, and a motorcycle. Joel introduced them at one of Liam's concerts and - whammy - they were both goners.

You barely saw her for the next four weeks because she was always with him. It was a record for Rachel. Of course, commitmentphobe that she is, she eventually panicked and dumped him, insisting he was just one more guy in the grand scheme of flings. Liam was heartbroken and spent many a night serenading her from the ground below your dorm room.

"So he'll be there?" asks Val, eyes wide with excitement behind her enormous glasses.

"He'll be there," you confirm.

"Like there was a doubt," says Rachel, offering you the joint.

"I'm driving to Nick's," you say, waving it off.

"Speaking of," says Val. "Will *he* be there? We want to meet him."

"You have met him."

"Sort of. I've said hello to him. Rachel is the only one who talked to him."

"And I was drunk," says Rachel. "So I don't remember."

"Bring him. We'll be nice. We just want to make sure he's good enough for our little girl."

Do you invite your non-boyfriend to a party where he'll be surrounded and grilled by people you've known for years? It would certainly aid in the showing-off portion of the evening.

To extend an invite, turn to section 158.
To extend your relationship, turn to section 150.

132

From section 127...

You're drunk. You don't remember how many drinks you've had, nor can you see straight enough to count the figurines you keep knocking down. You're not drunk enough to forget the lilty, feminine voice you heard earlier, though.

Is lilty a word? Yeah. It had a lilt. It was lilty.

"Well," says Valerie, antibiotics making her the designated driver. "I'm always glad when you two can benefit from me having a UTI."

You throw your head back. "Why me?"

Rachel slips an arm around your shoulder. "Guys are jerks. We totally should have busted him. And her."

"You don't know that he did anything wrong." Valerie sighs. This is probably the eighth round of *Why me? Because men are jerks* she's sat through tonight.

"Sure he did. Unless he hires a private nurse for the sniffles." She rests her head against yours. "And besides that, who wants a guy who doesn't think to tell Girl B to stay quiet while he's blowing off Girl A?"

You shake your head once. "Not me." *At least you're Girl A.*

Your server appears. "Another round?"

Rachel starts to say yes, but Valerie cuts her off. "No. Thank you."

"Dessert?" the server asks with a smile. Our Break Up Brownies are great for takeout."

"Oh, my god." You cover your face.

"Perfect," says Val. We'll take three to go."

Valerie goes to take care of the bill while you and Rachel gather your things. When she returns, you're wearing Rachel's jacket and sunglasses, she's wearing your scarf, and you've somehow switched purses.

Val shrugs. "Better than expected. Puke in my car and forfeit your brownie."

You're dozing off in the back seat when you hear your phone. You fumble around in your purse, cursing when you can't find it.

"Hello, jerk!" says Rachel from the front seat.

Fuck. She's got your purse. She's got your phone!

You're jolted sober. *"Don't answer it*!"

"Relax. It's a text." Rachel tosses the phone to you.

One new message from Nick. Wincing, you open it. It's a photo of him asleep on his couch, covered in a blanket, mouth hanging open, red nose, and tissues scattered all around him. The message reads, "If he kills me, it's worth it. Nick's Sister."

"Of course!" You palm your forehead.

"What?" Valerie asks.

"His sister. It was his sister's voice."

"Sure," says Rachel.

"No, look." You hand her the phone.

At a stoplight, Val leans over to look at the screen. "Would you look at that? How embarrassing would it be if we'd charged his apartment looking for skanks?"

"To be fair, we don't know that his sister *isn't* a skank," says Rachel.

"Oh, thank god," you say, relief washing over you. The mystery voice was Nick's sister - his sister who knows who you are!

Continue to section 129.

133

From section 113...

It's nice to play the role of Cool Girl sometimes, but siding with Team Penis in this moment would not only do Sally a disservice, but you as well. These conversations set precedents for one's own relationship, lighting a fuse on a bomb that sprays passive aggressive, paranoid shrapnel and begets unspoken questions like, "Is that how he would feel if the same thing happened between *us?*"

Yes, it's far better that you set the groundwork for *future* arguments with Nick, even if doing so moves one of them up to right now. You gulp down your last mouthful of rancid pizza and cola and wipe your hands.

"I dunno about 'normal,'" you say, balling up your greasy napkin. "But I can see where she's coming from."

Nick leans back slightly, deciding whether you're telling the truth or just having some fun with him. "Really?"

You shrug in a way you hope says, *This is my opinion, but I'm totally mellow about it so, no big.* "I don't know. I mean, I've never met Sally and I don't know a lot about Russ, but it's not like they just met yesterday. They're a couple, right? If you were thinking about your girlfriend, wouldn't it be reassuring to know she was thinking of you, too? And wouldn't you be hurt if you thought she wasn't?"

Nick rolls his eyes. "So if a guy doesn't talk to his girlfriend every single day, he doesn't care about her? That's ludicrous."

"Maybe." You toss the napkin in the trash. "But a quick text when he's busy or doesn't feel like talking is cheaper than flowers *and* will get him laid, far, *far* more often."

He coughs and pounds on his chest, choking on his pizza. "Noted."

Turn to section 89.

134

From sections 159 and 79...

It was hell waiting for it, but Date Number One is off to a great start. Nick was on time and heavenly to look at, Rachel and Valerie weren't hiding in the lobby to spy on his arrival, and NOPA was a perfect choice on his part.

You've learned Nick has a twin sister named Rory, his retired parents call the Bahamas home but spend most of their time traveling, and he was captain of his high school basketball team. You're currently explaining the history between you, Rachel and Valerie.

"So, you all live *together*?" Nick asks, scooping hummus with fresh pita bread.

You shake your head, smiling. "Feels like that sometimes. They live together and I live a few floors up. We shared a house in college, though."

"That's where you met?"

"I've known Rachel since ninth grade. My dad was transferred from Chicago to Palo Alto for work and she had just moved from Toronto to live with her grandmother. On the first day of school, I was hiding in the upstairs bathroom to eat lunch and she came in to sneak a cigarette. We were inseparable by the next period."

"Right on. Did you always plan on going to the same school?"

You swirl the wine around in your glass. "Sort of. Rachel didn't want to go to class, but *did* want the college experience, so we applied to the same schools, got into all three and decided on SFSU."

"And that's where you met Valerie."

You nod. "She was born here and wanted to go out of state for school, but her folks wanted her nearby. They compromised and she stayed in San Francisco, but got to live in the dorms. She had the single room across from our double and invited me over one day when I was stuck studying in the hall with a sock on my doorknob." Nick gives you a puzzled look. "Rachel's 'college experience.'"

He laughs. "Got it."

"Val and I studied together a lot, and she and Rachel *hated* each other at first, but they eventually found a Bert and Ernie kind of groove. Works for them, entertains me. Mostly."

Nick tells you about school, work and his future career aspirations. He loves his job and it sounds like he works hard at it.

"How about you?" he asks. "Tell me about the glamorous world of public relations."

You like your profession, but to say you're less than satisfied with your current work environment would be an understatement. Just the thought of your megalomaniac boss raises your body temperature. Valerie would kill you if went into complain-mode on a first date. Still, you don't want to come out of the gate editing yourself.

Put on your big girl panties and be honest, turn to section 283.
Skirt the issue, turn to section 41.

135

From section 89...

Few good decisions in your life were made in the heat of the moment. Despite the way your body responds to Nick's, you have a nagging feeling this could be one of those occasions. You slide your hands up his chest and over his shoulders, resting your forehead against his. You sigh. Apparently loudly.

"What's up?" Nick asks.

"I want to," you tell him. "But I guess I'm just not ready." Oh, how that phrase makes you feel sixteen again, and seventeen, and eighteen, and – well, it's familiar.

Nick's eyes widen. "You're a virgin, too."

"No, I'm not a- Wait, are you a *virgin?*" You whisper the last word.

He shakes his head. "No."

"Okay. Good. Not good. Or bad. Just…okay."

He stands up straight. "Okay."

"Are you mad?" God you hope he's not mad. Were you just being a tease? You weren't. No.

"Of course I'm not mad." *Phew.* "If you're not ready, you're not ready." He yawns. "I'm kind of tired anyway, so it wouldn't have been my best work. I could crash right now, actually."

You take a chance. "You could…sleep here. If you want."

"Thanks for the offer, but that's probably not a good idea tonight." Smiling bashfully, he looks down at his groin and you see what he means. Cold shower time. "Rain check on the sleepover, though. And I plan to collect."

You accompany Nick downstairs and say goodbye in the lobby.

"This week's a little crazy," he says. "I'll call you about the weekend?"

"Sounds good."

After a chaste kiss, he's gone. And you feel blah. And horny. You feel horny and blah. You return to your apartment and head straight for the pie. You consider bringing it over to Val and Rachel's to share but decide against it. Instead, you grab a fork, carry the whole pie to your couch, peel back the cellophane, stab the still warm crust, and sublimate.

Turn to 143.

136

From section 255...

Has to be done.

Right?

Yes.

Has to be done.

"No," you tell Nick after a long silence. "I can't wait."

He blinks. "Are you serious? We've been together for ages and now you just want to throw it all away."

"Exactly! We have been together *for ages*. If you were ever going to want to marry me, don't you think you'd have at least an inkling by now?"

He throws his hands up in frustration but says nothing.

Your vision blurs with tears. "Well, I know what I want," you say, your voice cracking. "I've known for a while. And while I want it with you, I won't wait around indefinitely for you to catch up."

"So, that's it." He swallows thickly. "Just *over*."

You wipe at the mascara under your eyes. "Yeah," you say, barely audibly. "I guess that's it."

You look around his apartment and it strikes you how lucky you are you never moved in with him. It would most definitely have left you heartbroken, probably more so than now, and made the inevitable post-break up escape torture.

You grab your purse and fill it with some of the essentials you left at his place. You give him a long hug and one last kiss before you drive home, managing to keep it together until you're in your apartment.

You cry non-stop for the next week, often wondering if you were right to end things the way you did. When you don't hear from Nick after three weeks, you know you were.

-END-

137

From section 108...

After a respectable one-week of Hottie McHotterson-fueled distraction, you're finally having an extremely productive day at work. Things with Nick are still going just groovy, with the usual touchy-flirty dynamic, and you're not in the least bit worried he's thinking about having a "once in awhile" visit with *her*.

Okay, so it's probably going to live in the back of your mind and crawl its way out to the forefront every so often, but for right now you are a productivity machine, crossing off half of the tasks on your lengthy to-do list before lunch.

You're about to tackle the woefully disorganized stack of files on your desk when an e-mail from Nick appears in your inbox.

Subject line: *I'm bored.*

Message: *What are you doing?*

Your heart swells. You simultaneously chair dance and swoon.

Nick has just sent you a casual e-mail - for no reason. Actually, there *is* a reason, which is that *you* were the person he reached out to when he was bored. You were his first thought. You were on his mind! You *are* on his mind. At this very moment!

If you weren't concerned that Rachel would attempt to have you committed, you would print off that e-mail and stick it on your fridge with a big heart-shaped magnet.

In the world of new relationships, this *truly* is a milestone. At least to you it is.

But... it doesn't change the fact you're getting a lot of work done, which will stop if you shift your focus to a live e-mail exchange with Nick. Of course, it's unlikely you'll be able to concentrate now anyway, given you'll be thinking about this e-mail for the rest of the day.

Put replying to Nick at the top of the To Do list, turn to section 109.
Put replying to Nick now on the To Don't list, turn to section 37.

138

From section 124...

"Shouldn't we be wearing dark clothes?" you ask from the front seat of Valerie's car. "And ski-masks?"

"It's daylight," says Rachel. "That would look suspicious."

"You're right," says Val. "In our regular clothes, this looks totally normal."

Rachel points to a convenience store down the street from Nick's apartment. "Pull over. And stay in the car."

"Won't be a problem."

Moments later, Rachel reappears holding three candy bars. She motions for you to roll down your window. "Apartment number?" she asks.

"107," you say. "Why?"

"Ground floor. Excellent. I mean, you'll see."

She approaches a boy, around eleven years old, skateboarding outside of Nick's building. After a quick conversation, she hands him the candy bars.

"She just offered a child candy." Valerie slides down in her seat. "If his mother comes out, we're leaving Rachel behind."

The boy walks into the building and Rachel hustles back to the car. "I wish I'd brought my suspense playlist for work," she says.

"Don't you mean getaway playlist?" asks Val. You notice the engine is still running despite her commitment to reducing her carbon footprint.

Five minutes later, the boy is at Rachel's window. Your stomach sinks when he reports that a blonde woman answered Nick's door and bought all of the candy.

"Great job, Bobby." Rachel hands him a twenty.

Wide-eyed, he asks, "What about the money for the candy?"

"Yours. Thanks."

"Thank *you*, lady. That chick was smokin'."

"I'm gonna puke," you say as Bobby leaves.

"Not yet," Rachel says. "Which window is his?"

Resigned, you point to Nick's place and she's gone again. You're kicking yourself for thinking things were getting serious with Nick when Valerie shouts, "*Oh. My. Fuck.*" You look up and see Rachel and Nick running across the barren courtyard. She slows down long enough to kick a small - like teeny - recycling bin into his path.

Maybe not so genius.

You leap out of the car when Nick shouts, "What the hell are you doing?"

"Nice to see you again," pants Rachel as she reaches the car. She dives into the backseat, leaving you alone with Nick - who looks sick. And angry.

"It's not as bad as it looks," you explain.

"Really? You didn't come here to spy on me?"

You sigh. "We did. When you canceled, I heard a woman's voice. Then Bobby said a hot chick is in your apartment and Rachel just wanted to see if you were...cheating."

"*Cheating?*" His face turns beet red. "You would have to be my *girlfriend* for me to cheat on you. And that hot chick is *my sister*, who nearly had a heart attack when she saw your friend looking in my window!"

"Oh, my god." *So queasy.*

"Are you crazy?"

"I'm so sorry. I don't know what came over me."

"So, yes."

"It was a stupid mistake. I don't know what else to say."

"Just...go." He turns and walks away, the belt of his housecoat waving in the wind.

After a moment, you get back in the car. Val and Rachel are arguing.

"I almost had it," Rachel insists.

"Yeah," Val says dryly. "If that recycling bin had been a fully equipped hotel kitchen, you *totally* would have pulled that off."

Rachel pats your shoulder. "Okay, so that was a bust, but if he's going to dump you over a little covert ops... Well, you probably dodged a bullet. And, hey, one day we'll look back on this and *laugh, laugh, laugh.*"

-END-

139

From section 156...

You're waiting in line for your Monday morning coffee at a cafe near your office. You don't tell anyone about this place because it rarely has a long line up despite being better than any chain.

And one other reason, which just walked in the door.

Meticulous Mystery Man. Or "Mmm" as Val's called him ever since you showed her the photo of him you slyly took one morning. He's so pretty. Tall with short, dirty blonde hair, clear green eyes and he's *always* wearing a three-piece suit and perfectly polished shoes. With cufflinks. And a pocket square.

When you told Rory about him, he assumed he must be gay. You were sure he was wrong, given how thoroughly he checks you out while you pretend to be busy with very important, urgent business on your phone. Rory insisted, though, driving you to work three days in a row before Mmm showed up. After he picked his jaw up from the floor, Rory sighed, decreeing all the good ones to be straight.

You don't know anything about him; not his name, nor why he looks so impeccable and expensive all the time. Which makes him the perfect safety crush. The unattainable, go-to image during self-gratification crush. Yet, this is the first time you've seen him, or thought about him, since you met Nick.

You move to the end of the counter and wait for your coffee. Before long, Mmm's standing beside you. Unusual. He usually gets a black coffee, puts a lid on it and goes on his studly way.

Today...*he speaks.*

"Morning." His voice is deep. You don't know what you were expecting, but you weren't expecting that. He extends a hand. "Maxwell Matthews."

Mr. Maxwell Matthews. MMM. Val would die.

You tell him your name and enjoy a few moments of pleasant, flirty small talk. Before he leaves, he asks for your number.

A year.

For a year, you've been running into to Maxwell Matthews without exchanging a single word but, *today,* now that you're seeing someone, he asks for your number. You make a split second decision to give it to him, knowing you can always turn him down later *if* he calls, but that you'll probably never get this opportunity again if you say no. Also, Valerie would hurt you while rambling something about eggs and a basket.

You're still surprised when Maxwell calls and asks you out for the weekend. It's a thrill, yes, but you don't know where you stand with Nick. You're pretty sure he'd say yes if you asked him if you're exclusive, but you don't *know.*

To keep your eggs in Nick's basket, turn to section 157.
To check out the basket (weave) on Mysterious Maxwell, turn to section 164.

140

From section 252...

When Nick arrives at your place, you're kicking back on the couch, enjoying a beer and the cool air blowing from your freshly installed air conditioning units.

"Was your dad here?" he asks, looking relieved he doesn't have to put them in for you.

"Nope," you tell him. "Why do you ask?"

"The air conditioner."

"Oh, I did them myself. Beer?"

"*Both* of them? You did the bedroom, too?"

You blow on your fingernails and polish them on your tank top. "Yup."

"Why didn't you ask me to do it?" he asks, suddenly looking offended.

"It was easy enough. You're not threatened by my ability to do manly things, are you?" you tease.

"*Please.* Just because you can lift an air conditioner, or two, doesn't make you macho, fair one. We'll see how you do changing a tire."

"I do actually know how to change a flat, but I might need your help if a burglar breaks in – I don't have much experience with baseball bats."

"Hilarious, tough guy," he grumbles, taking your beer.

Turn to section 309.

I4I

From section 177...

By the time Nick arrives to pick you up, you can hardly wait to give him the Patriots hat. You even checked the football schedule and learned the team plays this weekend, giving him the perfect opportunity to wear it.

You don't bother saying hello, or even closing the car door, before you thrust the most masculine gift bag you could find in front of his face.

"Surprise!" you announce.

"What's this?" he asks, examining the bag warily.

"Just something I saw and thought you'd like."

"You didn't need to do that."

"I wanted to." You push the bag at him. "Open it!"

He removes the navy blue tissue paper and pulls out the hat. "Patriots, great!" he says, and you *think* he means it.

"I thought you could wear it Sunday. You don't already have it, do you?"

"Nope. I don't have it." He clears his throat. "Actually, I don't really wear hats. They kind of give me headaches." He winces.

This is not how you thought this would go, and it looks like he can tell because he quickly adds, "But I'll display it proudly on my bookshelf, where it will stay in mint condition." He leans over to kiss your cheek. "Seriously, it's great. Thank you."

He puts the bag on the back seat as you close your door, and then you're on your way - in semi-awkward silence.

Not exactly the outcome you were hoping for.

Turn to section 199.

142

From sections 89 and 22...

It's been nearly two weeks since you and Nick started doing The Deed.

Good news: The sex is *pretty* great.

Bad news: Your relationship hasn't quite progressed the way you'd hoped.

He works countless late nights, which screws up your plans, such as Thursday's seven o'clock dinner date turning into him showing up at your place at nine. A glass of wine and a not-so-quickie later, he was on his way.

Tonight is your night, though, and you have plans to play pool. You're talking to Val when Nick calls on the other line.

"Hello, most gorgeous of gorgeous women," he says.

"What did you do?"

He forgot making plans to watch tonight's game with his brother-in-law, but he promises to come over and make it up to you afterward.

"Are you a pirate?" Valerie asks when you switch back.

"Say wha?"

"It sounds like he be after yer booty." She laughs. "Seriously. This isn't the first time he's bumped you."

"You're right. Work and family. Scallywag!"

"Maybe I'm wrong. At least he's coming to you. That's something."

At eleven o'clock, Nick texts: *Probably shouldn't drive. Can you come here?*

See? Too responsible to get behind the wheel just because he wants to see you.

On the drive over, you can't stop thinking about Val's warning that you're Nick's Booty Call Friday. You also picture her wearing an eye patch and shouting, "Arrrr."

All things pirate vanish from your thoughts when a slightly buzzed Nick opens his door and sweeps you up in a hug.

"I missed you," he says. You giggle uncontrollably as he smatters your neck with scratchy, stubble kisses.

Fifteen minutes later, Nick has *shown* you how much he missed you. You try not to think about the fact that, not only has the frequency of sex with Nick decreased, but the duration of each encounter is getting shorter.

It took longer for you to drive here.

You lie beside Nick. His face wears the expression of a guy who's enjoyed an evening of sports, booze and sex - because he has.

You smooth down your sex-hair. "I was thinking we could have dinner on Friday."

"This Friday? No can do. I'm babysitting Monster." He kisses your shoulder. "The whole weekend is shot for me."

"Work?" You hear it growing louder: *Arrrr*

"I'm working on Sunday, but I'm helping a buddy move on Saturday."

"How about Saturday night?" Louder still: *Arrrr*

"Moving days always become about sports and booze, but you could come by later." He nuzzles your ear.

No sir. Not today. "Right, so we could have more sex."

"You say that like it's a bad thing." He gives you that irresistible smile, which, though not completely powerless, is less potent than it once was.

"What are the odds of us ever going on an actual date?"

He wraps his arms around you. "I'm sorry. Things are crazy with work for the next little while."

"I *am* a pirate," you say.

"Huh?"

"Nothing."

You get up, hastily dress and gather your things. When Nick asks where you're going, you tell him you're not willing to wait around for the "next little while."

Savvy?

-END-

143

From section 135...

You don't even get a face-to-face break up? Break *up* or break *off*? Regardless, you deserve - at the very least - an ambiguous text message you can read into for a week and move on.

You haven't heard from Nick for almost two weeks. When you didn't get that call about the weekend, you texted to ask if he still wanted to make plans and – nothing. So you stayed in and ate all the junk food in your cupboards.

By Sunday night, you had carpel tunnel from repeatedly checking your messages and, okay, you sent *another* text asking if he was okay.

Nothing.

Two days after that, against your friends' advice, you sent one last text. He didn't respond.

It doesn't take Veronica Mars to figure out this is because you aren't having sex with him, which is both infuriating and unexpected. He seemed understanding, but it looks like "not mad," translates into, "not mad and not waiting."

It's now Friday night and you're on your third glass of chardonnay, feeling like giving Nick a piece of your mind. You dial his number, unsurprisingly get his voicemail, and leave the following message: "Seriously? You're just going to drop me because we haven't had sex yet? Which, by the way, you said you were totally okay with. Are we in high school? I don't even warrant a phone call? Bullet-dodged, I guess. Have a nice life."

You hang up, still feeling disappointed, but also slightly empowered for speaking your mind. You turn your head when you hear something slide under your door. You pick it up. It's a courier envelope that's addressed to you, but with the wrong unit number. You neighbor must have gotten it by mistake. You look at the sender box and feel nauseated.

It's from Nick.

Post-marked *Hong Kong*.

You read his letter quickly, not quite catching every word. The gist is that Nick was called away on business a couple of days after you last saw him. He lost his phone, laptop and luggage, and for some reason can't access his personal e-mail account. He doesn't have your number memorized but remembered your address, so he wrote to give you a heads up - *from Hong Kong* - that he'd be unreachable until he returns next Friday.

Which is *this* Friday. *Today.*

You remember the message you just left him. Sure, he wouldn't get your texts, but he'll get that message.

As if on cue, your phone bleeps with a text from Nick on what is probably a new phone: *I take it you didn't get my letter.*

-END-

144

From section 129...

"Of course, I understand," you told Nick before saying goodbye.

You do. Mostly. Except you don't.

You've been dragging ass all week after too many late nights binging on Orange Is The New Black with Rachel, arguing over who'd have an easier time in prison. (Rachel wins – shocking.) Usually that would make you a zombie come Friday morning, but no. Today you woke up immediately aware that you'd get to see Nick tonight. It fueled your day.

Why isn't it the same for him?

Pouting, you walk to the bathroom to wash off your makeup and change your clothes. But one look in the mirror and you think, _fuck this._

Fuck men.

Well…maybe not _all_ men.

You return to the living room to grab your phone. By the time you reach it, it's already ringing. Scott.

Trippy.

"I was just thinking about you," you say when you answer.

"Well that's a given, isn't it, luv?"

You're soon in a cab on your way to The Castro where you'll spend the night dancing with men who'll tell you that you're pretty and buy you drinks without trying to get in your pants. Some may want to try _on_ your pants, but that's always fun.

And you do have fun.

So much so that you wake up on the couch in the morning with a headache that pounds like a bass line and someone knocking at your door. You shuffle across the room and pat yourself on the back for living your life instead of moping over Nick.

"Who is it?" you croak at the door.

"Delivery," comes a voice from the hall.

You reach for the handle, noticing a trail of glitter on your arm. You'll have to ask Scott about that.

You open the door to a friendly, older fellow who hands you a steaming cup of coffee and a paper bag with a note taped to it. You thank him and close the door, overwhelmed by the delicious smell of croissants. You set the coffee on the hall table and open the note, which reads: *Thanks for understanding. Miss you and see you soon. N.*

Gold Star!

Turn to section 145.

145

From sections 126 and 144...

You and Nick are going strong. You see each other two or three times a week and he gives you every indication that he's *totally* into you.

He contacts you at least once a day. He asks about your friends and job. He sends you e-mails with adorable kittens or puppies and jokes he thinks you'll like. He even sent red chrysanthemums to your office, making you the envy of your co-workers.

Even your physical relationship has progressed. No, you haven't popped that relationship cherry yet, but things have gotten increasingly heated and you're not even really sure why you're waiting anymore.

You let Rachel and Valerie live vicariously through you at dinner tonight. Well, Valerie anyway. Rachel routinely rolls her eyes and makes gagging noises.

"So, are you exclusive yet?" Valerie asks, her eyes brightened by her turquoise cat eye glasses. "It's been a couple of months now."

You've been dreading this question - because you don't have an answer. You hold a dessert menu in front of your face, pretending to study it.

"We actually haven't really talked about it," you say casually. "Have I had the apple pie here? I could go for some apple pie."

She pulls the menu down and looks you straight in the eye. "Well, we know you're not seeing other people, but is he?"

"I don't think so." *Please be right.* "You think I should ask him?"

"No! Two weeks or two months, he has to be the one to bring it up."

To see if he wants to go steady, turn to section 151.
If you think slow not steady wins the race, turn to 160.

146

From sections 185, 177 and 262...

You wake up in Nick's apartment for the first time. You never thought about the fact you'd never slept there until Val pointed it out, and then you wondered if he was keeping a big bad secret - like he really does live with his parents.

You open your eyes and see Nick getting dressed.

"Good morning," he says, pulling on a tee shirt. "I thought I'd grab breakfast. Cream and sugar for your coffee?"

You nod sleepily, moving to get up. "I'll come with you."

He sits on the bed and kisses you, gently lowering you to your pillow. "It's raining. No need for both of us to get wet. Or dressed." He kisses you again and stands. "Feel free to wander around naked. I'll be back in twenty."

"So more like fifteen, then?"

He winks and leaves the room. A moment later, you're alone.

You put on Nick's sweatshirt, happily breathing in his scent before doing an admittedly paranoid check for nanny cams. Then you begin the exploring his natural habitat.

Anything in plain view is fair game: bulletin boards, photos, bookshelf...his desk. Six drawers – each equally tempting *and* in plain sight. It would be easy to snoop just a little before he gets back.

To do some private investigation, turn to section 206.
To respect his privacy, turn to section 212.

147

From section 236...

Filed under Things You Hate In Relationships is... *Silence.*

Not out-in-the-country-where-I-can-hear-the-grass-grow quiet, but the kind that comes when you and your boyfriend suddenly run out of things to talk about. It instantly opens the floodgates of worry: that he might be bored with you, that he may be thinking of someone else, that the honeymoon is over; that he misses that new car smell.

Tonight, you and Nick are lounging on his couch watching your usual Friday night schedule of TV you missed during the week, which is fine, except he's been quiet since you got there. None of your usual chatter over the dialogue, no pausing the show for a random thought.

It's different.

You try to spark some conversation, asking him about work, telling him about your day and strange news articles you read and so on, but he only gives you monosyllabic responses. Not a touch of witty banter.

Frankly, this is unsettling.

To thwart the silent killer, turn to section 149.
To have a silent night, turn to section 249.

148

From section 202...

You and Rory partner to plan a surprise party in celebration of your parents' upcoming 30th wedding anniversary. Of course, given he spends most of his time on another continent, your brother has been no help whatsoever.

He even spoiled the surprise when he accidentally sent your mother an e-mail intended for you, explaining that he was just too busy to help. So you're now planning the party *with* your mother. Your mother, who doesn't seem to care that Golden Child has better things to do than rejoice the union that led to his existence.

If you didn't love him so much, you'd strangle him.

A week out from the festivities, you're on the phone with your mom going over the guest list. As you feared, she asks if you're bringing Nick to the party.

The thought has crossed your mind, but since you haven't even spent much time with each other's friends yet, you're not sure a 30th wedding anniversary is the right place to introduce him to your parents, grandparents, and aunts who are very concerned with your depleting egg supply. And of course there's Uncle Lou, who likes to pretend he lost his glass eye and get your boyfriends to help him search for it.

Of course, if you don't invite him, you'll never hear the end of it.

To invite him to the torture chamber, turn to section 219.
To give him a reprieve, turn to section 208.

149

From section 147...

You wait to bring it up until the right time. Just before bed.

"Is something wrong?" you ask Nick as you slide in next to him under the sheets.

He considers the question, shrugs and says, "Nope."

"Are you sure? Because you've been really quiet. All night."

"Just quiet."

"Not to get all *feelings* on you, but it's just...unusual for you. If there's something wrong, you can talk to me about it."

"Why does something have to be wrong because I'm quiet?" He's not exactly laughing at you, but he's not exactly not laughing at you. "Is that a girl thing? The need to always be talking?"

"I don't always *need* to be talking."

"Quiet's not always a bad thing." He kisses you on the cheek and turns on his side. Facing away from you. "Goodnight."

And then silence.

Turn to section 241.

150

From section 131...

You will not be inviting Nick to Joel's party. Even if it means you miss the opportunity to make that particular group of girls you loathe jealous by showing off your incredibly hot, smart and funny...what exactly?

That's really the point, isn't it? You aren't a couple yet.

Inviting him might just freak him out. And while you'd love for him to get to know your friends, you'd *much* rather have Nick around in the near future, so mum's the word. Best to avoid bringing it up all together. Loose lips sink relationships, as Val would say - even though she's not saying it on *this* occasion.

Still, as the two of you walk downtown, hand-in-hand and happy, you feel a little sad that you can't just come out and ask him to a friend's party without worrying what it would "mean." That's what you're thinking about when you run into some of his friends.

"Nick!" exclaims a loud brunette before she gives him a friendly hug. "We were just talking about you the other day, weren't we, honey?"

"When are we *not*?" says her companion, rolling his eyes and earning a playful elbow. *So cute. Such a couple.* "How've you been, Nick?"

"I'm doing really well," he says, shaking the other man's hand. "It's great to see you guys. You look great."

His friends look to you and then back to Nick again.

"Shoot. I'm sorry," he says. "Pardon my manners. Mitch and Mary, this is my girlfriend..."

Come again?

"Girlfriend," repeats Mary before winking at Nick - *your boyfriend*. "I guess you *are* doing really well."

After a few minutes of pleasant chit chat, you say goodbye and continue on your way.

Nick takes your hand again. "Is that okay?" he asks. "It just kind of came

247

out."

"Definitely okay," you say, stopping to prove it with a kiss. "Actually, it's good timing. There's this party I wanted to talk to you about…"

Yay!

You have a boyfriend! (And a Plus One!)

Turn to section 165.

151

From section 145...

Going into tonight's dinner with Nick, you resolve to be a bloody grown up and ask if you're exclusive. With him. No big deal. You're adults, and there's nothing wrong with wanting to know where you stand. Still, you wait until dessert arrives to pop the question.

"This is amazing," says Nick, holding a forkful of chocolate cake out to you. "Try this."

You eat the cake. "Yum. Are we exclusive?"

He freezes. "That came out of nowhere."

"Did it? I mean, we've been seeing a lot of each other for a while now. I think it's going well, don't you?"

He nods slowly. "Sure, but…"

"But?" *But!*

He sets down his fork and takes your hand. "I don't want to upset you, but you aren't the only person I'm seeing."

Why would that upset you? "I'm definitely surprised. I just thought… Well, I *didn't* think you were dating anyone else."

"I'm sorry if I made you think that," he says sincerely. "But I wasn't sure if you were casual about this or not. We haven't even had sex."

"And that's a problem for you."

He slides you a *give me some credit* look. "I get the waiting thing - it can be fun. It *has* been fun." The corner of his mouth tugs upward. "But it usually means one or both of us isn't certain about where things are going. I'm not sure that's any different from seeing other people."

What kind of backwardly logical logic is that? "But if I have sex with you, you'd be willing to take yourself off the market?"

"That's not what I said. *At all*. I've never pressured you for sex." *This is true*. "I'm not a high school boy promising to be your boyfriend if you'll sleep with me."

"And, hypothetically, if I said I *did* want to be exclusive?"

"Then I'd be straight with you and tell you I'm not quite there yet and hope you'd give me a little time."

You can't really argue with that stupid honesty. "Okay, but I'm not sleeping with you if you're sleeping with other people."

"Same here." He laughs. "And I never said I was sleeping with anyone."

"Maybe I am."

He leans over and kisses you. "No you're not."

No. You're not.

Turn to section 162.

152

From sections 216 and 207...

Fast-forward to February and you still haven't heard "I Love You" from Nick. That's agonizing enough, but now it's almost Valentine's Day.

You hate everything about February 14th, from the over-priced chocolate to the red-and-pink-clad girls in your office who make a point of showing off the freshly delivered roses their boyfriends sent in advance of their dinner plans.

That is, before *this* Valentine's Day, of course. This year, you have a boyfriend, a red dress and reservations at one of the most romantic restaurants in the city. Just two days out from V-Day, all that's left to do is buy a card to attach to the perfect, powder blue Simon Spurr shirt you bought for Nick yesterday. You thought this would be a simple task but you've spent the last hour drowning in an ocean of sappy sentiment, leaving you ready to ask Cupid to shoot an arrow into your eye.

You're sure Nick will use this occasion to profess his love for you. After all, you've been together for over six months now. But when scanning the wide selection of funny, flirty and lovey-dovey cards (and a surprising number of dirty ones), you freeze. What the hell do you choose?

The easy thing would be the flirty, casual route. But if he does say he loves you, you're a chump. Of course, if you drop the L Bomb and he doesn't, you're an even bigger chump.

Crap.

You hate Valentine's Day.

To say I like you, turn to section 102.
To say I love you, turn to section 287.

153

From section 305...

Just three days later, you're feeling as good as new and ready for the weekend - extra-long weekend given you haven't been to work since Tuesday.

Nick came over to play doctor for a few hours and what a sweetie he was: getting you extra blankets, making you tea, and rubbing your achy shoulders. Everything was great.

Until he left.

Not wanting you to get off the couch, he leaned down to hug you - at the exact moment your nose chose for a sneak-attack sneeze. That in and of itself would have been manageable - maybe - but this particular sneeze launched a phlegm canon that landed squarely on the shoulder of his pea coat.

The two of you endured a painfully awkward moment before you reached for a tissue to clean it off. Once the initial shock wore off, he was kind enough to make a joke that maybe it was good luck - *great, you're bird shit* - but he was just as horrified as you were. You haven't heard boo from him since.

You're wondering if you should call him when Rachel phones you.

"Outbreak," she says. "I'm on my way home and I thought I'd bring dinner by. That is, if you don't have I-haven't-seen-you-in-a-week-and-can't-stand-it-for-a-minute-longer plans with Nick."

"Actually," you tell her, wincing in preparation. "He was here on Wednesday. He brought me cold meds."

"You let him see you sick? Were you suffering from delirium-due-to-cold? I've seen you sick. It's not pretty. No offense."

"Whatever for?" You role your eyes. "Anyway, he was sweet. Really."

"If you say so. So you are seeing him tonight?"

"Not sure, actually. I haven't heard from him since..." your voice trails off.

"Since?"

You explain the phlegm missile situation, telling her Nick really didn't seem bothered by it, and that you're sure it's just a coincidence he hasn't called. "He's not going to dump me over something like that."

"Probably not, but I'd give Florence Nightenmale some time to forget. And maybe a strip tease," says Rachel. You can hear her snicker. "All right, so you *don't* have plans tonight. I'm coming over. Should I wear a raincoat?"

Turn to section 171.

154

From section 255...

Your heart's been threatening to flutter right out of your chest all afternoon.

It's finally happening!

Six months ago, when you made the decision to just relax and let things with Nick happen organically, you knew Valerie and Rachel thought you were setting yourself up for heartbreak - because they told you.

Often.

But then you woke up to an e-mail from Nick this morning, asking to meet at your place after work to talk about something important.

This is it!

You can feel it.

You daydream the day away, faking a last minute doctor's appointment and leaving work early so you have a chance to doll yourself up a little before you see him. You're sure you're glowing when he gets there.

"Big day?" he asks when you let him in. "You look great."

He's not smiling and you figure he must be as nervous as you are. *Cute!* You sit on the couch together.

"So, what did you want to talk to me about?" you ask, trying to sound clueless.

"I'm not sure where to start." He rubs his palms on his thighs. "I've been thinking a lot about things. About us."

"Yeah?"

"Yeah. This is hard to say."

You can think of exactly *zero* proposals that began with those words.

"I met someone."

Nothing like a punch in the stomach to shock you back to reality. "Wh-who?"

"A vendor I deal with at the office. We've been working on a big project together."

The contents of your head swirl. "Is anything happening?"

"No," he says firmly, and you believe him.

"But you're thinking about it."

He nods his head slowly. "I'm so sorry. I care about you, *so much*, and I know you're set on a future together…"

"You care about me," you interrupt. "You don't love me anymore."

"I honestly don't know." He looks at his feet. "I mean, I love you, but since I've known Amy, I sometimes wonder if I'm *in* love with you anymore. And it's not fair to keep going like this when I'm even…thinking about someone else."

How many times have you told a guy you'd rather he just broke up with you if he found himself in this very situation? That anything else would be adding injury to insult. No one ever thinks they'll have to revisit those words. Nick sputters on, likely about how sometimes these things happen, or how it's for the best, or that you're a great girl who's going to meet someone perfect for you… it doesn't matter.

Ten minutes later, he's gone.

After countless tears, you finally go numb.

You wonder if you can get away with not telling anyone you broke up and avoid the "I told you so's" and sympathetic looks that are surely en route from everyone who loves you.

-END-

155

From section 160...

If you had only just started dating Nick, you'd probably let him fester over the idea of you having another suitor - and enjoy every minute of it.

But it's been nearly two months, you really like him, you're pretty sure he feels the same way, and as much as jealousy can sometimes be fun when you're on the receiving end, getting dumped is no fun at all - especially over something that isn't actually true. You place a neatly folded tee shirt on your duvet and decide to ease Nick's mind.

"Well, *I* managed to make it home just before dawn," you tell him. "Scott, on the other hand, was out all night. And most of the day."

After a quiet moment, Nick says, "Are you telling me you took that dick to a concert with front row seats and backstage passes and he picked up another girl?"

"Not exactly." Silence. "He went home with Micky. Wentz?"

"Micky Wentz is a dude." From adorably protective to adorably confused.

"I think that's what Scott was counting on."

"*Oh,*" he says as it sets in. "He's bi?"

"Try again."

"He's gay!"

"Extremely."

"Huh. Whaddya know," he says, reassured by his lack of heterosexual competition. "So I don't have to challenge him to a duel?"

And now adorably violent. "Not today anyway."

He laughs easily. "Now tell me about the concert. From the top."

You think you liked it better when he was jealous.

Turn to section 131.

156

From section 128...

Finally!

You hear Rachel's signature knock at your door. She's only fifteen minutes late, which is actually early for her, but it's awards night and you're on a schedule!

The most ambitious thing you can pull off with your hair is a Little House on the Prairie braid, so Rachel is your stylist for the evening. Other than a ponytail when working out, she never wears her hair any way but down, yet she can make anyone's hair do just about anything. Tonight, it's a classic up-do to match your new dress.

You wiggle your way to the door, the dress being a little snugger than you remember.

Rachel gives you a long look. Eyebrows raised, she says, "So is this awards dinner for your PR talents, or the ones you only get to use as an escort?"

"What?" You look down, hands padding over your dress. Even though you already know the answer, you ask, "Is this too much?"

"I think you mean too little. How did this even happen? I have to bribe or blackmail you to get you to wear a skirt more than three inches above your knee." Rachel gasps. "You're *finally* sleeping your way to the top!"

"That bad?" She follows you to the full-length mirror in your bedroom. "I had a pantsuit picked out but then Nick suggested this, and I know it's not my usual style, but…"

Rachel slips into her ditzy-girl voice and finishes your sentence. "But since the guy I like likes it, I figured I should buy it. Gross. Your boss is not going to be happy if you show up in this."

Rachel opens your closet and roots around until she comes up with a more professional choice of attire. "Here," she says, thrusting hangers at you. "Put this on." You silently curse and worship her sense of style. You've owned those clothes for months but never would have thought to pair them together.

"What am I going to do with this dress?" you whine. "It was on sale."

"I'll take it off your hands. It's *totally* my style. I don't even feel the urge to dye it black. Just think of it as an expensive lesson in not doing something just because a guy thinks you should."

"A bargain."

"It's hot. Just too hot for work. Keep it." She leads you to the bathroom and starts playing with your hair. "And no more pantsuits."

Turn to section 139.

157

From section 139...

You decide to call Nick and settle the question of exclusivity. You're positive that when you ask if you're a 'we,' he'll say, "Of course we are! Like you have to ask!"

He picks up on the second ring. "Please tell me you're calling with a serious, but not too serious, emergency that springs me from budget report hell."

"Oh, no," you say, relaxing somewhat. "If I had to spend my day working with numbers, so do you."

"Then I'll just enjoy this lovely distraction. What's going on?"

"Sorry, I didn't think you'd still be at work."

"It's welcomed."

You say that now. "All right. Well, earlier the subject of…us came up, and I wasn't sure how to answer…" You are horrible at this.

"I see." His tone screams, *I'd rather be budgeting.* "Listen, I'm having a lot of fun, and I want to keep seeing each other, but I'm not ready to be a couple yet."

You're pretty sure this means he's dating other people, which both stings and surprises you. How long are you going to have to wait until he chooses between you and one of the other women he's seeing? You just want to label this thing already!

Of course, you *could* go out with Maxwell and even the playing field some, but do you really want to start something new? What's a gal with an ambiguous relationship and a gorgeous would-be suitor to do?

To wait it out without Maxwell Matthews, turn to section 100.
Dump Nick and give Mysterious Maxwell a shot, turn to section 105.

158

From section 131...

Nick wants to cook for you tonight. You're trying not to read too much into it, but can't help being hopeful it's a sign of things to come. And you definitely feel more confident about inviting him to Joel's party.

You leave the girls and make a quick stop at your place before driving over to his. When you arrive, he leads you to the kitchen, which smells heavenly with his grandmother's Mediterranean spaghetti sauce cooking on the stove.

He effortlessly lifts you onto the center island. *Hot.* "Wine?" he asks.

"Thanks." You ogle his very fine ass when he turns away, and then admire the way his biceps strain against his black tee shirt as he uncorks the bottle. "No 'Kiss the Cook' apron?"

"I need an apron?" He sets the bottle on the counter and settles between your legs. He kisses you, firm and slow, and you link your arms around his neck. You lose yourselves for a moment, until you hear a persistent beep from the stove.

"The timer," you say breathlessly, unconvinced the sauce takes precedence over his mouth dragging along your collarbone and up to your throat.

He pulls back reluctantly, releasing his firm grip on your hips. That's when you notice your legs are locked around his waist. They should change that saying to "If you *can* take the heat, *make out* in the kitchen."

Nick serves dinner and you try hard to avoid spaghetti-face as you talk about your days. Seizing the moment, you tell him about Joel's party and how excited you are to see your old friends.

"You should come," you say. "Two weeks from Saturday. Rachel and Valerie want to meet you."

"I've met them," he says plainly.

"Yeah, but it was only for a minute."

"I dunno."

"Why not?"

"The hanging with each other's friends thing is pretty couple-y, isn't it?"

"Right." You look down at your plate. "And we're not a couple."

"That's not what I meant," he says. *It's not* not *what you meant either.* "I'll meet them soon enough. Okay?"

"Yeah, of course," you say, waving it off like it's nothing, which it's obviously not.

Turn to section 182.

159

From section 87...

All good things come with sacrifice, right? You read that somewhere.

"I wish I could, but I've already got plans," you tell Nick - the first of what you imagine will be more than a few little white lies.

"I figured it was a long shot. And now I've gone and revealed that I *am* available." He sighs dramatically. You wonder if he's on to you.

"I don't think any less of you for it."

"Glad to hear it," he says. "What's next week like for you?"

"How about Saturday?"

"That works. I was thinking dinner."

"I'm a fan of dinner."

"Do you like Greek? There's a great new place near me."

"Greek happens to be my favorite." *That's a good sign, right?*

"Excellent. I'll make a reservation and pick you up at 7:30 if that works."

"It does."

"All right. So, I'll see you then. In the meantime, I'll just freak out over what I'm going to wear."

He's funny. You so enjoy funny. "I'd appreciate something tight and low cut."

"Score. Saves me a trip to the mall."

After a little more banter punctuated with laughter, you get off the phone.

Good news: You have a date with Nick!

Bad news: You have to wait over a week for it.

At least it allows plenty of time for Rachel and Valerie to argue over whether or not you should wear something tight and low cut.

Continue to section 134.

160

From section 145...

You're nursing a hangover after The Broken Records concert with Scott. You had an unforgettable time - *with the band.* It was particularly memorable for the recently single Scott, who hit it off with the band's bassist, Micky. They dropped you at your place in the wee hours en route to Micky's hotel.

It's late afternoon when Scott texts to let you know he posted some pictures from the night on Facebook. You log in to check them out. The album is full of happy, smiley, sweaty pictures: shots of you, of Scott, of you and Scott, of Scott hugging you, Scott kissing your cheek, your bright mouth print on Scott's cheek, etc. Once again, you're reminded that if Scott weren't into dudes, the two of you could have very, very pretty babies.

He's tagged you in each photo, and you secretly can't wait for the stream of "I'm so jealous" comments. On your page, he writes, *Hey Beautiful. EVERYTHING about last night was amazing. Definitely sleep deprived. <Suggestively raises and lowers eyebrows.>*

Come evening your phone rings and you perk up when you see that it's Nick.

"Hey. How was the concert?" he asks. His voice sounds a little gruff.

"It was amazing!" you tell him. "We got to hang out with the band."

"Yeah, saw the pics online. Looks like you and *Scott* had fun. Late night?"

Oh man, is he ever jealous!

If handled carefully, this could play out to your advantage.

Of course, it could also blow up in your face.

To defuse the situation, turn to section 155.
To risk detonation, turn to section 161.

161

From section 160...

Oh, this is too good. You just can't pass this up.

You fake a feminine yawn before you answer. "Yeah. I'm *exhausted,*" you tell Nick. "I'm not even sure whether or not the sun was up when I got home. I think it was. Anyway, I should probably get into bed."

"Sure," he says, and you feel a *little* bad for finding pleasure in his dejected tone. "I'll let you go."

Not exactly what you were hoping for.

"Actually," he says. "Before you hang up…"

"Yes?" A pleasant anticipation spreads from your stomach to the rest of your body.

Nick inhales deeply before he speaks. "Feel free to tell me this isn't my business, but this Scott guy… Are you dating him?"

Crap. You weren't expecting him to just ask outright. You're not sure what you expected, but definitely not that. Your brain scrambles for an ambiguous answer, but Nick speaks again. "I know we haven't talked exclusivity or whatever yet, but I want you to know I'm not seeing anyone else."

You're overcome with relief. You knew it was possible he was dating other people. All you could do was hope he wasn't, and try not to obsess over it. Much. But to know for sure? That's a 10,000-pound anvil lifted off of your heart.

"Neither am I," you tell him, glad he can't see your elated smile.

"So…Scott?"

"Scott's a good friend. A good gay friend. Who likes dudes."

"Oh! He is. All right." With each word, he sounds less tense. "Well, I guess that's settled then."

Nice try. "Settled?"

"That neither of us are seeing other people."

"At the moment."

"I was thinking, you know, not at all."

You squeal internally, but manage to keep your voice even. "I could work with that."

You say an adorably awkward goodbye before texting the girls: *Guess who's got a boyfriend!?!*

Turn to section 165.

162

From sections 100 and 151...

In the last couple of weeks, your interaction with Nick has, let's say, tapered off.

You've seen him once, shared three short phone conversations, received two even shorter text messages, and you've sent one e-mail, which he has yet to respond to.

Your last date, a movie rental at your apartment, could only be described as uncomfortable. You sat together on the couch with a noticeable gap between you, a stark contrast from your usual interlocked positions. Oh, and you actually *watched* the movie. As soon as it was over, Nick bolted up from the couch and announced he needed to get home without citing a specific reason. Your customary routine of three-to-six goodbye kisses was downgraded to a quick peck on the cheek. That was more than a week ago.

Today, you've got that old familiar feeling of dread that comes with knowing the always uncomfortable *It's Not You, It's Me* speech is in the mail. When Nick's number shows up on your caller ID tonight, you're instantly queasy but pick up the phone anyway.

"Listen, I wanted to talk to you about something," Nick says after you exchange hellos.

"Sure," you tell him, cringing.

"You're really great, but I think we should end things." He blurts the words out quickly and exhales with relief.

When you don't say anything, he continues, "There's a lot going on at work and I'll be really busy for the next few months. I just don't think it would be fair to you to keep going if I can't give you my full attention."

Great, he's doing you a favor.

That's so sweet.

Whatever.

After an awkward goodbye you call Rachel and Valerie, who quickly arrive at your apartment, armed with booze and tissues. Tonight, you'll let them remind you that you can do way better than Nick (so true) and that there are plenty of fish in the sea.

On Friday, they'll take you out to the bar where this all started so you can reel in a new one.

-END-

163

From section 207...

You wait until Nick finishes telling you about his day before you ask, "Is everything okay?"

"As far as I know." He sounds puzzled and you can picture his quirked eyebrow. "Why do you ask?"

"Well, you said you'd call me back last night and I didn't hear from you, so I thought maybe your mom was calling with bad news."

"Nah. She just wanted to remind me it's my grandmother's birthday on Friday."

"So…"

"So…"

"You didn't call me back."

"Yeah, I got distracted by the game. It didn't finish until after eleven. Figured it was too late to call." He pauses for a beat. "It didn't seem like a big deal."

"It's not," you say in your sweet voice. "But next time, maybe send me a text? I'm a worrier."

"Sure," he says, his voice sounding a little tight. "No problem."

Absence of an apology noted.

Turn to section 181.

164

From section 139...

The evening starts out great, beginning with a call from Nick asking if you have plans for the night. You tell him you're busy and are purposely ambiguous with the details.

Next, you manage a flawless makeup application and quite possibly the best hair day you've had all year. By the time Maxwell Mathews arrives to pick you up, looking incredibly dashing in black slacks and a charcoal-colored sweater instead of his usual suit, you are actually pretty excited about your date.

That doesn't last long.

You walk downstairs to his Viper, a very expensive car, which you only know because Rory's dreamed of owning one since he was sixteen. You know a lot of girls would be impressed by that, and you're even one of them for a moment. That is until he finds three different ways to tell you how much he paid for "Precious" – yes, that's her name – during the fifteen minute drive downtown.

Total turn off.

When you arrive at a five star restaurant - okay, impressive - he makes a production of giving the valet a huge tip, presumably to make sure you notice. Again, turn off.

Once seated, he tries to impress you with his knowledge of expensive wines, ordering a three hundred dollar bottle without even asking if you wanted any, presumably because, at that price, how could you not?

He drones on and on about how great his job as a pharmaceutical rep is, and how he's poised to take home the single biggest commission *and* bonus his company has ever seen. What does he sell? Male sexual performance enhancers. What parent doesn't want to share that tidbit with their friends and neighbors when asked about their daughter's boyfriend?

The food was undeniably delicious - as was the wine, you must admit - but you don't think he's asked you more than three questions about yourself. He just rambles on about all of the things that make him great. You smile and nod a lot but, really, you're wondering if you could fake a trip to the bathroom and sneak out unnoticed or if he greased the maître d' to alert him to any escape attempts.

When dinner is over, he asks if you want to hit an exclusive nightclub nearby. You tell him the wine gave you a very expensive headache and ask him to drive you home. Back at your apartment, you can't remember the last time you were so thankful for a date to end.

What a waste of time.

Well, maybe not a total waste. It did demonstrate the value of dating more than one guy at a time, so you don't hang all of your relationship hopes on one.

At least you still have Nick.

Turn to section 101.

165

From sections 161, 166 and 150...

After two months of *extremely* patient waiting, on your part and his, you have decided to take things to the next level with Nick.

Okay, let's be honest, you were just waiting for him to call you his girlfriend.

All week, you've been planning the perfect romantic evening at your place, including dim lighting, wine and a special playlist created by Rachel, which you've already listened to in order to ensure she didn't sneak in Welcome to the Jungle or Nine Inch Nails.

Next up: sexy underwear. Valerie insisted you let them help you pick something out, given you're "clueless in that department." You resisted the urge to snark back that at least you weren't *chestless* in it.

"I don't see what's so wrong with my taste in lingerie," you tell them through the change room curtain as you layer new underwear over your own.

"*Lingerie?* I swear you're only woman left on Earth who hasn't heard Victoria's secret," says Rachel. "Boy shorts and a tank top do not a seductress make."

"I look *ridiculous.*" They charge through the curtain to view the white lace Brazilian panties and matching bra they managed to agree on.

"You look great!" says Valerie, clapping her hands together. "It's perfect."

"Seriously?"

"Yeah." Rachel nods her head. "It's just the right ratio of sweet to slutty."

"What?" you exclaim, looking down at yourself.

"I'm kidding. You look pure as the driven snow. Promise."

Once you've dressed and paid, the three of you head home.

"What do I do about dinner?" you ask on the way to the car.

"Easy. Steak and potatoes," says Valerie. "A safe choice that's hard to screw up. Hey, you can use your George Foreman Grill for the second time in two years!"

"No cooking," says Rachel, surprising you.

"Why not? I cook for boyfriends all the time. Haven't you heard that the fastest way to a man's heart is through his stomach?"

"It's actually through his chest. Or his fly. Regardless, once you show a man you can cook, he expects it. Nuh-uh. Take-out." She grins at you. "And just think, when you skip the meal due to weeks of sexual tension, you've got something to heat up and refuel."

Order a delicious not-at-home-cooked meal, turn to section 179.
Bring George out of retirement, turn to section 174.

166

From section 182...

When you texted Nick to cancel your next date because "something" came up, he suggested Wednesday instead. It took *everything* you had, but you ignored it. Two days later, he left a message about making plans for the weekend. You managed to ignore that one, too.

On Friday, you and the girls drive to Valerie's parents' place in Tiburon for a weekend of sun, drinks, cards and girl talk. Your friends applaud your willpower - and confiscate your phone.

When you get it back on Sunday night, he's sent you two texts, followed by a voicemail asking if you're okay. You don't respond.

The next day, just as you start to worry he's given up, the phone rings. This time, you answer.

"Hey," he says, sounding surprised. "Did you get my messages?"

"Yeah. Sorry I couldn't get back to you. I was gone for a few days."

"No worries. So...can I see you?"

"I'm pretty busy during the week. And I have that party Saturday."

"Do I still have an invite?"

Unbelievable! "Actually, I think you were you probably right about that. It would get awkward. 'Hey everyone. Here's the...guy I hang out with sometimes.' Know what I mean?"

"Introduce me as your boyfriend."

"I'm confused." *Indeed!*

"I know I was kind of a dick the other day, but I wasn't trying to be." You don't dare speak. "Jumping into relationships never works for me, but taking things slow can backfire, too. For instance, you might unintentionally make this really great, sexy, funny and beautiful woman you're dating think you're blowing her off. And then she goes MIA for a week and you miss her. Maybe even wonder where she is. And who she might be with. And you *hate* it."

This is too good. "What might a hypothetical dick do in that situation?"

"Probably call and text - a lot - until he reaches her and then ask if he can brand her with his name."

"Almost had me."

"And ask if she'll put him out of his misery and be his girlfriend."

"You're on. But the misery is just beginning."

"Bring it."

Turn to section 165.

167

From sections 187 and 183...

You're enjoying a lazy Saturday in bed with Nick when your phone rings.

You venture to the living room and pick it up, seeing it's your parents who just got back from visiting family in Chicago. You answer it and close the door to the bedroom most of the way to spare Nick the chitchat.

Your mom tells you she and your dad missed you and asks if you'll bring "that boyfriend of yours" to join them for dinner tonight. You accept her invitation, but only for yourself. Nick's pretty good at avoiding the subject of parents and you don't want to spring it on him.

You say goodbye and return to the bedroom, letting Nick pull you back under the covers and against his body. You tell him you need to cancel your plans that night to see your folks.

"So, is it a family-only occasion?" he asks.

"Uh, no. My mom invited you, but I just figured... Do you *want* to go?" you ask cautiously.

"Sure," he says, squeezing his arms tighter around you. "I think it's probably overdue, don't you?"

Maybe a little.

Inside, your mind reels with the possibilities of what this could mean, but you nod calmly and say, "Great. I'll tell Mom to change the reservation." You go to get up, but he pulls you back to him again.

"Later," he whispers against your ear and then disappears under the blankets, moving lower. And lower still.

Best morning ever.

Turn to 188.

168

From section 174...

Your head pounds so loudly it wakes you.

The bright light spilling in from your bedroom windows makes it hard to open your eyes. You slowly sit up and look around. Your clothes are scattered everywhere. There's no sign of Nick. You trudge your way to the bathroom and look in the mirror. A red and puffy-eyed raccoon stares back at you.

What the hell happened last night?

The last thing you remember is sitting down for dinner. That's a problem. You're naked, and you never sleep naked if you're alone, but now you're both. Your stomach flips. You're almost certain you had sex, but you have no clue if you used protection. You wrap yourself in your robe and head to the kitchen, stopping abruptly when you reach the couch. There's Valerie, fast asleep.

You shake her shoulder. "Did we have sex?" you ask frantically.

She jolts awake. "*Huh?*" She shakes her head. "What?"

You hurriedly explain your predicament. "I'm gonna yak," you tell her. "Is it too soon for morning sickness?

"Yes," she says, sitting up. "But don't worry. Nobody had sex last night."

Your panic is replaced with more confusion. "Then why are you-"

"Sleeping on the world's least comfortable couch? Nick called after you locked yourself in the bathroom."

"No!"

"Oh yes. I ran up here and you were in there - sobbing. Might be related to that empty bottle of red I saw."

You cover your mouth. *Shit!* You were so nervous last night, you forgot you *cannot* drink red wine without risk of calamity. Much like whiskey makes some people angry or aggressive, red wine makes you…almost worse. "I'm naked."

"All you."

Apparently, you refused to talk to Val when she showed up last night, so she had to get the story from a "panic-stricken, horrified" Nick. It went basically like this:

You were halfway through a bottle of wine when he arrived. You finished it together over dinner, along with the bottle he brought. The more you drank the more you flirted, and when he went to clear the dishes, you went for his belt buckle.

Nick tried to let you down gently and wouldn't change his mind when you insisted you weren't drunk. Your fermented, grape-soaked ego didn't handle that well.

"Sobbing?" You wince.

She grimaces. "Worse."

"Not the barking seal."

"Mid-seizure. With hiccups."

"I have to call him. Do crisis management before he dumps me."

"Yeah, about that…"

"He already dumped me?"

"*You* dumped him. And kicked him out. He did not object."

Say what?

"That's when you stripped and got into bed," she continues. "So at least you didn't embarrass yourself."

-*END*-

169

From section 176...

Yep. Hate 'em. You *hate* your friends right now.

Especially when Nick brushes your hair aside to kiss the nape of your neck, encouraged when it makes you shiver. His mouth continues along your shoulder and you squirm against him, feeling exactly how awake he is.

You try to think of the big picture, not the multiple *unassisted* orgasms Nick gave you last night - something so rare there should be some sort of government funded conservation effort for it. Telling Nick to hit the bricks instead of the sheets increases the likelihood you'll find yourself in this, and other, positions with him in the future. He shifts his weight until his body covers yours, his mouth continuing its expedition. South.

Must. Resist. Mouth.

"We can't," you manage, though your hands don't listen, having developed a thing for the feel of his back muscles in motion.

He makes his way back up to your neck, pressing his hard *everything* against you. "Can," he whispers against your ear.

When you roll him onto his back, his slow, smug grin says, *I win.* And he does. Almost. You raise his arms above his head and hold them there, taking his earlobe between your teeth. When you hear his little groan of satisfaction, you scatter off the bed and out of his reach before he catches on.

"Evil." He props his head on his hand and watches you slip on your pearl-colored robe.

"Trust me." You tie off the belt. "I'd *much* rather stay in bed with you, but I've got a crazy day."

"Then you definitely can't skip the most important meal of the day. Even if you've got to have it in bed to save time."

Maybe it's the result of sexual subterfuge, but you feel a little thrill at the power you seem to hold over Nick in this moment. You wonder if that's antifeminist, and then decide you don't care.

"Breakfast is first on my list," you say. "But I'll be late if I don't grab a shower."

He sits up, adorably eager. "I could help you speed that up. I give *great* loofah."

"Something tells me that has nothing to do with speed."

"This is true." He sighs and flops on his back again.

Ten minutes and a guest toothbrush later, you kiss Nick goodbye in the hall. When things quickly escalate, you give him a playful push out the door.

Wouldn't want to be late for not having sex.

Turn to section 185.

170

From section 268...

You let Valerie give you a thorough, if not mildly worded, cursing out for putting Nick first and then hang up to return to your busy game of waiting.

8:00 p.m. passes and no call.

9:00 p.m. passes and no call.

On Tuesday, you get a *really* brief e-mail.

Wednesday passes and *still* no call.

By Thursday, you're exhausted thanks to the hamster with a wild imagination that lives in your head, running laps on his little wheel as he shouts out helpful, elaborate theories as to why Nick hasn't called you. Hamster's favorite theory includes Nick being seduced by a hotel lounge cougar, ironically wearing leopard print, that preys on weary road warriors separated from their beautiful girlfriends.

How does that saying go? What happens in Toronto?

You sit on your bed in the middle of a standoff with your phone. There are two days left before he comes home so, the way you look at it, there are two options: call Rachel and ask her to bring you a handful of those little anti-anxiety meds, or just call him and put your mind at ease.

To check in, turn to section 247.
To wait it out, turn to section 238.

171

From section 153...

Secure – that's the word you'd use to describe your relationship with Nick. And reliable – reliable would work, too.

You know exactly where you stand. You don't have to wonder how he feels or if you have plans with him after work, because you already know he's on his way to your place. You spend nearly all of your time together.

Not because you have copious amounts of dopamine running through your systems (that ship has sailed, as it always does) but because you want to. You spend most nights together, wake up most mornings with each other, run errands together and eat most meals together. It's kinda perfect.

Still, as much as you love it - and you do - there are a lot of little things he does that are accumulating into *big* irritations. You're not a neat freak, by any means. You're as messy as you are tidy, so your apartment is clean about fifty percent of the time. You're prone to magazines lying around, clothes hanging over chairs, shoes in a pile next to your empty shoe rack, but that's *your* mess.

It's also *your* apartment, so you'll mess if you want to.

Nick, on the other hand, seems to have forgotten what a dishwasher is for. Or a hamper. He's constantly leaving plates on your coffee table, drinking glasses on your nightstand, and wet towels and dirty clothes all over the floor.

Up until recently, the steady stream of love drug made you perfectly happy to pick up after him, rationalizing that he was a guest and you were just glad to have him there, but now you've detoxed and you're pretty sick of it.

On this particular Saturday, like every other Saturday, you and Nick wake up and run out to grab breakfast, which you bring home to enjoy with the paper and the crossword.

You guys are so cute.

And this Saturday, like every Saturday, Nick finishes his meal, showers, dresses and flops down on the couch to watch sports highlights, leaving his dishes and the paper strewn on the table, and you don't need to look to know yesterday's clothes are next to his towel on the floor of the bathroom.

And here comes your new friend, Irritation, poking you in the shoulder frantically, as if to say, *See, he did it again!*

Now is as good a time as any to say something. Carpe diem, right? How hard is it to just ask him nicely to help you tidy up?

Of course, these things always start out well intentioned until, inevitably, one person gets defensive and it becomes a full-blown fight, which would ruin this cozy, secure little bubble you've got going.

To let it go for now, turn to section 175.
To address it now, turn to section 183.

172

From section 249...

It's decided. You are your own woman, unbound by the traditional rules of dating etiquette. You will profess your love to Nick when the right moment presents itself.

On this torrentially rainy Sunday afternoon, unwilling to venture outside and unable to find anything to watch on television, you challenge Nick to a friendly game of Scrabble. You're pleasantly surprised when he enthusiastically accepts your challenge and tells you about his weekly games with Nana while growing up. What's not to love?

One hour, five unsuccessful word challenges and an impressive number of twenty point words later, you've been trounced with a score of 375 to 230. The man knows how to work a Q.

"You're a Scrabble god," you tell him, fanning your arms in mock-worship.

"Tell me something I don't know," he replies proudly.

How's that for a right moment? "Okay, I love you."

What's that Simon and Garfunkel song your dad played over and over again while you were growing up? Oh, that's it: The Sound of Silence. Maybe not completely silent - you can hear rain pounding on the window and…are those crickets?

After an excruciating silence, Nick asks, "Play again?"

"Sure. Yeah."

The next round is even worse, mostly because you're distracted by humiliation, but also because your tiles keep forming words like "reject" and "mistake."

Whoever said love was a many splendored thing should be dug up and shot.

Turn to section 203.

173

From section 241...

If someone had predicted your serene Sunday with Nick would turn into you dumping him by the side of the road, followed by fifteen minutes of *awkward* while he drove you home, you'd have asked if they'd been into Rachel's secret stash.

But that's what happened.

"I can't believe you did that," gasps Valerie when you tearfully tell her and Rachel you broke things off with him.

"Oh, my god." You wipe away the stream of mascara running down your cheeks. You managed not to cry in front of Nick, but the floodgates have opened. "D-did I do the wrong thing?"

"*No.* Not at all. I just can't believe *you* did that. It's so…practical."

"Maybe I didn't think about it enough," you say, wiping your hands on your jeans. "I already miss him so much." You bury your head in Rachel's shoulder.

"I know you do you," Rachel says, wrapping an arm around you, giving you a gentle squeeze. "But trust me on this - two years from now, when *I've* got morning sickness because you're blissfully married and thinking about babies, you won't even remember Neal."

-END-

174

From section 165...

You've spent hours preparing for this highly-anticipated night with Nick. Thanks to your stellar multi-tasking abilities, you've shopped, shaved, plucked, moisturized, perfumed, sprayed, glossed, *and* cooked, with fifteen minutes to spare. You even managed to squeeze in a bikini sugaring to match your new Brazilian cut panties.

You've been so go-go-go all day that you haven't had time to think about anything beyond the next thing on your list. So when you top off your glass of wine and sit down to relax until Nick arrives, you're knocked over by a tidal wave of nerves.

You haven't been this nervous to have sex since the first time you had sex. You might even be more nervous now because, instead of just imagining vague possibilities for embarrassment, you actually know what to expect, which means you know exactly what could go wrong.

You've waited months for this, torturing yourself and your sex drive. It started out as self-preservation and eventually became more about not putting extra pressure on your fledgling relationship, but suddenly that's exactly what you've got - pressure. Weeks of anticipation building into to one…climax - a girl can hope.

You drink your wine and panic.

What if you're not any good?

What if *he's* not any good?

He could be one of those guys who's so good-looking that he's terrible in bed because he's never had *to be any good.*

You'd have to fake an orgasm.

You wipe your clammy hands on a napkin and reach for your glass. It's empty.

For more liquid courage, turn to section 168.
To ride out your anxiety cold turkey, turn to section 179.

175

From section 171...

Oh, how quickly things can change.

You're not sure what happened, but somehow, you and Nick have transformed from happy couple into scrappy couple.

You fight about everything. Big things, little things, important things, unimportant things, and about whose fault it is you're fighting. All the arguing wouldn't be so bad if the make-up sex (and regular sex for that matter) hadn't all but stopped.

Things were going so well. You really thought you were headed in the right direction – as in *up* the aisle. Not that you've thought about that a lot, though definitely more often than you have in the past.

This morning, for example, when you shut down his request for a quickie, it instantly becomes an argument about how rarely you have sex, which spirals into a fight about his hours, and then on to how much time you spend together (too much for him, not enough for you). When you squabble about whose turn it is to pick up dinner, he says he's had enough.

Instantly, you panic, wondering if your relationship has reached the invisible point of no return. Sure you've been fighting a lot, but he doesn't want to break up with you, does he?

That's not what you want.

You love him.

When you flat out ask him if he wants to end things, he says, "That's not what I *want,* but we can't keep going like this."

"What does that mean?"

He puts his hands on your shoulders. "Look, you know I love you, but fighting like this..." He shakes his head. "It makes me wonder if we're really compatible. You know?"

Ouch. "Well, how do we fix it?"

"I dunno. Let's, *both of us,*" he says carefully. "Make an effort to stop fighting for...six months."

Why not a year? "And if we don't make it?"

He grabs a towel and heads for the bathroom. "Then we go our separate ways - knowing that we really tried."

"And if we do?"

"Then maybe we can talk about getting engaged."

If any word could spur a peace treaty, "engagement" might be it.

Turn to section 184.

176

From section 179...

You hate your friends sometimes.

Especially right now as you greedily watch a sleeping Nick, buck naked, covered up to the waist with a thin sheet. You woke each other in a number of fun ways throughout the night before finally passing out. Now it's morning.

Unfortunately, your "morning after" conversation with Rachel and Valerie from yesterday is spoiling your spoils.

"Kick him out as soon as he wakes up," Rachel said. "He only gets enough time to hit the head."

"No way!" you told her. "I waited a *long* time to sleep with him. I have *earned* the right to sex all day if I want it."

"No offense, sweetie," said Valerie. "But he may not want to stick around. Boyfriend or not, you should treat this one like hanging up the phone. Do it before he can."

"We're past power plays now, aren't we?"

"Silly girl," said Rachel. "So naïve."

"I'd have thought you'd be firmly in camp 'get yours,'" you told her.

"I'm always in camp 'get mine,' but we're talking about *you.*"

"You're like the Grinches who stole Sexmas," you told them as they exited the elevator.

"Cindy Lou Whore," Rachel shot back.

After some back-and-forth, you told yourself you'd take your friends' advice. After all, they've slept with enough men combined to have actual statistical data on this issue. But that was yesterday.

Before you slept with Nick.

You watch as he begins to stir. His eyes flutter open and he grins sleepily at the sight of you looking back at him.

"Morning, beautiful," he says, pulling you to him possessively. He brushes your hair back from your face and trails kisses across your jaw and down your neck. "How'd you get all the way over there?"

Suddenly your usual routine of making coffee and doling out stamina-replenishing cereal for two doesn't seem like a bad plan at all.

To let him stick around, turn to section 178.
To kick him out, turn to section 169.

177

From sections 178 and 115...

Everyone senior to you in your department is at a weeklong conference in Washington. Left to captain the ship, you decide to run things exactly the way they do when they're in the office: tell everyone you have a meeting and then take a two-hour lunch with a friend.

The timing works out great since you haven't seen much of Val lately. You spend so much of your time with Nick, and she started seeing Travis, the biology teacher, whom she seems mighty smitten with. She's even breaking one of her cardinal rules of basing the number of times a week she sees a guy on how many months she's been dating him, seeing Travis at least three times a week for under a month.

After a quick lunch in the mall food court, you follow her from store to store and pepper her with questions while enjoying her attempts at deflection.

"Have you two studied reproduction yet?" you ask while searching a sporting goods store for a birthday gift for one of Val's brothers.

She stops sifting through a display rack of tee shirts and jerks her head up. "I can't remember if my brother likes the Chicago Cubs or the White Sox," she says, walking past you to a wall of hats.

Oh, she so has.

"According to my dad, no one who likes the White Sox should be encouraged through sports merchandise."

Along the wall, you spot a New England Patriots ball cap and get the warm fuzzies when you remember it's Nick's favorite football team. Yes, you are being *that* much of a girl - a girl who also has a serious appreciation for Tom Brady.

You have plans to see Nick tonight. Should you surprise him with it?

Giselle would buy it for Tom.

To take the hat home, turn to section 141.
To put it back on the rack, turn to section 146.

178

From section 176...

Screw your friends and their easy-for-them-to-say advice. They don't have a gorgeous man with remarkable stamina and upper body strength in their beds. You do.

Rather than chance morning breath (though you wouldn't be surprised if Nick's never had halitosis is his life), you turn in his arms until he's spooning you. You stroke your fingers back and forth across his forearm while his play in your hair. It's one of those utterly perfect quiet moments.

And then your stomach roars like a hungry kitten, making you both laugh.

"Breakfast?" you ask. "There's a great greasy spoon around the corner, or I'm pretty sure I've got a few boxes of sugary cereal in the kitchen. Of course, you could distract my stomach so we don't have to get out of bed."

"All three options sound good," he says. "But I need to get going." You feel his arms loosen around you, followed by a chill on your bare back as he climbs out of bed.

"Oh?" You hold the sheet against your chest and sit up, not hating the naked view as he gathers his clothes from the floor. You're not a fan of what you're hearing, though.

"Yeah, I've got a ton of things to take care of and today's my only day to do it. Next time for sure, though."

You brush your teeth while he dresses and kiss him goodbye at the door.

As soon as he's gone, you text Rachel and Valerie to tell them you'll see them at the brunch you were ready to blow off ten minutes ago. You've already decided to tell them you took their advice and kicked Nick out as soon as he woke up.

What they don't know won't embarrass you.

Turn to section 177.

179

From sections 165 and 174...

At exactly eight o'clock, Nick knocks on your door. You give yourself a hundredth-and-final check in the hall mirror: hair is still bouncy, panties are still not visible through your skirt.

You open the door to Nick's megawatt smile. He holds a bottle of wine in one hand and a gorgeous bouquet of red, yellow and white tulips in the other. It's almost as though he knows he's about to get lucky.

You thank him with a lingering kiss and then walk to the kitchen, stopping to pick up the vase you keep on the hall table. He follows and watches you swap out fake flowers for the real thing and add water. You dry your hands and turn around to find yourself face-to-face with Nick, who rests a hand on either side of you on the counter.

"Hi there," he says, his eyes full of all kinds of...sexy stuff. His proximity is by no means new, but you're nervous all the same and feel your cheeks flush. "You look beautiful." He leans in close.

"Nice try." You duck under his arm and grab the vase. "Dinner's getting cold."

He follows you to the table where the Italian take-out you ordered sits covered in the dishes your parents gave you when you moved out on your own. "Bocce," you say, setting down the vase. "I know you're a fan."

"Right now, I'm a fan of that skirt."

You give him a look that apparently says, *You should see what's underneath it,* because, before you know it, he's kissing you, firmly gripping your waist. You forget all about the food and kiss him back with everything you've got, completely messing up his hair with your fingers. He doesn't seem to mind as it gives his hands free reign.

"Bedroom," you murmur against his mouth.

He pulls back and looks at you seriously. "I'm not sure I'm ready."

Your eyes must bug out of your head, because he laughs before bending slightly to throw you over his shoulder. You squeal - and then feel cool air on your newly exposed behind - which is now in his face.

"You're right," he kisses your hip. "I do like what's under the skirt better. The first time might be faster than I'd hoped. Blame Brazil."

First time?

He carries you to the bedroom and drops you gently on the bed. There's no need to go into the details of what happens next - you're a lady, after all - but you will say he does *just fine* the first time. Even better the second time. And the third.

Turn to section 176.

180

From section 182...

Valerie's plan felt a little devious to you. You don't want to manipulate your way into a relationship. Besides, even if he's not ready to be a couple, you don't want to go days without talking to him.

Still, you can't really get past the bad taste in your mouth that comes from knowing the guy you're totally and completely into feels...who knows how about you. It's made you pretty quiet all night.

"Is something wrong?" asks Nick through a mouthful of food.

"No, I'm fine," you tell him, setting down your fork. "I'm just not hungry."

He looks at you for a long moment. "It's not because you thought I said we weren't a couple?"

Your ears perk up a little. Thought he said? Has he changed his mind? "Maybe."

"Man." He briskly rubs the back of his head. "I was afraid of this. I hate that I hurt your feelings..."

Here it comes!

He shakes his head. "I honestly thought we were on the same page." After a beat, he says, "I think we should break things off."

"*What?*" you snap.

"Whoa." He raises his hands defensively. "That's what I'm talking about. Look, I'm sorry if I made you think I was more serious about this, but I've been here before and I don't want you to resent me for not catching up fast enough. It's too much pressure."

Unbelievable. And yet, totally *believable.*

"I have to go," you say, standing up. "Enjoy your falafel."

-END-

181

From sections 215, 235, 163 and 288...

Before you became exclusive, Nick talked non-stop about an upcoming wedding in Mexico where he'll be the best man. After you made it official, he started adding you to the equation - illustrating how much fun "we" would have swimming in the ocean, walking on the beach and lazing in the sun.

He abruptly stopped talking about the trip four weeks ago. So when you were watching TV the other night and saw a travel commercial with a happy couple splashing around in the ocean, you couldn't resist remarking that it would soon be the two of you. He quickly changed the channel and, with it, the subject.

With T minus thirty days until he leaves, you hear him on the phone talking to Russ about rooming together at the hotel.

Hmm. What's he forgetting? Oh, right. *You*!

You could convince yourself he's a take-charge guy who's planning everything without asking you...anything. Or that he assumes you're a world traveler with no responsibilities, a ready passport *and* a willingness to share a room with his pal. You wonder if you should ask him about it or save yourself an awkward conversation. Anyway, you never told him you definitely wanted to go. Unless "I can't wait" counts.

For the direct flight, turn to section 226.
To standby, turn to section 218.

182

From section 158...

"He actually said that to you?" asks Valerie when you relay your conversation with Nick. You stopped at her place on your way home. "Guys are jerks."

"I feel like the jerk," you say, lying on the carpet and staring at the ceiling.

"How are *you* the jerk here?"

"I was literally just thinking about how well things were going. Not only is that not true, but thanks to *one sentence*, they may not be going at all anymore."

"So you aren't on the same page. It doesn't make you a jerk." She sits beside you on the floor. "And anyway, just turn it around."

She's wearing her *I've got a plan* face. "How?"

"If you're not a couple, you should live your life accordingly. Go AWOL for a week. Let him wonder."

"I don't wanna play games," you whine.

"It's really more of a clever ruse."

It's true. You have no commitments. You're free as a bird. Maybe Nick should have a chance to think about that. "What would I have to do?"

"Cancel your date tomorrow. No explanation. And *when* he contacts you next, no matter how many times, you ignore him. All week. On Friday, we'll go to my parents' place. They're in New York, so it'll be just us girls. But he won't know that."

Seeing you're unconvinced, Valerie continues, "Trust me. If you try acting like nothing happened, you're going to get all passive aggressive, which will just make things worse."

To take Valerie's advice, turn to section 166.
To leave things as they are, turn to section 180.

183

From section 171...

"Okay," you say, popping out of your chair and loudly clapping your hands together.

"What?" Nick says, mirroring the clapping but not taking his eyes off of the play-by-plays.

"Guess what day it is?"

"Saturday," he says, still not looking at you.

"Yes, but it's also Clean Up My Messy Apartment Day!" you cheer. "So, get up."

"Why do I have to get up? I distinctly heard you say *your* apartment."

"Yes, exactly! Apartment. Not hotel. Which means no maid service, mister. There's no one to pick up the towels on the bathroom floor or clear away the breakfast dishes. See where I'm going with this?"

He pretends to search for an answer. "You...think I'm a big slob?"

"Ding ding ding! And that's *fine* - in your apartment. But when we're here, I'd appreciate it if you'd pick up after yourself."

"Just to clarify – you're kind of a slob, too, right?"

"Yes, absolutely. But *here*, not at your place. Still with me?"

He nods and gets up from the couch, walking toward the bedroom. "Yep. Totally. I get it."

Is he getting his stuff?

"Are you mad?" you ask nervously.

"Why?" he asks, stopping in the hallway. "I'm glad you said something. Much better than just yelling at me for random, completely unrelated things like my mom and dad."

"Great. Thank you." You give him a soft kiss and head for the kitchen. "Hamper's in the closet."

Turn to section 167.

184

From section 175...

"What did you do?" asks Valerie when you share Nick's earlier ultimatum.

"I told him I'd think about it," you say sheepishly. "I've never been in this situation before. What *do* you say?"

"You could start by asking him if that ultimatum comes with a promise ring," says Rachel. "What does he think you are? A horse?"

"Huh?" you and Valerie ask simultaneously.

"He's dangling the engagement carrot in front of you. Or *carat*," she says, pointing to Valerie's diamond studs. "Like it's your fault you fight. If *you* can get *yourself* under control, he'll *consider* marrying you as a reward. Fucking bullshit."

"That's so not what he said!" exclaims Valerie. "He told her he loves her and wants to be with her, but doesn't want to fight all the time. And who would? What's wrong with setting a goal if they want to be together?"

"Go ahead. Tie a pretty ribbon around it, but it's still just bullshit with a bow." She turns to you. "Dump his ass."

You're more confused than ever. You love Rachel for being so protective, but she wasn't there. Nick wasn't putting it *all* on you. He did say you *both* had to make an effort. And why would he suggest it if he didn't want to be with you?

You're meeting him at your place in an hour. So what'll it be?

To keep the peace, turn to section 186.
To peace out, turn to section 192.

185

From section 169...

Ever since Nick left your apartment yesterday, everything seems *better*.

The sun burns brighter, food tastes better, your skin is all aglow, flowers are more fragrant - even the constantly barking dog down the hall with its uncanny ability to know when you're napping seems to want you to enjoy your post-coital bliss.

And you have been. Especially when reliving Saturday over and over again in your head. A truly perfect night that was well worth the money you spent on batteries while waiting for it. *Ahem.*

Yesterday, after Rachel confirmed (with some disappointment) that you were able to walk, you gave your friends the customary vicarious-living details, but when you slipped into what sounded dangerously close to erotic fan fiction, Valerie plugged her ears, repeating, "*La, la, la, la, la.*" Rachel made you promise to finish once 'the prude' was out of earshot.

You'd have thought the loop of images running through your head for an entire day would reduce the novelty somewhat, allowing you to concentrate at work today, but you were wrong. Your pornographic memory eased up somewhat, but only so your brain could transition to daydreaming about your future with Nick. Not about wedding dresses, which is so *not* you and far too early to think about anyway. Double dates and couples vacations, however? Fair game. And welcome. It's been so long since you last thought about this stuff.

When Nick calls you tonight, your good cheer must be as obvious as his own. He asks what's got you in such a great mood. You blush - partly shy, partly flattered he seems just as focused on you as you are on him. Should you tell him he's the reason for the extra pep in your step?

Last week, such an outward expression of affection would've been a major no-no, but that was then. Nick's your boyfriend now. You've had sex.

It's a whole new ball game.

To tell him you're happy about him, turn to section 115.
To tell him you had an all-around great day, turn to section 146.

186

From section 184...

It's been nearly a month since you agreed to focus your energy on not fighting with Nick, telling yourself it was for the greater good - your relationship. And you tried. You really, *really* tried.

The following is a shortlist of things you've put up with over the last three weeks without so much as sighing in his direction:

- He showed up late for two dates - leaving you sitting alone in restaurants for a combined total of fifty minutes - and he didn't even call to tell you.

- He stayed out all night with his friends and the girls they met at a bar. He told you he got in at 3:00 a.m., but you found out it was more like 10:00 a.m.

- He's treating your apartment like a hotel, bringing his dirty laundry over so you can "throw it in" with yours.

- He's managed to work how "hot" some random girl is into at least three conversations.

You've kept your mouth shut through all of it, telling yourself the mere possibility of a shiny white gold/platinum band at the end of this road makes it all worth it. But now, heading into week four, you've turned the other cheek so many times it's inside out.

There's *no way* you're going to make it the full six months.

And maybe that's why, when he shows up an hour late to pick you up for tonight's movie date, you're the one who's finally had enough.

"Ready to go?" he asks, when you open the door.

"We missed it," you tell him through clenched teeth. "Because you were late - *again.*"

"What time is it?" he asks, looking at his watch. "Shit, I didn't even notice. Rent a movie instead?"

"You're not even going to apologize?"

"It's just a movie," he says, raising an eyebrow. "What's the big deal?"

"The big deal is you're late *all the time* these days. And I'm sick of it."

He shoves his hands in his pockets. "Here we go…"

"Here we go *what*?"

"Let's have a big fight because we can't go *one* month without a blow-out."

And then, out of nowhere, you're hit with the proverbial lightning bolt of clarity.

Of course!

You've spent the last four weeks on your best behavior, but he's gone out of his way to piss you off, doing things he never used to do at all.

And you let him do it!

You used the idea of a *maybe* proposal as an excuse to let him treat you like crap.

"You asshole!" you roar, suddenly overcome with the rage that's been building for weeks. "You wanted this to happen."

"What?" he asks. You're not buying the dumbstruck look on his face.

"You wanted this to happen!" You repeat, as sure of this as anything in your life.

"You're acting paranoid."

"You've been a complete douche bag on purpose so I'd dump you. Because you don't have the balls to do it yourself! Or maybe you were seeing how far you could push the little wifey?"

"Honestly," he says, still playing it off. "You should hear yourself right now. This is exactly what I was talking about last month."

"No - you're totally right. We do fight way too much. And since it's clear I have much bigger balls than you, how about I do both of us a favor and just end this?"

"Wha-"

"Save it," you tell him. You pick up your key chain and remove the one for his apartment from the ring. You hand it to him. "Here," you say. "Mine please."

You take it, open the door and push him over the threshold, a fitting metaphor. He turns to say something, but you slam the door in his stunned face.

Is this how women end up marrying assholes?

-END-

187

From section 305...

Yeah, you're not actually at that place where superficial stuff no longer matters. You're sick, not delusional.

"Thanks," you tell him. "But Valerie actually got me stocked up before she left for work. And Rachel made me a killer hot totty that I suspect was mostly rye, so I think I'm probably going to zonk out shortly."

Yes it's a lie, and who the fuck cares?

"Are you sure you don't need anything? Not even company?"

"Always, but I don't want to get you sick."

"I don't mind your germs."

"Yes, but when I'm better and want sex, it would really suck if you were sick."

"You're a pragmatic woman and I love you for it."

You hang up and shove the tissues back up your nose as Rachel lets herself in.

"Hey," you say. "Good timing. I need a hot totty."

She reaches into the inside pocket of her leather jacket and pulls out a flask. "No," she says and returns it, reaching into the pocket on the opposite side and producing another. "Yes."

"Two?"

"You multi-task, I multi-flask. The other's vodka." She walks into the kitchen, returning with a shot glass, which she pours a shot of whisky into. "You good with that or do you need a chaser? Spoonful of sugar?"

"What I wouldn't do to see Mary Poppins recast with you as the lead."

"You, me and Julie Andrews," says Rachel, tapping her flask to your glass. "To your health."

Continue to section 167.

188

From section 167...

The morning after dinner with Nick and your family, you meet Rachel and Valerie for brunch.

"Was it awful?" asks a wide-eyed Rachel. She's only met The Parents once and it didn't go well - probably because she was smoking at their dining room table.

"No, it was actually perfect," you say. "Like, stupid perfect."

And it was.

You're still somewhat in shock as you tell them about the night, including the uncanny similarities between your parents, like the fact your mothers were in the same sorority, but five years apart. And how your fathers drive the same model Cadillac and build ships in bottles in their spare time.

Nick and your dad were like old buddies, both knocking back a few dark rum and cokes, cheering the same teams and both adoring you, of course. Never once has a first (or second, or third) meeting between your guy and your family gone so well.

"Hark!" says Valerie, cupping her hand around her ear. "Do you hear that? I think it might be - no, definitely - wedding bells."

Turn to section 189.

189

From section 188...

It's been nearly two weeks since Nick met your parents and you're both abuzz with love.

There's an unspoken understanding that your relationship has reached this new, solid place, and you can't help but feel secure and excited about your future together. This morning, that excitement shoots into overdrive.

You're just getting out of your car in the parking lot of your office when he calls.

"Hey, babe," he says cheerfully. You can picture his smile. "Plans tonight?"

"I'm supposed to see my boyfriend," you say coyly. "But I could get out of it."

"Great. Let's meet at your place at, say, six? There's something important I want to talk to you about."

"Good important?"

"*I* think so."

You say goodbye and immediately dial Valerie, repeating your conversation verbatim.

"I was right!" she exclaims. "He's going to ask you to marry him!"

"Do you really think so?" Because you're starting to think so. "I can't believe this is happening."

Ten minutes of shrieking and squealing (from Valerie) later, you go up to your office and spend the day fantasizing about tonight. After work, you zip home to change, fix your hair, and spritz on some perfume before he arrives.

At six on the nose, he knocks on your door. He looks *incredibly* happy to see you. You lead him to the couch and sit down.

"What did you want to talk to me about?" you ask.

"Okay," he says, suddenly nervous, which makes you nervous, but in the best way. "I've put a lot of thought into this and I think..." He pauses.

We should get married! We should get married!

"We should move in together."

Oh!

You honestly didn't see that coming. It never crossed your mind that this could be what he wanted to talk about. It's not marriage, but it's as close as you can get and still super romantic!

Of course, the Val's of the world believe moving in with a guy too soon is a sure-fire way to postpone a proposal, potentially indefinitely.

To take the plunge, turn to section 261.
To put a plug in it, turn to section 190.

190

From section 189...

"Wow." You settle against the backrest of the couch. "That's not at all what I was expecting."

"You thought I was pregnant, didn't you?" he asks. His smile is broad and bright - one you know he reserves for the happiest of occasions. "So?"

You reach for his hand. The feeling in your chest reminds you of the nervous sensation that builds as you inch your way up the tracks of a rollercoaster, your body anticipating the drop that inevitably sucks the air out of your lungs.

Deep breath.

"Don't hate me," you say. "But I have to say no."

Woosh.

Nick processes your answer, looking down at your fingers, still entwined. This is as stunned as you've ever seen him. You lean forward, angling your head to meet his gaze.

"I really am sorry," you say softly.

"That's so not what *I* was expecting," he says finally, briskly shaking his head. "I thought you'd be excited."

"I am. I'm blown away you even asked. It's just… I'm one of those no-living-in-sin-girls. Plus, my parents would kill me. And then you. Probably you first, actually."

"Oh." He swallows thickly. "I guess I didn't think of that."

"You were being romantic." You squeeze his hand. "Are you mad?"

"Nah," he says. You watch him gather some bravado. "Not mad. Just an ego-maniac who got a little ahead of himself."

You shift until you're sitting on his lap. You slip your arms around his neck as his wrap around your waist. "Kiss," you say.

He smirks and meets your lips. It starts out as a sweet, reassuring kiss but quickly intensifies.

The bad news? Not only aren't you engaged, but you *really* do want to live with Nick. If he'd asked you to marry him, you'd have booked a moving truck tonight. Nothing is harder than saying no to someone you love. But the good news? Nick wants to live with you! That's a step in the right direction.

Right now, though, he's got other ideas. Standing, he slides an arm under your legs, easily picking you up before he carries you to the bedroom.

Definitely could have gone worse.

Turn to section 194.

191

From section 102...

You and Nick spend most Friday and Saturday nights together with rare exceptions. So while you're not entirely surprised to hear that he and his buddies are having a Guy's Night. You *are* surprised to learn it's at a bar most people jokingly call "Silicone Valley" because the women there are made up of so much synthetic material, they could be recalled at any given moment. Not that you're judging.

This bugs you.

A lot.

"Thinking of switching plastic surgeons?" you ask.

He raises a brow.

"Was that catty?" You smirk. "Sorry, I just don't understand why guy's night has to happen at Disco Hooters."

"I didn't pick the bar," he tells you. "But I'll be sure to tell the guys you'd like to interview them on the subject for your thesis."

"Is that mocking? It sounds like mocking."

"I don't remember starting this," he says. "Listen, if it bugs you that much, I just won't go."

To drop it, turn to section 195.
To tell him you don't want him to go, turn to section 205.

192

From section 184...

The closer you get to home, the more certain you are Rachel's right, and the more pissed off you become.

You're glad to see Nick's already there when you open the door. No chance to cool off or change your mind. Still, mad or not, this isn't going to be easy.

He says hello and turns off the TV, waiting for you to join him on the couch. Maybe Rachel was more persuasive than you thought, but you could swear he seems a little bit...smug. Like he's sure you're about to agree to a cease-fire.

Maybe this will be easy after all.

You settle beside him, exhaling in a long whoosh. "So I thought about it."

"And?" he asks, his smug mug still staring you in the face.

"And I'm cutting my losses."

"What?" he asks, perplexed. He searches your face for signs you're joking.

"You were manipulating me this morning and I don't like it."

"What are you talking about?"

You raise your voice. Your finger wags in his direction. "In all the time we've been together, you've never once dared speak the word 'engagement,' but after a few weeks of fighting, suddenly you tell me if we can get along - for a very specific period of time - *maybe* you'll want to marry me? Like I'm so swirly over the idea of marrying you, or anyone, that I'll bend over sideways not to fight with you?"

"That's ridiculous." You've never seen him this mad: eyes dark and flashing, jaw muscles bulging not unattractively. *He's even hot when he's a dick.*

"It *is* ridiculous. And what would be even more so? Me signing off on this stupidity and walking on eggshells 'til death do us part."

"So you're breaking up with me," he says. "Just like that."

"All or nothing was your idea."

-END-

193

From section 273...

"Sorry, everyone," you say, reaching for your purse. "Gotta meet the boyfriend."

"Oh, no, no, no," says Rachel, pressing down on your shoulder.

"School night," you say with a smile Rachel should know means, *Keep it up and I'll tell them how old you really are.*

"I happen to know you don't have class in the morning."

"I happen to know you don't have class, period," you say. "Besides, he *does* have early class tomorrow morning. Every morning. And most nights."

"Is he like Good Will Hunting or something?" one of the frat boys asks.

You're are about to ask him if he's even seen that movie when Rachel loudly whispers, "She's sleeping with her professor - who is *totally* married." You gasp and she continues, "To his job. So my friend is constantly making herself available whenever it suits him."

"That sounds pretty good to me," the frat boy says, laughing and banging forearms with his friends, soliciting a smug smile from Rachel.

You're fuming. "I'll be on my way then," you say, getting up. *Sorry Val.* "P.S. guys, she's old enough to be your father's second wife."

Continue to section 297.

194

From section 190...

At a certain age, being in a serious relationship means being bombarded with questions from family, friends, and freaking strangers about when you and your man are planning to a) get married and b) have babies.

Honestly.

Who asks that?

Don't people realize the potential for awkwardness and embarrassment when they make such inquiries? You've been with Nick for nearly two years now, so it's your turn.

Good times.

You've given up your Friday night to attend a wedding shower for your co-worker, Marjorie. Only, at the last minute, she told you it would be at The Hen in The Fox House, a male strip club.

Instead of eating red velvet cake in a conference room, you're trapped in a bar with red velvet interior, surrounded by Marjorie and her married friends - all of whom are hammered off of cheap wine and who make you wear a penis sticker on your shirt.

The more everyone drinks, the worse the décor gets, the better the dancing gets, and the more they gush about how great marriage is, insisting you need to "get" Nick to propose to you soon or wait forever.

Thanks for the unsolicited opinions, drunk women I don't know.

Still, as annoying as it is, it does make you wonder why you and Nick haven't talked marriage yet. It's not like you want to tie the knot - or even get engaged -tomorrow, but you don't even talk about it. Not even in the abstract.

When he asked you to move in with him months ago, you took it as a sign he's serious about you. And he understands why you turned him down, so when he's ready to marry you, he'll ask. Still, you can't help but worry that not only are you and Nick not on the same page, but that you're on chapter twelve and he's reading the sports section.

And while living together *is* a commitment, it's a far cry from marriage. It's entirely likely he hasn't raised the subject because he just doesn't want to get married, and you're clueless because you're following some antiquated rule about never daring to be the one who brings up engagement.

Do you really want to wind up as someone's wedding shower anecdote about a friend who spent the best years of her life waiting around for Mr. Never Going to Happen only to die alone?

You pull into the parking lot and wonder what you should do. Part of you thinks if you're too scared to have The Talk with Nick, you are most definitely not ready for marriage. The other part says it would be stupid to let a group of strangers scare you into scaring him off if it turns out he's just not ready for this particular discussion.

To leave well enough alone, turn to section 196.
If you think you've left it alone long enough, turn to section 201.

195

From section 191...

Yeah, because that isn't a trap. A trap you've used before.

You rest a hip against the counter, folding your arms across your chest. "Yes, it bothers me," you say. "But not in an 'I don't trust you' kind of way. It's more like 'Wow, my boyfriend's totally setting back the feminist movement.' Have fun. Just be sure to bring an umbrella, you know, in case someone springs a leak."

Nick places his hands on your waist and kisses the top of your head.

"Trust me," he says. "If I wanted a girl who looks like a cheesy stripper, I would be with a girl who looks like a cheesy stripper."

"So I can cancel my spray tan then?"

Turn to section 285.

196

From section 194...

While brushing your teeth this morning, you applaud your decision not to have The Talk with Nick.

Two years in is hardly the time to panic about proposals - this isn't a chick-flick for cripe's sake. You don't have to marry someone six months after meeting him. You resolve to push the idea out of your head altogether when he says something that makes you spit your toothpaste all over the bathroom mirror.

His parents are visiting from the Bahamas and they want to meet you - tonight. With his mom and dad so far away, you'd gotten used to the idea of not meeting them. You once suggested the two of you go visit them, but he brushed it off. You suggested it again after he met your folks and he changed the subject.

"Your parents?" you ask after rinsing your mouth. "I was starting to think you murdered them for their apartment. Where'd this come from?"

"I know I've waited a long time. I put off introducing my girlfriends to my folks as long as possible - but I have good reason." He explains how excited his mother gets when he brings a girl home, followed by months of very unsubtle hints about marriage and babies, and finally his memory of the demon she became when his sister got engaged, which nearly ended the marriage before it began.

"What if she doesn't like the girl?" you ask.

"Then I'm barraged with equally unsubtle hints about breaking up with her. And provided with regular updates on which of her friends' charming daughters are available. Either way," he says, shaking his head, "It's torture."

"Aw, babe. You think I'm worth torture? That's so sweet."

"That and my mother won't leave me alone about meeting you."

The next thing you know, you're sitting across from his parents at his dad's favorite table at Morton's, making small talk.

You're actually thankful not to have had advance notice. There was barely enough time to pick a parent-appropriate outfit, let alone stress out over doing or saying something stupid. The next three hours fly by and his mother is thrilled about the serendipitous overlaps between your parents' lives.

Before you know it, you're in the car on the way home.

You quickly take stock of the evening and decide you did great! You were polite without being a kiss-ass, interested without being intrusive, open but not an egomaniac, and commented on current events without getting political. You even pulled off a few funny stories. You were a picture-perfect-parent-pleaser. And even better, you really like them, which rarely happens.

Not long into your drive, Nick's phone buzzes in the console. He checks it at the next light and hands it to you. "My mom." He grins broadly.

It reads: *She's a keeper!*

Yay!

You're a keeper!

Turn to section 258.

197

From sections 213 and 212...

On Monday morning of a long weekend, you power up your phone for the first time in almost three days. You turned it off when Nick arrived at your apartment Friday night, and he hasn't left yet.

Your mother left a voicemail on Saturday, so you figure you have at least one more day to call her back before she contacts your superintendent and asks him to check your apartment for dead bodies. Definitely too much Law and Order: SVU for mumsie.

There are ten text messages from Rachel and Valerie - each. Figuring you must be holed up with Nick, they first took your neglect with good humor.

If you manage to make it into an upright position today, call me, read Valerie's fourth message.

Now, on Day Three, they've become a little hostile, resulting in Rachel's most recent message/death threat, *12:00 pm at The Spoon. Be there or DIE.*

You stick your tongue out at the phone and place it on the nightstand. You've had a movie-perfect weekend with Nick so far: dinner, sex, sleep, sex, shower, breakfast, sex, lunch, movie, sex...rinse and repeat. You've been looking forward to brunch with the girls all week, but you already feel separation anxiety at the thought of leaving him.

"I should start getting ready," you begrudgingly tell him.

"Are you sure you're feeling up to it?" He holds the back of his hand against your forehead and makes a faux-concerned face. "You feel a bit warm."

If you feel a cold coming on, turn to section 209.
To avoid a cold shoulder from the girls, turn to section 230.

198

From section 201...

You had every intention of being Cool Chick - secure enough to go with the flow. Sure, you have the odd moment of panic, scared you're just breaking Nick in for the woman he marries two years from now, but you usually manage to squash it and go about your day.

But with each passing week, your inner doubts steadily grow, manifesting into some seriously passive aggressive (and jerky) behavior you thought yourself above. Behavior you've mocked.

Like leaving the paper folded to ginormous ads for engagement rings - ads created for exactly this kind of subterfuge - and the suggestion you hold off on planning a vacation next year, saying, "Who knows where we'll be then?" Grown up stuff like that. You're a woman possessed by clichés.

Nick doesn't notice for a while, but soon enough, you hear him sighing - involuntarily at first, but eventually pointedly. And today is the tipping point.

You're putting away dishes when he takes a call from his friend, Mike - a call impossible not to overhear given the size of your apartment.

Like when he says, "Congrats, buddy! I'm happy for you guys."

Must be moving in together.

"When's the big day?" he asks.

Big day they move in together.

"Of course, man. It'd be an honor."

To help him move.

Mike and Maya got together around the same time as you and Nick. Technically three months *after*, but who's fixating? You know this. Nick knows this. He knows you know this. You both know where it's going.

"Engaged?" you ask innocently enough when he walks back into the kitchen.

"Next spring." He points to himself. "Best Man. For the fifth time."

You laugh in spite of yourself. It's too much.

"What?"

"I just realized the most anti-marriage guy among your friends is the most popular Best Man."

He slides you a flat look. "Not funny ha-ha then."

"Whatever." You return to the dishes. "Good for Maya."

"Meaning?"

"Mike knows what he wants."

"Yes he does." He nods deliberately, slowly. "So does Nick."

Walked into that one.

Eventually he says, "This is about enough, yeah?"

"Enough?"

"Enough pretending you don't care about marriage despite your decreasingly covert ways of working it into nearly every conversation."

Oh, that. You stand straighter. "I made a bad call and I haven't handled it very well."

"*Well?*" He laughs wearily. "To think what 'worse' would've looked like."

"Forget it." You walk to the bedroom and start stuffing his things into his gym bag. "Forget all of it."

"This is *my* fault now?"

"*No.* This was all me." In the bathroom, you add his toiletries to the bag. "It was a joke to think I could wait indefinitely for you to make up your mind, but it clarified what I want."

"Which is?"

"For you to leave." You toss the bag at his chest. "Now would be good."

-END-

199

From section 141...

Consistency. It's one of the greatest things about being in a steady relationship.

You no longer wonder what you're doing on the weekend because you know you'll be with Nick. It's not a codependent thing. You can survive without him. You both just prefer to spend your free time together - and to use that time for a number of mutually enjoyable activities, sometimes multiple times a night.

Even after an exhausting week, you fight sleep so you don't waste any time together, which you put toward any number of mutually enjoyable activities... and so on and so forth.

It's kind of the best, and you kind of don't mind being the envy of every single gal you know. Except Rachel, who actually pities you. Val's happy for you, but thinks it's a little suspicious you've never spent the night at Nick's apartment.

Tonight you call Nick to check his ETA for dinner. You're surprised when he tells you his Estimated Time of Arrival is *not at all* because he's watching a playoff game at Ted's.

And then, as though he hasn't spent the last god knows how many consecutive Fridays with you, he asks, "Is that cool?"

No, it's not cool! A little notice would've been nice. You have friends, too. Friends you put on the backburner for him. Okay, not for *him* so much as for *you*, but still. You could be at Drag Queen Bingo with Rachel and Valerie right now. Instead, you're getting sort of stood up. *A little* inconsiderate, isn't it?

To let it go, turn to section 262.
To let it out, turn to section 106.

200

From sections 285 and 205...

You and Nick both own cars, but his beat up well-loved Camaro has seen better days. Probably in 1992.

Since you started dating, it's broken down at least four times, so he's taken to leaving it parked in his garage. By default, you've become the designated driver in your relationship, which means you spend most nights at his place and get the joy of driving home each morning to get ready for work. It's a major pain in the heated seat and, with gas prices being what they are, you have less money to spend on frothy things and stuff.

When you subtly suggest to Nick that he look into buying a new car - or at the very least, find a better mechanic - he tells you he doesn't see the need for it, rambling something about the environment and the fact he lives only a five minute walk from his office in the Financial District. And, of course, the fact that *you* have wheels.

Every girl loves it when her boyfriend begins factoring her into life's big… car purchases, but this doesn't do anything to solve *your* problems, like being late for work most mornings and how much you hate it when he changes the settings on the driver's seat and mirrors.

To keep on truckin', turn to section 266.
To drop the clutch, turn to section 279.

201

From sections 194 and 258...

"How was ovapalooza?" Nick asks, kicked back on the couch with the content expression of a man who didn't spend the night with a roomful of uteri.

"Torture." You flop down next to him. "I wish I had a penis."

He shudders. "That bad?"

You know how sometimes you script your words perfectly, but when it comes time to say them, you panic and blurt out exactly the wrong thing?

"Why don't we ever talk about marriage?" *Blurt.*

Nick chokes on his beer. "Please tell me you recognize how predictable this is."

Of course you do. "What?"

He laughs shortly. "Everything's going great until *boom*, complete strangers say we're moving too slow."

"Maybe we are. Most people talk about this stuff much earlier."

He rolls his eyes. "Missed that one on the last census."

"Women lose just about all say in anything significant once we cash in our relationship v-cards. After that, we wait for constant affirmation. The girlfriend label. The 'I love you.' The friends. The parents. And definitely the proposal. Everything's on the guy's timetable. At least during the renaissance we had, you know, sheep and titles to light a fire under a courtier's ass."

His lips twitch involuntarily. "What is the dowry on you anyway? I'm low on horses, which, as a nobleman, is an embarrassment to my family."

"I'm serious." You pout. "Think this is easy? Try being me right now."

He nods. "Fair."

"I just want to say what I'm thinking before I make myself crazy."

"Okay." He nods, but swallows audibly. "I'm listening."

"I want to get married," you say earnestly. "Not tomorrow, but within a few years. I *would* like to be engaged by next year. It's *not* an ultimatum, it's just an idea." He watches you intently, much calmer than you anticipated. "And I don't expect a huge ring. Or a wedding the cost of a down payment." You did it! Go, you! "What about you?" you ask.

"I don't know," he says simply. "Please don't take this the wrong way, but I haven't really thought about it."

Ouch. "How could I take that the wrong way? We've only been together over two years."

He exhales. "You asked. I may or may not want to get married someday. I don't know now. It's not something I'm ready to think about." His hand cups the back of your head. "We've got it good. Why can't we just see what happens?"

"Because I don't want to wake up fifteen years from now, single and staying that way after waiting around on a 'maybe.'" You can't believe this. You weren't even thinking about these things when you woke up today.

"I don't know what to tell you," he says, taking yours hands. "I love you, and I want to be with you for the foreseeable future, but I'm not going to promise to *eventually* promise 'til death do us part because a bunch of nosey chicks got into your head."

Oh yeah. So much better now.

He does have a point, though. Is there any sense in asking him to commit to the potential of committing? What's to stop him from telling you what you want to hear, giving you a false sense of security? And do you really want to wait and see, or would you rather grab hold of the situation?

To let things run their course, turn to section 198.
To take the reins, turn to section 253.

202

From section 213...

Thirty minutes and one trip down the street later, you're armed with the latest issues of Her, You, and Them. Each one is heavy on fashion and cosmetics, light on anything resembling an opinion on women's issues, and all feature a Hollywood starlet on the cover: one in her 20s, one in her 30s, and one in her 40s who could pass for her 30s.

Their biggest commonality, however, is their ability to make you feel unworthy of your ovaries. You're a good-looking girl - no doubt about it - and yet these glossy, perfectly posed and stylized beauties in high heels, peering at you from under their too-lush-to-be-real lashes, make you feel wretched in your faded yoga pants and chipped nail polish.

The fully clothed pages were bad enough, but by the time you get to lingerie, you're transported back to your junior high locker room and the time you asked your mom to write you a note excusing you from gym class until your breasts arrived.

And that was before plastic surgery and collagen injections took over the world. You plough through the pages of push-ups and corsets.

Who the fuck wears a corset who isn't starring in Reign?

You give yourself the usual "You could look like that with the right lighting, stylist and surgeon" pep talk, but it's too late. Over the next two hours, you console your body image by polishing off every bit of comfort food, sweet and salty, in the kitchen before promptly slipping into a food coma.

It's a good thing you haven't gone shopping yet because you just gained three pounds.

Turn to section 148.

203

From section 172...

"What the fuck happened to you?" Rachel asks when she finds you on the other side of her apartment door. "Are you turning zombie? Because I'll be sort of sad if you're... Hey dude, what happened?"

"Nick d-d-dumped me," you blubber, and she holds her arms out to you.

"*What?*" Valerie shouts from her bedroom, at the door an instant later.

"Come on." Rachel guides you to the couch. "Sit. Spill."

You accept a box of tissues from Valerie and take her silent cue to wipe the mascara out from under your eyes. "Crying is no reason to look a mess" is one of her mom's mottos.

You tell them about your "I'm in love" realization and how you sat on it until the right moment presented itself during a game of Scrabble. You tell them about the awkwardness that followed. You explain how you later meticulously and carefully packed away the game, delaying what you'd felt coming with each tile laid - the other three little words. Words dreaded by men and women alike: Can. We. Talk.

You give them the gist of what Nick said - that he thinks you were brave for telling him how you feel, but that he owed you the same thing. And as much as he cares for you, he's not in love with you. And because of that, he doesn't think you should see each other anymore.

So you're not.

Your friends flank either side of you on the couch. Val rests her head on your shoulder, but neither says anything. What's there to say? Other than, "Why would you tell him that?"

In the end, it doesn't really matter. The end result won't change.

You are single again.

Single and in love.

-END-

204

From section 319...

It's been thirty-two hours since Nick stormed out of your apartment following your first big fight. Fortunately for you, he forgot his wallet on your coffee table after paying the pizza guy, forcing him to contact you first to make plans to pick it up.

Your heart's been in your throat since he left. You're still mad at him, of course - he did more or less call you passive-aggressive - but you *hate* fighting and just want things to return to normal.

You let him in tonight and are instantly relieved to see his face, especially because it's obvious he feels badly, too. You sit together on the couch and he picks up his wallet from the table. He opens it and takes something out, careful to keep it covered in his hand.

"About the whole romantic thing," he begins. "Before you freaked out the other night, I was getting ready to give you this." He opens his palm and you see a set of his apartment keys.

"Oh, my god," you start to gush.

"Let me finish," he says, closing his hand again. "I thought it was pretty romantic, but then hearing what you said the other night kind of woke me up to the fact that maybe we have different ideas of what's important in a relationship, what's balanced..."

"Is this because of the present? I'm sorry. I should have said something sooner. It wasn't fair."

"It's not just about the present - though it doesn't feel good knowing you think I'd intentionally give you an insulting gift - it's about the fact you're obviously keeping tabs on my performance in this relationship and think I should be doing all of the work."

You wait for him to pause so you can tell him he's wrong, but he keeps going. "If you were craving romance so desperately, maybe you could have done something nice for me instead of waiting for me to do something for you, and making me out to be the jerk."

As it becomes clear you're not getting the key, you panic. "Babe, come on. I'm really not that shallow! I just got insecure and started worrying that you might be losing interest in me. It just came out wrong. I'm sorry."

"Maybe." He shrugs. "But the subtext is the same. I don't think this is going to work."

"That's it? Two days ago you made copies of your keys for me and today you want to break up?"

"Trust me," he says as you follow him to the door. "This wasn't how I expected the weekend to turn out either, but I think it's for the best. Sorry."

And then he's gone.

How the fuck *did that happen?*

-END-

205

From section 191...

You've never actually told a guy he can't go somewhere, but this isn't telling him, this is taking him up on an offer not to do something that makes you uncomfortable. You think.

"Okay," you say, leaning against the counter. "I don't want you to go."

"All right." He picks up his keys. "I won't."

And yet, it looks like he's leaving. You follow him, confused. "Then where are you going?"

"I said I won't go out with the guys, so I'm not going out with the guys. But I'm not staying here either."

"Wait. What just happened?"

He ties his shoelaces and straightens up, then walks toward you. "You basically just told me you don't trust me."

"I did *not* say that. If you recall, I made some pretty passive aggressive, and then outright aggressive, remarks in protest, but no one used the word 'trust.'"

"If you were going to a bachelorette party with strippers and I said I didn't want you to go, what would you tell me?"

You open your mouth and close it again. You have nothing to say, making him smirk in amusement. He places a hand at the back of your head and kisses your forehead. "Think about that. I'll talk to you tomorrow."

How did you miss that big shiny bear-trap? And it *was* a trap. Well, at least now you have the entire night free to work on your apology.

Turn to 200.

206

From section 146...

Okay, one drawer. Just one, though – no need to get creepy.

You're fully aware you may be opening Pandora's box, and might get some information you wish you hadn't, but the idea you could be missing out on information you'll be better off knowing is suddenly overwhelming.

You stare at his desk and try to sense which of those tempting little rectangles holds the most promise. You consider the top right - the one you would use most often if it were your desk - and the bottom left - where you would hide stuff you wanted out of sight, but not necessarily out of mind.

You decide on Drawer Number 2 and take a deep breath before diving in.

Boring!

Just random papers: his lease, car insurance, gym contract, etcera. Some of it's dated five years ago. Then you spot something at the very bottom of the drawer. You look closer and the air rushes right out of your lungs.

Underwear!

More specifically, its women's underwear, but most importantly, it's *not your underwear!* So whose is it? How long has it been there? Why does he still have it?

You can't ask him. "Hey, babe. I was digging through your stuff and found these. Can you ask your friend where she bought them? They're super cute and I should get a pair since you like them so much."

You hear the front door and plop the papers back on top of the mystery-thong, then quietly slide the drawer shut. You must get out of there immediately. When Nick enters the bedroom, you're hastily pulling on your jeans.

"Whoa," he says when you move on to your shirt. "The whole point of breakfast-in-bed is the nudity."

"Oh, my god," your fib begins. "My mother just called me from outside my apartment. I totally forgot she was driving in today."

You manage to get out the door in under two minutes and call Rachel, lucky to catch her and Valerie together in the car.

"Speaker, speaker, speaker," you demand, and then give them a play-by-play on Panty-Gate.

"Whose panties do you think they are?" asks Rachel.

"Ugh, don't say *panties,*" says Valerie, undoubtedly grimacing.

"I don't want to think about it," you tell them.

"Good luck with that."

"If there were papers in there from five years ago," says Valerie, "maybe that's how old the underwear is, too."

"Maybe," you say.

"Do not admit you found them. And don't snoop anymore."

"I won't."

Over the next few weeks, the discovery of strange lingerie stops lingering at the forefront of your mind. It'll pop up every now and again, but since you can't ask him about it without revealing your transgression, you've got no choice but to try and forget it.

In the future, you'll tell Pandora to keep her box closed.

Turn to section 213.

207

From sections 211 and 106...

You and Nick were talking on the phone last night when his mom called. He told you he'd call you back in five minutes. Nick enjoys phone conversations with his mother as much you enjoy a bikini wax (necessary, but thankful when it's over), so you worry when he doesn't call. Maybe his mother called with a family emergency or, *worse*, he forgot about you.

It kept you up until after midnight and you've been fretting about it all day at work. You're distracted, repeatedly checking for phone messages, texts and e-mails from him, and growing more concerned by the minute because it increases the likelihood that something bad happened - and the likelihood that the something bad is that he forgot about you.

Selfish much?

Finally, twenty-two hours and thirty-seven minutes later, Nick calls. You make small talk for a few minutes, but still no mention of last night. He doesn't even remember forgetting you?

How rude!

To forget about it, turn to section 152.
To remind him, turn to section 163.

208

From sections 209 and 148...

Like a gazillion other people around the world, you watch a lot of reality TV, read some gossip (thank you, Lainey Lui), and have a general idea of who's dating whom in Hollywood.

You admit your generation has a weird fetish for peeking into the private lives of others, but it's a fun way to shut your brain off for a couple of hours while feeling a smug sense of superiority.

Nick, however, is always on your case about it. He scoffed when he pulled up your Tivo recordings and saw a week's worth of Big Brother, and he asked for a glass of bleach to drink when you dared to watch The Bachelorette in his presence.

Last night, he saw the stack of old gossip rags Valerie gave you under your coffee table and said, "People who waste their time with that garbage are soldiers in a war against intelligent society." Way harsh, Thai! You totally pinned the magazines on Val, but it's all you've thought about since.

Does that mean he thinks you're stupid?

Crap!

You don't want him to think that. And anyway, maybe he's kind of right. It is kind of juvenile behavior for a grown woman, and if you cut back...you'd have more time for reading chick-lit.

On the other hand, you're not hurting anybody. And if people like you didn't keep up with the celebrity sports pages, how could the stars afford the very antics that entertain us? You're doing your part for the economy. Can't someone else deal with the rest?

To get back to real-reality, turn to section 223.
To soldier on, turn to section 214.

209

From section 197...

Two days after you bailed on brunch with Rachel and Valerie, you join them for dinner after work.

You hear Rachel as you approach the booth. "Nope. Nope. Maybe. Nope. Definitely. Definitely not."

"This has to be the most shallow dating app I've ever seen," Valerie says.

"Exactly."

"It's superficial."

"Which is why it works." When you reach the table, she gives you a sly grin. "Well, well. The prodigal slut returns."

"Not very PC of you," you say, sliding in next to her.

"Fancy that, Rach," says Valerie. "You said something and she responded. Didn't even take three days."

You roll your eyes. "So I spent a weekend with my new boyfriend. I haven't gone AWOL."

"Not yet," says Rachel. "But you're a hop-skip-and-a-hump away from becoming _that_ girl."

"What girl?"

"Can't Be Without My Boyfriend Girl," she says. "Aside from the general annoyingness that comes with the title, it's got a short shelf-life before _he_ starts to realize you can't be without him."

"Not to mention we're bitter and jealous," adds Valerie, handing you a menu.

You turn to Rachel. "You spend days at a time with guys."

She shrugs. "Once or twice." You glare at her. "Oh, you meant overall. Yeah, guys. Not boyfriends. Sex."

"Which is what we were doing," you whisper loudly. "Like, a lot."

"Okay," she says, going back to hunting for men on her phone. "I don't get you commitment-y types anyway, so what do I know?"

"Oh," says Valerie, her eyes flashing with amusement. "We've taken a vote and, since you prioritized Nick over us, you're paying for dinner."

"Worth it," you say.

Was it ever!

Turn to section 208.

210

From sections 256 and 245...

You're burned out from a long week of new client research on top of existing business. Having cleared your To Do list and calendar last night, you wake up on Friday deciding to take your quarterly "mental health day" and recharge your batteries.

You look out your window and are happy to see Mother Nature supports your plans, blessing them with sunshine and a cloudless sky. You put on some music on your way to the shower, in such a good mood that - were you in a cartoon - you'd have a forest's worth of adorable creatures as a team of stylists. And maybe one or two bunnies playing the flute.

The sunshine inspires a lunchtime picnic. You'd love to be the type of person who's secure enough to eat alone in a park while reading the classics, but you're not. So you decide to surprise one of your favorite people currently stuck indoors.

Geographic proximity to your favorite park, and deli, in the city narrows your choices for perspective picnic-mates to Nick (ham and cheese on rye – extra mayo) or Rachel (pastrami on focaccia – just say no to mayo).

You know Rachel can more or less call her own shots at work, but you don't know what Nick's day looks like, and calling to ask him would defeat the "surprise" thing.

To pick Nick, turn to section 235.
To surprise Rachel, turn to section 249.

211

From section 244...

A time-honored womanly tradition, you turn your cold drink with Nick into giving Nick the cold shoulder. You remain mostly silent except for a few "uh huh's" and an "I'm fine" or two.

Finally, he says, "I'm sorry you're upset about the party, but I really had no idea we could bring dates. It's never been an option before."

"It's just disconcerting to hear guests are welcome from the office fox who obviously has a thing for you." His mouth drops open slightly. "If you didn't want to bring me, you could have just said so."

"Of course I'd want you to come. And she doesn't have a thing for me." He smiles and reaches for your hand. "Take the word of your boyfriend over a stranger?"

He seems sincere, so you agree to go to the party with him.

On Monday afternoon, he sends you an e-mail titled: *Written apologies only.*

It's a forward from his boss: *There appears to be some confusion regarding Friday's holiday party. Despite the rumors, employees are not permitted to bring guests to the function.*

The upside, Nick didn't lie to you. The downsides - yes, plural - you didn't believe him *and* he's going to be at the office party getting drunk on the company tab - with Super Fox.

Merry fucking Christmas.

Turn to section 207.

212

From section 146...

It's tempting to delve deep into drawers containing unknown details about your man, but no good can come from it.

To keep yourself in check, you grab Nick's robe from the back of the door, head down to the living room and sit on the couch where you create a mental list of all of the things you wouldn't want him to find in your apartment.

1. Pictures of you with braces.
2. Pictures of you *before* braces.
3. Your collection of elementary and high school diaries containing unquestionably embarrassing documentation of your pre-adult geekdom.
4. An array of feminine hygiene products no man could understand.
5. Your collection of pictures of ex-boyfriends - everyone has one, but no one needs to see it. Though, now you're wondering if he has one.
6. Your vibrator.

Just as you wonder how hard it would be to install locks around your apartment, the front door opens and in walks Nick with breakfast.

"Did I give you enough time to snoop?" he asks you when he hands you your coffee.

"Don't be silly. I hired a P.I. when we started dating, so I know *all* of your dirty little secrets."

He takes your hand and leads you back upstairs. "I can't get enough of a woman who isn't bothered by a criminal record and a little pagan worship."

Turn to section 197.

213

From section 206...

Like many women - at least you hope you're not the only one - every so often you realize your underwear has begun to resemble the old rags your mom keeps for cleaning windows.

This happens less often when you're single, since you couldn't care less about underwear or shaving your legs when no one you're sexually attracted to will see them. But now that you and Nick mate as frequently as rabbits, you either need to get your buns over to the mall or start going commando. Given how tight most of your jeans are, you rule out the latter.

Rachel and Valerie picking out your underwear while mocking your taste is as annoying as an ill-fitting thong, so you have two options.

First, you could turn to this month's fashion mags for inspiration, repeating the mantra, "It's make-up and airbrushing. It's make-up and airbrushing," as you flip through models in size XS panties and DD cups.

Second, you could take Nick on a field trip to the mall and let him pick out whatever he likes for you, which could be fun - and potentially embarrassing.

To settle in for a night of self-hatred, turn to section 202.
To ask Nick to pick something out for you, turn to section 197.

214

From section 208...

You is who you is. No two ways about it.

So what if Nick thinks your pastimes are frivolous? His are hardly leading the charge for social change. Like when you arrive at his place on Saturday night to find him enthralled in an Ultimate Fighting Championship match on his gigantic TV, hollering like a barbarian.

Somehow, you don't think this is what Gandhi meant when he said, "Be the change you want to see in the world."

Without taking his eyes off the screen, he says, "This is almost over, babe. Fifteen minutes, max. John Moraga is the man."

You've never been a fan of blood, so you take out the most recent copy of Them Weekly and successfully tune out the steady stream of grunts and crunching sounds from the TV.

When it's over, Nick turns to you for the first time since you arrived. He nods toward the magazine draped across your legs. "Trying to beef up that IQ?" he teases, swooping down for a kiss.

"In a toss-up between gossip and watching two grown men beat the shit out of each other for money, I almost always choose glossy over bloody."

He throws his head back, laughing. "You're comparing UFC with *that*?" He points at your lap. "Sports happen to be as enriching as they are a great form of exercise."

It's your turn to laugh. "If you're playing them. More people watch sports than participate in them, which is usually accompanied by beer, sitting, and ads full of chicks with big, fake tits." You hold up your magazine. "I've got two out of three right here."

"Why do people care so much about celebrities? It's stupid." He smiles apologetically. "No offense."

"Why would that be offensive?" you say dryly. "And, since you asked, it's a hard-wired biological response to admire and dote on the 'celebrities' of one's culture. I saw a scientist talking about it on Dateline. At least I think that's what he said. I'm a little dim-witted."

Determined to prove sports take celebs in a cage match, Nick grabs the magazine. He fans through it, stopping abruptly before turning back a few pages. "Hey, that's Joe Moraga."

"He's dating a super model." You push him gently until he flops backward on the couch. "Sit. Read. I'll go get us some beer."

Turn to section 236.

215

From section 239...

It didn't take much convincing before Nick accepted the offer of your services in returning his habitat to liveable standards.

This morning, you show up at his place wearing your cutest cleaning clothes and holding a mop. Throughout the day, the two of you actually have a great time as you team up to vacuum, sweep and mop floors, wash and dry dishes, clean mirrors to a streak-free shine and, yes, conquer an entire month's worth of laundry.

When you finish hours later, you can actually feel a certain animated bald guy giving you two-arms-crossed in approval of Nick's bright and shiny apartment. Exhausted, you both flop down on the couch, clinking together the necks of two ice-cold beers.

"Thank you so much," he says, and gives you a beer-soaked kiss. His spirits are ten times higher than when you arrived.

"Anytime," you say, leaning a tired head on his shoulder. "Snowboarding tomorrow?"

"Sorry," he says. "Can't. I just got a text from Russ. They need an extra guy for basketball tomorrow, so I said I'd play."

You've got *to be fucking kidding.*

"Next weekend, for sure." He kisses the top of your head.

Turn to section 181.

216

From section 244...

Nearing the end of another boring Monday, you're dreading the thought of heading back to the craziness of Christmas crowds at the mall to find a dress for Nick's office party.

You could just wear a dress you already have that he's never seen, but it's far more important you find the perfect one to upstage his female coworkers - you know, like the mature, secure woman you are.

Ten minutes before five, you receive an e-mail from Nick. It's titled: *FW: Holiday Party Clarification.* It's from his boss, reading, *There appears to be some ambiguity regarding Friday's holiday party. Despite the rumors, employees are not permitted to bring guests to this function. Sorry for any confusion.*

Nick adds a personal note that says, "I hope you're still buying a dress because I'm taking you out on Saturday!"

Aren't you glad you're such an understanding girlfriend?

Turn to section 152.

217

From section 223...

Last night, you rushed home after an endless day of guiding reporters around a trade show.

In record time, you transformed yourself from sweaty and haggard into fresh, smooth and glossy for your date with Nick. And then you sat around and waited. Not wanting to bug him if he was trying to get out of the office, you waited for nearly an hour to call him. When you did, it rang three times and went to voicemail.

Two hours and two generous glasses of wine later, any "I had a long day, too" empathy you had went out the window.

You went to Rachel and Valerie's to distract yourself and ended up drinking more. Before long you stopped venting about how pissed off you were and began sharing fears that Nick's standing you up was a sign that his interest was waning. And a cowardly sign at that, which just made you angry again. By the time you passed out in your bed a few hours later, you were furious.

When you wake up this morning, thirsty and with a bit of a headache, you instantly remember Nick never showed last night. You stand up, grumble, mope and curse some more before your phone rings. Nick's name shows on the Caller ID.

Oh, good. Maybe he's calling to let you know he's running fourteen hours late.

To give him a piece of your mind, turn to section 237.
To give him the silent treatment, turn to section 246.

218

From section 181...

You and Nick have a pretty comfortable communication pattern going on. You talk nearly every day, and send daily texts and e-mails when you're both busy.

In the last four days, though... You've left him two voicemails, an e-mail and a text, none of which he's returned.

Not a peep.

You're lying on your bed next to Rachel, just like in high school. You do it every now and again, only now you drink wine instead of soda, and Rachel isn't sneaking out your bedroom window to smoke cigarettes on the roof - she's rolling a joint. Just as you finish telling her that Nick's been incommunicado, your phone chirps to alert you to a text.

That's kind of a peep.

sorry. been busy. c tomorrow, reads his message. You show it to Rachel.

"Too busy for full sentences and proper grammar or too busy to talk to his girlfriend?" she asks.

"Be nice! You know what it's like getting ready for a vacation. It's chaos."

"Sure, if you're a woman. How hard can it be for a guy? You said he has his passport, he bought clothes - I'm guessing graphic tees, a few pair of board shorts and flip flops - and he booked his ticket, right? How much else could he need to do?"

"He's probably finishing up a lot of work at the office."

"Aw. You're so cute," she says, tilting her head. "Sorry, babe, but I think the writing's on the wall. En español."

"Then translate, Cha Cha."

"He's all but ignoring you just days before a drunken bender in the tropics with his college buddies." She sips her wine, shaking her head. When she sees you haven't caught on, she says, "He's gonna break up with you."

You love Rachel, and you can see why she might think tomorrow's goodbye dinner with Nick may be your Last Supper, but you know you guys are happy and that he's going to miss you on his trip.

"Don't believe me?" Rachel asks in response to your eye roll. "Tell him my theory tomorrow night."

To let her think what she wants, turn to section 227.
To prove her wrong, turn to section 220.

219

From section 148...

It can't hurt to ask, right?

It's not like you just started dating. Besides, you'd love to show off your hot new boyfriend to family, friends, and relatives who look at you sympathetically when you show up solo to a family function – right before they sit you at the kiddie table.

You spring the subject on Nick before he leaves your apartment for work.

"What'chya doin' next Saturday?" you ask as you straighten his tie.

"No plans for me. You've got that party for your parents, right?"

You smile widely.

"You want me to go," he says.

"Would you? My mom asked me. She really wants to meet you."

"I don't think so, babe. I think it might be a little soon, don't you?"

"It's not that soon. We've been together for a while now. And it's a special occasion."

"Exactly." He kisses your cheek and walks toward the front hall. "With all of your relatives. That's extra pressure in a situation already full of it."

You follow behind him. "Please? Do it for me?"

"Sorry. I've rushed into that stuff before and it's never a good outcome. Don't you want to take things slowly? Do it right?"

"I guess so," you say with a small pout.

"Thanks for understanding. I gotta go or I'm gonna be late." With a quick kiss, he's out the door.

Feeling a little rejected, you spend the rest of the day thinking up excuses to give your parents as to why he's not coming.

Winner: His family just happens to be having a party of their own that night. *What a coincidence!*

Turn to section 250.

220

From section 218...

When Nick arrives to pick you up, you're simultaneously happy to see him and sad to know this is the last time for a whole week. Still, you're determined not to let it ruin your night.

"Hey stranger," you say, sliding into his passenger seat. "I feel like I haven't seen you in ages."

He gives you weak smile.

"I'm just teasing." You put a reassuring hand on his arm. "I'm sure this week has been nuts for you."

Nick doesn't say a word. He just stares out the windshield.

"So, are we going?" you ask cautiously, even though you're pretty sure you already know the answer. Rachel was right.

"We should talk."

He proceeds to give you a seemingly well-rehearsed speech about how - even though he thinks you're beautiful, smart and funny - he's just not in a place where he wants to be serious right now. He thinks it's best the two of you take a break.

As surprised as you are to hear this, in spite of Rachel's prophetic warning, you suppose you may have been coming on a little strong lately. And it's just a break - if you're cool about it, he should relax.

Of course, in the back of your head, you hear Valerie telling you a break is just half of a break up. And Rachel cursing.

To take a break, turn to section 222.
To break up, turn to section 229.

221

From section 306...

It's been six months since you and Nick had the big talk about marriage.

A lot of women in your position would probably have walked away from the situation – cut their losses – but not you.

Lots of guys say they don't want to get married. It's like the party line taught to them by their friends, brothers and uncles. Sooner or later, they all end up married. So you decide to let Nick warm to the idea gradually rather than throw away the last two years together over one conversation.

When he comes home from work tonight, you're setting the table for dinner, musing to yourself over how proud you are for being more fight than flight on this one.

"Perfect timing," you say with a warm smile. "Dinner's ready."

He looks at you dumbly for a moment and then lets his laptop bag drop from his shoulder.

"Can we talk first?" He won't look you in the eye, and a heavy feeling spreads through your stomach.

"Sure." You sit next to each other on the couch. "What's going on?"

His face is pale. "I thought I knew what I was going to say." *Gulp.* "But now..." *Gulp.*

"Say something before I puke, okay?"

"Upfront, I want to say I'm sorry and I, I did *not* plan this." Your stomach hits the floor. "I met someone else."

"What? Who?" Despite feeling like you were tasered with 50,000 volts of electricity, you're surprisingly calm.

"One of my clients. We met a month ago during a new business pitch."

"A month ago?" You stand up. So much for calm. "And you've been seeing her since?"

"It just..."

"I *will* punch you in the face if you finish that sentence."

"I don't know what happened." To his credit, he looks genuinely distressed. Then you remember he was inside someone else's vagina and stop caring about how he feels. "I just thought she was exciting. I-I had to see if there was anything there. It got out of control and now..."

"Go ahead, Mr. Excitement. Now what?"

"She's pregnant."

Your stomach seeps through the floor and drapes itself over your downstairs neighbors' couch.

"*What?*" you scream - shriek, really. "And she's having it."

He nods.

"Well, I guess she's out of luck if she's expecting Daddy to marry Mommy."

He's quiet.

"You're going to marry *her*? What happened to *never*? To 'isn't a lifelong commitment enough?'"

"I meant that at the time. But I don't know now. It just feels like the right thing-"

"You are unbelievable! *Get out!*"

Incredulous, he says, "Are you serious?"

"No, hang out. We can pick baby names!" You grit your teeth. "Get out. Right now." He stands and you all but shove him toward the door, right into the hall. You heave his laptop out after him, hearing a satisfying crunch when it hits the floor. You lock the deadbolt.

"What about my stuff?" he yells through the closed door.

"I'll send it to you!" you yell back. "In the meantime, ask your baby mama to find you some *exciting* new clothes."

By week's end, you've changed the locks, packed up his things, except what you want to keep (or just don't want him to keep) and have it delivered to his office - in boxes with "CHEATER" written all over them in thick black marker.

You didn't *mean* to.

It just sorta happened.

-END-

222

From sections 220 and 226...

What's that old expression? It seemed like a good idea at the time? That sums up your decision to grant Nick a relationship vacation before he left on his week of Mexican debauchery.

You spent the first two days after he left feeling pretty good about the situation, convincing yourself he'd come back missing you like crazy and sorry he suggested a break at all. You also didn't tell Rachel or Valerie and did a great job of avoiding them (and reality).

By Day Four, insecurity and imagination got the better of you. You couldn't sleep, wondering what (and who) Nick might be doing.

On Day Five, you were getting ready to leave the office when Valerie sent you an e-mail titled: *You REALLY need to see this.* The belly flop your stomach did was your intuition's way of telling you that as much as you needed to see it, you didn't want to.

Her messages reads: *Open the attachment and answer your phone.*

You obey, with the fleeting hope you just opened a Trojan horse and not a game-changer. Right in front of you is a picture of Nick - in a pool with a random blonde in a barely-there bikini sitting on his shoulders, wrestling with another couple. You want to hurl. You answer your phone without taking your eyes off the screen or even saying hello.

"That's him, right?" asks Val.

"Where'd you get this?" you ask.

"My brother's at my parents' place for reading week. It's from his Facebook page. He doesn't know *her*, but the other girl lives in his dorm." She pauses. "There's a lot more. Same girl, but different days. I'm sorry."

Not as sorry as you are, of course.

You hang up and lock your office door.

You call in sick for two days, which you spend holed up in your apartment.

You came clean with your friends about Nick's freedom pass and they've been kind not to give you a hard time. You've even started to feel a little better, thanks to Valerie's refusal to send you more pictures. And Rachel forcing you to unfriend him on Facebook to prevent digital stalking.

Rachel did her thing and had the phone company block him from calling you, and deleted all traces of him from your phone. Same thing with your e-mail accounts.

Now, instead of turning into a blubbering baby or playing coy and trying to win him back, you get to disappear and let him wonder what happened to you.

Genius.

-END-

223

From sections 208...

You meet up with Valerie for lunch and an update on her new beau, Steven the artist.

She's taken to forwarding you and Rachel candid shots she takes of him when she thinks he's not looking. He's hot, no doubt about it.

As soon as the server's gone with your orders, you pounce. "So, how's Stevie?"

"Gay," she replies, matter-of-factly.

"*What?*" Even people walking on the street stop to look at you. "No he's not. Is he? Why do you think so?"

A smile plays at the corner of her lips. "For starters, he hasn't tried to get my clothes off yet - not even a little under-the-sweater action."

You nod sympathetically. "I'd make the jump from gentleman - or breast-man - to homosexual, too."

"He likes Maroon 5."

"Lots of straight guys like Maroon 5."

"How many of them have you slept with?"

You think for a moment. "Okay, none, but that's circumstantial."

"And this?" She tosses the morning paper in front of you. It's neatly folded to the male-to-male sex ads in the back.

Dead center is an ad for a male escort; and there's no denying the ruggedly sexy man - in a teeny towel, with godly hair and dewy skin - is Steven. Only the name accompanying the picture is "Jasper."

You resist giggling, not sure this actually classifies as funny...yet. "He's a struggling artist," you say. "Maybe he just modeled for extra money."

She points to herself. "I had the very same thought. So I called the number."

Thank you! "And?"

"He answered."

You can no longer contain your laughter. Val explains that she's fine with it as it clears the Sweater Kittens of blame.

"Before I forget." She pulls a copy of Them Weekly from of her bag. "For you."

"I'm good, thanks."

"You have a copy?"

"Nah. Just taking a break from that stuff."

Knowing you love to gossip about strangers you refer to by first name, she asks, "Why?"

You suck on your straw and try to avoid eye contact. "Not a lot of time."

She gives you a flat look. "Too busy with your humanitarian work?"

You sigh and explain your conversation with Nick the night before.

"That's bullshit!" she says. "And so what if he doesn't like 'that stuff'? We do!"

Attempts to convince her you're not doing it for Nick are futile.

"You can't see it through my sunglasses, but I'm rolling my eyes," she says. "Mind if I call Jasper? I want him to know he's not the only one living a lie."

Turn to section 217.

224

From section 227...

You wake up this morning with a huge grin. Nick comes home today.

For the past week, you've kept busy with work, yoga, and drinking a lot of wine with the girls. Still, the days dragged on and you can't wait to see him.

He's supposed to come over to your place mid-afternoon, so you've been busy cleaning, shopping and preparing everything you need to cook his welcome home dinner. When you still haven't heard from him by four o'clock, you can't take it anymore and call him.

"Hello," he answers, and it's so good to hear his voice.

"Hey!" you exclaim. "Welcome back. How was it?"

"Great. I think I need a liver transplant, but it was a good time."

"I can't wait to hear all about it. What's your ETA so I can start dinner?"

"Actually," he says, and your heart drops immediately. "I'm bagged. I don't think I'm going to make it tonight."

"But I have a whole feast planned that's guaranteed to make you forget seven days of the same buffet food." He doesn't say anything. "Okay, how about tomorrow?"

"Tomorrow's no good. I'm having dinner with my sister."

You're overcome with a feeling somewhere between dread and butterflies.

"So when would you like to get together?"

"I'm sorry. I'm coming," he says, giving you whiplash. "I'll be there in an hour."

Turn to section 228.

225

From section 226...

"Yeah," you tell Nick. "I actually agree. A break is a good idea."

"It is?" he asks, noticeably skeptical.

"For sure. There are a couple of guys I've been meaning to sleep with, so this would be the perfect opportunity."

"Seriously?"

"No, you jerk! Of course not seriously. Do you really think I'm going to give you a seven-day all-inclusive Hoochie Pass and then welcome you and all of your newly acquired STIs back to my bed if you decide that's what you want? Not gonna happen."

With that and good slam of his front door, you're on your way home - and wishing him a serious case of Montezuma's Revenge.

And crabs.

-END-

226

From section 181...

"Dude, this is going to be awesome*!*" says Nick, before he hangs up the phone and rejoins you in his living room.

"What's going to be awesome?" you ask him with faux cheer.

"Oh. Mexico." He picks up the remote. "Wanna check out that Bond movie we missed?"

Nice try.

"So, about this trip," you say. "Were you thinking about telling me you changed your mind about taking me along?"

Direct hit. You watch Nick scramble for a response and wonder which of you is more uncomfortable.

"It's just-" He scrubs his hand over his face. "Not all of the guys are bringing girlfriends, so they're worried it's going to become a couples' trip."

"A bunch of couples at a wedding does sound weird."

"You know what I mean."

"No, I don't think I do. What do the guys worry will happen, or should I say won't happen, if the girlfriends are there?"

"Guy stuff."

"Drunken, girl-scoping, all-night partying guy stuff?"

"Spoken like a girlfriend." He points at you as if to say, *Exactly!*

"Unless you want to participate in said guy stuff, what does it matter?"

Silence.

"Nice," you tell him, standing up.

"Hang on," he says, gently taking your hand before you can walk away. "I've been thinking that maybe while I'm gone, we should, you know, take a break."

Where the hell is this coming from?

Did Nick just downgrade your relationship status from Happy to Needs a Break? You thought things were going great. You don't fight, you're not crowding him, and you always have a good time together - in and out of the bedroom.

What the fuck are you supposed to say here?

Maybe he's getting a lot of pressure from his pals to be unattached while they're away. "Like the old days," or some other such bullshit. Guys can be jerks like that. Of course, he may just be using them as a convenient scapegoat.

What to do, what to do?

To give it a break, turn to section 222.
To break up, turn to section 225.

227

From section 218...

When you left Rachel's the other night, you couldn't help but worry she might be right that Nick's sudden lack of communication is foreshadowing of your upcoming life as a single woman.

It still bugged you a lot at work yesterday, your mind a tennis match between annual budget forecasting and imagining what it would be like to go back to solo Saturday nights. But then he picked you up for dinner tonight, greeting you with a lingering kiss, and you began to relax.

By the time you place your orders at your bon voyage dinner, you're back to your old secure self. He tells you about his last-minute vacation preparation errands, like indoor tanning sessions (apparently guys do that, too), the search for the perfect sunglasses, and late nights finishing month-end reports and preparing transition materials for co-workers covering for him while he's away.

Take that, Rachel!

After dinner, you go back to his place and watch him pack the last of his things for his 7:00 a.m. flight. Then you give him a proper send-off (*wink-wink*) as a protective measure against bikini-clad babes and frisky bridesmaids. You say a groggy goodbye at 5:00 a.m. when he drops you off at your place en route to the airport.

The moment he pulls away from the curb, you miss him.

Turn to section 224.

228

From section 224...

The next hour waiting for Nick is the most agonizing stretch of time you've ever endured.

You recognize this old familiar feeling as one that shows up right before someone rips your heart out. You wonder if it's anything like how elephants feel before they go off to die alone in the jungle.

You want to call the girls, but if you're wrong, you'll have riled everyone up for nothing and look like a jerk. Of course, if you're right, they'll be camped outside your door until he leaves, ready to console you with hard liquor.

Instead, you walk in circles around your living room and touch up your hair and makeup ten times. If he is thinking about dumping you, flawlessly applied foundation will surely change his mind.

When Nick arrives, your heart swells a little at how good he looks with tanned skin and a week's worth of scruff on his cheeks. He doesn't look tired, more like really uncomfortable.

He walks in and gives you a brief hug and a kiss on the cheek before walking past you to sit on the couch. You sit next to him, but keep your body angled straight ahead, unable to look at him. After a long silence, he finally speaks.

"So," he says in one long exhale. "I did a lot of thinking while I was gone."

"About?" You stare at the Monet reprint mounted on the wall.

"About us. I think we should split up."

The words are an instant migraine, pounding painfully as he rambles on about how you're a great girl and a lot of fun, but he just doesn't want to be in a serious relationship or lead you on. It's the script guys carry around in their wallets next to condoms: *In Case of Emergency, Break Up.* You know there's no point in trying to change his mind, so you let him finish and watch him go.

Five minutes later, Rachel and Valerie walk through your door, carrying a full bottle of Jaeger. You do shots and take turns cursing "that asshole" until you finally pass out.

-END-

229

From section 220...

You really, really, really don't want to end your relationship with Nick, but it's better you do it now than have him do it later.

"I don't think so," you tell him once you gather your resolve.

"I'm sorry?" he asks, eyes wide. He looks genuinely surprised at your response.

"I don't do breaks," you say plainly. "Particularly not breaks that involve you taking a guilt-free jaunt to Mexico and then coming back to decide if you want to be with me. You're either in or out - so I'm out."

With that, you wish him a safe trip and climb out of the car as gracefully as possible before you can say anything stupid and ruin a perfect exit.

-END-

230

From section 197...

You drag yourself from your Nick-filled bed for a quick shower. Or a quickie *in* the shower given he joins you.

An hour later, you arrive at The Spoon. Rachel and Val are at your usual table in utter hysterics.

"What's so funny?" you ask, draping your purse strap over your chair.

Tears stream down Rachel's face. She's still laughing, but there's no sound.

"She finally found my porn name," says Valerie.

"And the winner is?" you ask.

"Jodie Fister," Rachel manages. "I googled it and it's wide open." They give in to a new wave of laughter and you smile apologetically to the elderly woman eating alone at the table next to you. She winks.

Valerie wipes at her mascara under her glasses. "You made it!"

"Of course," you say, as though blowing them off never occurred to you.

"Whatever." Rachel looks up at the ceiling. "I can just see you - lying there, brow all furrowed, wondering if we'd buy the 'I'm not feeling well' excuse."

"Shut up." You laugh because she knows you all too well.

"How'd you get away?" Val asks.

"I told him I miss my friends and, frankly, could use a little me-time."

"So he's waiting at your apartment, then?" asks Rachel, waggling her brows. You smirk and flag down the waitress.

Two hours later, with a full belly and up-to-date on your friends' lives, you return home to find your gorgeous, still naked boyfriend in your bed.

Turn to section 231.

231

From sections 246 and 230...

Nick's very close with his friends and talks about them all the time. Especially Candy - short for Candace.

You've never met her, but she sounds blonde.

"Candy has the coolest car," or "Candy went skydiving last weekend." Definitely better than, "Candy has, like, forty-five bikinis," or "Candy can put both legs behind her head."

You suppose.

"Is that a stage name?" Rachel asks over lunch when you fess up about Nick's sweet tooth.

"Exactly!" You throw your hands in the air. "It's like a porn-star time bomb."

"You're mean," says Valerie. "You're stereotyping based on her name?"

"Yup."

"Of course." Rachel grins wickedly and elbows you. "Think she can get her legs behind her head?"

Gah!

"Help me," you plead. "I'll lose my job if I don't stop obsessing."

"Change the subject when he mentions her," suggests Valerie. "He'll get the hint."

"And until then she obsesses over the human pretzel?" asks Rachel. "Fuck. That. Noise!"

Valerie straightens her glasses. "Okay, Mistress Miyagi, what would you do?"

"Act like you want to be friends with her." She leans on her elbows. "Be all 'Hey, this Candy sounds flexible - I mean fun - we should go out.' If he's all for it, you're in the clear. If he wigs out...those bags under your eyes might not be for nothing."

At dinner with Nick, it takes less than ten minutes for him to mention her.

"Candy's going to Brazil for two weeks," he says. "How awesome does that sound?"

"Pretty awesome," you say cheerfully, hoping he doesn't sense the actual reason for your enthusiasm. "Vacation?"

"Sport Illustrated shoots the next Swim Suit Issue there. She's a model."

Did your heart just stop?

Yep, Somebody get the paddles.

To let Nick keep his friends close, turn to section 269.
To keep the Brazilian bikini model closer, turn to section 233.

232

From section 253...

That Valerie is one clever little minx.

The three of you conspire to plot a picture-perfect scenario to make Nick seriously contemplate a life without you - since he doesn't appear to be doing it on his own. And because her brain just works that way, Val even puts together a phony paper trail to support *Operation Future,* which you set in motion tonight.

Nick meets you in the lobby of your office building after work, when you just happen to get a call from "the receptionist" saying she just accepted a personal package for you. Nick waits while you hide out on the 2nd floor for five minutes and take out the large manila envelope already stuffed in your bag.

You make sure he sees the words "Happy St. Patty's Day!" written in green marker and then carefully ignore the envelope on the way to your place. You walk in the door and casually toss it on the kitchen counter before kicking off your shoes.

Three, two...

"Okay, so can we talk about the St. Patrick's Day package you got in July?" Nick asks, eyeing the package curiously.

You smile coyly. "You know people are always after me lucky charms."

"I wanna know," he whines.

"It's just some stuff Valerie sent over about Ireland." You open the envelope and pull out maps and brochures with handwritten notes from Val, along with snapshots of a gorgeous, Irish-looking house. "She and Rachel are going in a couple of months."

"And she wanted to rub it in."

"Not exactly..."

Just as Val prepped you, you spin a web about how she and Rachel are taking six-month sabbaticals to travel to Ireland and stay with Valerie's aunt and uncle in that big beautiful house in the pictures.

You say you didn't think anything would come of it - those two are always planning imaginary trips that never happen - but Rachel's current contract was coming to a close and Val's brother offered to cover her clients, so they started making plans. And when, funnily enough, your boss brought up how understaffed your Irish subsidiary is, you joked that you could probably help them out.

"Anyways." Big finish! "If I pay my housing expenses, they'll get me a temporary work visa and cover my travel. I made the mistake of telling Valerie and now she's hounding me to go."

You've purposely kept focused on the glossy, green materials in front of you rather than look Nick in the eye, but you see his body stiffen in your periphery.

"So," he says slowly. "Are you considering it?"

You look at him. "No. I don't know. Not really?" *You are way too good at this.* "It's kind of a once in a lifetime opportunity, you know? Can't help but think about it a little." You shake your head. "It's crazy. Who picks up her life and moves it for six months?"

Nick stands pensively for a moment. You're pretty sure you've got him right where Val wants him.

Turn to section 11.

233

From section 231...

Breathe. Do not show fear.

"Candy sounds like a lot of fun. I bet we'd totally get along!" you say with as much enthusiasm as you can muster. "Hey! Let's have drinks with her when she gets back. I'd love to get to know her."

Nick coughs loudly and pounds on his chest with his fist. "Went down the wrong pipe," he finally chokes out.

"Have some water." You hand him his glass. "So what do you think about drinks with Candy?"

"Um, maybe." He gulps the water. "She's pretty busy with her modeling - in and out of town all the time. I'll, uh, definitely mention it to her, though. How was work?"

Not exactly the, "Yeah, you two would be total BFFs! Let me set something up," you were hoping to hear.

For a brief moment, you wish he'd choked.

Turn to section 268.

234

From sections 250 and 172...

You try everything you can think of to cheer Nick up.

You offer suggestions on how to turn the situation at work around. He says you don't understand because you don't work in "the industry."

You ask if we wants to see that new action flick with Jessica Biel, even though it will make you want to buy acting lessons for her and ass implants for yourself. No sale. You offer to order pizza with hot peppers on his half, when you know the juice will seep over to your side and ruin it. He's not hungry. You finally convince him to relax and watch the hockey game while you rub his shoulders and scratch his head. That he accepts - for over an hour.

When he cheers for Boston's shootout victory, you think he may be turning a corner and suggest moving to the bedroom. He tells you he isn't really in the mood and asks if he can sleep alone tonight.

Almost glad for the reprieve, especially now that the beer's gone, you leave your car at his place and cab home. En route, Val texts to ask if you want to get a drink.

You tell her no thanks, you're not really in the mood.

Turn to section 239.

235

From section 210...

"Mayo?" says Rachel as she bites into her sandwich. "Jealous of my cellulite-free ass or something?"

Following a totally embarrassing attempt to surprise Nick at his office, you grabbed your picnic basket and headed to Rachel after all.

"I'm sorry," you tell her with a frown.

"I'm kidding," she says with her mouth full. "It's great. Thanks for the surprise."

Rachel tells you she found *the* song she's been hunting down for days to fit a particular scene. You try to listen, but your mind keeps floating back to Nick.

"Do you always invite people to lunch and ignore them?" she asks, poking you with her potato salad fork. "What's eating you?"

You share the details of your trip to Nick's office, including the fact that, on your arrival, the receptionist had to call him out of a client meeting - with his boss - to see you.

"So this is a second-handwich," she says with a wink, always trying to lighten the mood. "Was he mad?"

"Not mad exactly, but definitely not happy. I'll go with annoyed."

"Yikes. Well, you said he was having problems with his boss. Maybe he was worried it would look bad."

"Possibly."

"Or maybe he got a glimpse of his wife dropping off his lunch after taking the twins to pre-school. Are you going to finish your sandwich?"

Turn to section 181.

236

From section 214...

It's September and you're Sunday-mourning the end of summer when you arrive at Nick's house. He, on the other hand, is noticeably happy. He sweeps you up into a hug and your cheek rubs against the rough fabric of his Patriots jersey but you don't mind - you're thrilled he's so happy to see you.

"Sunday Football is back, babe!" He hands you...your very own jersey.

Your dad is big on football and hockey, hoarding the family television most nights throughout fall and winter. You often watched with him growing up, so you have a pretty good understanding of how football works, you just aren't really a fan.

That's not to say you've never leveraged your knowledge of when to cheer and when to shout expletives at the screen to score points with the guy you were dating. The obvious cause and effect of this is that you've watched a lot of football, but it always makes them happy and gives you time to spend together that you might not have otherwise had.

Still, looking down at the polyester straight jacket in your hand, you wonder if you should play for Team Nick or request a trade to Lunch with the Girls.

To suit up, turn to section 147.
For early retirement, turn to section 97.

237

From section 217...

"And you didn't even bother to call me? What is that?" are the final words in the verbal assault you just launched on your inconsiderate boyfriend.

The whole tirade took roughly fifteen Mississippis and you're out of breath when you finish.

"Are you done?" Nick asks with a steely edge in his voice.

How dare he get condescending with *you*?

"I'm sorry I couldn't call you last night to let you know I wasn't coming," he says. "Unfortunately, I had to rush to the emergency room to be with my sister and niece, who broke her arm at the park."

Fuck...

You scramble for a way to backpedal. "Well, you could have called me from there. I was worried."

Yeah, worried.

"I was in such a hurry to get to the hospital that I forgot my phone. I don't have your phone number memorized, so I couldn't call you. I wasn't terribly worried about it, though, because I figured my girlfriend would give me the benefit of the doubt. Apparently, I don't know her as well as I thought. Lana is fine, by the way. Thanks for asking."

Fuck. Fuck. Fuck.

-END-

238

From sections 170 and 240...

While Nick cooks dinner for you at his place, you grab a photo album from his bookshelf. Plain sight and all that. You giggle at knobby knees, unfortunate clothing, and his high school ponytail. You laugh non-stop until you come to a snapshot of Nick kissing an ex-girlfriend.

She's really gorgeous.

The three B's: Blonde. Built. Blue eyes.

You wonder what her name is. She looks like a chick whose name starts with a hard "k" - like Katie, or Krissy, or Kylie. The really perky-sweet type that girls say they hate but secretly want to be more like.

You follow Nick and Hard K enjoying themselves - and each other - everywhere from restaurants to weddings to amusement parks. Spring, summer, winter and fall. Quite the happy couple, they're always laughing, smiling, hugging...

"Did I hear laughing?" Nick appears behind you. When he sees you holding the album he blurts out, "That's a *really* old album."

Honing in on his nervousness, you point to a particularly pretty close-up of her. "Sweetie, who's she?"

Oh, it's a hard "k," all right. Candace.

As in Candy.

As in *Brazilian bikini model*.

Oh. My. God.

He never mentioned they dated. You'd have remembered.

To call him out, turn to section 256.
To keep your mouth shut, turn to section 263.

239

From section 234...

Following the recent drama at work, Nick's been trying to get back into his boss' good graces by putting in a lot of extra hours.

You've barely seen him over the last few weeks, so to say that you're really excited for your day trip to Dodge Ridge would be the understatement to end understatements. You call him to confirm your plans for the morning and see what you should pack for your first snowboarding lesson.

"I hate disappointing you," he says. "But with all the time I've been spending at the office, my apartment looks like a crash site and I could barely drag myself home tonight. I think I need the weekend to get my act together. Do a month's worth of laundry. Call Hazmat. Know what I mean?"

You do understand. PR isn't ranked as one of the most stressful jobs on the planet for nothing, but you're already pouting inside because you won't get to see him. Again.

Unless…

Unless you could find a way to salvage the weekend with a win/win compromise.

Offer to help him with his chores, turn to section 215.
Offer to bring him dinner Sunday night, turn to section 248.

240

From section 268...

You and Valerie feel like you're in a surreal episode of Top Model where you get ten minutes to put together the best outfit possible with the chaos you're given.

You successfully style Rachel in a striped shirt, polka dot skirt, green hiking boots, a bow tie, sombrero and a feather boa, and walk (slowly) ten blocks to a crowded sports bar. After a few hours, the novelty wears off - probably because Rachel is blocking passes left and right despite looking like an acid trip-inspired Halloween costume.

You've done a pretty good job of distracting yourself up to now. Your friends haven't even had to mock you for unsubtly checking your phone. Probably because you turned it off, deciding it would be sheer torture otherwise.

Of course, as soon as you say goodbye to them in the elevator, you take the phone from your purse and turn it on, hoping you have a message from Nick.

You don't.

Not even a text.

You're more than a little disappointed, but you knew it wasn't a sure thing. Either way, you're more struck with a sense of pride in yourself for going out and making a memory with your friends.

You go to sleep content and wake in the morning to find an e-mail from him. He says he's sorry he didn't get a chance to call last night, that he misses you and can't wait to see you when he gets home.

Turn to section 238.

241

From section 149...

You and Nick are running errands when you get stuck behind a wedding procession exiting a church. There are at least 100 people out there and an endless line of town cars blocking the road. Nick is particularly annoyed by this delay.

"I don't get it," he says, shaking his head at the people. "What's the point?"

"Of the big wedding hoopla?" you ask.

"Of marriage in general. It's such a stupid tradition."

The thing about avoiding the subject of marriage is that it can take a while to learn your boyfriend hates the idea of "'til death do us part."

"Well, I think *big* weddings are a waste, but what's wrong with wanting to commit to someone?"

"It's not the 1500s. You can do it without a contract making it as hard as possible for the other to walk away when things don't work out."

When. Romantic.

"So no marriage for you then?" you ask calmly.

"I seriously doubt it."

Even if it's not a never, it's still disconcerting. You're not exactly racing to the altar or dreaming of Nick in a tux (at least not for that purpose), but you're fairly sure you want to get married someday. And you'd hate to waste the pretty on a guy who'll never budge.

Still, you've known lots of guys who've said exactly what he has, only to wind up hitched with a kid on the way within two or three years.

To see what happens, turn to section 250.
To decide what happens, turn to section 173.

242

From section 311...

"Honestly?" you ask.

He looks at you warily. "Of course, honestly."

"Okay, I hate camping," you admit. Better to tell him the truth now than have him surprise you with The Grand Canyon for your honeymoon.

"Really?" *Yep, there's his disappointed face.* "What do you hate about it?"

"Everything." You fill him in on your childhood experience, including l'eau d' trout.

"Come on," he says. "That was years ago. Camping with me will be much more fun than camping with your brother. And I'll be the only one climbing into your sleeping bag tonight, I promise."

"Okay." You force a smile and try to push your reservations (for a nice bed and breakfast!) to the back of your mind. "I'll try."

"That's my girl. Now let's get this tent up. I'm dying to fish."

Oh joy.

In the morning, you awake from the worst two hours of sleep in your entire life, and peek outside the tent. Nick is packing up the car. Did you sleep until Sunday? Unlikely. Did he decide he hates camping, too, and now he's whisking you away to a spa? Probably not.

"What's going on?" you ask grumpily.

"Good morning, sunshine," he says, his tone sharp and sarcastic, without even the hint of a smile. "You can rejoice. We're leaving."

"Leaving? But I said I would try."

"And when did you plan to start? Because it certainly wasn't last night when you sulked about my choice of getaway, complained the camp site was on the wrong side of the trees for sunset, refused to eat dinner because it was 'gross,' or sat in the car until bedtime to avoid mosquitoes."

Were you really such a spoiled brat last night? Yes. You definitely were. "Well.

What do you want to do now? It's still our anniversary."

"I'm not really feeling all that celebratory today, so why don't we just head back to the city? And don't you worry. I've learned my lesson. I won't surprise you again."

Despite your sore back, you feel awful for ruining his weekend. Of course, you did get sprung from hell early for bad behavior, so it's kind of a wash.

Happy Noniversary!

Turn to section 257.

243

From section 36…

You spend the night in your childhood bed and have breakfast with your parents before heading home to tell Nick what you've decided.

Or at least, what you think you've decided.

Okay, it's actually a test.

So fucking what?

All's fair in love and whatever.

You walk in the door to find Nick folding the same laundry from the night before. He looks up at you, checks for puffy eyes and then gives you one of those heartbreaking grins of his.

"You came back to me," he says, tossing a folded tee shirt on a stack and moving toward you.

You meet him halfway and hug him hello. "I did," you say, breathing in that very uniquely Nick smell, worried it'll be the last time.

"Are you…staying?"

"Think so."

"That's unsettlingly indecisive." He releases you and starts his usual nervous fidgeting: crossing and uncrossing his arms, rubbing a hand over the back of his neck, the whole nine.

"I don't *need* to get married." He relaxes significantly. "But I still want security. I don't want a contract that says you'll never leave me, but I'd feel better if we had measures in place to protect us if something happens to the other."

He looks puzzled. "Like life insurance?"

"And wills. And power of attorney. Just imagine Val and Rachel fighting over who gets to take me off life support." Done. Exactly as planned. You wait for his reaction.

"You mean…down the road. Like years from now."

"Well, I don't mean tomorrow, but we've already been together for years, Nick. If we're staying together, if we're committed to each other, it's the responsible thing to do."

Nick's a big, strapping guy. Rarely does he look frazzled or weak. Right now, he looks like he'd cut out his own liver with a ladle to get out of this conversation, which tells you everything you need to know.

You sigh. "Don't worry about it." You can't help your frown.

Whiplashed, he says, "I am so lost."

"You've never thought about that stuff?"

"No, but…who does?"

"I do. Not all the time, but it crosses my mind. Because when I think of the future, I see us. What do you see?"

He tilts his head thoughtfully. After a beat, he says, "I guess I just don't think of the future that much."

You place a hand on each of his shoulders. "Yeah you do. You think about your career all the time. Where you want to live. Where you want to travel. But where am I in that?"

"What happened to 'not tomorrow?'"

"I meant it." And you did. "But you're asking for a huge compromise on something important to me when I don't even factor into your future. That's not fair."

He knows you're right.

You know you're right.

And then you and big, un-frazzled, always strong Nick cry and spend one last weekend together, mostly in bed, maturely figuring out how to go your separate ways.

-END-

244

From sections 249 and 248

Christmas is, hands down, your favorite time of year. Nick's, too.

Sharing each other's seasonal joy, you team up on shopping. After a few hours in the crowded mall, you're disheveled and weighed down with bags, searching the directory for a place to get a cold drink.

And that's when you hear an unfamiliar, singsong voice chime, "Hey, handsome. Funny running into you here!"

You spin around and come face-to-face with every mortal woman's nightmare: Super Fox. Like Candy, she's beautiful, blonde and built, but worse than that, she seems to have an invisible lighting crew and the superhuman ability to walk for hours in high heels. You smooth down your hair and adjust your pant leg over your running shoes.

"Super Fox!" replies Nick (okay, he called her Anna), sounding far more excited than you'd like. "How's it going?"

"Great," she says. "Just shopping for the Christmas party. I found the perfect dress!" You scan her pretty paper bags and can't help but notice the lingerie store logo screaming, "Picture me half naked." She extends her hand to you. "Hi, I'm Super Fox." (Okay, she called herself Anna.)

"Oh, man. I'm sorry," says Nick. "This is my girlfriend."

"You didn't tell me you have a girlfriend." She giggles. "I guess we'd have met at the party on Friday, though."

Funny, or maybe not so funny, Nick told you the office party was staff only.

"It's nice to meet you," you croak, like a frog next to a beautiful princess. "Will we meet your boyfriend at the party?"

"I don't have a boyfriend."

Of course not.

She waves goodbye with a perfectly manicured paw and you scramble to make sense of what just happened. What the hell? Why wouldn't he want you there? It doesn't…

Unless she's the reason!

"That's weird," says Nick, sweating a little. "I could swear we weren't allowed to bring dates."

To give him the benefit of the doubt, turn to section 216.
To tell him your doubts, turn to section 211.

245

From section 250...

You wait a moment to be sure he's finished before you speak.

"Wow," you say, stroking your hand down his back in a non-aggressive attempt at comfort. "I mean, what a little dick. You're calmer than I'd be."

"Thanks," he says, and you feel him relax, but just barely. Yeah, you're not gonna hover.

"I hope I'm not about to make your day worse, but Valerie called on the way over and she's got some serious man trouble. Tears and the whole bit. I told her I'd go there after I welcomed you home with this tasty beer."

"You know what," he says, gratefully accepting the six-pack. "That's totally okay. I'm not going to be great company anyway. How about I take you to dinner tomorrow?"

You beam at him. "Perfect."

He gives you a long, knee-buckling kiss and walks you to the door with plenty of time to salvage your Friday night by helping Rachel and Valerie get *into* some man trouble.

Turn to section 210.

246

From section 217...

A few moments later, your phone announces a new voicemail. You glare at it and press 'listen,' already mad at whatever bullshit excuse Nick has for bailing on you last night.

And then you couldn't feel like a bigger asshole.

"Hi, beautiful," his message begins. "You must be pissed or worried, or something." He sounds exhausted. "I'm really sorry I couldn't call last night. Lana broke her arm on the playground and I had to rush to the emergency room to be with Rory because my brother in law's out of town. I forgot my phone and I don't have your number memorized, so... I hope you understand. I'm gonna take a nap, but I'll call you in a couple of hours."

You've never been so happy you screened a call in your entire life. You can only imagine the words you'd say - and be unable to take back - had you answered the phone. Poor Lana.

Three hours later, you meet for lunch at the mall and pick out the perfect get well soon gift for his niece. You even send him off with a little something for her from you.

Of course you do. After all, you're a totally supportive and understanding girlfriend, right?

Turn to section 231.

247

From section 170...

Oh screw it!

You're being silly. Nick will be totally happy to hear your voice. You remember the name of the hotel he's staying at, look up the number online and call the front desk. You ask the clerk to connect you to Nick's room.

He picks up after the fourth ring.

"Hello?" he says, in a groggy, muffled voice.

"Hi," you respond enthusiastically. "It's me! You sound like you're sleeping."

"I am sleeping." He does not sound enthusiastic.

"At 10:00 p.m.? They must be running you ragged."

"No, 1:00 a.m. Toronto? Three hours ahead?"

Definitely not enthusiastic.

"Oh, my god. Time difference. Completely forgot. I'm sorry."

"Is everything okay?"

"Fine. I just..." You cringe. "Wanted to say hello."

"Hello. Can we talk when I get back? I need to be up really early."

"Sure. Okay. Goodnight."

"Goodnight."

You hang up the phone and flop back on your bed, mad at yourself for your late night phone-pas. So much for easing your anxiety.

Crap.

Turn to section 250.

248

From section 239...

You arrive at Nick's place on Sunday night carrying a bag of greasy Chinese food and beer.

He's waiting in the doorway as you step off the elevator, looking as happy to see you as you are to finally see him. He takes your bags and sets them on the hall table so he can lift you into a tight hug and give you a thorough kiss. Then he takes your hand and leads you through his now spotless apartment to the living room table. There sits a huge bouquet of red and orange Asiatic lilies.

"Secret admirer?" you ask.

"Probably a few, but those are for you. Read the card. I'll be right back with plates."

You open the small envelope implanted in the arrangement. "Thanks for understanding. You're the greatest. Nick."

You *are* the greatest.

Yay!

Turn to section 244.

249

From sections 263, 147 and 210...

You're *in love* with Nick.

For real.

For real, for real.

Often in the past, you'd have to consciously think about, and decide, whether or not you loved the guy you were dating. Usually after someone else brought up how long you'd been together. But this time there's no doubt about it.

It's "make him a mixed-tape, can't remember the last time you thought about another guy, overlook the fact he's a loud chewer" love.

You call him Pooky. He punctuates sentences with "Babe."

The thrill of becoming one of those girls you hate.

You often find yourself on the verge of blurting out the biggest of little words to him, always stopping short. Every girl you know has been conditioned to think being the first one to say, "I love you" is relationship suicide. And it usually is, but probably not with Nick.

Your keen powers of observation tell you he feels the same way about you.

To tell him, turn to section 172.
To keep it to yourself, turn to section 244.

250

From sections 241, 219 and 247...

Nick returns from a weeklong business trip in Toronto. You arrive at his apartment and present your weary traveler with a six-pack and a smile, planning on a relaxing evening of absolutely nothing.

And then waking up and doing all kinds of something.

He opens the door and you give him a few quick kisses followed by a hug and an enthusiastic, "I missed you!"

"Hey," he grumbles back. Not unfriendly, but he doesn't seem half as happy to see you as you are to see him.

Following him to the living room, you ask, "What's the matter?"

You sit on the couch, but Nick remains standing as he takes you through his trip. It's a little hard to follow since you still aren't quite sure what it is he actually does, but the gist is, a "douchebag" junior member of his team kept vital information from Nick prior to a big meeting, hoping he could present it himself and impress the execs - and he did. But, yada yada, it went south and made Nick look incompetent in front of the client and his boss. They lost the business.

Nick sags down next to you, his expression somewhere between anger and sulking.

Your heart says, "Help him! Be a supportive girlfriend."

Your head keeps directing your eyes to the door.

To make the best of it and cheer him up, turn to section 234.
To make an excuse and get out of there, turn to section 245.

251

From section 285…

"Okay," you tell Nick with a phony air of indifference as you pick up your phone.

"Okay what?"

"Don't come with me." You call Rachel and she answers on the second ring. "Hey. Plans tonight? Great. Meet me downstairs in twenty. It's time for my tattoo!"

"Finally!" she screams and you pull the phone away from your ear.

"You're doing it anyway?" Nick asks when you hang up.

"Yup." You put your phone in your purse and walk toward the door. "Your tacky girlfriend will be home later if you wanna drop by." With that and a smile, you're out the door.

Come nightfall, you're admiring the new friend fluttering on your shoulder when you hear a familiar knock.

That didn't take long.

You carefully arrange your robe around your shoulders before opening the door to Nick. He stands with his hands in his pockets and his head tilted slightly downward, a remorseful look on his face.

"What brings you by?" You flash him the smile of a woman satisfied with her choice.

"This isn't the butterfly conservatory?" he asks, looking at you from under long lashes.

You shake your head, but let him in. He follows you down the hall. You untie your belt and let the robe fall to the ground, leaving you naked with the exception of a small bandage protecting the pretty pigment.

You let him pull it back carefully. "Wow," he says. "It's actually really pretty."

"I know." You grab his hand and lead him to your bedroom. "Come on, I'll let you make it up to me, but I'll need to be on top."

Turn to section 254.

252

From section 98...

Judging from the sheen of your damp skin when you wake up this morning – dewy is one thing, but this is just gross – it's obvious summer is finally here! And uncharacteristically warm. Time for pints on patios, alignment-obliterating flip-flops, and most importantly, the beach!

First things first though, you need to dig the heavy, archaic air conditioning units you inherited from your grandmother out from the back of your closet and install them in your living room and bedroom windows.

You look forward to this chore about as much as you do your annual pap smear, but always reject your dad's offer to take care of it for you, proud you've got the pipes do it yourself - capable woman that you are.

Standing in front of your closet, you wince at the clothes and bags jammed in there precariously, ironically next to the closet organizer you bought two years ago and never installed. That's when you remember you have a big strong boyfriend.

Isn't this what they're for?

To DIY, turn to section 140.
To let Nick do it for you, turn to section 299.

253

From section 201…

You tell Nick you'll go with the flow - for now, but not forever.

You reiterate that you want to get married eventually and understand he isn't sure yet, but that you also don't want to stay together indefinitely with a question mark hanging over your heads. You give him nine months to meditate on whether marrying you is in his future.

What can you say? One year was too long and six months seemed too short. You'll have been together for three years by the deadline, so it seems appropriate. And, okay, maybe you took the average number of months it takes fictional couples to get engaged and multiplied it by ten, but you think that's actually pretty reasonable. You also feel you've done a good job at relaxing and keeping things as pressure-free as possible.

That is, up until now.

It's been seven months, three weeks and two days and he still hasn't brought it up. You figured he'd reach the six-month mark and come to his senses, but no, he's dragging it out. It's killing you - and soon, you'll be the one to crack.

"Give me the 'bed of your own making' and 'careful for what you bitch for' speeches," you tell Rachel and Valerie.

Rachel snorts. "I was actually going to say, 'grow up, go home and tell him that you gave him nine months too long, so snap to it or peace out.'"

"How are you not a motivational speaker?" Valerie asks her.

"Something about criminal activity and the fact no one can find a clean copy of that sex tape I made a few years ago." She looks you in the eye. "If he hasn't thought about this yet, he's an ass, and you should dump him on his."

Valerie gives a sad, half smile. "She's right. You have to call his bluff. Though, I'm not sure I'd go to DEFCON 2 just yet."

"Why not? It gives him six hours to respond before she dumps him."

"Or," says Val. "You could take advantage of the fact he *expects* you to be nice and diplomatic about it. Make him unwittingly give you what he doesn't yet realize he wants-slash-needs. And afterward…let him act like it was all his idea."

"Well, now you're speaking my language," says Rachel. "Canadian."

To go to DEFCON 2, turn to section 255.
To go to VALCON 1, turn to section 232.

254

From sections 251, 270, 266 and 279...

Some girls like Cabo, others Miami, but for you and your friends, it's all about The Vegas.

Every year, you, Rachel, Valerie and a few gal pals indulge in seven days of drinking, dancing and gambling during a whirlwind tour of Paris, Italy and Egypt - all on one strip. It's the highlight of your year!

That was before Nick, of course.

Things have been so great between you and, with the trip just two weeks away, you hate the thought of leaving him - even if it means amazing shopping at designer outlets that even *you* can get excited about, and legally walking around the city with a frozen daiquiri in your hand. Making the situation even harder, last night Nick told you he already missed you and wished you were staying home with him instead.

That's what you're thinking about right now, sitting in your office re-reading Valerie's e-mail asking for the go-ahead to book flights and hotels - whether you should back out of the trip and stay home, or maybe convince Nick to take a week off, too, and have a staycation with you.

It would be easy to blame work, to tell your friends that your boss scheduled a new business pitch for the same week and insists you be there.

Easy indeed.

To make excuses, turn to section 267.
To make reservations, turn to section 286.

255

From section 253...

Rachel is right.

Yes, you gave him a deadline, and, no, you haven't quite reached it, but it's not like you told him you'd never mention it again. He must have a general idea of what he wants by now. And if he doesn't, if he hasn't at least given it serious consideration, maybe you *should* just walk away.

Of course, there's no easy way to broach the topic. You can't just say, "Hey, decided if you want to attach yourself to me for life yet?" Fortunately, your preoccupation with finding the right segue unwittingly creates one.

"Did the hamster in your head take up spinning?" Nick asks.

"Hmm?" You snap out of your daze. "What do you mean?"

"What's happening in that gorgeous brain of yours?" He points a finger at you. "And don't say 'nothing.'"

No time like the present - except maybe later. "I'm not sure I should bring this up, but it's bugging me."

"Get it off your chest. Is it the wet towel on the bed thing?"

You shake your head. "The 'think you'll ever want to marry me?' thing."

His head jerks back. "Has it been nine months?"

"Eight." You wince and ask, "Have you thought about it?"

"Some. Honestly, it's stressing me out, too. It's a lot of pressure on something that should happen naturally, you know?"

"I guess," you say, your disappointment obvious. This is not encouraging.

"I just don't want to force such an important decision and regret it later. Can't we just be together and see what happens?"

Where there's a will, there's a wait, turn to section 154.
To wait for no man, turn to section 136.

256

From section 238…

"Candace is your ex!" you shout. It was supposed to be a question, but you were overrun by the rage that accompanies feeling like a fool whose boyfriend hides the hot ex he sees all the time. "You dated her through at least two Christmases, half a dozen weddings and Disneyland, and instead of telling me, you talk non-stop about how freakin' great and model-ly she is?"

In the time it took you to freak out, his face transforms from sheepish to surprised to cold. Who knew eyebrows could furrow like that?

"Well," he says, his tone so frosty you're surprised you can't see his breath. "If you had let me explain, I would have told you I was with Candy for four years. And I loved her. Until she went to Europe, came back, and dumped me for her new girlfriend. Not something I brag about."

You did not see that coming. You imagine he didn't either.

You make quickly with an apology: you don't know what came over you, you're not normally like this, you feel really bad he went through that, you're sorry you jumped to conclusions, and so forth.

"It's okay." He takes your hand and leads you to the kitchen. "I'd probably feel the same if you didn't tell me you have a history with a guy you spend a lot time with."

There doesn't appear to be any irreparable damage.

Hopefully.

Turn to section 210.

257

From section 242...

One week after you were crowned Unhappiest Camper, things with Nick haven't returned to normal.

You're also still disappointed you never actually celebrated your anniversary. To kill two birds with one gesture, you decide to take Nick to your parents' cottage for the weekend and have an anniversary do-over.

When he arrives with your usual Friday night take out tonight, you barely let him through the door before springing your idea on him.

"Okay," you begin, motioning for him to sit on the couch. "You know how you're saying you're not mad at me, but actually *are* mad at me because I was a big baby and ruined the special weekend you went through so much effort to surprise me with?"

He nods slowly, eyeballing you suspiciously.

"Well, I had an idea on how I could make it up to you, at least a little. In three weeks, I'm taking you for a weekend at my parents' lakefront cottage." He goes pale. "They won't be there, don't worry. What do you think?"

Nick scrubs a hand over his face and then rests his hands on his knees, staring silently at the wall. After a long moment, he says, "I don't think I can."

"Why not? It's got the best of both worlds - water and nature for you, a bed and a bathroom for me!"

"It sounds great, really, but I won't be here that weekend."

"Oh. Well that's okay. We could have it the following two Saturdays, too."

Another long silence before he says, "I need to tell you something."

Your head spins with possibilities: He's cheating on you with a park ranger. He found someone less selfish and they're eloping that weekend. He's eloping with a selfless park ranger that weekend.

"My boss called me in today," he says, and you relax a little. "I was a little panicked at first, thinking I was getting laid off or something, but he's giving me a promotion."

"That's amazing!" you exclaim, throwing your arms around his neck. "Do you have training that weekend or something?"

"Not exactly," he says, gently pushing your arms down to your sides. "There's more. The job is in New York."

You heart stops. "You're taking it," you say, sure you're right.

"He asked me to take the weekend to think about it, but I'm going to, yeah."

You feel the emotional equivalent of someone stabbing a balloon with a pin. You don't deflate, you *pop*. "So, it's a no-brainer then. Nothing to keep you here, right?"

"There's nothing easy about this, if that's what you mean, but it is a huge career move for me and I've worked really hard for it. I won't get another chance."

"So, we break up?" *Or you ask me to come with you and start a new chapter together? God, would I even go?*

"No, no. I don't want that at all. I think we should give the long distance thing a shot. My salary will be almost double what it is now, so flying you in or coming back to visit you will be easy! Think about it, babe. New York."

"You really think it could work?"

"Why not?"

Because I'm already losing sleep at the thought and you haven't even left yet. Because what happens in New York stays in New York. Because you'll forget me a month after you get there…

To go the (long) distance, turn to section 304.
To throw in the towel, turn to section 322.

258

From section 196...

About two months after meeting Nick's parents, you started becoming a little...obsessed about marriage.

It started out small. You'd find yourself admiring wedding dresses on magazine covers, which you'd never done before in your life. You started actually listening to people drone on about their wedding plans, making to-do lists in your head instead of the usual grocery lists.

Then last week your Tivo joined in, automatically recording every single reality show about marriage, which you now watch whenever he isn't around.

It's all you think about.

Even Rachel and Valerie seem tuned into you when they arrive with DVDs for movie night. You scan the stack of chick-flicks they bring and groan. The Wedding Planner, 27 Dresses and Something Borrowed.

"Are you trying to kill me?" you ask, flopping down on the sofa.

"Absolutely," says Rachel, giving you her What the Fuck look. "And if this doesn't do it, I've got Pretty Woman and Dirty Dancing downstairs to finish you off."

"At least they aren't about weddings. Ugh."

"Oh, so we're finally going to talk about this?" Val smiles and excitedly rubs her hands together.

"Do we have to?" you and Rachel say in sync.

At Val's insistence, you summarize your recent marriage-mania and ask if they think you should talk to Nick about it before you lose any more of your mind.

"Why not?" says Rachel, loading in the first DVD. "You've got your zillionth wedding shower of the year next week, so use it as a natural segue."

"Uh-uh." Valerie shakes her head, cleaning her retro, amber-colored glasses with a shammy. She grins wickedly. "We can do better. Think cousin Colleen!"

Valerie reminds you how her cousin finally managed to get her long-time boyfriend, Ricky to propose. After being patient for five years to no avail, she gave him a little nudge by letting him think she was about to buy a condo to live in by herself. Scared he was losing her, Ricky proposed within the week.

You remember thinking it was genius at the time. And she *is* still married. Besides, almost desperate times call for almost desperate measures.

To talk weddings after the shower, turn to section 201.
To put the con in condo, turn to section 88.

259

From section 53...

"I want to believe you," you say.

Nick's face brightens. "So believe me."

"The story's too perfect."

"Because it's true." He gives you the full power of his smile, reminding you exactly why it's better to err on the side of caution here. He wouldn't be the first guy whose good looks made you look the other way only to regret it later. You were (mostly) over it, so stay (mostly) over it.

"Nick, you're right. I barely know you. What I do know is that I'm 99 percent certain I entered my whole number into your phone, and 100 percent certain I spent most of the last three weeks feeling like an fool."

He looks genuinely disappointed. "What's in it for me to lie here?"

"Oh, I can think of at least one thing."

His head jerks back slightly. "You really think I'd do that?"

You shrug.

"So I've basically wasted the last three weeks."

"At least one of us has."

"Wow." He shakes his head. "Okay. I'll leave you to it then."

He turns and walks away, past Valerie, Rachel and the guy in the spiked bracelet, past the bar, past the coat check and out the door. You catch Val's eye and motion toward the bar. She meets you at Levi's post, leaving Rachel with Spike.

"So...that looked intense," Valerie says while you wait in line. You repeat what Nick told you. "You really don't believe him?"

"Would you?"

She starts to answer but is interrupted by Levi. "Two out of three of my favorite ladies," he says, and winks at Val.

"Hey, Levi," she says sweetly.

He wipes his hands on a towel and nods his chin at you with a cheeky smile. "Where'd the stud go?"

"Stud?" you ask.

"The guy you were just talking to. Bought you a drink a few weeks ago? He's been here every week since looking for you, ignoring every pretty young thing who bats her eyes at him."

"Shut up!" Valerie exclaims. You cover your mouth with your hands.

Shit. Shit. Shit.

"Go!" Valerie says, giving you a gentle push. "Maybe you can catch him."

You run as quickly as your boots will let you, right through the exit and out to the street - like something out of a rom-com, minus the soundtrack. You look left and right, and even stand on your tiptoes to improve your view, but there's no sign of Nick anywhere.

It's okay. You'll call him. You'll call and apologize for-

Shit.

You don't have his number.

-END-

260

From section 314...

The last few weeks since Nick found you again have been just about perfect. Every morning, you wake with a smile on your face and you find yourself humming, whistling, and even singing while you get ready for work.

You aren't even fazed by the usual lack of personal hygiene of those around you on the subway. You smile at the grumpiest of characters, and use the word "super" far more often than anyone really should. You're exceedingly cheerful to coworkers, many of whom accuse you of being pregnant thanks to your perpetual glow. And when the Mom-Squad in the lunchroom treats everyone to a play-by-play of what they find in their little darlings' diapers, you don't even gag on your chocolate pudding cup - not because it's not gross, but because you're far more focused on Nick.

Nick, who you spend more evenings out of the week with than not; who keeps you up most nights, not by trying to get in your pants, but by making you laugh to the point your cheeks hurt, and kissing you until your lips are plumper than an Instagram feed full of selfies.

You're sleep deprived but barely notice, just happy to be with him, whether for a movie, brunch, or people watching in the park. When you're not together you're in regular contact, talking on the phone, texting, or forwarding each other videos of sleepy kittens. At night, you lay awake thinking about him, and imagine he's doing the same - it's very Molly Ringwald of you.

"Instant monogamy!" says Valerie, as she removes three wine glasses from a cupboard and sets them on the kitchen table she shares with Rachel.

"The five-minute rice of relationships," mocks Rachel, plunging the arms of a corkscrew down, plucking the cork from a wine bottle with a pop. "Just add sex."

"You had sex?" Valerie passes a glass to Rachel.

"No," you tell her. "And no one's using the C-word either."

Rachel raises a brow. "Clitoris?"

"That and 'couple.'"

"Well, maybe so, but you spend more time with him than us," says Valerie. "And I haven't once heard you complain that you haven't heard from him, or say you can't make plans with us in case he calls. Couple."

Rachel fills the last glass and distributes them. "By that logic, we're a couple, Val."

"We're not? Even with all that use of the C-word?"

Not even their weirdly dysfunctional relationship can ruin this for you. "I guess we're not *not* a couple," you say.

Rachel sips thoughtfully. "Have you asked him?"

Or, maybe they can ruin it for you. "No. And since when are you about labels?"

"I'm not, but you are. Has he called you his girlfriend?"

"Formality," says Val, waving Rachel off. "If he were to introduce you to someone right now, I'm sure that's what he'd call you."

"And if she were to introduce him to someone as her boyfriend right now, I bet he'd hide behind the nearest tree."

You fidget with the stem of your glass and tune out Rachel and Valerie's debate over which of them would wear the pants in their relationship. Instead, you wonder why you haven't had The Talk with Nick yet.

Val's right when she says you sound like a couple. And isn't that the best part? That you don't spend all of your time with and without him wondering what you are to each other? Wouldn't suddenly asking for a label be the surest way to pop this little honeymoon bubble you've got going on?

You're pretty sure your lack of sleep is now going to be the result of not knowing where you stand. The way you see it, you've got two options.

To ask if you're his girlfriend, turn to section 292.
To ignore your girlfriends, turn to section 303.

261

From section 189...

It's been two weeks since you and Nick moved in together.

Rachel, Valerie, Rory, your mother, your boss, and even your old landlord, told you the merge was a bad idea. They all thought you were putting too much pressure on a young relationship.

But what do they know? You think it's one of the best decisions you've ever made - not to mention a true test of what it would be like to spend the rest of your lives together officially. It's genius.

And so far, you have been so right.

Things are going smoothly, and you're already pros at compromise. For instance, you both agreed it would be best to get a new apartment. You didn't want his parents thinking you're a gold digging freeloader, and he didn't want to live in a world where Rachel and Val just drop by on a whim. You chose a place in his neighborhood, as it wouldn't change either of your commute times for work.

He let you have the master bathroom to accommodate all the products you have and never use. He made room for you in the closet by donating most of his wardrobe, things he has but never wears, to Good Will. You don't wear most of your clothes either, but he hasn't noticed.

You took a lot of his parents' beautiful furniture to save it from storage, and sold most of your stuff to Val's youngest brother for his first apartment. You used that cash to buy what little else your new place needed.

Waking up to each other every morning is even better than you'd imagined. So is having most of your meals together, not having to make plans to see each other and, blessedly, no more traveling home in the freezing cold morning to get ready for work.

It's domestic freakin' bliss.

Turn to section 265.

262

From section 199...

"Hello," says Nick when you don't answer right away. "It's cool I'm with the guys tonight, right? Or did I screw something up?"

"No," you say quickly. "No screw up. Have fun with your friends." And just to be a little passive aggressive, you add, "I actually wouldn't mind a night of secret single behavior, myself."

He laughs. "Whatever that means, I don't like the sound of it."

"Clearly you've never watched Sex and The City."

"I've seen enough to know referencing it doesn't make me feel better."

"Me time. To indulge my baser instincts."

"Baser instincts?"

"You know, walking around naked while nibbling the nits I pick from my scalp. Scratching myself. Watching porn."

"Oh, that's all fine. As long as I still get to claim you as my property."

"Without question."

"And take you and your flea-free scalp to dinner and a movie tomorrow."

"We look forward to it."

You say goodnight and hang up the phone. Sure, you're bummed, but it's hardly the end of the world. You grab your bag and head out the door to catch up with the girls.

Drag Queen Bingo it is.

Continue to section 146.

263

From section 238…

"Nice pictures," you tell Nick, trying not to grit your teeth as you return the album to the shelf. "Is dinner ready?"

He nods and you follow him to the kitchen table where you begin your meal in uncomfortable silence. At least, you're uncomfortable. You can't be sure if he is because you haven't made eye contact since you sat down. You steal a quick glance at him. Yes, he's uncomfortable, too.

"Listen," he says slowly. "I know it probably looks really bad that I didn't tell you about me and Candy."

You think before answering. "Well, no, it doesn't look great. But I'm sure you had your reasons." *Like you're still in love with her.*

"Candy and I were together for around four years. Then she came back from a month-long family trip to Europe and introduced me to Kris." Just as you're thinking it's remarkable he could remain friends with someone who cheated on him, he adds, "Her new girlfriend."

"Whoa."

"Yep. Turns out Candy's gay. It's kind of embarrassing to tell your current girlfriend that your last girlfriend left you for another chick. So I didn't."

"Yeah. Not something you just blurt out." You start eating again. "Well, it's nice that you guys are still friends."

Hooray! Candy's a lesbian. Candy's a lesbian!

Turn to section 249.

264

From section 288…

You're aware guys aren't always born with the same desire to procreate as women. Hell, *you* weren't even born with it. And so it's entirely possible that Nick could change his anti-offspring position in a few years, maybe even sooner.

Still, you'd hate to waste too many of your childbearing years - and the good skin that comes with them - waiting for that to happen. Who wants to risk winding up eggless and alone?

Okay, that's probably a little extreme.

"What?" asks Nicks, recognizing from your expression that the hamster in your head is doing his daily cardio.

"It's just… Well, I'm pretty sure I want kids. Or at least, *a* kid."

"Now?"

"No!" You shake your head emphatically. "Not now, but eventually."

"So why are you worried about it today?"

Because now you can't help but wonder if he's actually saying, "By the time you want kids I won't even be around, so don't sweat it."

"It honestly hadn't even crossed my mind until now. But now that it has…"

He tilts his head. "What?"

"You know how I feel about you, but I think it's a bad idea for someone who wants kids to get serious about someone who doesn't. Even for a little while."

"Very funny." He laughs uncomfortably as he examines your face. "You're serious. Aren't you?"

Your eyes widen. "I think I am."

He rubs the top of his head. "I did not see that coming. Like, at all."

You sigh. "Me neither."

-END-

265

From section 261…

In the seven weeks since you moved in with Nick, domestic bliss has given way to domestic bust.

Two weeks into it, you were enjoying cozy meals, reading in bed together every night and sharing all of the household duties from shopping to cooking to cleaning. All of that began to crumble by week three when Nick got really busy with everything from work to working out to his regular monthly poker game with the guys.

Since then, you've been picking up his slack.

It's not so bad – you kind of like taking care of him. Besides, you know how important his job is to him, and who are you to complain if he wants to sculpt that pretty body of his? You also think it's great to have independent interests so you don't wake up one morning and realize you have no friends or hobbies, and end up resenting each other for it.

Besides, you're sure if things were reversed, he'd gladly return the favor. That's what relationships are all about.

To keep pitching in, turn to section 272.
To throw in the dishtowel, turn to section 294.

266

From section 200...

As much as you'd like everyone to believe it's "natural," your beauty regime takes a reasonable amount of time, and a specific series of products, to achieve. And you are not in a place with Nick where you're ready to let yourself go.

Though you're thinking about it.

When you stay at Nick's for a weekend, your overnight bag is heavy, weighed down with everything from clothes to makeup remover to your hair dryer.

You look like a hot Sherpa.

And you're tired of packing, unpacking and repacking it, of forgetting essentials. Things would be so much easier if you had just one measly little drawer (okay, a decent sized drawer) at his place where you could keep duplicates of beauty necessities and what he calls your "FHPs" (feminine hygiene products).

You hear Valerie's mom in your head from the last time you joined their family for dinner, "If you want to keep a man, you must remain mysterious. *Never* leave anything at his place. I saw it on Oprah." Of course, Val's parents met in high school and were married before her mom moved out of her strict Catholic parents' house, so you doubt she's ever had the joy of the walk of shame.

Something's got to give.

To ask him for a drawer, turn to section 284.
To spend more time at your place, turn to section 254.

267

From section 254...

Not two minutes after you reply privately to Valerie and explain that you have to cancel because of a work conflict, insisting the rest of them go without you, she calls your direct line.

"What the hell!" she yells before you can say hello. "That's the only week we're all available!"

"I know," you say, in your whiniest, most disappointed voice. "It sucks, but I can't get out of it."

"You're sure you're not just canceling because you'd rather stay home and be all lovey-dovey with your boyfriend? Because that would be really uncool."

"I'm sure," you tell her, imagining her wearing her serious librarian frames and wagging her finger at you.

"So, if I asked you a series of rapid fire questions about this new business thing, you'd be able to answer them with no hesitation?"

"Fire away."

Thanks to your keen powers of anticipation, you've already predicted and prepared answers for each of the questions she asks; from what type of business you're pitching (online retail), to which colleagues you'll be working with (you get to pick your team, a small consolation, and you're just pulling together names now), to why your expertise is so important that your boss would take away your vacation time (umm, has she heard you talk about your boss?).

After her inquisition, Val appears satisfied you aren't just being one of those chicks who lets her friends down and gives up the things she enjoys for her boyfriend.

Even though you are.

Turn to section 271.

268

From sections 233, 269 and 97...

Nick's been in Toronto on business for a week and you miss him.

A lot.

When he left for the airport, he warned you his schedule was pretty grueling but promised he'd try to call on Monday night around 9:00 p.m. when he knew he'd be in his room.

Here you are at 7:30 on Tuesday, watching your favorite news program, *Entertainment Tonight,* and willing time to move faster when your phone rings. In your hand.

He's early!

Oh.

No.

It's only Valerie.

"Get your coat and meet us downstairs," she orders.

"Now?" you ask. "Why?"

"Remember how I bet Rachel she couldn't wait five whole dates to sleep with Not At All My Type But Utterly Doable Lawyer Guy?"

Of course you remember. How could you forget the twenty minutes you spent agreeing on a nickname? "I believe we settled on Utterly *Fuckable* Lawyer Guy."

She ignores you. "Big surprise, three dates later, The Human Chastity Belt admits defeat. I'm collecting right now."

"And you want me there in case I have to break her knee caps?"

"You'd better have your shoes on by now. That second hand store down the road closes in forty-five minutes and I need time to style the fashion masterpiece Rachel will wear as we saunter slowly through Union Square in search of the busiest, most highly male-populated bar we can find. And she has to buy drinks. I'm driving, so I'm relying on you to rack up a serious liquor bill."

As seriously, definitely, completely tempting as that sounds, if you go, you won't be able to talk to Nick when he calls.

Val hears your hesitation. "If you would rather wait around for your boyfriend to call than help one friend humiliate another, we need to talk."

Yeah, like she's never done it herself.

To ask her to take pictures, turn to section 170.
To see it for yourself, turn to section 240.

269

From section 231…

"I love Brazil," you tell Nick, trying not to choke on your risotto. "My family went there for Carnival when I was ten." *Cue subject change.* "This risotto's great - want to try some?"

You feed him a creamy mouthful of rice from your fork, doubtful that Miss I-Put-the-Lust-in-Sports-Illustrated would dare eat such a savoury dish - not with fat *and* carbs.

Trying desperately to tame your inner catty, you stick with the plan and recollect that trip with all the enthusiasm and detail you can pull together - breathtaking parades, colorful costumes and live music, yada, yada.

You've successfully changed the direction of the conversation, sure, but you know damn well you're in for a long night of worrying about Nick's level of interest in Candy's Brazilian. Photo shoot.

Turn to section 268.

270

From section 284...

For the last couple of weeks, Nick's been working early mornings and late nights on a huge project he thinks will get him promoted.

You admire his determination, but it's really starting to affect your relationship. You see him far less often and when you do, he's just *not* interested in having sex. He's always too tired or stressed out. It's been nearly two weeks since you slept together without the sleeping.

You knew you'd stop having sex with the frequency of rabbits eventually - just as soon as you built up a tolerance to the feel-good chemicals your brain over-produces at the start of relationship. That's how it goes. It's just never happened so...abruptly before.

When you awake in his bed this morning, you do your best to interest him in a Saturday wake-up call only to be rebuffed for more sleep. You head into his bathroom and shut the door, turning on the hot water in the shower before undressing. You give yourself a quick once over in the mirror, confirming your figure hasn't changed since you met Nick. Nope. Still a certifiable babe, so it's unlikely you're the problem. And "tired" never seemed to be a problem for him before.

You shower and dress, stepping out of the steamy bathroom to find Nick on the bed and typing on his laptop. He sets it aside and pops up. "Perfect timing," he says. "Gotta grab a quick shower. They need me at work in an hour."

He closes the bathroom door and you frown, disappointed your plans for the day are once again ruined. Determined to make the best of it, however, you decide to check out Kristen Bell's new rom-com on your own. You sit down and pick up his laptop to check show times, noticing his work e-mail account is still open on the screen.

Temptation, thy name is e-mail.

To snoop through his inbox, turn to section 274.
To stay out of his inbox, turn to section 254.

271

From section 267...

Like most women out there - or so you'd assume, you've never done a survey or anything - you've always dreaded the suggestion of a threesome.

You've managed to avoid the subject up to this point, figuring it was because you've only gotten serious with "wholesome" guys. Like Nick. That is, until two weeks ago when you watched a movie where the victim was murdered by her boyfriend after a messy threeway.

"Ever done it?" Nick asked, as if he were talking about riding a bicycle. Or a tricycle.

"Murdered a boyfriend? Not yet," you said, and turned toward him. "But the night is young."

He gently poked your ribs. "A threesome, killer."

"No," you said simply, hoping he'd leave it at that.

"Would you?"

"I don't know."

Who would have thought those tiny little words would cause such a commotion? You only said what you did because you didn't want to come off as a prude - and because you didn't think he'd actually want to have one.

Sure, you've thought about it once or twice before, but not in a serious way; more like a "healthy fantasy with cameos by Hollywood's hottest leading men" way. Since that conversation, though, he's brought it up a few more times and may actually be starting to sway you.

It might be fun - at lot of fun even. But it could also be a big, messy disaster.

Easy-Threesie? Turn to section 276.
Two to horizontal mambo? Turn to section 275.

272

From section 265...

Nick's at his now weekly poker game, so you invite the girls over for Chinese. Two bottles of wine later, you feel a little bit tipsy and Rachel takes advantage of this mild vulnerability.

"So, it's been two months," she says, emptying the rest of the bottle into your glass with a controlled twist of her wrist. "How's shacking up treating you?"

"It's great," you tell her, nodding your head with exaggerated enthusiasm.

"I call bullshit," exclaims Valerie, uncorking a third bottle.

"What?" you say. "It's true."

"Which is why," says Rachel. "Instead of annoying us with every excruciating detail of how 'great' it is, you've barely mentioned Nick in over a month."

You tilt your chin up slightly in defiance. "Maybe I'm just maturing."

"Spill," Valerie scrutinizes you over her Vera Wangs.

"We're fine. He's just really busy and I'm picking up the slack."

"Define 'slack.'"

"Shopping, cooking, cleaning..."

"Everything," says Rachel.

"I guess, but I don't mind. It's what it would be like to be married."

"There are two things wrong with that statement. One, this isn't Mad Men; and two, you're not married."

"Whatever."

"Whatever? Two months in and you're already a live-in maid."

This makes you laugh. "Honey, I love you, but you've never lived with anyone, and you don't know what you're talking about."

"Even if I couldn't put my legs behind my head, I'd still know what it looks like, sister. I'm telling you, you're asking for trouble."

Turn to section 278.

273

From sections 280 and 294...

You've joined the girls for weekly Wednesday margaritas - your answer to Nick's weekly basketball game with the guys.

You've had fun, gossiping and teasing each other mercilessly, currently working to suppress your laughter as Rachel and Valerie bluff the admiring frat boys at the next table, telling them the three of you are college seniors.

You're about to signal for another pitcher when you catch sight of the clock on the wall across from you. It's nearly ten o'clock, your usual bedtime with Nick. The way things have been going lately, it's pretty much the only guaranteed time you have to check in and catch up on each other's days.

You're torn. Nick's almost never home, but that's not your fault, nor should it mean you rearrange your schedule around his. Even though you really want to see him.

Do you head home for face time with your man or stay with your sorority sisters who are currently schooling their hapless suitors in the syllabus for Human Sexuality?

"I'm going to be up all night studying my oral with Rachel," says Valerie, tracing the rim of her wine glass with her finger. "Again."

To head home, turn to section 193.
To order another pitcher, turn to section 293.

274

From section 270...

The newest message in Nick's inbox is from Mandy Jones, who you imagine is probably a cute, tiny brunette who wears tight fitting sweaters and flirts with anyone under the age of forty - mostly because he's never mentioned her before and the e-mail is titled, *Need You.*

Hey Gorgeous, It reads. *I just can't seem to stay away from you. Must be fate. See you in an hour?*

Nick opens the bathroom door just as you finish reading the message, scaring the hell out of you. "Sorry," he says when he sees he startled you. "Would you grab a fresh towel for me, please? Thanks, babe." He closes the door again.

Phew!

And, jerk.

You hit the back button on the browser and close the lid on the computer before getting a towel from the linen closet. You open the bathroom door and toss it on the counter.

"Hun," you say. "I gotta go. I'm gonna catch a movie but I need to go now if I'm going to make it."

"What movie?" he asks. "Maybe we could see it tonight."

Right. "Chick-flick."

"As you were. I'll call you later."

Of course, there will be no movie for you. Instead, you'll spend the day talking with your friends and obsessing about Mandy Jones and her needs.

Turn to section 282.

275

From section 271…

"Let's do it," you tell Nick. You're both sitting in the same place you were when the subject first came up.

"Do what?" It takes a moment, but his confusion finally gives way to realization and his eyes light up. "A three-way?" he asks incredulously. "Stop it."

You just stare at him, a promising half smile on your face.

"Are you serious?"

"Yes." You nod emphatically.

"Um. I don't actually know what to say to that. No one ever thinks they'll get this far. Awesome? Is awesome appropriate?"

"I think I'm awesome, so sure."

"Okay, so…with who? One of your girlfriends?"

"Actually," you say, running a fingertip down the center of his shirt. "I'm thinking more like one of your buddies."

"What?" He jumps up from the couch. "No way!"

"Sorry. I get it. How about Scott?"

"Nope." He gives a brisk shake of his head.

"Why not?"

"Because I'm not gay."

"Huh. Me neither, which rules girls out." You shrug. "No threesome, I guess."

Knowing he has no counter argument, Nick sits beside you, defeated.

And that's that!

Turn to section 307.

276

From section 271…

So you're going to have a threesome…

Realizing what a huge step a three-way is in a relationship, you want to be prepared. You can't talk to your friends because, not only are you fairly sure they have no experience in the area (even Rachel), it would mean telling them your plans. Not happening. So you type "threesomes for beginners" into your web browser and here you are - everything you wanted to know about embarking on three-way sex but were afraid to ask.

From how to pick your third to proper etiquette to post-experience emotions, you feel like you completed a correspondence course on the *ménage à trois*. And, sure, you're a lot nervous, but you're excited, too.

Nick's shocked when you give it the green light, and he's floored by your list of rules and guidelines, but nothing could've prepared him for when you suggested he recruit Candy (his ex-heterosexual ex-girlfriend) to help you find your third.

She's more than willing to help - maybe as her way of saying, "Sorry I forgot to mention I'm gay." You even become Facebook friends.

She introduces you to Lisa, a bisexual acquaintance of hers, and you all hit it off. She's pretty - but not prettier than you. She's sexy - but not skanky. And she lives five hours away, rarely coming to San Francisco. She's perfect! After discussing boundaries and safety, you set a date for one week from that night.

And before you know it, you've done it!

Which you still kind of can't believe. It's a bit of a blur, but you enjoyed it - in the moment, anyway. The moment Lisa left, reality set in and your anxiety took over.

Was she better than you in bed?

Sure, you have the prettier face, but does she have a better body?

Did he like her too much?

Will he want to do this all the time now?

With her?

Nick, to your dismay, has the opposite reaction. He looks...happy, like he just climbed Mount Everest - and Mount Everest has two vaginas.

When he asks you how you feel about everything, you panic and tell him it was great, too afraid to tell him what you're actually thinking, which is, *Why the hell did we do that?*

And that's the beginning of the end of you and Nick.

Normally you'd be really passive aggressive until he figured out what's wrong, but this time you jump right into active aggressive.

If he's lost in thought, you ask if he's thinking about Lisa, with an extra side of resentment. If he doesn't want to have sex, you huff about how you aren't enough for him anymore.

But it's not until you question his every interaction with other women - coworkers, strangers, and your friends - that he finally snaps, telling you he's had enough of your "paranoid jealousy" and breaks things off.

Two years go by and you don't hear the first thing from or about Nick.

Until today.

While scanning your newsfeed, you notice good ol' set-you-up-on-the-threesome-that-ended-your-relationship-Candy's photo album titled, "The Wedding."

Something compels you to click on it. The first pictures aren't all that interesting; cliché sunset, beachfront stuff, and then...

No Way. No %#@ing way!*

It's Nick.

And his wife.

Lisa.

That bitch.

You invite her into your bed and she screws you before she totally *screws* you? This can't be happening. You flip through dozens of pictures of the happy couple before, during and after their sunset ceremony and you want to vomit.

This was not covered in the article.

-END-

277

From section 293…

You love your friends, but they don't always know what they're talking about.

Neither of them has lived with a guy. Heck, you can't even remember the last time either of them was actually in a serious relationship. Things with you and Nick are normal. Completely.

That's what you told yourself when you left your friends six months ago, anyway.

For the most part, things at home are the same. Nick still works a lot, still works out a lot, and still has precious little free time. You still do the majority of the housework, shopping, planning and organizing.

There have been a few changes, though. Most notably, those little pieces of intimacy between you and Nick that you've been clinging to are disappearing.

He stopped using his pet name for you, stopped finishing your sentences (in fairness, he's rarely actively listening), and even stopped calling to say he loves you when he has to pull an all-nighter. And there's less touching. You rarely cuddle, you can't remember the last time you had Saturday sex, or any sex for that matter, and he rarely kisses you goodbye when he leaves for work in the morning.

Everything feels different.

You've been telling yourself it's just a rough patch, that relationships are hard work. Only, you're painfully aware you're still the only one putting in the work and now, it seems, the only one at all concerned with the status of your relationship.

On a gloomy Saturday morning, you resolve not to let your relationship slip further away. You're going to talk to Nick and see if you can't get things back on track.

Just as soon as you finish tidying the hallway.

You're straightening shoes when you accidentally knock over his laptop bag, spilling some papers. You curse and bend to pick them up, only to immediately lose your breath. On top is yesterday's newspaper, folded to the classifieds - more specifically, to apartment rentals. You dry heave, taking in the listings circled in red ink, with notes like, "Too small," "Too expensive," and finally, "Make offer."

"I was going to tell you," Nick says quietly behind you.

You spin around to face him and feel your lower lip tremble. "When?"

"When I found a place. I knew it would be hard afterwards, so..."

"So you're just leaving?"

"Not *just* leaving. I mean, I don't think either of us is all that happy lately."

"Things have been different, sure, but *I'm* happy," you say, instantly knowing it's a lie.

"Really? You like sitting around waiting for me to get off of work, making dinner for one and cleaning up after me?"

"So work *less*," you plead. "Let's spend more time together. Moving out is only going to make it worse. Unless you don't want this to work." He doesn't answer, so you go on. "You don't."

He shakes his head sadly, focused on the floor. "It's not what I want anymore. I want to be single again."

You know that's break-up for "I'm not in love with you anymore," and that it likely means he's already thinking about other women, but you don't want to acknowledge either anymore than he does.

Instead you shove a few necessities in a bag, slip on your shoes and head over to Rachel and Valerie's before you have a chance to break down.

You stay there until a one-bedroom opens up…right upstairs.

-END-

278

From section 272...

The kitchen sink has been leaking for the last three weeks. The steady *drip, drip, drip* is making you crazy.

You've lost count of the number of times you've asked Nick to fix it, and the number of times he's told you he'll get to it soon. And since he's having friends over to watch football today, you know you're going to have to deal with the drip for at least another week.

When most of his friends arrive, you get your things together to run some errands and avoid the rowdiness to come - not to mention the constant twang of water on aluminum.

You hear a knock and open the door, surprised to see Pete, AKA: The Piper - a nickname he was given because, not only does he have the best arms you've ever seen, but he's also a plumber.

Mere coincidence?

Or is the universe sending you a knight in shining wrench?

To ask Pete to take a look at your pickled pipes, turn to section 280.
To not pester Pete with your plumbing problem, turn to section 281.

279

From section 200...

When Nick fails to pick up on cues that you're the doing all the legwork or, more specifically, right-foot work, in your relationship, you steer things in another direction.

Over the next couple of weeks, you do your best to show him how much easier life would be if he'd either resolve his vehicle situation or buy a transit pass.

First, you cancel a date for a Christian Bale movie you know he's dying to see because you "have a flat," and when he asks you to take BART to the theater, which is near his apartment, you tell him it's too much work and you'd rather just stay home.

The next week, you're at his apartment and things are starting to get *interesting* - that or this is one of those occasions where a guy actually does have something in his pocket. You abruptly tell him you've got to get going before you're too tired to drive. He suggests you stay the night, so you tell him you're meeting Rachel at the gym really early and don't have gym clothes with you. That one leaves him feeling a little...blue.

The next night, he calls to see if you're coming by so the two of you can finish what you started and you tell him you'd love to, but shouldn't drive given you've had a couple of glasses of wine. Then he asks you to help him pick out a new car on the weekend.

Nice job, you!

Turn to section 254.

280

From section 278...

Dusting off one of your feminine wiles, you stand on your tiptoes to kiss Pete's cheek and say a sweet, "Hey, handsome."

"Beautiful," he says, giving you the full wattage of his dazzling dimpled smile. "On your way out?"

You nod. "Library."

"Brains, too," he flirts. "I didn't know people still used libraries."

You giggle, and it's delightfully genuine. "I'm teaching myself how to fix a leak."

He gestures toward the noise in the other room. "Nicky can't take care of it?"

"Oh, sure. He's just been super busy, and I figure I can't make it much worse."

"You know," he says, and the dimples return. "I happen to know an extremely talented plumber. He could probably take care of that for you right now. Maybe cost ya...a beer and another kiss."

"Oh, Pete, that's right!" you say, resting a hand on his really solid bicep. *Really solid.* "I forgot you were a plumber. But you're a guest, I couldn't..."

He holds up a hand. "Nonsense. It'll just take a minute."

"You're my hero," you say as he heads downstairs. He returns just as Nick comes for a round of beers.

"Pete, buddy, you made it." Nick gives him the patented guy half-hug. "And you brought your tools."

"Your *much* better half told me you've got a leaky faucet," Pete says. He puts his gigantic arm around your waist, and you know he's just having some fun with Nick. "I hate to see a damsel in distress, so I insisted she let me look at it. Actually," He turns to you with a subtle wink. "We could get under there together and I could show you how it's done."

"Isn't he great, babe?" you ask, looking adoringly at Pete.

"The greatest," Nick says dryly. "Pete, I appreciate it, man, but if you hand me your tools, I'll take care of it quick."

Under Pete's watchful, and thoroughly amused, eye, Nick fixes the leak a few moments later.

"Nice job, man." Pete clasps a big hand on Nick's shoulder. "Lucky you, too. I was about to try and steal your woman."

"Better luck next time," Nick says, handing Pete a beer and planting a big open-mouthed kiss on your lips.

You are good!

Turn to section 273.

281

From section 278...

Monday. *Drip.* Tuesday. *Bloop.* Wednesday. *Bloop.* Thursday. *Drip.* Friday. You guessed it - *drip.*

You've been patient. Extremely patient. Were he alive, Gandhi would call to ask your secret. But by Saturday, you reach a breaking point.

Over your coffee and the paper on a beautiful morning, Nick's phone rings. A moment later, he says, "For sure, man. Gimme twenty."

"Going somewhere?" you ask innocently when he hangs up. Maybe his buddy's in a jam. Car trouble. Hospital. Needs a condom.

"That was Joe. The guys are getting together to play some pick up."

"You're serious?"

"Seems like a silly thing to joke about."

"What about the sink?" Your mouth is tight as you try to keep your suppressed anger from escaping. Drip. Drip.

"I'll do it later. I've got all weekend."

"Great, except you've been saying that for three weeks."

"It's not that bad. Another day isn't going to kill you."

"Says the guy who's never here to hear it."

He looks at the ceiling and exhales. "So that's what this about."

"What are you talking about?"

"You're pissed I have a life. Maybe you should try it."

This should end well.

Turn to section 295.

282

From section 274...

The following Saturday morning, you're taking another shower at Nick's place, having arrived late last night after he got home from "work."

You turn off the water and hear him call upstairs that your coffee is almost ready. You seize the opportunity, throwing on his roomy black robe, barely bothering to dry off, so you can dash over to his computer while he's in the kitchen.

You're in luck - the laptop is on the bed, opened to his work e-mail. Adrenaline courses through your veins when you see an e-mail from Mandy Jones topping his inbox, one he's already read. You peer down the hallway before opening it.

You were amazing last night, she writes. *Can't wait to do it again. Mandy XOXO.*

Un-fucking-believable. He's really cheating on you.

What a dick!

You take a moment to compose yourself and when you feel calm enough, you go to rip a strip off him. His back is to you when you reach the kitchen.

"So," you say, leaning against the doorframe. "Anything interesting happen at work last night?"

"Not particularly," he says, turning around and raising his mug to his mouth.

"Really? Mandy seems to think so."

He stills. "What are you talking about?"

"Oh, I dunno, maybe the 'last night was amazing e-mail' she sent you."

"I knew it!" He face is instantly dark. He sets his mug down. "You've been reading my e-mail."

"You're mad at *me* for busting *you* for cheating on me with some hussy at work?"

"Hussy!" He barks out a laugh. "Come with me."

You follow him back upstairs to his computer and watch as he clicks through various folders, finally selecting one called *Holiday Party.* He scans the images and clicks on the one titled *Me and Mandy.* It fills the screen.

Fuck.

Mandy is most definitely not a hussy, at least not now - who knows what she was like thirty years ago? She's easily fifty-five years old, with curly silver hair, large glasses and a clearly motherly adoration of Nick.

This makes no sense.

Nick explains that he didn't think much of it when you jumped out of your skin after he startled you at his computer last week, but when you started asking a lot of questions about his job and who he was working with, he got the nagging feeling you'd been snooping. He hoped he was wrong, but he asked Mandy to send that e-mail as a test.

You got e-mail bombed.

You apologize, explaining you're not normally a snooper, but the e-mail you came across *accidentally* seemed to explain why he'd been so disinterested in you, and that it's been eating you alive all week. Nick doesn't care.

"I'm so sorry," you plead. Again.

"Me too," he says. "I'm sorry you didn't just tell me what was bothering you, and because you obviously don't trust me."

"I do trust you. It was just an insecure moment. I'm really, really sorry. Can you forgive me?"

He shrugs. "I guess." *Phew!* "But I can't date you. You should go."

Your protests are useless, so you return to the bedroom and dress before emptying your drawer.

Fool. A guy who's cheating on you doesn't give you a drawer.

When you're finished, you find him waiting at the open front door.

-END-

283

From section 134...

You meant to tell Nick there are elements of your job you don't love, and some office politics that leave you feeling a little undervalued and underappreciated.

Instead, you're headed into minute ten of an exacerbated diatribe about your boss, Marissa, who was hired courtesy of her father-in-law who runs the agency's New York subsidiary. She takes "fake it 'til you make it" to a whole new level and is genuinely oblivious to the fact you're the one actually running her department.

She recently told you she's concerned your frequent late nights and non-billable hours indicate you're "not adequately handling your workload" when, in reality, you're fixing *her* mistakes to prevent your clients from suffering her ineptitude. You repeatedly slip into your super-fake, super-cheerful and super-condescending boss-voice, which plays better if someone's known you for a while.

Nick has been listening with rapt attention, leaning forward on his elbows, slowly nodding or shaking his head along with the narrative, and laughing when appropriate. He even enjoys boss-voice.

"Anyway," you begin to wind down, pretty sure you're starting to look crazy. "I'm told that just fantasizing about her being hit by a speeding bus isn't a chargeable offense." You look down at the table, suddenly feeling awkward.

When you look up again, Nick's focused intently on you. He gets up and stands beside you. Your tilt your head back to look at him. His leans down, slides a hand behind your neck and kisses you. A slow, lingering kiss that makes you glad you're sitting down.

After a moment, he pulls back and returns to his seat. You notice most of your fellow diners are watching you, their expressions ranging from amused to annoyed.

"Sorry," Nick says, flashing you that boyish grin. "You looked like you needed that."

"Um. Yes. It did make me feel...relaxed."

"I'm glad," he says, and passes you a desert menu. "You should consider slotting it in between sudden death fantasies and yoga. You know, break up the monotony."

Okay, so he either doesn't think you're insane, or he does but still finds you attractive, which - let's face it - you'll take.

Continue to section 32.

284

From section 266...

When you arrive at Nick's apartment, you let your overnight bag drop to the floor with a dramatic *thud,* letting out a pronounced "Oomph" for emphasis.

"Um," says Nick, poking at the bag with his socked toe, "If you're trying to get rid of a body, there are far more discreet places to do it than my apartment, though I'm flattered you thought of me."

"I wish it was a body," you tell him. "Then I'd only have to carry it once and be done with it." Planting your hands firmly on your hips, you look him straight in the eye and say, "I need a drawer."

"A drawer," he repeats, buying time. "For what?" Buying more time. He's too smart to play this dumb.

"I'm tired of lugging this stuff around all the time. If I could leave a few things here it would make me happy, giving me more time and inclination to make *you* happy."

A look of sheer terror appears on his face. You're not sure he's breathing.

"Get over yourself," you tell him, fanning his face with your hands. "I don't want to move in. I just want to save myself the massage therapy bills sure to result from schlepping this bag around three times a week. Of course, if you prefer, we could spend more time at my place. With Rachel and Valerie always an unannounced visit away."

"How big of a drawer do you need?" he asks, clapping his hands together with sudden enthusiasm.

That's more like it.

Turn to section 270.

285

From section 195...

You were twelve years old when your Aunt Shirley had a beautiful silvery blue butterfly tattooed on her lower back. You were in awe. And when your mom gave her much younger sister a hard time about it, you promised yourself you'd have one just like it someday, keeping a photo of it in your wallet for years.

You came close last year when you and Rachel went to Niagara Falls for a high school friend's wedding. An open bar led to a triple-dog-dare, which led to a cab ride to Naughty Needles Tattoos and Piercings Parlor.

She jumped into the chair first, anxious to have the Chinese character for "warrior" branded onto her shoulder. Thanks to the steady stream of expletives that flowed out of her mouth from the moment the needle touched her skin, however, you chickened out. On Monday, Rachel learned it was actually the character for "fool" blacked into her skin for all time. Now she tells people it means "irony."

You've got a whole new wave of courage today, though. Probably due to the fact you've been entertaining yourself with a marathon of Inked at Nick's place while waiting for him to get home from the gym. He's barely in the door before you ask him to come and hold your hand when you go under the needle. Right now.

"Sure thing." He laughs, peeling off his sweaty tee shirt. "And you can hold mine while I get a Prince Albert."

"I'm serious!"

He grimaces. "A tattoo of what?"

"Bigger boobs."

He's quiet.

You sigh dramatically. "A butterfly. Look." You thrust the worn photo of Aunt Shirley in front of his face.

He groans. "But tattoos are so tacky. No offence to Aunt Shirley, but I don't want a girlfriend with a tramp-stamp. And I'm definitely not going with you to get one."

Doesn't want? What the hell are you supposed to do with that?

To take the out, turn to section 200.
To bring a friend, turn to section 251.

286

From section 254...

As hard as it was to leave Nick for a whole week, you're so glad you did.

You had a blast reconnecting with your friends - and your tan. Still, you missed him terribly, never going longer than an hour without wondering what he was doing at that exact moment and wishing he were there with you.

When your plane touches down on the tarmac, you're thrilled to be home. You immediately pop out of your seat and push past angry passengers in order to de-plane and make it to baggage claim as fast as possible.

Like karmic repayment for good deeds done, your giant suitcase is magically the first to appear on the baggage carousel. You practically dislocate a shoulder heaving it onto the ground and wheel your way to passenger pick up. Your heart all but leaps out of your chest when you see Nick waiting with a bouquet of fresh flowers and a smile bigger than yours.

You walk to him as quickly as your suitcase allows and let him scoop you up in his arms. Between all of the kisses and him repeatedly telling you how much he missed you, you don't notice your girlfriends have caught up until you hear them shout "Barf" and "Get a room" en route to Val's car.

Absence.

Heart.

Fonder.

Turn to section 307.

287

From section 152…

In the grand tradition of go big or go home, you picked out a big red card with shiny cursive writing that rhymes off a handful of things you *love, love, love* about Nick and secured it to the big gift box holding his shirt.

After a dimly lit dinner, and the silent pleasure of being envied by all the single girls spending Valentine's Day with their girlfriends, you and Nick are almost at your apartment door when he remembers he left your gift in his car. For a moment there, you were worried he'd forgotten.

He runs downstairs and you open up a bottle of wine, filling two glasses and setting them next to his gift on your kitchen table. He returns and places a smallish envelope next to the big box with his name on it. He insists you go first.

Your mouth feels like cotton as you tear into the envelope. You pull out an… invitation? No. It's a gift card for a deluxe manicure, pedicure and facial at a new organic spa downtown. It's a great gift, no doubt, but you are painfully aware there's no card. No lovey-dovey sentiment, not even the dreaded "From Nick."

You think of your card.

You might throw up.

Pull yourself together.

"This is great," you tell Nick, planting a sweet kiss on his lips. "Thank you so much!"

"You're welcome," he says, pleased. He rubs his hands together. "My turn!"

Obviously taught well by his mother, he reaches for the big red envelope first, eyeing you playfully as he opens it. Then he reads it and you watch his expression become…uncomfortable, maybe? Embarrassed? You're sure as hell both of those things. To move things along, you practically shove the box into his hands, forcing him to drop the card. He opens the lid, revealing his swanky new shirt. He is thrilled! You are thrilled, too, because it's the distraction you need to slide the card under a placemat.

Grabbing your wine glasses, Nick motions toward your bedroom. "Okay, you. Get in there and make with the naked."

Excellent! You both want to move past this as quickly as possible.

Turn to section 288.

288

From section 287...

Nick's niece, Lana, just turned three. To celebrate, her parents are throwing her a giant party today, with all of the kids from her neighborhood and daycare.

After the party, Uncle Nick, who offered to help wrangle the little ankle biters, arrives at your apartment, where you've been tearing your hair out trying to finish a new business pitch all day.

He immediately collapses on your couch.

"Rough game of Pin the Tail on the Donkey?" you ask.

"There were kids *everywhere,*" he says.

"At a three year-old's birthday party? The anarchy!"

"You don't understand," he continues, looking bewildered. "There were at least thirty of them; running around, screaming like little maniacs, crawling all over me like I was a jungle gym."

"That's so cute!"

"Not cute. Annoying. Not for me, thanks."

"You don't want kids?" you ask, assuming it's safe if he raised the topic.

"Nope."

"Come on. Not even a little?"

He shakes his head.

You've never been a chick to fantasize about being a mother, "Oohing" over people's babies and "Ahhing" over their 3D ultrasounds, but you do know you most likely want kids. Maybe *a* kid. When the time is right. Far, far into the future.

Still, just hearing Nick be so adamant about not wanting kids sets off your biological smoke alarm.

To press snooze, turn to section 181.
To wake up, turn to section 264.

289

From section 306...

"Hey, so how do you feel about pizza?" Nick asks when you don't say anything else.

"No," you tell him, almost passively, surprised to hear the words coming out of your mouth.

"Okay. Chinese?"

You shake your head. "I mean, no to talking about this later." You exhale a shaky breath. "I don't think I can stay with someone I know won't ever marry me. I want to get married. At least I'm pretty sure I do."

"Come on. You'd break up with me for 'pretty sure?'"

"You just said it wouldn't be fair to expect you to get married if you didn't want to. Why should it be different for me?" And then you're crying.

"Don't cry, babe." He smooths your hair with both hands. "Why are we even worrying about this right now?"

"Are you ever going to change your mind?"

"No," he says automatically, before he throws his hands up. "I don't know."

"I don't want to lie to myself and pretend like I'm not the kind of girl who'd say she was cool with wait-and-see and then spend all of her time hoping you'll change your mind. Because I am very much that girl."

Nick shakes his head in disbelief. "You went to the shower happy, you come home and we break up?"

You try to swallow the lump in your throat. "I don't want to break up with you. We just... We should have talked about it sooner."

You sit in silence for twenty minutes before he goes for some air. It hurts, for sure. It hurts a lot. But you know - okay, you think - you made the right decision.

You should have everything you want, and so should he.

-END-

290

From section 311...

"No, I like camping," you lie out of love. "I'm just not sure I packed for it."

"Got ya covered," he says, proudly picking up a pink backpack. "My sister's favorite comfy camping gear. All set."

"That is *so* nice of her."

The night is like one really long fake orgasm.

You smile your way through two unsuccessful attempts at setting up the tent, eventually figuring it out yourself. Your smile chatters when the sun goes down and he hasn't gotten the fire started - finally starting it using the car's cigarette lighter. You even bluff your way through canned beer while covered face-to-foot in borrowed clothing to ward off deer flies. Later, you actually *do* fake an orgasm, and sell that convincingly, too.

Despite the worst sleep you've ever had, you keep up the façade through a cold breakfast, a boring hike (if you've seen one tree...), lunch from a can, and a fruitless fishing expedition.

Tonight's colder than last night, but your mood improves some - partly because you leave wilderness hell in the morning, but mostly because you're getting used to canned beer.

Whatever gets you though the night...

You finally head back to the city and your misery steadily dissipates the closer you get to your shower. By the time you reach your place, you're in a genuinely good mood. And it's clear Nick had a great time, which was the point.

You're unwinding in the great indoors after work on Monday when Nick calls.

"Miss me already?" you ask.

"Yes, but that's not why I called." He's got serious voice. *If he's going to dump you after what you just endured for him...* "I told Mandy about our trip and she bet me twenty bucks that you didn't actually, well, enjoy it. I'm twenty dollars richer, right?"

"Um." You're glad he can't see you wince. "If you lie to Mandy?"

"You said you liked camping."

"I don't. I hate it," you say with bittersweet relief. "But you went to so much trouble and *you* like it, so I figured a couple of days wouldn't kill me. Unless we were eaten by a bear."

He sighs deeply and you know he feels bad - precisely what you were trying to avoid. "That's really thoughtful of you, but it was *our* anniversary. You should have had fun, too."

"I was with you, so I had fun." One more fib won't hurt him.

"Not acceptable," he says, followed by a short pause. "Can I call you back in a few minutes?"

"Uh, sure. No problem."

You wonder if you should have just come clean with him at the campsite, but decide this was still better than ruining the weekend for both of you. Your dad would say a little self-sacrifice builds character.

Fifteen minutes pass before you get a notification of an e-mail from Nick titled *Anniversary 2.0*. You open it and smirk when you see he's forwarded reservations at a posh boutique hotel for next weekend - complete with couples' massages. Your mom would tell you a little self-sacrifice builds good karma.

Turn to section 305.

291

From section 307...

The next day, Valerie and Rachel drop off your present. You open the door and find them wedged in the doorway, blocking your view. Behind them is Hank, a gorilla-sized guy who lives on their floor.

"Hank is my birthday present?" you ask suspiciously.

He blushes all the way up to his bald spot. "Just the heavy lifter."

"Go to your bedroom and don't come out until we tell you," orders Valerie, excitedly pushing you in the right direction.

You hurry into the next room and close the door, waiting impatiently until Rachel calls for you. Back in the living room, Hank is gone and in his place stands a beautiful wooden jewelry chest, perfectly matched to your bedroom furniture. It stands four feet off the ground, with six velvet-lined drawers of varied sizes.

Gorgeous and - since the girls know full well you just throw all of your jewelry into one drawer - very thoughtful.

"This is amazing," you gush, giving them each a hug. "Thank you!"

"You're welcome," says Valerie, beaming proudly. "So, did Nick give you anything to put in it?"

Embarrassed, you show them the makeover certificate and wait.

"Why did he stop there?" says Rachel. "He could've given you a voucher for the implants he's always wanted."

"Tell me you said something to him," says Valerie.

"He looked so happy," you tell them. "And it was his birthday, too. I didn't want to makeover-react and ruin the night."

"Fine." She holds her hands up in front of her. "Just don't be surprised when you get cellulite cream for your one-year anniversary."

Turn to section 301.

292

From section 260…

You go to your apartment to wait for Nick and think. You remind yourself this guy likes you so much he spent weeks tracking you down, spends most of his free time with you and, despite frequently sharing your bed, has never pressured you for sex *or* run at the sight of you without makeup. You're a couple. All that's left is the formality of labeling it.

You hear a familiar knock and open the door to a sexily rumpled Nick wearing your favorite suit. One look at his lopsided smile and you pull him in for a soft, slow kiss that almost makes you forget everything. You follow him to the couch where he pulls you onto his lap.

"How was your day?" you ask.

"Good." He strokes a hand over your hair. "Long, though. How about you?"

"Nothing special." *Here goes.* "Was just at Rach and Val's. Got grilled a little."

"Are you up to something salacious?"

"If you consider yourself salacious. Good word, by the way."

"A thesaurus is the Kama Sutra of diction to you, isn't it?"

"Indubitably."

He rubs a thumb across the back of your hand. "They grilled you about me?"

"Us."

You feel him stiffen beneath you, and not in a good way. "What was the question?"

"Whether or not we're *together*."

His thumb stills. "What'd you say?"

"That we haven't talked about it."

He rubs the top of his head, which you've learned means he's uncomfortable. You meet his eyes. "Freaking me out a little."

He looks down. "I'm seeing someone else."

You. Are. Stunned.

That never crossed your mind. You're together so often, you can't imagine he'd have time for someone else.

"I met her before I met you," he says. "It's not that serious."

"But you're sleeping with her."

"I have, yeah."

"I see."

He squares his shoulders with yours. "I really like you. You know that. But we jumped into this pretty fast. I didn't want to just slap a label on it, or, you know, make big changes."

You say nothing.

He closes his eyes. "That didn't come out right. I just didn't want to add the pressure of a commitment yet. It comes with a lot of expectations we may not be ready for."

Yeah, like not sleeping with other people.

"It's only been three weeks," he continues. "It feels longer, and it's awesome, but we're just getting to know each other."

This must be what it feels like to be on The Bachelor - knowing you're just one of the girls he's fooling around with, wondering whose secondhand spit you're getting when he kisses you.

Do you want to live like that until he picks someone? Or do you cut your losses even though, really, he's not wrong? Maybe you shouldn't keep all your cruelty free, organic eggs in one incredibly attractive basket.

"And if I went out with some guy tomorrow?"

"I'd hate it." He tucks a stray hair behind your ear. "I'm not looking for other women, but I can't ask you not to see other people."

"When you're seeing someone else."

He sighs. "It's really not that serious."

"That doesn't make me feel great."

"I don't want you to feel bad." His shoulders slump. "Maybe we should rewind a little."

Oh, no way. "Start taking turns for phone calls? See each other less? Cruise bars on the weekends?"

He leans back slightly. "You're mad."

You are, though you don't really have a right to be. He hasn't lied to you. He's not cheating. You're the one making assumptions. Still, you have to wonder how long you'd be blissfully ignorant if you hadn't brought it up. And you can't go backwards. You rest a palm on his cheek and look into his eyes, wondering how often *she* does the same thing.

"No," you say.

"You're not mad?"

"I don't want to rewind. I kind of wish I hadn't said anything, but I did. Believe me when I say it's better if I spare us both the ugly side of my personality that would emerge if I tried to forget you're seeing someone else."

His face falls. "If I stop seeing her?"

You consider this. "It won't change the fact I already feel like we're together and you don't."

You stay seated on his lap for a few more minutes before he gets up to collect the things he's left at your apartment.

He leaves and you head back to the girls' place. You let yourself in and walk straight to Rachel, who hands you a lit joint.

"So, not a couple then," she says, blowing out a stream of smoke.

-END-

293

From section 273...

People who aren't cohabitating with their significant others don't get how great it is. Nearly two months after moving in together, you and Nick have quite the little routine going.

Sure, he's a busy guy with a lot of obligations, which bothered you at first, but you knew that going in. And relationships - the good ones - are about compromise. Things are hectic right now and you don't see each other as often as you'd like, and, yeah, you've been taking on the lion's share of the housework, but it's temporary.

You've come to recognize it's best he put this time into his career now rather than later, to ensure you're as secure as possible for the next step - be it marriage, kids, whatever. Rather than fight against the tide, you've learned to go with the flow.

This is exactly what you tell Rachel and Valerie at breakfast.

Rachel picks up the menu and squints, scanning the choices with a dark blue fingernail before flipping it over and doing the same. "Did they start serving delusion here?"

"Next to the fruit cups," Valerie says, pointing at the bottom of the plastic menu.

"You guys are, like, *so* funny," you say.

"We're funny?" Rachel chokes on a laugh. "He works a lot for 'your future,' which I'm sure are *your* words, and you become The Time Traveler's Girlfriend, heading to the 1960s, cooking and cleaning and enjoying time together when he has it."

"That is not at all the plot of The Time Traveler's Wife," says Valerie. She turns to you. "Seriously, though, forgoing the spontaneity and romance unique to the first few years of a relationship in order to practice your wifely duties is pragmatic."

"You're making fun of me," you say, and she shrugs as if to say, *Duh.* "It's not like that. And who said the romance was gone? I'll have you know we are plenty romantic."

Their expressions tell you they want proof. "We're super affectionate, we cuddle on the couch when we watch TV, and we…"

"-finish each other's sentences…" the three of you say at once.

You flip them off.

"What day do you have sex?" asks Rachel.

"Sat-," you begin. "*Shut up*. Who here has lived with a boyfriend? Just me? Oh."

"All right. But don't come crying to us when he tells you he needs space, or that he's bored, or that you're too available. Actually, of course, come cry to us - we're not monsters - but expect a big 'I told you so.'"

To make like a bee and get busy, turn to section 52.
To keep the hive stable, turn to section 277.

294

From section 265...

Last Thursday night, you made dinner for you and Nick - again - and the moment he was finished, he moved to the couch, pulled out his laptop and worked while watching sports highlights.

Again.

You stuck to your guns and used the opportunity to bring up how much he's been slacking on household responsibilities. At first he gave you some push back, reminding you how busy he is, how tired he is, and why a super clean apartment isn't a huge priority for him right now. Eventually, though, he came around and promised to start pulling his weight. And he did.

For three days.

When he slips back into his old ways, you're at a loss for what to do next. You meet Scott for lunch, sure he'll have insight on how to get a man do something without being a nag.

His one and only suggestion is Manny Maids, the cleaning service he uses weekly and just "loves, loves, loves!" It's like any cleaning service, but instead of a woman, you get a super-buff guy who shows up (in your choice of muscle shirt or assless chaps) to wash your floors and clean your bathroom.

"Trust me, luv," he says as he forwards you the address. "Any straight lad who comes home to Paulo fluffing his pillows will happily empty the dishwasher and throw in a load of darks now and again."

You make the call and by the time Nick gets home from work the next day, you're relaxing in your favorite chair with a book. Paulo, wearing a fitted black tee shirt and jeans that look tailor-made for his ass, vacuums under the couch - which he lifts off the ground with one hand.

Bless you, Mother Nature.

To say Nick's surprised to be greeted, "Ciao" by a sexy, Dyson-wielding Italian man is an understatement. You're immediately summoned into the bedroom.

"Hey, babe," you say, acting like everything is normal. "How was your day?"

"Who is that?" he asks, pointing toward the living room where the vacuum is still running.

"Oh, that's Paulo. Our new maid."

"Maid? He looks like a body builder."

"He is! He just does this on the side."

"Good for Paulo. When did we decide to get a maid, anyway?"

"We didn't. I did. Sorry I didn't discuss it with you, but I didn't want to add more to your plate. I know you want to help more, and I don't want to be a nag, so…"

"So you hired Sylvester Stallone?"

"1980s Stallone maybe, but I like to think of him as a 2011 Joe Manganiello. And besides, he came highly recommended by Scott."

"I don't want some dude cleaning my apartment."

"Well, someone has to do it, and it's not just going to be this woman anymore. So either you pitch in or Paulo goes on the payroll."

Nick lets out a low growl. "Fine."

You for the win!

Turn to section 273.

295

From section 281...

The rest of that conversation went something like this: Nick called you controlling and said you need to get over the fact he's not as OCD as you are. (*How dare he!*) He also reminded you he already has a mother who nags him and isn't in the market for another one. (*How dare he, squared!*)

You told him you would get out more if you weren't constantly cleaning up after him, and that the only reason you put up with it is the hope you'll get quality time with him when he finishes another sixty hour workweek - though it seems he'd rather spend his free time with his friends.

He didn't stop moving while you argued. He brushed his teeth, changed into his gym shorts, filled his water bottle, laced up his shoes and slammed the door behind him when he left, ending the argument exactly seven minutes after it started.

God forbid he keeps them *waiting.*

Over the next twelve hours, you pace nervously around the apartment. You've fought before, sure, but this feels different.

Nick gets home around midnight, bringing with him the odour of stale draft beer. He gets into bed and passes out without saying a word to you. This morning, after exactly zero hours of sleep for you, the two of you sit silently together at the table.

It's twenty minutes before he finally speaks. "I think this was a bad idea."

"What? Living together?" you squeak. "But...it was your idea."

He shakes his head. "I know. I just didn't think it was going to be like this."

"Like what?"

"No space. Being constantly accountable."

The fact he can't look you in the eye shows you his mind is made up. "So you're breaking up with me. That's just it."

He finally looks at you and nods. He tells you he already talked to your landlord who'll let you out of the lease in two months. Nick will move back to his parents' condo while you find a new place (and replace all the furniture you no longer have).

Asshole.

Who you still love.

-END-

296

From section 297...

Your cousin Becky is getting married!

That exclamation point is not one of excitement; it's one of resentment bordering on anger. Bex is just six months older than you and, for your entire lives, she's done absolutely everything first.

She walked, talked and was potty trained first. She rode a bike, took ballet and started school first. She got her period first and, of course, lost her virginity (*way*) first. Now, go figure, she's getting married. First.

The worst part, worse than the fact she's marrying a guy named Rex (*really*), is that she asked you to be in the bridal party.

It's like she wants to hurt you.

No surprise here, Bex is already making a name for herself as a Bridezilla. She won't leave you alone. You used to talk *maybe* a few times a year, but now she calls about the wedding at least as many times each day. Dresses, churches, the perfect party favor, and the agony of picking the perfect shade of white for her dress - you've heard every mind-numbing, excruciating detail.

Twice.

Tonight, while she drones on about Rex's difficulty narrowing down his friends from ten potential groomsmen to five (*he's, like, so popular*), you're not so much looking forward to the wedding as you are rooting for the divorce. You say goodbye and grab a fork from the dish rack, pretending to repeatedly jam it in your eye.

"I for one am just so looking forward to this wedding," Nick says, looking up from his laptop.

"I think I'm starting to hate her." You groan. "Are you allowed to hate your cousin?"

"Yes. Man, I don't get it. One day. So much drama. You never see guys - excuse me, rarely see - guys getting so worked up about this stuff."

"You're more of an 'elope to Vegas' kind of guy?"

"More like a 'not get married at all' kind of guy."

What?

Where did that come from? You've been together for years and he's never said anything like that. He can't mean it. He probably just means that all guys say that, but still get married anyway, right? Only using slightly different wording.

Should you talk about this?

To ignore it, turn to section 107.
To address it, turn to section 310.

297

From sections 193 and 52...

In the past year, you've noticed a definite spike in the number of baby and wedding showers you've been asked to attend.

They're all the same: one or two people you know and lots of people you don't know or can't stand being around, watching someone open the same presents, eat the same food and have the same boring conversations.

What keeps you going is knowing those who subject you to this torture will maybe, one day, have to suffer through your wedding and baby showers - preferably in that order. That and the ten baby blankets you bought in bulk so you'd just have to pull one out of the closet and stuff it in a gift bag on your way out the door.

Tonight - a Friday, no less - you're at an "optional but strongly encouraged" baby shower in the boardroom for Laura. She's lucky you love her.

After a flurry of ribbons, bows and wrapping paper makes it look like a stork puked all over the conference table, your boss passes out cake and the gossip begins. Normally, you sit back and watch the vultures pick the bones but, today, you *are* the gossip.

"So," asks Laura, completely comfortable wearing a colorful wreath of bows around her neck. "Should we be setting a date for one of these parties for you?"

"Me?" you ask through a mouthful of strawberry shortcake. "I'm not even married."

"I mean a wedding shower." You know she's purposely torturing you, but she looks as horrified as you are when, suddenly, all of your co-workers are staring at you. "We haven't really talked about it."

"You live together, right?" asks Gillian from Accounting. You nod. "Better get talking about it. You've got one year to get engaged after moving in together or it is never gonna happen. My sister's been living with her boyfriend for eight years and she's *still* waiting for a ring."

Apparently you and Laura are the only people in the room unaware of this rule, as you both watch everyone's furious nods of approval and listen to their tales of spinster friends or cousins who lived with boyfriends for years with no result.

They're right!

Aren't they?

Suddenly you feel dizzy. Maybe you should talk to Nick after all. No one wants to be *that* girl.

To talk to Nick, turn to section 306.
To ignore your co-workers, turn to section 296.

298

From section 110 and 315...

Unbelievable!

Six months ago, you canceled plans with Rachel when Nick called with a last minute invite to a basketball game. You didn't even like basketball (still don't), but you ditched her for him because it was just so sweet of him to think of you when he had a dozen b-ball-loving friends who'd have killed to go. Then you felt the wrath of Rachel, and rightfully so, for abandoning her for a guy.

Now, your department head invites you to dinner next week - at one of the city's nicest restaurants, with all of the company bigwigs - *and* asks you to bring Nick, which is unheard of for someone at your level.

When you called Nick to invite him - brimming with excitement to have finally made the VIP list at work – he told you he couldn't make it. Why? Because he already has plans to watch a hockey game with a buddy that night – on television.

Of course, you were dumbfounded he would pick HD sports over what's obviously an important career dinner for you, and immediately flipped your lid.

You pointed out that you'd done the same for him not so long ago, but he wouldn't budge. Apparently this buddy just broke up with a girl he was dating for five minutes and needs Nick's support. After a couple of hastily chosen expletives, you hung up on him.

That was two days ago and you haven't heard from him since. You're still mad, but you hate fighting with him and just want the nervous knot in your stomach to go away.

Should you call him and just make up?

To call him, turn to section 318.
To wait him out, turn to section 308.

299

From section 252...

Dressed in shorts and a skimpy tank, you greet Nick at the door with a cold beer and a hopeful smile.

"Uh oh," he says, instantly on to your game. "What do you want?"

"For you to install my giant air conditioners so I can cool this place down."

"Giant, eh?" He eyes you carefully - all part of your plan. "Sounds like a big favor. All right, I'll install them, but you can't change when I'm done."

"Deal!" A slightly sexist one, but whatever.

In your bedroom, he takes a giant step backward as you open the closet.

"What?" you ask.

"Every time you open that thing, I see myself knocked out by a bowling ball."

"No bowling ball. My machete collection, maybe."

When the temperature drops, you take a cue from your mom and gush to Nick about how lucky you are to have such a big strong, blah, blah, and so forth. He beams with pride over your recognition of his innate manly abilities, even taking on the macho posture your dad gets when she does that.

"No problem. Anything else I can help with?"

"Actually, I do have this closest organizer but I don't have the right tools to screw it in."

Oh yeah, you said that.

He clears his throat. "I've got some tools in my car. I'll go grab them."

"Great!" You clap your hands together. "And I'll get you another beer."

Okay, that last part wasn't your mom, you hope (*shudder*), but certainly effective.

Turn to section 311.

300

From section 307...

"So," he says, looking at the open envelope in your hand. "Do you like it?"

"It's great," you say, your voice less convincing than you'd have liked.

He tilts his head slightly. "But?"

"Honestly, I guess I'm just not sure how I feel about my boyfriend giving me the gift of a head-to-toe make-over."

He looks confused, and then a little panicked. "I thought you chicks loved this stuff."

"Us chicks do love this stuff, when we buy it for ourselves. When you buy it for me, it's kind of like you're saying you want me to change into something... better."

It takes a minute, but he finally realizes his mistake. "Wow, that's the most unromantic gift ever, isn't it?"

"Maybe a little misguided, but I know you meant well."

"Okay, I have an idea. Wait here," he says and leaves the room.

He returns a moment later and tells you to close your eyes and hold out your hand. You do and he places something tiny and cold in your palm. "I was thinking about this anyway," he says. "Open your eyes."

You look down and see a silver key.

"It's for my place!" he says, proud of himself.

"Now, that's a romantic gift."

Bring on the birthday suits!

Turn to section 320.

301

From section 291…

Time flies when you're not having fun.

It's been two months since your birthdays and that was the last time you and Nick did anything even remotely romantic. Well, that's not entirely true. Last week, he surprised you with chocolate - but then ate most of it, so it doesn't count.

Together nearly a year now, your regular romantic dinners and cozy cocktails have given way to take-out, beer and wine in front of your television. If you weren't still having sex regularly, you'd panic into the pepperoni pizza you're currently sharing.

Still, as he reaches for another slice and turns up the volume on the television, you can't help but wonder, is this how it starts? Or, *gulp*, ends?

Obviously, something needs to be done before your love story goes from epic to epitaph, but how do you go about it?

To address the issue head on, turn to section 319.
To find a subtle approach, turn to section 302.

302

From section 301...

You spend the remainder of the show preoccupied with finding the subtlest way to let Nick know you're craving a little romance without making it into a thing.

If only the perfect opportunity would just fall into your lap.

"Oh, hey, before I forget," says Nick as the credits roll. "My college roommate's in town next week and wants to get together on Friday. Think you can rustle up some plans with the girls?"

Well hello there, Opportunity. Come on in! Something to drink?

"Rachel," you say and stand to clear your plates. "Val's...doubtful."

"Did you have a fight?"

"No." You laugh softly. "New guy. They're in the schmoopy romantic, attached at the hip, lovey-dovey phase. She'll rejoin the rest of us soon enough."

"Whoa now. Aren't we in the abyss anymore?" he asks, following you into the kitchen.

"Of course, we are," you lie, kissing him on the cheek. "It's just a different abyss - the comfortable-couple abyss. Don't you think it's different from when we started dating?"

"Sure it is! We have sex now."

"You know what I mean."

"Come on. We do romantic stuff all the time. Our birthdays?"

"Totally romantic," you say, nodding emphatically.

"See, and that was just..."

"Two months ago?"

"That long? Okay, well let's not switch abysses yet. You never know what can happen." He gives you a soft kiss and pulls you into his arms.

"All right," you say, nuzzling into his neck. "I'll cancel the movers."

Turn to section 312.

303

From section 260…

One hour and two glasses of wine later, you all but run up the stairs to your apartment knowing Nick's waiting at your door.

Once you see his face, the way his tailored suit hugs his solid frame, his slightly loosened tie and mussed hair, you completely forget the conversation you just had. Your libido takes over. You rush over and fling your arms around his neck, swallowing his greeting with your mouth, and sighing when he returns the kiss. You don't even care that your nosy neighbor, Ida Splenta is surely spying on you through her peephole.

His fingers travel from your waist to your back pocket, finding your keys. Without looking, he unlocks the door - a skill he's acquired over the last few weeks. Once inside, he kicks the door shut and you slide your hands down his chest and under his jacket, easing it back and over his shoulders, tossing it somewhere in the vicinity of your coatrack.

He walks you backward to your bedroom until you the backs of your knees meet the mattress. Smiling, you slip his tie over his head and unbutton his shirt, which he sheds as you take off your sweater. Moments later, you're tangled together on your bed, nothing but your matching bra and panties and his boxer briefs between you. Hands and mouths everywhere.

You don't want to wait anymore.

Wordlessly, you reach over to your nightstand and remove a condom from the drawer.

"Wait," he says, and his hand closes over yours.

This is unexpected.

You get a sinking feeling. "What's wrong?"

A torturously long moment passes before he answers. "Nothing's wrong, exactly, but I should tell you something."

You're sure he's about to say he has an STI. And not the kind wiped out with a strong antibiotic. The kind that drops by for a visit once every once in a while.

"I've sort of been seeing someone else," he says, wincing as though bracing for impact.

Yup. Not what you were expecting.

"Sort of?" you say. He lies beside you now, watching your face carefully. "How long?"

"Here and there for a couple of months. Nothing serious."

Here and there? Nothing serious? Like this isn't serious? "I'm such a fool." You cover your eyes with your arm.

"Don't say that," he says, gently lowering your arm.

"I actually thought we were together. Like together, together."

He's quiet for a moment. "So I take it you aren't seeing anyone else."

You glare at him. "Silly me, I thought the fact you spent three weeks looking for me, and the bulk of the last few weeks *with* me, meant you weren't sleeping with multiple women."

He abruptly sits up and swings his leg over the bed, reaching for his pants. "A theory supported by the fact I just turned down sex *you* initiated."

"Oh, I'm sorry. You get a gold star for being sexually monogamous with *her* and just sleeping with me."

His jaw tightens. "You're acting like I was cheating on you, even after pointing out that we've never talked about exclusivity. How can you be-"

You raise your voice. "Because you've been *acting* like a boyfriend. I spend more time with you than I do with my friends. You stay here at least three times a week."

He matches your volume. "Because I like being with you!"

"But not *just* me, right?"

He fastens his belt and looks up at you. There is bona fide anger in his eyes. "Actually, yes, just with you. If you had let me finish, I'd have told you I plan to break things off with her tomorrow and wanted to tell you before taking things any further."

"So you cheated on her with me."

"Why stop assuming now?" He laughs ruefully. "We weren't exclusive, or I would never have started seeing you. I haven't slept with her, or even seen her, since you and I started dating. I'd have ended it weeks ago, but I had to wait for her to get back from Tokyo because when I'm done using a woman for sex, I like to break it to her in person."

You feel like you swallowed a 20-pound dumbbell.

You watch him finish dressing and realize he's right. He doesn't owe you anything. You never had The Talk. You never asked if he was seeing anyone else - you just assumed he wasn't because you aren't. He didn't have to tell you anything he just told you, and what do you do? You fly off the handle before he has a chance to explain.

"I'm sorry," you say quietly, searching for something to say that will erase the last five minutes.

"Yeah, me too," he says with a sigh.

-END-

304

From sections 316 and 257...

Hey, you mature, supportive and trusting Super Girlfriend.
You are wonderful.

The last three weeks before Nick moved were harder than you'd anticipated, but you both made the most of your time together. You searched through endless Craigslist ads for an apartment, you channeled your inner Midwesterner to help him pick out a climate appropriate wardrobe, and then pack said wardrobe. You let him teach you how to use your laptop's web cam (even though you already know how to use it) so you could talk face-to-face whenever you wanted. You even drove him to the airport.

In the two months since, you've been patient when things turned out to be even more difficult than you feared. You've never used the webcams; hell he's been so busy with his new job, he barely has time to sneak in a phone call to you every other day. You didn't even sulk when he canceled his first trip home to see you because of a last minute trip to Hong Kong. Of course, that one was helped when he sent you a first class ticket to New York for the upcoming long weekend. You've been in a pretty good mood since.

You can't wait to spend three whole days with him doing everything and nothing. There's even talk of the Hamptons, for which you just purchased a sexy white bikini that cost a third of your paycheck. You're placing the prettily packaged parcel on your passenger seat when Nick calls.

"Calling to let me know where the limo's picking me up Friday?" you say. It's quiet on his end. "Babe? You there?"

"Yeah." He clears his throat. "Do you have a sec?"

Sure he's about to cancel on you, *again*, you can almost see what's left of your patience escaping through the open window. "Of course. What's up?"

"It's about this weekend..."

"Do you need to reschedule?" *In through the nose, out through the mouth.*

The next few minutes are kind of a blur, but you make out the following words: "Met someone… think I'm in love… want to be honest… didn't mean for this to happen…. harder than I thought… really sorry… forgive me."

You hang up without saying a word and then sit silently for a few minutes before calling Rachel and Valerie to come collect you and your car. Good friends that they are, they take you home, ply you with liquor and, instead of letting you feel stupid and embarrassed, help you fantasize about destroying Nick, his new apartment, his new convertible *and* his new girlfriend - all at the same time.

-END-

305

From section 290...

Yu hab a tewable code.

You were up all night coughing and sneezing and today has been all about sneezing and coughing. Under self-imposed quarantine on your couch, you're catching up on the soaps you watched as a kid and occasionally replacing the tissues shoved up your nose to stop it from running.

As miserable as you are, it still beats work.

When Nick calls you on his way home, you tell him in your sore-throatiest voice that you're sick.

"Sorry to hear that, hun," he says. "But I'm definitely liking the voice." This makes you feel marginally better. "What say I stop by with some of that chicken soup from the deli down the street and a bottle of that knock-you-the-fuck-out medicine?"

If you could breathe, you'd sigh. You're just not sure you want him to see you. Like *this*. He's never seen you sick before. Unplugging your nose with some nasty-tasting nasal spray is easy enough, but you can't look much better than you feel - though, your footie pajamas are pretty adorable.

Still, his very sweet offer shows you're long past that kind of superficial crap mattering, and you could really go for some chicken soup.

To let Nick make a house call, turn to section 153.
To heal thyself, turn to section 187.

306

From section 297…

When you get home from the shower, Nick is sprawled out on the couch, beer in hand, watching the end of the football game.

You slip off your shoes and sit down beside him, taking the beer from his hand.

"Ugh," you say, and take a long pull from the bottle. "I *hate* baby showers."

"Score one for the penis!" he says, grabbing another beer from the cooler resting at his feet. "Any fist-fights?"

"No, but one chick asked me so many questions about us and when we'd get married and breed that I seriously considered clotheslining her."

"That bad?"

"At least twenty questions," you say, shaking your head for emphasis in the hope he's buying your Girls Who Want to Get Married Are So Ridiculous act.

"This is why I hate marriage," he says. "Everyone acts like it's this special club you must, must, must be a member of. It's bullshit."

"Well. It's not *all* bullshit."

"It's a piece of paper," he says, throwing his head back with a short laugh. "I have never wanted to get married."

Hmm, sorry, what? "Well, if it's *just* a piece of paper, then why not get married because it's important to the person you love?"

"Because I don't want to. Would you really expect me to get married just because you wanted it? How is that different from me asking you *not* to get married because I don't want to?" You let that hang in the air. "Wouldn't it be enough if I told you I wanted a life and a family with you?"

"You want to have kids?" you choke. "Like, soon?"

"No! Okay, let's slow down here. I think it's a little premature to even be thinking about this. Maybe we should table it for later."

Later?

How do you "table" your boyfriend telling you he doesn't want to get married?

You want to get married!

You're almost sure of it.

Of course, he could change his mind. It's not like you want to get married tomorrow. Who knows what he'll think a year from now? You're already living together. He's obviously serious about you.

Of course, this could just be the next stop on the road to being "that" girl.

How can you spend so long with someone and just now learn they don't want to get married? Are you willing to compromise on this? Wait it out and see if he changes his mind, resigning yourself to be okay with it if he doesn't?

Or should you press the issue and be willing to walk away now, no matter how much it hurts, instead of two years from now?

To speak now, turn to section 289.
To temporarily hold your peace, turn to section 221.

307

From sections 286 and 275...

It's your birthday!

It also happens to be Nick's birthday, too - quite serendipitou*s*.

You've had a great day, with unexpected gifts and a lovely lunch with Sheri and Laura, followed by two-dozen white roses from your parents delivered to your office. Tomorrow night, you celebrate with the girls, but tonight, you celebrate with Nick - preferably in your birthday suits.

After a cozy dinner, you're excited to give him the designer watch you saw him admiring last month, bouncing in the passenger seat the entire drive back to your apartment and then practically dragging him inside.

No surprise, he loves, loves, loves his watch, insisting you shouldn't have, but unable to keep the huge grin off of his face.

Yay!

Now it's your turn.

Double yay!

Nick pulls an envelope out of his pocket.

You're intrigued.

Plane tickets, you decide.

You tear it open.

It's… It's…a gift certificate for a complete makeover - hair, make up and wardrobe consultation.

Right, because nothing says "I love you" like asking you to change your entire appearance. You can already picture Rachel and Valerie's horrified faces when you show them tomorrow night.

Looking up at Nick, you can see he's quite pleased with himself.

To lie and say you like it, turn to section 291.
To tell him the truth, turn to section 300.

308

From section 298…

It's been four days since you fought with Nick. Four days with no contact.

So far, you're amazed at your will power in not calling him to apologize for something that was his fault in the first place, but now your resolve has begun to dissolve. You lay on your couch, staring at the phone resting on your stomach, willing it to ring. And it does, tickling your belly as it vibrates.

It's him - you win!

You let it ring a few times before answering.

"Hello," you say, hoping it sounds like you weren't waiting for his call.

"How's it going?" he asks awkwardly.

"Good," you lie. "It's going good."

"Listen, I just wanted to apologize for the other night. You were right. The dinner is important to you and I should go. I talked to Dave and he's actually got a date that night, so everything worked out."

You can't help but wonder if this remorse surfaced before or after he found out poor, heartbroken Dave was bailing on him for a girl, but you decide to let it go given he knows he was wrong *now*.

Turn to section 316.

309

From sections 140 and 317...

Some might think it strange that Nick hasn't spent much time with your friends, but with everyone's busy schedules of...stuff, it's been hard to find a time for everyone to sit down and get to know each other. But tonight, you're finally having dinner with your guy and the girls.

By the time your meals arrive, you're elated. Everything's going great. Everyone's getting along and it's hard (even for you) to get a word in edgewise, what with all the chatting and laughing. And just when you're thinking it doesn't get better than this, you hear something sure to make things worse.

Nick: Men totally get the shaft when it comes to parenting rights. It's brutal.

Valerie: How do you figure?

Nick: Think about it. If a woman gets pregnant, the man has no say at all about whether or not to keep the child, and when it's born, the guy has no choice but to support it, but gets little to no say in how the money is used in the actual rearing of the child.

Valerie: Somehow I think you'd change your mind if *you* were the pregnant one. Women have to carry the child, so they should have more rights.

Nick: But everything *else* should be equal, right? Or maybe women deserve special exceptions to equality when it suits them?

Valerie (turning to you): What do you think?

Thanks a-fucking-lot.

Truth be told, you agree with Valerie - as does Rachel, who's been *mmmhmming* and *yeah-ing* alongside her - but if you admit it, Nick might feel like you're ganging up on him. If you side with him, Rachel and Valerie will be pissed.

To side with your boyfriend, turn to section 315.
To side with your best friends, turn to section 313.

310

From section 296...

"Like never? Never ever?" you ask, hoping - praying - he's just being a guy.

He looks up from his laptop and shakes his head. "I really don't think so."

You feel like someone is sitting on your chest.

How could you have gotten this far into a relationship and have no idea he doesn't want to get married? Not just to you, but to anyone.

"It's really that important to you?" he asks, when he sees how disappointed you are. You nod dumbly. "You never really talk about it."

This is true. Fucking Catch 22's. "Why don't you want to?" you ask.

"Why *do* you want to?"

"They're called ovaries."

He laughs gently. "That's not a good enough reason."

"Because it's what you do next," you say. "Get married. Have kids. Build a future. Retire. Die."

"I'm pretty sure we can still do the rest of those things without being married," he says, setting his computer aside and standing.

"But what about security and financial protection?"

"It's called a domestic partnership," he says, walking to you and placing his hands on your shoulders. "What else ya got?"

"The presents?" you ask with a wry smile.

He laughs again. "Look, marriage works for my parents - for lots of people - but I don't want it. And I honestly don't think I'm going to change my mind."

Oh. Well, no big.

He lowers his head until your eyes are level. "Are you going to be okay with that? I mean... I wouldn't blame you if..."

You gasp. "You want to break up?"

"No! Of course I don't. But you should get everything you want from life. I don't want to be the reason you don't."

To agree not to be betrothed, turn to section 50.
To tell him you need to think on it, turn to section 36.

311

From sections 299 and 313…

Tomorrow is your and Nick's one-year anniversary! That's one year since your first date, not the day you met, which has its own anniversary - not that you'd admit it.

When you think of how you used to worry about whether he'd call or if you'd see him that week, it seems so silly. Especially after Nick remembered the occasion on his own *and* insisted on surprising you with your first trip together. It's so romantic and so…unlike every other relationship you've ever had.

You promised yourself you wouldn't hypothesize about your amorous weekend, not wanting to build up unrealistic expectations. It was an ill-fated plan. Within twenty-four hours, you were fantasizing about couples' massages, hot tubs, dancing, and horseback riding on the beach. Rachel stopped talking to you two days ago, nauseated by your whimsy.

When he knocks on your door tonight, you're ready to jump out of your skin. He's excited, too, if his huge boyish grin is any indication. He blindfolds you with red silk before carefully guiding you and your luggage (full of attire for a beachfront ranch and spa) to the car.

He buckles you in and you're off - with no idea where you're going, but positive it will be somewhere special. Two or three hours later, he turns onto a dirt road, convincing you that you're in the country.

"We're here," he declares, and you tear off the blindfold.

Trees.

Tree after tree after tree.

One more and, yep, it's a forest.

You look for horses, but there's nary a hoof-print in sight. Instead of massage tables, you see picnic tables.

No. Anything but…

"Welcome to Lake Tahoe - more specifically Lover's Leap," Nick announces, parking the car and climbing out. "We're camping!"

No, no, no, no, no!

This isn't right. You hate camping. Ever since your dad dragged the family out to Redwood National Park when you were a kid. You hated the cold, the mosquitoes and the canned food, but mostly you hated Rory for slipping a trout into your sleeping bag. A few hours squished against it like a sardine left you smelling like a fish counter for a week. You haven't camped since and don't want to now.

You head to the back of the car to help unload the trunk. No wonder he blindfolded you - it's bursting with the world's oldest collection of camping junk and surely would've given away his surprise.

And given you a chance to fake pancreatitis.

He explains he "pillaged the family gear" in his parents' storage locker last night. You perk up when he says he looked at air mattresses, but quickly deflate when he says he decided against it. Apparently it wouldn't be "real camping."

How on Earth are you going to get through two days of this?

Having yet to hear a word from you or see you smile, Nick says, "Oh, no. You hate it."

To be the bearer of bad news, turn to section 242.
To grin and grizzly bear it, turn to section 290.

312

From section 302...

On Saturday, you awake to a call from Nick, who's in a great mood.

"Good morning, sunshine," his voice booms. "Get up and get dressed. I've got a surprise."

"Sounds romantic," you say sleepily. "What do I do once I'm dressed?"

"Drive over to my place. I'd come get you, romantic guy that I am, but I can't leave my apartment."

"Handcuffing yourself to a bed and hiding the key isn't romantic."

"Closer than you think. Now get a move on...he said romantically?"

You jump out of bed, fly through your morning routine and zip over to Nick's. You try his door, but it's locked. There's an envelope at your feet that says, *Open Me*. Inside is a key with a note attached by pink ribbon. *Use me*.

So Alice in Wonderland.

Intrigued, you let yourself in and are immediately overwhelmed by the smell of bacon. You follow it to Nick's dining room, amazed to see a breakfast feast of three kinds of eggs, bacon, croissants, fruit, juice and coffee. Looking back at the mess in his kitchen, it's obvious he actually prepared it himself.

"How's this for a romantic surprise?" He pulls out a chair for you.

"This is incredible," you say as you sit. "Where do I start?"

"Not this part - the other part," he says, looking down at your hand.

You look down. "The key?"

"Not *the* key. *Your* key."

"*My* key." You stand and give him a smacking kiss. "You're the king of romance, babe."

Turn to section 320.

313

From section 309...

When the server offers the dessert menu, Nick declines, saying he's not feeling well. He's barely looked up since you agreed with Valerie.

Equal parts welcoming the excuse to leave the tense situation and dreading what will happen once you do, you say goodbye to the girls and head out to the car. You make a couple of attempts at conversation, hoping to breeze by the issue, but the silent treatment he gives you speaks volumes.

"Do we need to talk about this?" you ask.

"Talk about what?" he asks. "The fact that you totally hung me out to dry back there? That wasn't embarrassing at all."

"I'm sorry you were embarrassed, but how exactly did I hang you out to dry?"

"By siding with your friends over me," he says, shocked he needs to explain.

"I didn't side with anyone. I just happen to agree with her. Should I have lied about my opinion? Did you wake up in 1962, or is your ego just that fragile?"

Nick considers this, finally laughing. "I'm being a jerk, aren't I?"

"See, and now I agree with you."

Turn to section 311.

314

From section 53...

You hold out your palm. "Give me your phone."

"My phone?"

"The one in your hand?"

He eyes you warily. "Are you going to smash it?"

"You'll just have to see," you say with a smirk.

He hands it to you open to your contact info. "It's the zero," you say, and hit the back arrow. "The sixth number is zero."

His face relaxes when you hand it back to him. "So, you're not mad?"

"Well, I'm disappointed you gave up after only eighteen numbers, but-"

He grabs your face with both hands and cuts your words off with his mouth. Your hands automatically slide up his chest, over his shoulders, and link behind his neck.

Oh, mama.

A few moments later, he releases you. "Thank you."

"For what?" you ask, just a little out breath.

"Most girls don't believe me when I feed them that story."

You playfully punch his shoulder. "Jerk."

He laughs. "Come with me."

"Where?"

"To whichever of our apartments is closer."

You don't hesitate when he takes your hand and leads you toward the exit. You look around for your friends, noting Rachel's protective scowl and Valerie's happy wave.

His place is closer.

He kisses you in the cab to his apartment. Then he kisses you again in the elevator, oblivious to, or not caring about, the biker with a Shih Tzu who gets in after you. You reach his front door and he unlocks it with one hand, leaving the other linked with yours. Once inside, he leads you directly to his couch where you make out until you pass out. Happily.

You're a little disoriented when you wake up the next morning, wondering for a moment why your pillow is so firm. Then you remember it's not a pillow, it's Nick's chest. You raise your head to find him already awake, a bright smile on his face. "Breakfast?" he asks.

You smile sleepily at him, nodding vigorously.

Continue to section 260.

315

From section 309...

What's that old adage? If looks could kill?

Well, when you tell Valerie you think there's "definitely some room to move in making parenting rights equal for men," the razor sharp glare she shoots at you through her chrome Ralph Laurens nearly flatlines you. Even Rachel looks to be contemplating what to wear to your funeral.

Nick's ego remains intact - he may even be a little smug - and you manage to get through the rest of the meal, but jump at the check before your server can say "dessert." Fortunately, you don't even have to fake a sudden headache.

In the morning, you head over to The Spoon for what's sure to be an awkward, already scheduled breakfast with your friends. You arrive at the restaurant and aren't totally surprised to find Rachel sitting alone at a booth for two.

"How much trouble am I in?" you ask, settling in across from her. "One to ten."

"Solid ten. Dude..."

"I panicked! Of course I agree with her, but it was the first time you guys really hung out with Nick and I didn't want him to feel like it was three-on-one."

She shrugs. "I guess, but *she* doesn't see it that way."

"How long do you think she'll be mad?"

"Funny you should ask." She grins evilly.

You curse when she pulls something from her coat pocket. "What?"

"Just passing along your penance. You're to write out 'I will not sell out my friends or my beliefs to make my boyfriend happy.' Five *hundred* times."

"You're not serious." You take the paper from her.

"Oh, but I am," she says, far too amused. "Ready to order?"

Turn to section 298.

316

From section 308…

This morning, you realize you're just a few weeks away from your one-year anniversary with Nick.

Wow.

It seems like yesterday you were doing emotional cartwheels over the six-month mark. You want to do something super special to celebrate, spending the afternoon researching romantic weekend getaways, printing out info for bed and breakfasts in Napa, Palm Springs and Catalina to show him tonight.

Nick stands and gives you his customary kiss hello, but there's a noticeable contrast in your demeanours. You're excited and he's… Something is definitely up.

He's not unhappy to see you, but he seems nervous, too. Maybe he got the anniversary excitement memo. How adorable would it be if he pulled out his own list of getaways?

Aw.

You place your drink orders and launch right into your pitch. "Guess what? Our one-year anniversary is just around the corner! Can you believe it?"

"Seriously?" His head jerks back in surprise. "Wow."

"My thoughts exactly. What do you say to a weekend away from the city?"

You were expecting enthusiasm, but Nick says nothing. He looks uncomfortable and maybe a little pained.

"Or not," you say. Your 'this is weird' meter beeps again. "We could stay here and have a great time, too."

"No, it's a great idea," he reassures you. "But I have to tell you something."

"Something good, I hope," you say with a tight smile. You've had butterflies before, but this feels more like moths.

"Something good." He drums on the table with his fingers, a nervous tick. "My boss offered me a promotion."

So why isn't he smiling? The moths wig out.

"A big promotion," he continues. "Two levels above my current position."

"That's amazing! I'm so proud of you. Something else to celebrate, right?"

"Yeah, it's great." He nods. "Great and in New York."

New York. You never would have imagined such a grand and inspiring place could burst your bubble, rain on your parade and knock the wind out of your sails all at once, but it has.

"Congratulations," you tell him half-heartedly. "Did you take it?"

"I have until Monday to answer, but I'm planning to, yes."

"I guess that's settled then." You snort. "Easy decision."

"Please, don't be mad. It's not an easy decision. Not at all. But I'm afraid it's an obvious one. Opportunities like this don't come around twice and I've been working so hard."

"When do you leave?"

"Three weeks."

You silently curse your high school English teacher, Mrs. Gallant for introducing you to dramatic irony. "So it's curtains for us then?"

"No. It doesn't have to be. We'll do long distance. I'll be making twice what I am now. I can easily travel back and forth, or fly you in. New York, babe. It's not all bad."

"You really think that's going to work? Seeing each other once a month, or less?"

"I think it's worth a shot, don't you?"

A shot. Easy for you to say, Big Promotion in New York Guy.

You can already feel the anxiety of wondering what he's doing thousands of miles away. "And if it doesn't work?"

"Then we tried." He takes your hand. "You know I'd prefer it if the job was here, but it's not. And I know you want me to succeed and be happy."

Really, you want *you* to be happy, but you'd be a complete bitch if you didn't support him. The question is, do you support him as his girlfriend and trust your relationship is strong enough to withstand different time zones, or do you end it now and save yourself even bigger heartache down the road?

To go the long distance, turn to section 304.
To go the lone distance, turn to section 322

317

From section 323…

Note to self: Buy a more comfortable couch.

You were no doubt angry Nick fell asleep last night, putting the kibosh on the big finish to your romantic evening, but after another glass of wine, you realized it wasn't his fault and transitioned from mad to disappointed.

Okay, maybe you were still a little mad. You did leave his legs hanging over the side of the bed before you camped out on the couch, tossing and turning until finally falling asleep.

You awake to the smell of coffee permeating the blanket over your head. Crawling out of your cocoon, you see Nick kneeling beside you, holding out a coffee cup with a guilty smile on his face.

"I'm such a jerk," he says when you accept it. "I can't believe I fell asleep. Why didn't you wake me?"

"I did." You laugh. "Twice."

"Are you mad?"

"I was at first," you admit. "But you couldn't help it. No big deal."

"I'm gonna make it up to you right now. Let's go."

"Where?"

"I'm taking you to breakfast and then we're doing anything you want."

"Anything?" you ask with a mischievous grin.

"Short of self-mutilation and shaving my head, sure."

"Oh, you are *so* going to regret this."

After breakfast, Nick sticks to his word and spends a day doing things most guys avoid at all cost; starting with two hours at the mall watching you try on at least two dozen different outfits for an upcoming conference you're attending, followed by a Reese Witherspoon double feature and a week's worth of reality TV. And not a single complaint.

Turn to section 309.

318

Form section 298…

You called Nick, but he didn't answer, so you left him a message saying you didn't want to fight and asking him to call you so you could work things out.

This brings the tally of days since you last spoke to five. You can't remember the last time you went this long without talking to each other since you started dating. That knot in your stomach is becoming a noose by the time you finally hear from him tonight. You're relieved, but still wary when you answer.

"Hello?" you ask tentatively.

"Hey," he says, casually. "What's up?"

"Not much. I called you the other day."

"Yeah. I'm sorry I didn't call you back, but I needed some time to cool off. The way you handled that situation was really childish. Swearing at me and hanging up? I'd hope I've earned a little more respect than that."

You're being scolded! He sounds like your father back in high school - when you'd swear at him and slam doors. Okay, you see his point, but he should apologize, too.

"You're right," you concede. "I was being completely juvenile, but I hope you understand why I was so mad."

"I'm honestly not sure I do. It bothers me you don't take it seriously when I say a friend is counting on me."

He's seriously starting to sound like a girl. "He was *'dating'* her for all of three weeks! I doubt he even knows her birthday. And that's not what I was - no, am - mad about. I'm mad because when *my* friend needed *me*, you pressured me to go with you!"

"I didn't make you do anything you didn't want to do."

"Oh, I see. So you just don't *want* to come to this dinner with me."

"It's more like I don't think I should. It might not be the right time for me to start rubbing elbows with your bosses."

What? You've done office functions together in the past. It's never been a problem before. Unless… "Why would now be a bad time?"

He sighs deeply. "Okay, here it is. I've been doing some thinking and I'm just… I'm not sure we're right for each other. In the long-term. I've actually been thinking a lot about being single again." He swallows hard. "So I don't think it would be right for me to go with you to such an important function."

That bullshit scolding he gave you earlier is starting to make sense now. He's making excuses to dump you! "Because you *might* break up with me or because you *are* breaking up with me."

"Because I am, I guess."

Unbelievable, squared!

You'd probably be sad if you weren't so pissed off right now. And you're nothing if not consistent, so you curse him a big blue streak and hang up on him.

-END-

319

From section 301...

"Uh oh," says Nick, snapping you back to reality. "What's wrong?"

"Huh? Nothing," you tell him, sinking into the couch.

"Then why are you doing the stare-into-space-with-furrowed-brow thing? That usually means I did something wrong."

"Okay, since you asked." You wrap your arms around yourself. "Why don't we do anything romantic anymore?"

He looks at you incredulously. "What are you talking about? Do you remember our birthdays? Totally romantic."

Remembering his gift of a head-to-toe makeover suddenly makes you angry. "That was two months ago," you say, raising your voice slightly. "And the dinner may have been great, but I'd hardly call your gift romantic."

"You said you liked it," he says, rubbing the back of his head, confused by the sudden turn of events.

"Because I didn't want to hurt your feelings on your birthday but, really, you could have just given me a list of all of the things you'd like to change about me!"

"Right, so instead of being honest at the time, you wait two months and throw it in my face. That's a little passive aggressive, isn't it?"

"I am *not* passive aggressive," you tell him. "I never would have said anything at all if you did something romantic once in a while."

"Really? When was the last time *you* did something romantic for me?"

He's got you there, but it's too late to back down now. "I'm the woman," you insist. "It's your job to do the romantic stuff."

"And the woman's only job is to whine and bitch about not being treated like a princess." He nods slowly. "I see how that works."

"Come on! Does it really take so much effort to come up with an occasional gesture to show your girlfriend how you feel about her?"

"Okay. How about a gesture that shows you what I'm feeling for you right now?"

You're half-expecting him to flip you the bird, but instead, he walks past you and into the hallway where he grabs his keys off the table and keeps going - right out the door.

Turn to section 204.

320

From sections 300 and 312...

You know a few of Nick's friends from the night you met, and since then have shared a handful of hellos with a few of them during comings-and-goings from his apartment, but you've never spent enough time with them to win them over.

In your experience, friend approval generally comes in one of two forms: one, after spending a couple of hours with your funny, charming and beautiful self, one of his friends will put an arm around you and say to the guy in question, "Buddy, this one's a keeper." Or two, you'll head to the bathroom and slyly turn around in time to catch his friends giving him the enthusiastic nod of approval and maybe even a high-five.

Either way, an endorsement from his pals is crucial in taking your relationship to the next level, so you've really been looking forward to tonight's party with his friends.

You take extra care getting ready, trying to make it look like you didn't try at all. You keep the drinking to a minimum, are talkative but not a chatterbox, and have managed to keep your foot out of your mouth - so far.

You're much more comfortable than you expected. His friends are a lot of fun and you hit it off with pretty much everyone you talk to. While chatting with the girls, his buddy Russ' girlfriend, Sally, who is a little tipsy, suggests it would be fun if everyone rented a cottage together for a weekend getaway. When another girl seconds the motion, they all start chattering away.

It's so exciting that everyone's so excited!

It just so happens your family has a big, beautiful cottage on the water at Stinson Beach, and your folks are always urging you to use it more often.

How much fun would that be?

To offer up the family cottage, turn to section 321.
To offer to bring snacks, turn to section 98.

321

From section 320...

Thanks to two glasses of liquid courage, you have no problem chiming in when the gaggle of giddy girls contemplates how to go about renting a cottage.

"We could use my parents' cottage," you offer. "It's pretty big. Sleeps eight comfortably, or twelve uncomfortably."

And the room goes quiet. All eyes zero in on you. The girls' eyes gleam at the potential of solidifying their cottage fantasy, but the rest of the room - more accurately, the men - collectively turn their heads in your direction and wince, most sucking air in through their teeth.

Nick looks stunned.

After an agonizing moment, people return to their conversations, and you down the rest of your drink. You spend the next hour pretending you aren't out-of-your mind uncomfortable until Nick finally asks if you're ready to go.

You're painfully aware you didn't receive so much as a single nod from his friends. No endorsement. He drives in silence and you can't help but wonder if his pals may have suggested he throw you back into the sea. This isn't helped by the fact he's headed toward your apartment, not his, which you thought was the plan.

"That was fun," you tell him warily, unable to stand the silence.

"Yeah," he mumbles, without taking his eyes off the road.

"You're mad at how I offered my parents' cottage, aren't you? I must have sounded totally pretentious."

"You didn't sound pretentious."

That's a relief. "What then?"

His silence is your answer.

"You're mad I offered it at all."

More silence.

"Really?" you ask him, disbelief making way for anger.

"You wouldn't be upset if I'd done the same with *your* friends?"

"Upset that my boyfriend felt comfortable enough to make an offer like that to my friends? More like outraged."

"You don't need to be sarcastic."

"Then explain to me why what I did was so awful?"

"It's just going to start a fight."

"It's a little late to be worried about that."

"All right, fine. You don't think you were being a little…presumptuous?"

"About?"

"I don't want to hurt your feelings, but what if I'm not ready for a couples' weekend?"

"Why would that hurt my feelings? We've been together nearly a year and supposedly love each other, but you're not sure if you're serious enough to have me spend more than a few hours with your friends. That sounds perfectly reasonable."

"This is exactly what I was afraid of. I didn't say I'm not ready. It just would've been nice if you'd asked me first - you know, in case I wasn't."

Turn to section 323.

322

From sections 316 and 257…

You have a fleeting thought that you wish you'd read your horoscope today. Maybe it would've somehow vaguely predicted this unexpected turn of events, giving you a chance to, you know, do something to get Nick fired.

But no, he gets you with a classic blindside, and a variant on the old "Don't you want me to be happy?" line.

"Of course I want all of those things for you," you say, meaning it. "But I want to be happy, too. And I know me. I will not handle long distance well. I'll get insecure, and jealous, and paranoid… We'll wind end up hating each other."

Nick's silent for a moment, but finally nods. "Okay," he says. "I understand." He turns his attention to his menu, seemingly unaffected by the fact you just broke up with him.

Say what?

He's not even going to give you the courtesy of trying to change your mind?

"Okay?" you ask expectantly. "Just okay?"

He sighs. "I just dropped a bombshell in your lap. It's a lot to ask of anyone, and you were honest. I respect your decision."

His voice is calm - almost unaffected. It kind of feels like he was expecting you to break it off and is now just putting on a good show about wanting to stay together so he doesn't look like an asshole.

A moment ago, this seemed like the hardest decision you'd ever made, but upon seeing his reaction you realize it was actually an easy one. After all, if he were truly serious about you and wanting to see where things went, he probably would've asked you to go with him.

Funny thing is, you probably would have.

-END-

323

From section 321...

Nick drops you off at your apartment and you spend the next few days trying to see the situation from his perspective. Eventually you remind yourself that men and women - people in general - have different comfort zones in relationships.

The fact you see something a certain way doesn't mean he does, or that he should have to. So, while you're a little stung by what he said, you're channeling the energy you would have spent moping into planning a romantic evening to put you back on track.

This morning, you wake up early and decide to play hooky from work, instead spending most of the day cleaning and shopping, followed by very carefully cooking (and not screwing up!) his favorite meal, but leaving dessert to the masters.

And, of course, you spend a decent amount of time preparing yourself for his inevitable appreciation of all of your hard work.

Wink. And ouch!

Things get off to a great start. After a long week, Nick's thrilled to walk into the mingling aromas of a perfect pot roast and store-bought homemade pecan pie. And you're thrilled he's thrilled! After his second helpings of dinner and desert, you continue to channel your inner Donna Reed and send him to the living room to watch whatever game is on TV while you clean up.

You emerge from the kitchen ten minutes later and find Nick passed out on the couch, head back, mouth slightly agape, and snoring lightly. You kneel beside him and nuzzle his neck before trailing soft kisses across his jaw to his ear until he opens his eyes. "Wow," he says dopily. "Dinner almost knocked me out."

"Almost?" you ask, still kissing his neck. "Then you'll have to follow me so I can finish the job."

Sounded sexier in your head.

He lets you pull him up and lead him to your bedroom. You leave him sitting on the bed and duck into the bathroom to slip into the something less comfortable Rachel picked out for you earlier. A moment later, you re-enter the bedroom and find him lying on his back, again.

You straddle him. "Not so fast, Mister."

Eyes closed, he murmurs, "Babe, I'm full and exhausted. As much as I would love to, I'm incapable of ravishing you at the moment."

You playfully persist, unbuttoning his shirt, but the sudden sound of a chainsaw coming from the back of his throat tells you it's a lost cause. You spend a full day gloves-on cleaning, apron-clad cooking, at-home waxing and he falls asleep?

He didn't even bother to look at the way-too-expensive lingerie you bought solely to seduce him, which is currently riding up your butt. You can't help but feel furious he didn't even *try* to stay awake.

So much for reaffirming your love. Argh!

To wake him up and kick him out now, turn to section 110.
To let him sleep and kick him out in the morning, turn to section 317.

324

From section 327...

It's amazing there's any flooring left in your living room following two hours of pacing, both while getting up the nerve to call Nick and while waiting for him to arrive.

You tell him the only way you can manage - you show him the pair of positive tests and say, "So...yeah."

Then *he* paces the floor for the next two hours. He doesn't say much, other than the occasional utterance of, "But we were safe."

And then it sinks in for you. The tears finally come. Nick stays the night with you, and holds you during rotations of sobbing and sleep. When the alarm clock goes off at 6:30 you both call in sick to work. Then you leave a message at your doctor's office, grateful when they call you back to tell you they can squeeze you in this morning.

You dress and accept the cup of herbal tea Nick brings you from downstairs, which immediately makes you think of all the things you'll have to give up for now - or for the next eighteen years. Still, you can't help but notice he had the presence of mind to avoid coffee - and wonder what that means.

Nick sits in the waiting room while you talk to Doctor Mannheim. She has you pee in a cup, which she quickly dips two thin strips into before giving you a pelvic exam. You dress while she goes to ask Nick to join you.

His face is as green as yours is white. He holds your hand, his leg rapidly bouncing with nervous energy.

"Okay, kids," she says, settling on the plastic chair across from you. The big smile on her face makes you cringe. "You're *not* pregnant."

You both stare at her. Nick speaks first. "But there were tests. There were two tests."

"Four tests," she says, holding up one of the strips. "Negative."

You both sit in shocked silence.

The doctor looks at you kindly. "Did you bring them?" You retrieve the bagged tests from your purse and hand them to her. "Yeah. 'Sure Thing' Figures, stupid name, faulty product."

You find your voice. "F-faulty?"

"Yes. Unfortunately there are a lot of women either unnecessarily worried or, sadly, rejoicing right now. They all come out positive. They're being taken off shelves as we speak."

"But *you're* sure."

"No baby."

You are filled with relief - and something else you can't quite name, but it's not good. You see Nick's shoulders relax. You look at each other, both with smiles that don't quite reach your eyes. The heavy feeling in your stomach is still there. You wonder if he has it, too.

The trip home is silent. You walk into your apartment and straight to the couch, where you sit with your legs curled under you. Nick makes a detour to the kitchen and grabs two beers from the fridge before he joins you. It's 11:00 a.m.

He hands you an open bottle. "I figure, since we're not going to be parents, a little day-drinking isn't going to hurt anybody."

You take a long pull from the bottle. "So, that happened."

"Yeah." He rests a hand on your knee. "How do you feel?"

You think for a moment. "Grateful. But at the same time, I've got this horrible feeling of…dread. It's stupid, because I'm not pregnant. I never was, but…"

"Yeah."

"How do you feel?"

"Like I understand my dad a little better." He looks at his shoes. "He and my mom got married because she was pregnant."

You didn't know that. There's a lot you don't know about Nick, and he you. "That was a different time," you say, even though you've had the same thoughts. "Do you think he regrets it?"

"No. They're happy. They'd already been together for a couple of years."

"Not like us," you say plainly.

"That's really not what I meant."

"No, I know," you assure him. "Things just feel so…"

"Serious?"

You sigh. "Exactly."

Two days ago, you wanted nothing more than to be alone - and naked - with Nick as often as possible. You aren't in love with him, but you were on your way. If you had to guess, you'd say he was, too, but this cold dose of reality just shut the door on your honeymoon period. It's gone.

You sit awkwardly together for a few minutes, delaying the inevitable. When you say goodbye at the door, he hugs you tightly.

"I'm sorry," he whispers against your hair.

"Me, too."

-END-

325

From section 90...

You bracket his face with your hands and press your lips to his. "No."

He leans back to look at you. "This is confusing."

"No, you can't walk me up, but I don't have to go yet. More kissing."

"Copy that."

You two could enter an Olympic synchronized kissing event, soon a tangled mess of arms and lips. More than once, you consider changing your mind and taking him upstairs, but resist. When your lips begin to feel swollen to the point of injectables, you decide to call it a night. Or a morning.

You fully open your eyes and are shocked to see the sun coming up.

Nick's surprised, too. "Seriously? I figured it was maybe midnight."

"I guess it's a good thing we didn't go upstairs," you say, and smooth down your hair. You know it's futile even if you can't see your reflection through the foggy windows.

"Guess so," he says, massaging the back of his neck. "Tired?"

"Not really."

"Watch the sunrise?"

You nod, getting out of the car to stretch before settling on the hood. He wraps a jacket around you and you rest your head on his shoulder, mentally noting the excellent staying power of your tube top. Thirty minutes later, the sun is up and you head upstairs alone with a smile on your puffy lips.

Continue to section 83.

326

From section 75...

For a few moments, your lady parts and your brain debate the best way to handle finding oneself in a sexually monogamous relationship with a genetic miracle (with a great personality) who's also seeing someone else.

You try to convince yourself that, technically, he's already choosing you over her. Then you wonder if, had you been unavailable tonight, she would be the one in his bed hearing about how he's not sleeping with you.

Next, you tell yourself that dating multiple people is a common and healthy practice, and that maybe you should find another basket to leave an egg in - or better yet, bread. You'll keep your eggs to yourself. You could reassign one or two feminine wiles not currently focused on Nick and suss out a suitable alternate. How hard could it be to find another guy like Nick? The last time only took a couple of decades.

Ah, hell.

Clearly, you're already stuck on Nick. You spend a good portion of time thinking about him. When you can't sleep, it's because you're envisioning elaborate, unrealistic (and way too early) glimpses of your future - something you know is wrong because they're the only thoughts about Nick you don't share exhaustively with your friends. It's all relatively normal for a new relationship, but now that you've had sex with him, things are automatically intensified.

Curse you, odds of sex on the first date ever leading to anything good!

"So," you say slowly, looking directly into his eyes.

His smile fades. "Ominous."

"I just wish we'd talked about this before. It's only been a few minutes since you said you were seeing someone else and I've already run the scenarios in my head."

"Outlook not good?"

You rub a palm down his stubbly cheek. "Me pretending I don't care, wondering why you haven't broken up with her yet, worrying you'll meet someone else, giving us a quadrangle. Or I meet someone else. I could meet someone else."

His mouth twists into a half smile. "Crossed my mind."

"I just don't see this ending without me - or maybe you, it could be you - becoming passive aggressive, or flat out jealous. But it's avoidable."

"You want me to stop seeing her?"

Yes!

"No. No, I think we should probably just part ways now. No bad blood. No expectations. Clean break."

There's no mistaking the look on his face. He's disappointed. "You wouldn't rather just see what happens?"

"I know what happens," you whisper, and kiss the tip of his nose.

-END-

327

From section 324...

Rachel throws open the door to your apartment. "Sorry I'm late!"

"Really?" says Valerie from her spot beside you on the couch. "Nice."

Rachel winces and hip-checks the door shut. "I mean, sorry that took so long. Huge line up at the drug store."

Late. This week, you've been late for everything. For work, the dentist, your rent check, and now - well, now you're late for your period, which is always on time. Always.

You realized this while watching Clueless with Val for about the hundredth time. She called Rachel who went straight to the drug store for a pregnancy test.

While waiting, you and Val tried calculating the odds of you getting knocked up despite being safe every single time you slept with Nick. But as you've lost count of the number of times you've been together, and don't track your ovulation, you gave up.

Rachel's arrival brings more dread than relief. You watch her take two boxes out of a plastic bag. "Your lucky day! BOGO on pregnancy tests. More money for diapers!"

Val levels her with a glare.

"What? A little humor would kill us right now? I figured she should do two tests at once so she won't worry the result's a false...whatever."

"That *is* sound thinking." Val turns to you. "Ready?"

"No," you say. Your voice sounds hollow in your ears.

"Wanna do it anyway?"

"No."

Your friends lead you to the bathroom and read out the instructions: Wait for mid-stream, pee on both sticks, agonize for two minutes, cry or rejoice depending on whether you get one line (great) or two (awful).

Longest two minutes of your life. The three of you sit tensely and silently on the couch. You watch the clock like you did when you were eighteen and waiting for the mail guy to deliver an acceptance letter from your first choice school. Now, not only are you still paying off your student loans, you may also have to think about sending someone else to college - your kid. With Nick.

"Time," say Rachel and Val in unison.

You close your eyes and repeat the word "negative" over and over under your breath. You reach for one stick.

Two pink lines. Your stomach hits the floor as you grab the other test.

Two pinks lines.

You're fucking pregnant.

The blood drains from your face and you don't even feel Valerie wrap her arm around your shoulders. "It's gonna be okay."

"They're both positive," you squeak. "How is that okay?"

"You still need a blood test."

You perk up a bit. "Right. Maybe they're both wrong. I mean, same test, same brand, same urine, maybe…"

You all know holding out to hear both tests are false positives is the equivalent of false hope, but if it'll get you through the initial shock, no one's going to deny you your denial.

Only one thing left to do now. Tell Nick. Your bright, shiny - and apparently fertile - new boyfriend. The irony that you put off sex in order to avoid letting things get too serious too quickly isn't lost on you.

Of course, you could wait for the blood tests and *then* ruin his life. It'll take at least a couple of days to get in to see your doctor. Why should both of you go out of your minds waiting for confirmation that you're gestating a human in your womb?

Tell him now, turn to section 99.
Wait for the blood test, turn to section 324.

328

From section 48...

Nick holds the restaurant door open for you. You thank him and step outside, walking to the side of the road.

When you raise your arm to hail a cab, he asks, "Sure I can't change your mind?" *Can't he?* "If you're not comfortable going to my place, there are all kinds of places around here."

You eye him. "Sounds like a trap."

"Like the kind where you end up swinging in a huge net rigged to a tree?"

"No." You wave, playfully dismissive. "I can spot those puppies a mile away."

"Then I don't follow."

"If I say no to your place but say yes to a drink nearby, it looks like I was just worried about what would happen if we were alone."

He gives you a cocky smile. "Well, that *is* the reason, isn't it?"

Yes!

"Well, it's not *not* the reason." The cab now idling beside you honks once.

"I'll tell you what," Nick says, gesturing to a dark lounge two doors over where the tables are lit with candles. "We'll go there, have a drink or two, and under no circumstance - not even if you beg - will I let you come home with me."

You smile wryly. "I sense a loophole."

There's that lopsided grin you're growing increasingly appreciative of. "Good point! Right. Nor will I be persuaded to go back to your place. Or hotels. Or your car. Or my car."

"Interesting."

You hear the buzz of the cab's window sliding down. The driver yells, "In or out?"

Nick looks at you, a hopeful smile on his face. "In," you say, and take his hand as you walk toward the lounge.

A little over an hour - and a couple of drinks later - you're back on the sidewalk. A cab pulls up and Nick opens the door for you. You climb in and smile up at him. "Thanks for tonight," you say. "I had fun."

"You're welcome," he says, and leans down until you're eye to eye. "And thanks for not begging me to come home with you."

"Anytime." He kisses you and, as your breath leaves your body, you wonder how he manages that soft-and-firm-at-the-same-time thing. The driver clears his throat, startling Nick, who pulls away abruptly. His head makes a thud when it hits the roof. You press two fingers to your lips and try to bite back a laugh as he winces.

"Are you okay?" you ask.

"I could have a concussion," he says, rubbing his head. "Probably shouldn't sleep."

You smirk. "Nice try."

"I could have a concussion," he says again. "Probably shouldn't sleep."

"Then maybe you should stay up with me all night," you say.

His eyebrows shoot up. "Yeah?"

"Not a chance. Set an alarm for every fifteen minutes."

"Worth a shot." He smiles and does a quick safety check before closing your door.

You give the driver your address and the car merges with traffic. You wave to Nick and settle against the backrest, a huge smile on your face.

Continue to section 69.

329

From section 331...

You can't unring a bell. And you don't want to.

"Forget it," you say, and fuse your lips to his.

His fingers press into the fabric of your jeans. "This is forgetting it?" he says, and gently scrapes his teeth along your jaw to your ear.

Did you just mew? "Forget forgetting it."

"Forgotten."

He easily lifts you up with one arm and you wrap your legs around his waist, kissing and nipping at his neck as he carries you to the bedroom. You're momentarily airborne before bouncing lightly on the mattress. You peel off your top and rest back on your elbows, watching as he reaches back and removes his shirt in one swift movement.

And then he's on top of you. He supports you under your arms and pushes you back on the bed until your head finds a pillow. As your mouths move together, you work on his fly and he kicks off his shoes. You undo your own jeans and lift your hips so he can pull them down your legs. You feel his weight again, his lips on yours, and know there's no way you could have pretended nothing happened.

An hour later, you lay wrapped in a sheet, your head on his chest, listening to his heart. Your eyes flutter close as he traces the length of your arm.

"So much better than sex amnesia," you say.

"So much."

You lay happily empty-headed for a moment before it bolts into your mind: *What does this mean?*

More sex, yes, but what about for the two of you? Are you together? "Friends with Benefits?"

"I hate that expression," he says.

Stop thinking out loud.

You squeeze your eyes shut. "Sorry. I just… My brain woke up and–"

"Now we need to have The Talk."

"Well, not *The* talk, but *a* talk."

He rests an arm above his head. "You start. Try using words like, 'I feel…'"

"What does this mean? To you. Because - and I should have mentioned this - I'm the sexually monogamous type. And I have no idea if you are-"

Nick cuts you off. "I *am* a sexually monogamous person." *And?* "And I'm not sleeping with anyone else."

Your muscles relax, but then he says, "But I also think it's a bad idea to label anything while we're high on chemicals."

"Oh." *Blasted oxytocin.*

"The extra pressure usually backfires. Know what I mean?"

Yes. You nod.

"But don't get me wrong. I'm not looking to be with anyone else."

Not looking to be.

The potential for sexual monogamy with this decent, inconveniently gorgeous guy is tempting, but you can see your future: you, the smitten kitten, wigging out, waiting for him to take the question mark off your relationship, perpetually paranoid because there's nothing to stop some gorgeous, new woman from slithering out of the ether and stealing him away

You groan. "Everything you say is perfectly rational and reasonable!"

"Thank you?"

"No, that's bad. I know me. It'll be great for a couple of weeks, and then my imagination and impatience will turn me into some nightmare girl, and you'll be all, 'Bro, what happened to that cool chick I was having excellent monogamous-casual sex with?'"

You're sitting up now, your knees pulled up to your chest as he rubs your back in small circles.

"Okay," he says slowly. "First, I would never say 'bro.' And second, I think you might be having-"

You face him, eyes wide. "An anxiety attack?"

"I was going to say 'a moment.'" He leans back, pulling you with him. "I'm not sure what to say."

You raise a hand in resignation. "No. Don't say anything. It'll just be perfect." You exhale deeply, ruffling your hair. "It's too ironic."

"What is?"

"The reasons you don't want to label things are the exact reasons I'll be worried if we don't. We'd both feel some kind of pressure, and that won't work." *You are going to hate yourself for this.* "I already really like you, but you're right - our brains are soaked in oxytocin. So I can't see you anymore unless I'm willing to end up heartbroken or half-crazy. If we stop now, I'll be over it in like, a day or two."

He tightens his arms around you. "A day or two? I'm worth at least two weeks of wallowing."

"Maybe one." You smile. "You understand?"

"Not really, but I happen to really like my bunny and don't relish the thought of you boiling him."

"Good. Being a jerk will make this easier."

God, you hate it when rational thinking takes over *before* you have the chance to make sexy mistakes.

-END-

330

From section 331...

Public places. There are few that you and Nick haven't been to over the last three weeks as you try to avoid being alone together. Idle hands, or really *not* so idle hands, and all that.

You've been to the zoo (despite Val's many humanitarian objections), or at least the parking lot, where you gave a PG13 show to a family grabbing their picnic lunch from their car. You've been to the movies, where you were actually kicked out for acting like "a couple of horny teenagers." And you've been asked to leave two restaurants before diners lost their lunch. You usually wind up in your car (easier to make out in than his) where things inevitably progress to a borderline R-rated level.

It turns out abstaining from sex is a sure-fire guarantee the two of you can think of nothing but sex when you're together - and when you're not.

Tonight, you have plans to see Avenue Q - first time for him, third time for you. You've got thirty minutes until Nick picks you up. You're half-dressed in jeans and one of your prettiest bras, plucking hanger after hanger from your closet, frustrated that you can't find a middle ground between Jump Me and Chastity Sweater.

You hear a knock at the door and remember that Rachel said she might drop by to grab the umbrella she left here yesterday. Perfect timing - she can pick a sweater for you. You walk to the door, ignoring the fact you're still shirtless because it's just Rachel. You fling open the door, as surprised to see Nick as he is to see you - in your bra. "So, I'm a little early," he says.

You hide behind the open door as best you can. "Got that. Come in. And close your eyes."

"You realize this is nothing I haven't seen," he teases, humoring you with a hand over his eyes.

Three weeks. You've waited three weeks. You've known him for a month, which, in dog years, means you're married - or something.

"Screw this," you say, and plant a kiss on his lips, sliding your arms around him.

You feel him smile against your mouth. "Oh, you meant literally."

You pull the hand from his eyes. "Shut up."

"Shutting up." He bends slightly and you squeal as he throws you over his shoulder, fireman style, walking quickly to your bedroom where he sets you down at the foot of your bed.

You go for his shirt first, pulling it up over his head. "Shoes," you tell him, and he kicks them off.

"Jeans," he says, and you reach for the other's buttons at the same time. Seconds later, you're both finally naked and you push him back on the bed.

"We're gonna miss the show," you tell him, straddling him as you kiss your way up his neck to his earlobe, which you tug at gently with your teeth.

"I'm okay with that," he says, cupping the back of your head and using those biceps to flip you underneath him. "But this better mean I'm your boyfriend."

Oh yes, yes it does.

Turn to section 327.

331

From section 16...

Nick calls to tell you he's on his way over. You leap into action; showering, dressing, and putting on just enough makeup to look like you aren't trying.

With a few minutes to spare, you take out the well-worn copy of Wuthering Heights Val loaned you that you keep meaning to read but never quite get around to. You randomly dog-ear a page and toss it on to the couch in an 'Oh, there's a knock at the door, I'll just put down this book I've been engrossed in and go see who's there' fashion.

And there it is: three short knocks. Your stomach turns inside out and you force yourself to count to ten before you walk to the door. You steal a peek in the hall mirror.

Ready.

You open the door and find Nick, dressed in dark jeans and a long-sleeved grey tee shirt pushed up just above his elbows, with his hands in his pockets. The combined effect reminds you how solid the muscle is just under that fabric. That shirt is perfection.

Of course I slept with him. Find me the straight woman who wouldn't.

You must be staring. He frees a hand and waves it slowly in front of your face. "Hello?" he says, a slow smile expanding over his face.

Jelly. Your knees are jelly.

"Hey," you say quickly. "Sorry, come in."

Embarrassed, you lower your head as he walks in and focus your attention on closing the door. You turn and collide with the concrete grey wall that is his chest. You look up as his arms encircle your waist, and then he's kissing you - slowly, intensely. Breathless, you place a hand on his chest. Suddenly you hate that shirt. He presses three final kisses against your mouth.

"You're blushing," he teases, his smile causing vibrations that reach all the way down to your...toes.

"Your fault."

His hand skims the length of your back. "Why do seem so nervous?"

"Not nervous," you say, taking his hand and leading him to your living room. "Maybe a little."

Mercifully, he drops it, his gaze shifting to the couch. "Wuthering Heights?"

"Yup. Heathcliff. Moors. Brooding. Epic stuff," you say, far too quickly. "Oh, who am I kidding? I haven't even read the first page of that book. For all I know, it's about a cat. I *am* nervous."

He smiles, crinkling the skin around his eyes. "Why?"

"Because this is the part where I tell you that I don't normally do stuff like... last night."

His eyebrow lifts with his smirk, as though attached by a string. "Which *stuff* exactly?"

You're exasperated, throwing your hands up. "All of it. Way too soon."

"Too soon for who?"

"For history. No good."

"Should I take that personally?" Still smirking.

"I think you know what I mean." It's infuriating that he finds this cute.

"You're worried that because we had sex, we're doomed."

"Exactly!"

He nods, quiet for a moment as he looks around the room. "Okay. Reset."

"Reset?"

He places a hand on each of your shoulders. "Sex reset. I mean, I'm *not* going anywhere, but if you'll feel better, it never happened."

You eye him cautiously. "Just forget it?"

"Forget what?"

How are you supposed to *forget* anything? And come to think of it, why should you? He's here. He didn't disappear. He's willfully giving up more sex to ease your mind. These arguments could really go either way.

To press reset, turn to section 330.
To press play turn to section 329.

ACKNOWLEDGEMENTS

Love Him Not would be sitting on a hard drive somewhere if not for my big brother, Roy Reed. The Bert to my Ernie. The reason I'm not attracted to Johnny Depp. Thanks for tucking me under your wing and fostering my creativity while pushing me to follow through on my ideas. To be a Reed is to endure and, boy, did you Reed a lot for this book. Even when I'm extremely unlucky, I'm lucky to have you. Your patience is endless, your shoulders are mighty, and your brain is remarkable.

My man, Nathane Jackson, you are a little bit of everything - family man, friend, athlete, scholar, healer and loyal partner. You didn't waiver when saddled with a sick girlfriend in a young relationship, even when it turned our lives upside down in ways we couldn't imagine. You prove that family isn't defined by paper or blood.

My mother and hero, Helen Reed, you're the smartest, bravest and most resilient woman I know. You taught me how to be fierce, how to survive, how to be heard, when to fight, and when to hold my tongue. (The last one's a work in progress.) Like your mother, you prove badass runs in our veins. Shady Pines, Ma.

My father, Stanley Reed Jr., worked tirelessly to give us a good life and died far too young. In addition to bestowing on me the greatest nickname a girl could ask for, he taught me to fish, to appreciate puns, and to write my name using pancake batter. My memories of him are few in number, but there's not a bad one in the bunch.

My stepfather, Richard Milton - a modern day Rhett Butler and damn good euchre partner - always there to help, to fix, to teach, to joke, and to keep my boyfriends in line (and employed). Our last talk took place over the first draft of this book. While his life was ending, he found enthusiasm for my future.

Erin Page, my big sister with the huge heart. My brother, Adam Reed who was born to be as devoted a father and husband as his own. My nephew and niece, Tyler and Carlin - you grow far too quickly. Stop.

My terrific sister in law, Natasha Brandt, I can't thank you enough for not leaving Roy as a result of the endless hours he spent on this book, as well as for putting up with me and making me feel welcome in your home.

My niece, Kayla "Boo" Page - you constantly inspire me to revel in what makes me unique. My greatest wish for you is that you never lose your quiet confidence or forget that you are brave, beautiful, so very funny, kind, talented and creative.

My second family, the Jackson clan, especially John, one of the most generous men and supportive fathers I've ever known. Also Uncle Tom, Heather, Meryn, Jeff and Mike Jackson, Jane Eaton, Colleen and Gary Kozak, Don Spry, Gail Lostracco, Victoria Belliveau, Stefanie Powell and the rest of the gang. And my late mother in law, Valerie Jackson - thank you for raising a "real attractive guy," and for showing me how to battle illness with humor and courage.

Charlene Challenger, my wonderful editor and tremendous friend, you have my limitless gratitude for your unflinching belief in me. You made this a better book, made me a better writer, and you made the whole process hysterical. Your generosity and solidarity are never-ending. Forever too much pants!

Andy Rich, your ability to suffer thousand-word, rambling emails is unmatched. Thanks for pouring time, energy, humor and (when fitting) outrage into this project for nothing in return. Your mind is epic, and I remain mystified (and disappointed) that you've yet to take over the world.

Sincerest thanks to great friends and extended family: Curt Corriere and Andy McKaig, you incredibly giving, compassionate and thoughtful people, you. Also Mary Justynski Caroline Geofroy, Sheri Lee Campbell, Russell Challenger, Istvan Dugalin, Cindy Watson, Andrea Traynor, Russ Visch, Nelson Coombs, Dan Vernon, Mel Conadera, Blake Morrow, Pat Travers and Patrick Byck. Thanks for not saying, "Oh, she is never going to finish it." To my face, anyway.

Thanks to Sam Hiyate, Devon LaBerge and Rebekka Unrau at The Rights Factory for convincing me to try traditional publishing - and for not hating me when I turned down multiple offers to forge my own path.

Much appreciation to the incredible folks who not only helped shape my public relations career, but also generously encouraged me throughout this process: Scott Steinberg, Nick Malaperiman, Mark Harwood, Robert Coffey, Daniel Morris, Renata Richardson, Tiphaine Locqueneux-Bianch, Anita Wong, Gayle Robin, Karin Scott and Kim Saunders.

To those dedicated to making me well, Dr. Lavan Chandran, Dr. John Dempster, Laura Bauslaugh, Avideh "Ninja" Motmaen-Far, Katharine Liberatore, Denise Moore, Bronwyn Dickson, and Dr. Michael Bernstein.

Finally, buckets of gratitude to formidable funny lady, teacher and babe, Kate Ashby. You taught me there's beauty in vulnerability, opportunity in silence, and that it's okay, if not recommended, to get out of my own head.

Despite the incredibly generous donations people made toward crowdfunding this book, Indiegogo's well-documented site malfunctions and %&@#!* business practices prevented me from reaching the campaign goal and fulfilling your "Perks." Instead, I offer you my infinite gratitude. I know. It's not the same.

Adam Reed, Adam Sadowski, Alex Vasquez, Alexander Joo, Alison Reid, Allison Ryan, Ana Plenter, Anastasia Soutos, Anders Svensson, Andrea Jermacans, Andrew Chlebus, Andrew McKaig, Andy Bellatti, Anita Wong, AnnaMaria DeMara, Anthony Burroughs, April Sienes, Arthur Slade, Ashley Joyce, Avideh Motmaen-Far, Beata Rydyger, Britta Gardiner, Bryn Williams, Byron Gaum, Cameron McLean, Carolyn French, Casey Morton, Chad Beamish, Chantal Mauro, Charlene Lokey, Chelsea Quendt, Cheryl Brandon-Rekstis, Christiaan Welzel, Christine Ditzel, Christine Frame, Christine Killik, Cindy Watson, Colleen Kozak, Corrina Green, Curtis Corriere, Daniel Morris, Daniel Vernon, Daniela Avarino, David Dingle, David Dunbar, David M. Lawson, Donna Charpentier, Elana Priesman, Emilia Farrace, Encarnita Klement, Eric Eckstein, Eric Franciosa, Erin Page, Francine Sebastiano, Frank Verrilli, Freya Ravensbergen, Gail Lostracco, Geoff Rekstis, Glen Mulvihill, Greg Carver, H. Single, Hannah Cho, Heather Jackson, Heather Stock, Helen Tansey, John Dempster, Holly Daly, Ian MacIntyre, Ivan Dikic, Jabbar Washington, Jackie Hooper, Jason Hughes, Jennifer A. Temple, Jennifer Grossett, Jennifer Herd, Jennifer Kavur, Jennifer Monchamp, Jerry Morelli, Jessica Kasparian-Buganto, Jessica Tan, Jessica Troie, Joanne Gero, John Benyamine, John R. Jackson, Juanisa J. McCoy, Judy Thai, Julianna Shapiro, Justin Mohareb, Kari Lakomski, Kassia Stairz, Kate Blair, Katharine Liberatore, Katie Rankin, Katrine Volynsky, Keri LaPlante, Kyle Gentle, Laura Bauslaugh, Leah Canali, Leila Smith, Lucas Dawson, Luccio Capalbo, Lynn Beamish, Madalin Malloy, Malcolm Dyke, Margaret Jane Eaton, Marius Lopez, Marshall Zwicker, Mary Justynski, Mary Phan, Maryl Celiz, Mathieu

Yuill, Matt Blair, Matthew J Yipchuck, Maxime Ca, Melissa Pressacco, Melyssa Stoute, Meryn Jackson, Michael Berenstein, Michelle LeSueur, Mike Adams, Mike Martin, Mike Thiessen, Mindy Markovich- Sedlock, Nancy Rollins, Natalie Kuyumcu, Patrick Mahoney, Priscilla LoStracco, Rachel Olsen, Rommel Conadera, Roy Reed, Russ Visch, Ryan Bint, Ryan Dee, Ryan Perrotte, Ryan Stevenson, Stephan Bohemier, Sally Jacquart, Sara Curtis, Scott Sellers, Sean Leber, Sefu Bernard, Shannon Lee Simmons, Sheldon Henry, Sheri Lee Campbell, Simon Vivien, Stacey Zigah, Stephen Grossett. Steve McCormick, Susanne Blair, Tatiana Campbell, and Ted Brockwood.

www.ingramcontent.com/pod-product-compliance
Lightning Source LLC
Chambersburg PA
CBHW051055030726
47504CB00006B/1640